SCHABRACO AND OTHER GOTHIC TALES

AN ELEGANT AND USEFUL PUBLICATION
For the Fair Sex.
ADAPTED FOR FAMILIES AND BOARDING SCHOOLS.

On Monday, July 2, 1798, will be published,

In a convenient size for the pocket, fancifully done up in coloured paper, and embellished with, 1st, a Portrait of Mrs. Hannah More, beautifully engraved by an eminent artist; 2d, a superb Coloured Plate of the present Fashionable Dresses for the Ladies.

NUMBER I. (Price 1s.)

OF THE

LADIES'
MONTHLY MUSEUM;
OR,
POLITE REPOSITORY

OF

AMUSEMENT AND INSTRUCTION:

Being an assemblage of whatever can tend to please the Fancy, interest the Mind, or exalt the character of

THE BRITISH FAIR.

BY A SOCIETY OF LADIES.

We may read, and read,
And read again, and still find something new,
Something to please, and something to instruct.　　　HURDIS.

LONDON:

PRINTED FOR THE PROPRIETORS,

AND SOLD BY MESSRS. VERNOR AND HOOD, IN THE POULTRY, AND BY
EVERY BOOKSELLER IN THE THREE KINGDOMS.

Communications addressed to the Editors, Post paid, will be thankfully received.

PROSPECTUS.

IT has long been matter of surprise, that while several successful attempts have been made to vary or extend the periodical publications, designed for the amusement or instruction of Gentlemen, the Ladies should have hitherto had no alternative of selection; and that they should all have been confined to the same monthly mental repast, however discordant their tastes and delicate their appetites. Of some abortive schemes to new garnish the entertainment, and to furnish fresh condiments, it is unnecessary to speak: they were mere temporary expedients to catch the attention; and possessed in their very essence the seeds of speedy dissolution.—Like fantastic ornaments, they were calculated only for the fashion of a season, and were supplanted by other plans of a similar tendency and duration.

Whatever may be the fate of the present work; which is offered to the British Fair, its projectors and conductors have well weighed the importance of the office they have undertaken, and feel a full impression of the respect which is due to their lovely patronesses. They are, however, encouraged to hope, that a publication; expressly under the direction of females, will not for this reason be the less acceptable to their own sex; and as they mean to exclude whatever a lady ought not to write, their subscribers may be sure of finding nothing but what a lady may safely and innocently read. To give ardour to virtue, to warn from the most distant approach

Advertisement and prospectus for *The Ladies' Monthly Museum.*

SCHABRACO

AND OTHER

Gothic Tales

from *The Lady's Monthly Museum*, 1798–1828

Edited with an introduction and notes by
JENNIE MACDONALD

VALANCOURT BOOKS

Published by Valancourt Books, Richmond, Virginia
http://www.valancourtbooks.com

ISBN 978-1-948405-57-7 (trade paperback)
ISBN 978-1-948405-59-1 (hardcover)
Also available as an electronic book.

Cover by Daniel Benneworth-Gray
Set in Dante MT

CONTENTS

List of Illustrations

INTRODUCTION

IT has long been matter of surprise, that while several successful attempts have been made to vary or extend the periodical
publications, designed for the amusement or instruction of Gentlemen, the Ladies should have hitherto had no alternative of
selection; and that they should all have been confined to the
same monthly mental repast, however discordant their tastes
and delicate their appetites.

Prospectus for *The Lady's Monthly Museum*

On July 2, 1798, a new magazine appeared on London's periodicals
scene. Adorned with an engraved portrait of celebrated author-
essayist Hannah More and embellished with a hand-coloured fashion plate, the first issue of *The Lady's Monthly Museum* (hereafter
LMM) bowed as prettily as any debutante. It had been introduced
by an advertisement containing a prospectus, which announced
the new publication's intentions to entertain and instruct a niche
market of the "British Fair," specifically those girls and young
women attending boarding schools. Like a chaperone alert to
protecting her charge, the prospectus and prefaces that accompanied each volume worked tirelessly to assure a skeptical public of
the *LMM*'s aim to serve as role model and *amusante* and to guard
against immorality, vouching safe the forthcoming content. The
quotation on the advertisement from James Hurdis's poem *The
Village Curate* effectively served as a motto for the magazine, promising "Something to please, and something to instruct." A delicate
line to balance upon was thus drawn. Throughout the magazine's
life, it worked to entertain its demanding readers and to qualify and
assert its educational value to potential critics.

The end of the eighteenth century saw public debates raging
on the best approaches to education, particularly of girls. Aligning
itself with Hannah More from the start, the *LMM* appeared to be
promoting conservative and moral education over the practical

education advocated by liberal voices such as Maria Edgeworth and Mary Wollstonecraft. Ever fond of elaborating *bon mots*, a later volume declared in the conservative vein, "Reading gives us a relish for solitude; fills the mind with knowledge, and enables us to form a sound judgement [*sic*] of things; it banishes idleness, and its fatal consequences, and teaches us to make a good use of time, and to acquire virtue" ("On Reading," Vol. 15, Oct. 1813). To achieve this aim, the prospectus promised that the "materials which will be presented in agreeable variety to the eye of their lovely readers, will consist of original Novels, Tales, and Romances, of the purest tendency," moral appeal, "adorned with all the embellishments of fancy," romance and adventure. And yet, to enchant and amuse its readers, the *LMM* had to include dramatic and exciting works of fiction and poetry with the potential for criticism and censure. The *LMM's* inclusion of work in the Gothic mode provides an intriguing thirty-year exercise in dancing with two partners, moral education and thrilling entertainment, narrated by a parental voice eager to please both.

Published from 1798 to 1828,[1] the history of the *LMM's* Gothic productions is grounded in four major Gothic voices: Horace Walpole, Ann Radcliffe, Matthew Gregory Lewis, and Jane Austen. Walpole, whose *The Castle of Otranto* (1764) combined the monsters and fanciful tales of medieval romance with modern sensibilities, had died in March of 1797, just a year before the magazine's debut, but his novel had for decades been reborn in reprints and theatrical adaptations, as well as pirated and blue book versions. Radcliffe's blockbuster novels, *The Romance of the Forest* (1791), *The Mysteries of Udolpho* (1794), and *The Italian: or Confessional of the Black Penitents* (1797), were still current in 1798. In them she institutionalized the phenomena of the explained supernatural, whereby seemingly supernatural events that initially inspired terror were later found to have perfectly natural causes. Importantly, she incorporated Edmund Burke's theory of *A Philosophical Enquiry into the Origin of Our Ideas of the Sublime and Beautiful* (1757) deeply into her narrative practice, elevating the Gothic tale to critical acclaim. In his *The*

---

1 At which point it embarked upon a series of mergers with other women's magazines in an effort to pool their resources and stay afloat.

Monk (1795), Matthew Gregory Lewis introduced his impression-able monk, Ambrosio, who embraces evil in the form of the dia-bolical Mathilda. Less well-known is the fact that Austen's brilliant Gothic parody, *Northanger Abbey* (1817), which she originally titled *Susan*, was being composed at the height of the Gothic maelstrom[1] and was completed in 1803. During the time of *Susan's* composi-tion, the *LMM's* lively Gothic dynamic ranged from the terrifying tales of "Schabraco" and "De Valcour and Bertha" to the romantic "The Maid of St. Marino," medieval tales like "Edric of the Forest," and the satirical "The Journalist, or Debut of a Female Author. The rich stew of Gothic work in the *LMM* offers a unique insight into the mix of contemporary popular literature that contributed to Austen's great and only foray into the Gothic mode.

Publication History

The Lady's Monthly Museum was not a particularly innovative title. Charlotte Lennox had published a magazine called *The Lady's Museum* from March 1760 to January 1761. Nominally, though, the concept of a museum well suited a literary miscellany in an era accustomed to the notion of public collections of disparate and curious items. Museums, like libraries, were considered appro-priate places for young women to venture on their own and with friends. The title, in fact, was a bit malleable across the life of the magazine and even within single issues and prefaces where it was variously referred to as: *(The) Lady's / Ladies' Museum*; *(The) Museum*; *(The) Lady's Monthly Museum*; and *(The) Ladies' Monthly Museum* (starting from Vol. 15, July 1813).

On its first publication in July 1798, however, the new title in full was *The Lady's Monthly Museum; or, Polite Repository of Amusement and Instruction*. It claimed as a novelty, and interesting guarantee of propriety, to be under the editorial guidance of "A Society of Ladies," and its London publisher was the respectable firm of Vernor & Hood. For various reasons, the production of the *LMM*

---

1 According to Mayo, "The registers of new fiction indicate that about a third of all fiction published in volume form between 1796 and 1806 was frankly 'Gothic' in character, or at least included important scenes of sentimental terror" (349).

was dramatically reorganized twice, resulting in the categorization of three "series" during its overall run from 1798 to 1828:

First Series: Vol. 1 (July 1798) to Vol. 16 (June 1806)
New Series (n.s.): Vol. 1 (July 1806) to Vol. 17 (Dec. 1814)
Improved Series (i.s.): Vol. 1 (Jan. 1815) to Vol. 28 (Dec. 1828)

Each volume consists of six monthly issues, January-June and July-December, with the first volume commencing from July 1798. According to Alison Adburgham, from January 1829 the *LMM* was reorganized anew for four volumes to June 1832 as *The Ladies' Museum*, which eventually merged with the *Lady's Magazine* and with *La Belle Assemblée* as the *Lady's Magazine & Museum of Belles Lettres* (210).

Resources

The *LMM* has yet to feature in full as a subject of extended critical inquiry. In her ambitious "rescue work [salvaging] pre-Victorian periodicals from the limbo of forgotten publications" (9), *Women in Print: Writing Women & Women's Magazines from the Restoration to the Accession of Victoria* (1972), Adburgham, considering the *LMM*'s role in the evolution of fashion periodicals (it regularly published hand-coloured fashion plates with accompanying descriptions), observes that it "had a much longer life than any of the publications devoted entirely to fashion; and for all it was a mixed bag, it was an elegant little magazine" (210). Edward W. R. Pitcher's ambitious index of contributors to the magazine had to be limited to *The Lady's Monthly Museum First Series: 1798-1806. An Annotated Index of Signatures and Ascriptions* (2000). Robert D. Mayo's *The English Novel in the Magazines, 1740-1815. With a Catalogue of 1375 Magazine Novels and Novelettes* (1962) and his 1950 article, "Gothic Romance in the Magazines," offer thoughtful ways to approach the *LMM*, as one of many periodicals, but none of these useful commentaries focus solely on the *LMM*. In his Introduction to the Valancourt Books edition of Ann Radcliffe's *The Italian* (2006), Allen Grove notes that because of the ephemeral and hard-to-find nature of later eighteenth-century periodicals, "most scholarship on Gothic fiction ignores these shorter stories and fragments, in the process overlooking a significant piece of literary history and an important part of the context in which we should analyze a novel such as *The Italian*" (xxviii). The present collection attempts to fill in part of that overlooked history.

Indeed, some of the most interesting observations about the magazine can be found in its own prefaces, which introduce each issue. Pitcher advises against reading any of the *LMM*'s content as literal truth, given that

> Not only could the conductors of literary magazines interact with the readership in ways unavailable to the authors of monographs such as novels, they could also merely affect to be doing so. Quite commonly, "letters to the editor" are letters by the editor, or his stable of staff-writers; articles allegedly contributed by writers working independently of the periodical might be written by those under contract to it. (6)

The prefaces, nevertheless, offer a view of a periodical concerned with providing a good product, keeping its subscriber-readers happy while mollifying critics by its repeated promises of moral and literary excellence, and especially its own continued existence and profit. Over and over readers are assured of the *LMM*'s desire for approbation; its efforts to secure worthy submissions and "embellishments" or "finery" (portraits, illustrations, and fashion plates); and its attempts to stay relevant, competitive, and affordable. One learns, for example, that in 1805 the estimated number of the *LMM*'s "Fair Readers" was approximately 50,000, "allowing for several readers to each copy" (Mayo, "Gothic," 773, n. 22). By July 1813, the magazine that initially cost one shilling still could be had for only *"the subordinate price* of EIGHTEEN-PENCE for each number, with any similar publication, they will find the charge bears no proportion to the value of the number, and, taking into consideration both quality and price, it stands unrivalled" (Vol. 15, iv). From time to time innovative content was announced: from Vol. 13 (Jan. 1821), "four pages of Music, with an accompaniment for the Piano-Forte . . . will be so inserted, that they may be taken out, and bound up separately ... [to] form a handsome Volume of valuable Music" (iv); in Vol. 11 (Jan. 1820), the proprietors were eager "to receive authentic communications of scientific or interesting discoveries, remarkable occurrences, or original anecdotes of eminent persons" (iv); and male portraits, starting with George VI, were to be included from Vol. 15, January 1822. A late word on "the sterner sex" was declared in Vol. 28 (July 1828): "The sterner sex have too long arrogated to themselves mental superiority; the more abstract sciences have been considered peculiarly their province; but, if we are not mistaken, this is a mere assumption. At all events we shall show that philosophy may be rendered accessible to ladies; and that, too, in a very attractive form."

Authors and Contributors

While "the sterner sex" provided editorial guidance[1] as well as much of the LMM's literary content, a key aim of the prefaces was to maintain relationships with professional outside contributors. Perhaps the best-known female professional was prolific novelist and children's author Mary Pilkington, who signed her pieces variously "M.P.," "P.," or "Mrs. P." The LMM celebrated this frequent contributor in Vol. 13 (Aug. 1812), with an engraved portrait and "Memoirs of Mrs. Pilkington," which noted, "Our pages have often been indebted to her for compositions of sterling merit" (64). Tiny glimpses of working relationships with the LMM can be seen in a standard feature, "Acknowledgements to Correspondents,"[2] where the editors advised hopeful contributors of the status of their submissions. In Vol. 4 (April 1800), for example, correspondents were notified that "The Complaint of a Ghost shall appear in our next" (324). Authoress "E.F." might have seen this plea in Vol. 2 (Sept. 1807): "We hope, in conjunction with many of our corre-

---

1 Pitcher argues that "The titlepage lie that 'The Lady's Monthly Museum' was conducted 'by a Society of Ladies' to 'Exalt the Character of the British Fair' is only one of several deceptions practised by this popular magazine begun in the year of *Lyrical Ballads*. The magazine was run by men who affected to be female or male 'modern philosophers' whenever the disguise served to defeat the advocates of rationalism, radicalism, and republicanism" (1).
2 Also called "Answers to Correspondents" and "Notes to Correspondents."

spondents, to hear shortly from the authoress of the elegant and interesting tale of the 'Cave of St. Sidwell.'" Occasionally news of familiar authors featured in a preface. The author of "How have I lov'd amid the dark'ning grove," "Oscar," was a frequent and popular contributor to "The Apollonian Wreath," the *LMM*'s poetry section. In July 1818, the *LMM* preface laments "the loss of one gentleman from ill health who has for some time been a principal and most able contributor to the poetical department, and most fervently pray for his restoration." Sadly, in January 1819, readers found a "Sonnet / Sacred to the Memory of / OSCAR, / who died in the bloom of youth and beauty":

> A Poet long known to the Readers of the Ladies' Monthly Museum,
> whose name will ever be cherished with affectionate Remembrance,
> as long as Benevolence and Genius shall find Friends and Admirers,
> and whose early and premature Death will ever draw forth the tear of
> commiseration from the eyes of every lover of genuine poetic talent.
> (Vol. 9, 53)

At least three poems mourning Oscar's passing were published in the magazine, one in January 1819 (dated December 1818), followed by two more in March 1819.

Another important task for the prefaces was inviting "correspondents," or reader-subscribers, to submit work for publication. This was always of tenuous benefit, as amateur submissions frequently fell far short of the quality required and often overwhelmed the *LMM*'s editorial capacity. Mayo comments, "Widespread interest in self-expression, the insatiable urge to scribble, [and] the desire to shine as a literary light . . . led amateurs of every rank and condition of life to bombard booksellers as well as editors" with their written efforts (*English* 320). "On the whole the fiction of these ingenious correspondents is highly derivative," he observes, "but it is at the same time extremely illuminating, since in being written *by* magazine readers *for* magazine readers it provides a very sensitive barometer for their shifting tastes and attitudes over the course of a number of decades" ("Gothic" 772). The *LMM* quickly adopted a tough love approach to such "scribblers," publicly notifying them of rejections in the "Answers to Correspondents" list. But it also embraced what it saw as a moral duty to instruct, improve, and encourage ambitious writers, "hoping, by a little timely encouragement, to encite [sic], and by practice enable them, to produce hereafter works in their nature more extensive, and in their effects more important" (Vol. 5, July 1800, ii) and came to see itself as "the nursery of Genius, and as the Repository of the productions of their lighter hours" (Vol. 17, Jan. 1823, [iv]).

Subscribers

From its start in 1798, the *LMM* was aimed at building boarding school subscriberships. A year later the proprietors happily announced,

> It is with infinite satisfaction we find, that the delicacy of Sentiment, and chastity of Selection, which we have most sedulously adhered to in the Conduct of our Work, have rendered it, in numberous [sic] Instances, a welcome Visitor at the most respectable Seminaries of Female Education. We have been favoured by many Governesses of Ladies' Boarding Schools with most flattering Testimonies of Approbation, and Assurances of Support, on the Condition (which we hope never to infringe) of persevering in the Plan that we have hitherto pursued. (Vol. 3, July 1799, i)

By July 1801, the *LMM* was reaching an international audience, pleased to announce that "a large number of the Lady's Museum is, as opportunity offers, exported to the Continent of Europe, to the East and West Indies, and to America, particularly in Complete Sets," which, are "always kept ready, in various bindings, by Messrs. Vernor and Hood, No. 31, in the Poultry" and "are much in vogue, not only as elegant Presents to Female Friends, but also as Parental Rewards for Filial Virtue, and Prizes for Scholastic Merit and Diligence" (Vol. 7, ii).

In one very important way the targeting of a boarding-school student subscriber made interesting sense. Away from home, isolated at least initially among strangers, and presented with new and curious information, such a girl resembled that classic character of Gothic fiction, the Gothic heroine alert to emotional sensibility. John Brewer sums up the perceived dangers to this "usual object of sensibility's critics" as "a woman who indulged or was controlled by feelings provoked by literature and romance," potentially such as exciting Gothic works in the *LMM*. Brewer's description of "the ill-disciplined reader of novels, the giddy girl who loses all practical sense of the world because she is misled by the romantic tales of sensibility [and] it was feared that such women were easily seduced and likely to lose their virtue" (121) was exactly the sort of reader the *LMM* sought to both entertain and educate. John Stoler expands on the relationship of readers to Radcliffe's novels, observing, "these same women could share in the age's common denominator—feeling, which requires no special knowledge or education—and therefore could embrace the cult of sensibility. Not reading as critics and scholars, they took the trappings of Radcliffe's works as their substance [and] turned to fiction not analytically to examine subtexts and themes but as a release" (21). "Radcliffe's novels," however, "present mixed messages of their own: they entice their female readers by offering fanciful adventure and by appealing to the vogue of sensibility while at the same time praising the commonsensical values of domesticity to which women were expected to conform in a male-dominated society" (22), exactly the balance the *LMM* strove to achieve in its Gothic content.

Publishing the Gothic and Controversy

Similar to a bold but naïve debutante at her first public appearance, the *LMM*'s first issue burst upon the scene appropriately introduced and attired but offering rather shocking evidence of its ambition to court favor. The prospectus had promised "The materials which will be presented in agreeable variety to the eye of their lovely readers, will consist of original Novels, Tales, and Romances, of the purest tendency, adorned with all the embellishments of fancy." Several of the *LMM*'s very first Gothic offerings, however, were quickly challenged by guardians of the gentle readers, and an exchange of commentary was published in subsequent issues. The primary offender was a four-part serialized tale called "Schabraco. A Romance."

Mayo reads "Schabraco" favorably in regard to the divisions between its installments, finding, "In each case the partitioning of the action is not mechanical but functional, and has been effectively used to enhance the interest of the story for magazine readers." Although Mayo derides "Schabraco" as "a vulgar and transparent imitation of Mrs. Radcliffe's *Italian*" ("Gothic" 786), the story moves briskly along, involving the reader's concern for a young man seeking to to know more about a mysterious figure and finding himself entangled in frightening and dangerous scenarios. Evil plans are hatched, a series of strange events occurs, and the drama is raised to a feverish pitch. The author, however, assiduously invokes Radcliffean explained supernatural techniques and delights in painting sublime and picturesque imagery, as in this early passage:

> The morning was calm—the prospect sublime. A bright sun tinted Calabria's mountainous tracks; even Messina's lofty buildings caught a faint but mellow lustre. The most transcendent feature in a scenery so grand, when it first remotely caught his astonished eye, was scarcely visible;—Mount Ætna yet veiled her majestic figure in the fog that hung about her lower sides. Her towering head, indeed, was illumined with the brilliant ray, which shone with a radiance uninjured by the mist that enveloped its lower sides; which even as he looked, drew up like a vast curtain, and gradually discovered a wild confused mass of picturesque imagery. (Vol. 1, August 1798, 90)

Such embroidery, however, was lost on vigilant parents and other guardians of the *LMM*'s devoted readers. In a letter published by the magazine with surprising alacrity and equanimity in November 1798, boarding-school student "Tell-Tale" reports a father's alarm and dismay at his daughter's being encouraged to read "such things" as "mark the Gothicism of the rudest ages, and not only divert your study and attention from real life, but embarrass your affections with fictions and ideas not only of no use, but seriously pernicious, as they inflame the passions, and tincture both the fancy and the heart with extravagance and romance" (392). Rather than shrink from the challenge, the *LMM* in its "Acknowledgements to Correspondents" list responded, thanking "Tell-Tale and her half-dozen of female critics ... for her candid relation, as we might not otherwise have known aught of the matter" (Vol. 1, Nov. 1798, 420). In the headnote to the complaining letter, though, "The Proprietors" declared themselves to "have it much at heart to render [the *LMM*] worthy of public approbation and patronage. And for this end they invite and solicit the impartial opinion of all their correspondents, that, from various tastes, they may learn what is best, for the benefit of the whole" (Vol. 1, Nov. 1798, 385). Two responses were printed in the December 1798 issue, the first from "The Author of Schabraco" and the second from "Eliza," a fellow author and probably also an *LMM* contributor.

"The Author of Schabraco" and "Eliza" both meet the criticism by asserting trust in readers' ability to read with judgment and good sense. Having contended with the key criticisms raised by "Tell-Tale's" letter, "The Author of Schabraco" confesses "the task of self-defence by no means an easy one" and observes "To my contemporaries, whose little effusions are implicated with Schabraco ... notwithstanding the odium we have justly incurred, there is every reason to believe, that while Virtue and Prudence hold the Reins of Fancy, she will never outrun the Public Suffrage" (Vol. 1, Dec. 1798, 471). "Eliza" declares she

> has great reason to believe that a piece entitled *"Patience Rewarded, A Moral Tale,"* would not have half so many readers as *"The Mysterious Wanderer, A Romance."*—The former is overlooked; all the fine sentiments and religious tenets disregarded; and the unfortunate book ... torn up, leaf by leaf, to curl the auburn locks of a beauty for an approaching ball,—while the romance is perused with rapture. (Vol. 1, Dec. 1798, 471-472)

If she has offended, "Eliza" concludes, "my intention was merely to plead an excuse for those who have undertaken the amusement of the public without any design to pervert the *morals* or injure the *constitution* of youth" (Vol. 1, Dec. 1798, 472). The *LMM*'s perhaps over-zealous aim to entertain resulted in scaling back Gothic pieces for subsequent issues, but works in this vein appeared fairly frequently throughout the magazine's run, and it is interesting to see how they reflect the changing interests of the times. In January 1808, the *LMM*'s new feature "The Literary Spy" articulated a renovated view of "Novels and romances" that could be said to extend to the shorter forms embraced by the magazine, as well: "however generally deprecated, [they] are yet universally read, and when written with elegance, improved by purity of moral, we know of no pursuit more likely to improve the manners, and awaken the sensibilities of the heart, than a moderate perusal of them" (Vol. 4, 19). The elimination of imaginative tales was a foolhardy venture; the *LMM* now involved its readers as active and thoughtful participants. And the magazine's Gothic productions offer arguably the most gratifying ground on which to engage, enjoy, and interrogate the reading experience.

The Selection Process

Selecting the pieces for this collection was both a pleasure and a challenge. Reading through thirty years of likely pieces initially proved daunting, as so many offered unexpected ideas and all were intriguing. In the end, I found Walpole's concept of the "two kinds of Romance, the ancient and the modern" guiding my choices. They had to exhibit "boundless realms of invention" as evidenced in plotting and material trappings like settings and objects that reflected a vision—with room for the magical or fantastical—of the medieval world; they also had to feature "mortal agents" or characters "according to the rules of probability; in short, to make them think, speak and act, as it might be supposed mere men and women would do in extraordinary positions" (65). Importantly, each piece had to evoke an emotional atmosphere intrinsic to the characters' experience and appeal to an emotional awareness and response on the part of a twenty-first century reader. I think it essential that in the spirit of eighteenth-century sensibility today's readers feel invited to sympathize on some level with characters and/or the narrative voice, and I hope the selections make that possible. Because my concern was to meet these three criteria, I did not restrict the selection process, with the result that the collection includes a range of genres.

Four disparate pieces present different views on the concept of romantic literature: "The Journalist, or Debut of a Female Author"; "The Complaint of a Ghost";[1] "Established Rules for the Composition of a Modern Novel, or Romance"; and "On the Effects of Chivalry."

The seven poems include ballads and sonnets, legendary and imagined ghosts, and tragic and ghastly stories: "Adventure at Netley Abbey," "The Abbey," "Henry's Shade," "The Lady of Elfinglen," "The Prince of the Lake," "How have I lov'd amid the dark'ning grove," and "Written during a late Evening Walk."

The one "Enigma" and "Solution of the Enigma" is included as an example of how even the word puzzles the *LMM* published to confound its readers consisted of Gothic imagery and ideas.

"Castle Walstenforth: A Dramatic Romance, in Three Acts" offered readers a text to enact as a private theatrical production, a popular entertainment in such settings as private homes and boarding schools. Compared with poetry and fiction, the publication of a play in the *LMM* was a rare occurrence.

The fiction selections include earnest, Radcliffean-influenced romances, a satire, and a modern (1811) narrative. Mayo offers a useful nomenclature for discussing the fictional narratives: "fragment," "tale," and "novelette." "There was," he observes rather dryly, "no essential difference between the three species . . . except with respect to length" ("Gothic" 778). I have accordingly considered these categories in terms of approximate word counts and based on what the original titles indicate: fragment (up to 3,300 words), tale (up to 6,700 words), and novelette (up to 18,000 words).

The fragments delight with their brevity, compact action, and urgent idea of retelling the story. With the exception of "The Vampyre;—A Fragment" (an extract from Dr. Polidori's 1819 novel); "A Fragment"; the satirical "The Ruin of the Rock, A Fragment"; "Sir Edmund; A Fragment"; and "Sir Egbert: A Gothic Fragment" all feature different configurations of a knight accompanied by a squire, a lady in distress, and a villain.

---

1 The risible complaining ghost blames Walpole for yanking him out of peaceful oblivion to be enslaved for the purposes of all kinds of writers.

The tales offer the widest variety of storytelling. "Edric of the Forest" involves its titular knight in the battles of the 1740s when the return of Charles Stuart prompted the Scottish rebellion. The haunting "The Lost Falcon," supposedly a translation from the German, evokes an eerie fairy tale. "The Haunted Mine" suggests a pastoral Gothic set among common people.

Mayo is particularly fond of "The Gothic novelette [which] though ill-suited for survival in a realm dominated by the two and three-volume novel, was admirably qualified to meet the conditions of publication in the miscellanies, since it projected the story on a scale that permitted its completion within a few months, and by reducing to proportion all its features produced a form of magazine fiction which was truly functional" ("Gothic" 785). "The Maid of St. Marino" and "Schabraco" represented a major part of the *LMM*'s first issue and as a pair offer a useful comparison. Both draw upon Radcliffean elements such as setting and the explained supernatural, but while "Schabraco" prompted outrage due to its depiction of heinous crimes and an especially wicked monk, "The Maid of St. Marino" appears to have escaped censure by adopting a sentimental tone to counter its protagonists' moments of peril and hints of the supernatural. Included with "Schabraco" here are the several letters that elaborated the controversy.

The exciting story of "De Valcour and Bertha" piles on the classic Gothic elements: a ponderous bell, a remote mountain castle, secret assignations, a mysterious orphan, a wicked stepmother, violent weather, murders, a secret society, abduction, imprisonment, and supernatural effects. Julian de Valcour and his paramour Bertha make for a brave team, and Bertha on more than one occasion has to fend for herself in surprising ways.

"The Cave of St. Sidwell" takes the reader into the life of a hermit and the orphan he rescues. The collection of characters includes a dissolute wife, a band of robbers, and an injured stranger. Poison, female curiosity, found letters, murder, an important birthmark, an education in sensibility, and an important transformation texture the Gothic atmosphere.

The complex "The Banditti of the Forest" is perhaps the most "literary" of the novelettes in its inclusion of poetic epigraphs and intertextual reference. An unusual narrative voice seems almost avant-garde in its slippage from past tense to present tense during exciting moments, as well as changes in point of view. Elaborate tales within the story add unusual narrative layers, particularly one unique relation by the African Sebastian. Like "The Lost Falcon," the German setting signals a shift from the conventional Italian locales.

Finally, "The Child of Suspicion" reads as a Regency Gothic set in contemporary time with contemporary attitudes and concerns informing the story. A decaying estate requires an infusion of funds, which leads to its lord making a very strange match with a toad-like woman of questionable background. The fate of a young couple wishing to marry hangs in the balance and the lovely heroine contends with multiple challenges to her sense of self and integrity.

Conclusion

Publication on a monthly basis enabled the *LMM* to respond quickly to public concerns and adjust its plans and expectations. It especially enjoyed the latitude to observe the evolution of ideas and trends in literature and entertainment and to solicit and encourage up-to-date subjects, forms, and ideas from its authors and contributors. A survey of its Gothic-informed literature provides a view of an intense period of aesthetic, social, and literary production as a periodical parallel to the literary scene of the time and its shifts from medieval Gothic to historical Gothic to more diffuse pastorals, fairy and ghost tales, and modern Gothics that found their ironic champions in such parodies as *Northanger Abbey*.

The present collection is offered in the spirit of the *LMM*'s mission to entertain and instruct and with the hope that more work on the *LMM* and its contemporaries published expressly for women will be forthcoming. The riches are worth the mining. As an unnamed author asserted in February 1814, "There is no part of Knowledge which is not an object worthy of our Attention . . . A single blade of grass will suggest to us meditations innumerable, excite a thousand new ideas, and conduct us towards the most enlarged principles, and illuminate the mind with the most brilliant rays of information" (Vol. 16, 156).

Editor Biography

Jennie MacDonald received her PhD in literary studies at the University of Denver, where she focused on eighteenth-century novels and plays. Her dissertation was a critical edition of Robert Jephson's *The Count of Narbonne* (1781), the first stage adaptation of Horace Walpole's seminal Gothic novel *The Castle of Otranto* (1764). While at DU, she served as Assistant Editor for *Restoration and Eighteenth-Century Theatre Research* and as Managing Editor for *Law & Policy*. She recently contributed chapters for material culture collections featuring printing, the toy theatre, and American post-colonial theatre. Other publications have included book, theatre, and opera reviews, as well as encyclopedia articles on Gothic novels and plays, adaptation, paratext, and visual culture.

Bibliography

Adburgham, Alison. *Women in Print: Writing Women & Women's Magazines from the Restoration to the Accession of Victoria*. London: George Allen and Unwin Ltd., 1972.

Austen, Jane. *Northanger Abbey*: and *Persuasion*. London: John Murray, 1818.

Brewer, John. *The Pleasures of the Imagination: English Culture in the Eighteenth Century*. New York: Farrar Straus Giroux, 1997.

Burke, Edmund. *A Philosophical Enquiry into the Origin of Our Ideas of the Sublime and Beautiful*. London: Printed for R. and J. Dodsley, in Pall-Mall, 1757.

Grove, Allen, ed. Introduction. *The Italian* by Ann Radcliffe. Chicago: Valancourt Books, 2006.

Mayo, Robert D. *The English Novel in the Magazines, 1740-1815. With a Catalogue of 1375 Magazine Novels and Novelettes*. Evanston, Ill.; London: Northwestern University Press; Oxford University Press, 1962.

—. "Gothic Romance in the Magazines." *PMLA* 65.5 (1950): 762-789.

The Lady's Monthly Museum, or Polite Repository of Amusement and Instruction: Being an Assemblage of Whatever Can Tend to Please the Fancy, Interest the Mind, or Exalt the Character of the British Fair. By a Society of Ladies. Three series. London: Vernor & Hood, 1798-1828.

Lewis, M. G. (Matthew Gregory). *The Monk: A Romance. In Three Volumes*. London: Printed for J. Bell, 1795.

Pitcher, Edward W. R. The Lady's Monthly Museum *First Series: 1798-1806. An Annotated Index of Signatures and Ascriptions. Studies in British and American Magazines.* Vol. 2. Lewiston, N.Y.: The Edwin Mellen Press, 2000.

Radcliffe, Ann. *The Italian: or Confessional of the Black Penitents: A Romance.* London: Printed for T. Cadell, Jun. and W. Davies (successors to Mr. Cadell) in the Strand, 1797.

—. *The Mysteries of Udolpho: A Romance; Interspersed with Some Pieces of Poetry.* London: Printed for G. G. and J. Robinson, Paternoster-Row, 1794.

—. *The Romance of the Forest: Interspersed with Some Pieces of Poetry.* London: Printed for T. Hookham and J. Carpenter, 1791.

Stoler, John. "Having Her Cake and Eating, Too: Ambivalence, Popularity, and the Psychosocial Implications of Ann Radcliffe's Fiction." In *Jane Austen and Mary Shelley and Their Sisters.* Edited by Laura Dabundo. Lanham, N.Y.; Oxford: University Press of America, Inc., 2000. 19-29.

Walpole, Horace. Preface to this Second Edition. *The Castle of Otranto, A Gothic Story.* 2nd ed.. London: Printed for William Bathoe in the Strand, and Thomas Lownds in Fleet-Street, 1765. v-xvi.

White, Cynthia L. *Women's Magazines, 1693-1968.* London: Michael Joseph Ltd., 1970.

A Note on the Text

The selections in the present volume were typeset from the first editions of the magazine. Although it is tempting to standardize the texts, because they span thirty years, many authors, and various editorial and printing practices, retaining the vagaries of the originals was deemed preferable so modern readers can observe differences evident in a publication with a long and complex life. Every effort was made to reproduce the texts as they originally appeared in order to present as closely as possible the works as their first readers encountered them. To this end, spelling variants, unusual punctuation and grammatical structures, most typographical errors, and original footnotes have been preserved. Importantly, in the case of serialized longer works, the breaks between installments are presented here to aid an understanding of how authors and the publishers built narrative suspense and continuity. Where clarity was at risk due to errors in the original version, minor silent corrections have been made. These include, for example, adding absent periods and opening and closing quotation marks. Obvious and potentially confusing misspellings have been corrected; however, variant spellings common at the time, such as "buz," "chace," "cloaths," "villany" and so forth have been retained as originally printed. Also noted in the footnotes are author information when known; historical figures and events; literary quotations and references; places; and unusual, rare, or obsolete terms, with most definitions sourced from *Oxford English Dictionary* (*OED*), 2nd ed., Online Version. Dates given for quoted source material are for the year of first publication (or for translations the year first published in English), with the understanding that *LMM* authors may have drawn upon later editions or versions.

GOTHIC SELECTIONS FROM
THE LADY'S MONTHLY MUSEUM

Advertisement

---

1 From *The Village Curate, A Poem*, by James Hurdis (1788).

PROSPECTUS.

IT has long been matter of surprise, that while several successful attempts have been made to vary or extend the periodical publications, designed for the amusement or instruction of Gentlemen, the Ladies should have hitherto had no alternative of selection; and that they should all have been confined to the same monthly mental repast, however discordant their tastes and delicate their appetites. Of some abortive schemes to new garnish the entertainment, and to furnish fresh condiments, it is unnecessary to speak: they were mere temporary expedients to catch the attention; and possessed in their very essence the seeds of speedy dissolution.—Like fantastic ornaments, they were calculated only for the fashion of a season, and were supplanted by other plans of a similar tendency and duration.

Whatever may be the fate of the present work; which is offered to the British Fair, its projectors and conductors have well weighed the importance of the office they have undertaken, and feel a full impression of the respect which is due to their lovely patronesses. They are, however, encouraged to hope, that a publication, expressly under the direction of females, will not for this reason be the less acceptable to their own sex; and as they mean to exclude whatever a lady ought not to write, their subscribers may be sure of finding nothing but what a lady may safely and innocently read. To give ardour to virtue, to warn from the most distant approach of vice, to paint the social, moral, and religious duties in colours calculated to allure; to form the amiable temper and correct the manners of the blooming maid; to add energy to the resolution of the good wife and the tender mother, are objects inseparable from the design of this publication, and which can never be overlooked, without forfeiting a claim to that favour which they now respectfully solicit.

Already possessed of a large quantity of original Composition, and promised the most respectable assistance, the Editors have no cause to apprehend that they shall lose by a comparison with any established work of this nature, even in a literary point of view; but as they are rather ambitious to gain reputation by their future conduct than to excite notice by their previous professions, they waive all attempts at fashionable compliment and courtly insinuation; satisfied briefly to state the peculiar advantages of their plan, and to leave the issue of success to its faithful execution.

The materials which will be presented in agreeable variety to the eye of their lovely readers, will consist of original Novels, Tales, and Romances, of the purest tendency, adorned with all the embellishments of fancy. It is intended, however, that every article in continuation shall be finished within the same volume, that the attention may neither be distracted by distant combinations, nor the pocket taxed by the necessity of pursuing unending narratives.

Next to those pieces in which fancy will have the principal share, particular regard will be paid to Essays and Letters, calculated to form the female mind to virtue and propriety in every relative situation. Biographical memoirs of distinguished Ladies, Characters, Poetry original and selected of every species, Charades and Enigmas will also be leading features in the work.

Another part of the plan, which is as novel as it is requisite, is to give an impartial review of such new publications as are peculiarly adapted for ladies and children of both sexes. Whatever cannot be recommended in general, will be quite disregarded. It is rather with a view of pointing out excellencies, and to assist in directing the choice of young persons and mothers to what is worthy of their selection than to establish a tribunal of criticism, that this idea was started, and will be steadily pursued.

French having now become an essential branch of female education, as an exercise for juvenile talents, a short tale, anecdote, or piece of poetry, will appear monthly in that language, of which the best translation given, will be inserted in the succeeding number.

Nor in a publication exclusively devoted to the use of the Ladies of every rank and every age, must an attention to reigning fashions be omitted. If virtue in a lovely form is universally allowed to be most fascinating,—Beauty and Virtue, attired by the Graces, must be quite irresistible. It is not the fortune of every one to move in a sphere or to occupy a station where the prevalent taste can be caught by the eye and copied in the dress; and therefore not only a verbal description, but also a COLOURED plate of fashionable modes will be given in each number. Another plate will in general represent some interesting scene from a real or fancied subject, or be a striking portrait of some female character. Such are the intended embellishments from the art of design; and where the most liberal regard will be paid both to the quantity and the quality of the letter-press, more cannot reasonably be expected, nor can they be really wanted. It may, however, be proper to add, that not only fashionable dresses, but also fashionable amusements, will be faithfully recorded; and of consequence new plays and other public attractions will be regularly noticed. To afford room for more valuable and more interesting matter, politics will be entirely discarded,— the occurrences of the day will be left to their proper vehicles—the newspapers; and of the usual lists, none will be included, except those of marriages.

These are the outlines of the plan. The size of the publication will be equally remote from cumbrous inelegance and petty minuteness. It is intended to combine a tasteful exterior with intrinsic worth; and will every six months form a volume, which it is presumed will be found deserving a place in the chamber, the parlour, or the library.

THE MAID OF ST. MARINO.[1]

AN HISTORICAL LEGEND.

HAPPY in the enjoyment of such advantages as were peculiar to the inhabitants of St. Marino (a small but long-famed republic in the dukedom of Nabino), Jaques Mingotli and his wife Marian were thankful to their tutelary saint for a retirement so favourable to the possession of domestic peace.—Jaques had quitted Marino at an early age, unknown to his friends, for the purpose of engaging in the holy wars; and after various dangers had retired to take possession of his long-betrothed Marian, and the little property bequeathed by his father, for whose sake the Council permitted him to reassume the privileges of a republican.—For several years succeeding their union, the liveliest traits of conjugal unanimity were exhibited in the conduct of this prudent couple, notwithstanding Marian might have demanded the exposition of certain mysteries attending her husband's arrival at Marino; but she carefully suppressed any indulgence of an unwarrantable curiosity, and appeared contented with the motives he was pleased to assign for committing to her the care of a child, apparently under the age of seven years, to whose language himself was a stranger; but when acquainted with that of Italy, she used to speak of England—of Salisbury—and sometimes mentioned the names of Richard and Beangana, King and Queen of Britain.[2] Her own name, she said, was Lucia, to which she used to add the title of Lady.—The plain

---

1 Vol. 1 (1798): July, 6-10; Aug., 98-102; Sept., 190-195; Oct., 274-279; Nov., 357-362. Reprinted in at least two later magazines, including *The Amusing Chronicle, A Weekly Repository for Miscellaneous Literature* (1816); and *Blackwood's Lady's Magazine* (1849), which invokes the Gothic fiction of a "found manuscript" by adding the comment "From the Note-Book of a Republican of the Seventeenth Century."

2 Richard I of England, r. 1189-1199, also called Richard Cœur de Lion (Richard the Lionheart), and his queen, Berengaria of Navarre, which establishes the time period for this "historical legend" in the later 12th century.

cloathing, simple diet, and restricted amusements allowed by the republic, were quite unsuitable to our little stranger's ideas.— There was an air of disappointment, mixed with an unconscious regret, in her acceptance of the honest civilities she received; but time, and the unwearied tenderness of Jaques and Marian, soothed, if they did not wholly eradicate, the imperfect sense she seemed to retain of former greatness. It was somewhat remarkable, that among the tokens of magnificence which were conspicuous in the dress she wore when first presented to Marian, was a seal ring, of uncommon magnitude, which depended from a ribbon fastened about her neck. Of this memento Jaques was particularly careful, hoping it might one day forward a discovery of her origin, for he frankly confessed he knew not to whom she belonged; although the circumstance which threw her upon his mercy, gave him reason to think his young charge was of high descent, but of that circumstance he chose not to speak; and Lucia, after seven years' abode at Marino, claimed, by her willing obedience, the full and entire affection of her humble foster parents; while the serenity and cheerfulness, which were the characteristics of a state governed by moderate and wise principles, extended their influence even to the bosom of Lucia. About this period of her age, an incident which occurred in the republic awakened our happy family from their beloved tranquility, carried distress to the heart of their adopted child, and wrung the particulars of Lucia's introduction to Jaques from his generous heart; which, when known, did not in the least elucidate the obscurity that veiled her birth:—A decrepid soldier appeared before the first Council, to solicit for his residence on their healthy mountain. His figure was noble, and, although declining, did not bend beneath the weight of years, but from a lameness hereafter to be explained. His eye sparkled with a lustre which bid defiance to infirmity and incidental occasions. His grizzled locks, retiring from the pale and hollow temple, gave a simple majesty to his expressive countenance, while the modesty of his manner added unusual force to that request the rules of Marino forbid. It caused, notwithstanding, some disquiet to the community. It was inimical to ancient customs, broke in upon their established rights, and threatened an innovation of those laws so many revolving centuries had seen observed; but distress urged its claims, the feelings of pity were secured, and charity did the rest.—Lestrange, for so the veteran called himself, soon became a welcome visitor to Jaques, and an object of much interest to the gentle Lucia.—He spoke of war, and his countenance was illumined with martial ardor—of peace, and a soft melancholy stole over his features;—but when solicited to talk of *himself*, or his former situation, a tear, a sigh, even a faint blush passed along his cheek, proving the delicacy of that chord which vibrated so painfully to the touch or remembrance of recollected sorrows.—Lucia, to whose artless questions he paid a marked attention, saw and respected the reluctance he shewed to answer certain interrogatories. The simplicity of her education (for nothing superfluous was taught in that excellent community) had neither contracted her feelings, or prevented a display of the perfections she inherited from nature; and when spared from those occupations, an indefinable aukwardness made irksome, her chief delight was to ramble along the edges of that vast height which supported the town, accompanied by Lestrange, whose remarks, amusing, instructive, and elegant, opened a new scene to her ductile mind. She attended with wonder and delight to his familiar and beautiful explanation of the brilliant orbs which derived peculiar lustre from the brightness of an Italian atmosphere; and, while tenderly assisting his feeble steps, felt a pride in the idea that she was in some measure of consequence to his ease. Fifteen months had quickly elapsed in these reciprocal offices of kindness, and the loves of Lucia and Lestrange became good humouredly proverbial; when, on one particularly serene evening, tempted by an unusual flow of strength and spirits, Lestrange ventured with his lovely companion beyond the bounds of Marino. He was deeply engaged in describing the course of the moon, as she gilded the cypresses which formed a grand avenue to the principal church, when suddenly stopping, and looking into the glen below, which was formed by an inferior mountain, he seemed almost petrified by the appearance of three men, who stood attentively observing him. Lucia turned a fearful look towards her friend, upon hearing him exclaim, 'He was betrayed,' and could scarcely support herself; while he, pointing to the men, told her *they* were deputed to drag him to a shameful and undeserved death. 'Yes,' said the venerable man, 'all is lost, I cannot escape. Ah! horrible.

The rack must again be my portion.'—He was proceeding, when Lucia suddenly darted away, and flying to Jaques, told him the circumstance. Endeared by the sanctity of his manners, his former occupation, and the veneration so willingly paid by a reflecting creature to worth, Lestrange found in Jaques a ready friend: he hastened towards the spot pointed out by Lucia, but before he could reach it, met him in the custody of those men from whom he professed to apprehend so much danger, and with painful astonishment beheld them conducting his valued companion to the Council Hall; where, to his utter dismay, he heard the helpless prisoner accused of a horrid murder, committed some years since, attended by circumstances of peculiar cruelty, on suspicion of which he had endured the second degree of torture, and that his *obstinacy* had so far surmounted bodily anguish as to be prepared for the third degree; but owing to a mistake in an evidence, the lenity of his judges had permitted him to escape. 'And on what,' asked the chief magistrate, 'do you ground your present conviction that he *is* the criminal?'—Alonzo, the person who thus asserted his guilt, hesitated, for Lestrange lifted up his penetrating eye, as if eager to know the motive for such a persecution. 'Speak,' he cried, 'was I not acquitted?' Alonzo took courage: 'It is not in this court we can bring forward a case of this nature; it is laid before the King of Naples, who has issued his sovereign grant to the heirs of Vanzenza, for seizing you wherever you might be found.' To an information so decisive, Lestrange now opposed the strictest silence, nor could their utmost efforts to draw from him either defence or confession avail; but when Alonzo argued the necessity of his being again put to the question, which he hinted might then be done, the President arose, and with a composed, yet indignant aspect, stood mute for a moment; then turning to the accusers: 'It appears,' he cried, 'that you are strangers to the laws of this republic, or suppose us to be actuated by the barbarous measures of some other communities. Learn, that we do not arrogate to ourselves the despotic power to inflict punishment before conviction, nor is penal torture known to *us* but by name; at any rate, your request strikes at our glorious privileges, consequently is an insult.'—Lucia, who had followed her beloved instructor to the hall, now understood the scope of his pursuers' infernal designs.

[*To be continued.*]

———————————

[*Continued.*]

AT the mention of torture, she cast a look of such sympathetic anguish at Lestrange, as reached his heart, and a tear evinced it. "They shall not take him from us," exclaimed the agitated maid—"He is innocent, Signors—He cannot be guilty—Save him, then—O! save him from—" She would have proceeded, but her generous warmth was checked by the president, who calmly forbid her interference; and then asked the poor captive, for the last time, if he chose to avail himself of an opportunity which could not be prolonged. Lestrange then spoke, which the solemn silence of his friends (and *all* present *were* his friends, excepting those who sought to criminate him) declared the awful impression his situation had made on their hearts. "It only remains (he cried, bowing with dignity to the council) for me to declare, as I do most truly, that I am guiltless of a crime, at which humanity shudders, even that of murdering my beloved benefactor; a crime, the supposition of which has already brought upon this emaciated frame a variety of sufferings, and which now threatens further vengeance; though from what quarter, I hardly know. This declamation I owe to your candid forbearance; had my cause been canvassed at St. Marino, instead of Naples, I had not now stood here as a delinquent; but complaints are useless, and I submit to my fate!" The sober firmness of his manner, the majesty of truth which illumined his aspect, and the horrid expectations he encouraged, were circumstances that engaged the most favourable opinion of the Signors; and even, in some degree, imposed a temporary awe upon his guard: but it soon subsided; one of them waved his hand for attention, and approaching the tribunal, addressed the president as follows. "You, who profess implicit faith in our church, will not, I trust, impugn her decree. Read this, and then dare to be refractory." "I see," cried Signor Ludorico, "the doom of this unhappy man is inevitable. The ruler of whatever government shelters him, is hereby commanded to deliver Roderigo Vanzenza (which name you acknowledge,

speaking to Lestrange, who bowed submission) into the hands
of Alonzo Ferrura, and, in default of its immediate compliance,
will be subject to the censures of holy mother church." Every one
seemed struck with the importance of this mandate, against which
there was no appeal; and Vanzenza (no longer Lestrange) was formally delivered up to the strangers. Jaques Mingotli, who dreaded
the honest indignation of his distressed Lucia, would have withdrawn with her from the audience, but she burst from him—caught
the hand of her dear tutor, and drawing him to her bosom—"You
will not go, my friend?—Leave not your poor Lucia—I am your
child—The child of your love—Forgive me, my other father, I love
you most dearly—but O! who can account for the pleadings of my
heart for this dear object?—Take him not away—See, they tear
him from me!"—They did, indeed, with an unpardonable ferocity,
strive to separate a couple, at whose singular attachment all Marino
had wondered; but in their rude endeavours to effect their painful
parting, the ring, which Lucia had worn of late, was torn from
the string, and it fell to the ground; when Vanzenza stooping, and
eagerly catching it up—"Powers of mercy!" he cried, "from whence
came this, Lucia?—Who—who gave you a token so precious?" "I
know not," answered the trembling girl, while he once more folded
his arms about her; but, as if the bodily pangs to which he was condemned were to be preceded by mental ones the most acute, he
was no longer permitted to stop, although he entreated, even upon
his knees, for one half hour; and, amidst the execrations of the
audience that dared not to interfere, the screams of Lucia, and his
own heart-rending petitions for time—the wretched Vanzenza was
torn from his friends, and soon found himself without the environs
of Marino.—Alonzo no sooner saw he was beyond the power of a
Republic so venerated for its integrity, and so beloved for its mercy,
than he readily accounted to Vanzenza for this second attack on his
liberty.

But, prior to his account, it will be necessary to bring forward
those events which had thrown this unhappy gentleman into the
power of Alonzo; and this will be most effectually done by reciting
the substance of a memoir, finished while he was at Marino, and
which was found by Lucia in the chamber where he usually lodged,
who wept over the affecting particulars, while her heart throbbed

with an unusual sensation as she traced the feelings of a soul over-whelmed with agony.

From the contents of this memoir it appeared, that Roderigo, a younger son of the house of Vanzenza, had attended Beangana, the affianced bride of Richard the First, in the capacity of usher to that noble lady; but that, in consequence of a report that Count Francis his brother was murdered, at his paternal seat, he imme-diately returned to Naples, at some little distance from whence the Castle was situated. Here the report was confirmed; but in a manner that chilled his blood. Fatigued and harassed both in body and mind, he could scarcely articulate his request to Tancred, an ancient and favoured domestic, for permission to see his widowed sister Juliana. Affected by his distress, the good creature, instead of complying with the request, urged him to take some refreshment. Roderigo looked up with an air of surprise—"You evade my ques-tion, Tancred. I would see the Countess. My brother is murdered; from *her* I would learn the particulars. Distressed as she undoubt-edly is, Juliana will nevertheless receive with redoubled tenderness a participating friend and brother." Tancred shook his venerable head—"Alas! no, my Lord—The Countess has never been visible to strangers since her husband's death. Even the Signor Taverini was scarcely admitted. Her grief exceeds all due bounds—and then—and then—pardon me, Signor—but the report—" "What report?—but begone, old man, nor tempt my rage.—*Strangers*—said you?—Is the lamenting brother of Count Francis classed with *strangers?*—Yet stop.—Where is this Taverini, who is admitted to privileges unallowed to Roderigo Vanzenza?"—Tancred hesitated, and was about to speak; when, at the appearance of a Cavalier, muf-fled up in a black cloak, he bowed, and was retiring. But Vanzenza, seizing his shoulder—"Speak," he demanded, "who is this Taver-ini?" "*I*," craid the Cavalier, letting fall the cloak which had covered the lower part of his face—"I am Signor Taverini," exchanging the most indignant looks with Roderigo—with one who seemed ready to defy him to the teeth. "And *I*," answered the agitated Count, "am Count Vanzenza, brother to the late unhappy Francis." Tav-erini stepped back.—"You are come," he rejoined, "in an unlucky moment—the Countess's grief—" "Cannot exceed mine, Signor. Tancred, shew me to her apartment." Tancred moved reluctantly, but commanded by *him*, who was now his Lord, he dared not dispute. And stopping at a room, which opened upon a corridor that faced the noble garden, he gladly retired. This room was hung with all the insignia of the most pompous mourning; and at the farther end, in a small oratory, he beheld the Countess in a robe of black. Her face was turned from the door; but hearing him enter—"I thought you long," she said. "These are melancholy moments to pass alone!" The softness of her accents alarmed Roderigo, who had often remarked her haughty tone, even when addressing her late Lord; but distress, thought he, can quell the highest spirit. He was now advancing, when a violent shriek from Juliana arrested his step—"Save me," cried the amazed Lady—"He comes again to dip his hands in blood!" Appalled at this terrible exclamation, Vanzenza turned to Taverini, (who entered in haste) for a solution of such an extraordinary address.—"She is frantic, my Lord. Her words are not to be regarded. Some terrible reports have obtained since her Lord's death."—"Reports, again!" interrupted the astonished nobleman. "To what do they belong?—of what nature?" "I can only say," returned Taverini, "that the chambers facing the sea have exhibited some horrible appearances, which indeed could not be concealed from Lady Juliana; and she is now convinced, that our late honoured friend, who you have been told was found dead in one of those rooms, owes his death to—" "O," cried the Countess, "to a monster, who dares insult me by his presence!" Roderigo's countenance darkened with suspicion; he frowned awfully upon Taverini.—The words he had just witnessed were of import; however, this was no time for investigation, and he approached his sister with a view of offering that consolation her sad situation demanded. She grew calmer, but chose not to enter into any conversation; and this reluctance he attributed to the presence of Taverini. Finding her gloomy reserve encrease, rather than diminish, he quitted her presence, under the idea that his brother had received some foul play, and fully determined to watch the motions of him who he now violently suspected to be the author of the present calamity.

[*To be continued.*]

—————

[Continued from page 102.]

As Count Vanzenza was now the ostensible Lord of his brother's household, he naturally expected the homage due to his claims; but in the countenance of every domestic he fancied a reluctance to attend him: a dislike, approaching to horror, seemed to supersede the concern they might be supposed to feel for their late loss. One only of the numerous train paid the respect his state exacted, and this man was Tancred. The Count observing his readiness to oblige, commanded his attendance at supper. Tancred appeared pleased at the distinction; and, during his Lord's repast, related the following circumstance of Count Francis' demise, with its consequences.

It was usual, he said, for Taverini, who was a relation of Lady Juliana's, to sit at table with her long after her husband had retired for the night; and this, the old man feared, was a cause of much contention between the noble couple; particularly, on the night of his death, the Count had gone to his chamber in open displeasure, and he believed slept alone. That about four in the morning a cry of murder sounded through the Castle. Terrified at the unusual disturbance, he ran up the great stairs, and met Lady Juliana in her night dress, her hair dishevelled, her hands clasped, and, exhibiting every mark of distraction, exclaiming—"My love, my life, my murdered Francis!" That, without stopping, he ran forwards, and discovered his Lord lying on a bed, with every appearance of being strangled. His casement was open, part of a napkin lay on the window; on the ground Tancred saw a lock of black hair, a piece of a shirt, and an old hat. It was plain the assassins escaped by means of the window, and that the poor victim had struggled hard for his life.

He then went on to mention the extraordinary, but ineffectual, means taken to discover the murderers; and how very active *Taverini* had been on that head. Vanzenza shuddered.—"But now, my Lord," concluded the garrulous orator, "comes the worst of the story. Ever since the night he was buried, those chambers" [pointing to two, opposite Roderigo's apartment] "are troubled—there my dear master appears nightly;—and—but that—." "*But what,*

Tancred?"—"Why, that is all, and please your—." "Something yet remains to be explained, Tancred; your hints, and those of Juliana, mean a dreadful mystery. Speak, then, on your duty I charge you, speak." "I cannot, so please you—I dare not," cried the ancient creature, dropping on his knees—"Oh, it is a secret, so awful!—but watch with me, my Lord, this night, and you—." "Slave," exclaimed the enraged Count, while he half drew his sword, "am I to be trifled with?" "O, no, your lordship—forgive me; it is not my own invention; but when the apparition—See, my Lord, that door—I think it moves—It opens—!"

Tancred was not deceived; the door did open—a shriek was heard—and the words "Vengeance, vengeance on my murderer!" followed. Vanzenza was petrified, and could scarcely raise the terror-struck Tancred, who, grasping the Count's knees, begged him to leave the Castle, for his life was not safe. "How! my life!" "O, my Lord, all the servants think—." "Think what?" "That *you* are your brother's murderer."

"Powers of goodness, what means this madman?" His apostrophe now met with a fearful interruption from the chamber of death, for he plainly distinguished this sentence—"*Roderigo is a fratricide!*" The voice that uttered an accusation so shocking, sounded hollow, yet piercing, and Tancred tremblingly asserted, that every one beneath that roof had heard those very words repeatedly. He was going on, when the approach of several people seemed to relieve Vanzenza's benumbed faculties, who, stepping forward, perceived several domestics, well armed, and headed by two officers of the police armed also; and before the Count could demand their business, at an hour so unusual, he was surrounded by them, seized, and strongly secured. In vain did he attempt to learn the cause of this violence; in vain struggle to disengage himself; the combination was too powerful for effectual resistance, and he was dragged to the great entrance of the Castle, where several horses were in waiting, on one of which he was mounted, and conveyed to Naples, where, to his utter astonishment, he was accused (such was the superstition of those times) as accessary to his brother's death; and this, solely on the strength of that mysterious information which had been frequently repeated, and which himself had witnessed on the preceding night.

His defence, which was manly, spirited, and pathetic, procured him neither credence, nor mercy. The evidence of a supposed apparition destroyed every effect of simple truth; and, although it amounted not to full conviction, was sufficient to justify his persecutors in their application of the torture. Vanzenza bore this barbarous proof of concealed villainy with wonderful constancy; and, after two years' imprisonment, he was permitted to depart from Naples, and, although acquitted, with a strict prohibition never to appear within the Neapolitan jurisdiction; consequently he was precluded the possibility of attempting any investigation of his late dreadful prosecution.

To add to the Count's distress, he was informed that his beloved wife and family were involved in the extended ruin. Banished from their peaceful Villa, at Riombino, no one could tell what was become of them; and as Vanzenza had been merely a soldier of fortune, he was well assured, if living, poverty at best must be their portion. Thus oppressed, deserted, afflicted with cruel pain, and an incurable lameness, the consequence of the torturing rack, he sought some sequestered abode, where he might breathe out an existence embittered by such various calamities; and after wandering about for three years, enduring all the vicissitudes incident to his sad situation, it occurred to him to try his fate, at St. Marino. How he succeeded, has been seen; for although pennyless, he was not rejected; although friendless on his arrival, he soon procured by that letter of recommendation, an open candid manner, every convenience necessary to his comfort. We shall conclude this abbreviation with the finishing lines of his memoir, and which ran as follows.

"Hail to this peaceful, this long-sought retirement. Hail to that Being, who, for wise and gracious purposes, has conducted my steps far from the haunts of cruelty and blood; where superstition has no power, where infernal treachery can no longer tear the heart strings of unoffending innocence. Here I can coolly revise the incidents of a life oppressed by dark and unknown assassins. Dear, murdered Francis, repose in silence. The truth *will* appear; thy injured heir *will* be reinstated; if not in his own person, yet in his offspring. But, ah! Leonora; dost *thou* not taste the bitter cup of which thy Roderigo has so deeply drunk? Hast *thou* not sunk beneath—But—be still, impatient spirit, nor slight the blessings still left in thy possession; again thou seest in every countenance a friendly regard. Yonder sweet maid, that ministers with so much delighted attention to the wants of suffering humanity, adds to thy comfort, and gives thee inexpressible pleasure. Her soft eyes, beaming with pity, reminds me, that gentleness and mercy have taken up their abode at Marino. She is *the child of Humility!* and Hope itself cannot look that way . . . . Beangana, too, thou best of mistresses,—alas! could'st thou have interfered . . . . . Richard, noble, unfortunate king of England—hard was thy fate; and dare Roderigo murmur!"

From this last hint, it appeared that the misfortunes of that noble pair precluded the Count's attempts to solicit their assistance; so that his enemies had completely triumphed. How they effected his second seizure he gathered from Alonzo, who informed him that Signor Taverini had lately brought forward two of the Lazorini at Naples, who, though in general an inoffensive body of people, occasionally produced corrupted members; and these had positively sworn to the murder of Count Francis as committed by three of their brethren—*themselves*; and although strongly tempted by Taverini to join the infernal compact, decidedly refused to take an active part. He also said, they were engaged to appear against his prisoner on his arrival at Naples. Alonzo then spoke of the infinite trouble himself and companions had met with in their search after the Count. To the latter part of this information that unhappy nobleman was deaf. *Taverini*, the relative of Lady Juliana, and usurper of his rights at the Castle, now confessedly his prosecutor, took up all his thoughts. His former suspicions gained strength; there was a coalition, he now fancied, between the two; and he felt eager to face them: but he had no council, no protector. His royal friends, Richard and Beangana, were no more. The judges were already prejudiced—had already evinced their sense of his imputed guilt, by inflicting the torture. What, then, could he again expect—but similar treatment? Thus mentally arguing upon the possible, and the probable, Vanzenza reached Naples, and again took possession of the wretched dungeon in which he had formerly experienced so much suffering and sorrow. Lucia, too, whose tenderness and spirited defence he could not forget, now pressed upon his memory with pungent recollection. The ring he had seen reminded him of one formerly in the possession of Count Francis, and presented to him as a token of friendship by the mother of his Countess. But here his hope of elucidation dropt. There were more rings of the same description; and he sighed at the idea of that happiness he enjoyed when first taught to look upon the revered Princess Beangana as his patroness.

(To be continued.)

[Continued from page 195.]

SEVERAL weeks had tediously elapsed in an hourly expectation of being again called to defend a cause so horrible to the feelings of Vanzenza.

Confined in a dark, damp, and dreary dungeon, he almost wished for the period of his enlargement, although clearly of opinion his death must speedily follow. At length the awful day arrived which was appointed for his final examination.—A circumstance of this nature could not be concealed, and the court was crowded with a most splendid assembly of both sexes.

Accompanied by the Lazeroni, who were decently attired, appeared Signor Taverini, who, placed near the judges, cast looks of contempt, mixed with an expression of fear, upon the humble yet composed victim he had so long attempted to crush, whose squalid appearance and dejected figure could not overcome a dignity which attended his calm and steady examination of his enemies.

The testimony of the Lazeroni was to this effect—That they had been tampered with by Roderigo Vanzenza to assassinate the late Count Francis; and upon urging their reluctance to undertake such a deed, he engaged three more to assist them, when, overcome by the splendor of the proposed reward, they partly agreed to join in the villanous attempt.—At this time the supposed criminal was with his family upon a visit at Riombino; but as soon as he had made this arrangement returned to his post under the Princess.

Upon comparing the consequences attending the execution of their promise, these two men refused to ratify it, and the business was done by the other confederates, who were since executed for a similar transaction. They then asserted, that, stung by the reflection of being involved in such a compact, they determined to disclose the whole matter to Signor Taverini, which happened some time after Roderigo had been liberated, and swore point-blank to the truth of these assertions.

As this evidence was deemed absolutely decisive, the court proceeded to sentence Roderigo Vanzenza to be broke upon the wheel; and this doom was pronounced amidst the tears and exclamations of that noble audience.

The Count then stepped forward, and entreated to be heard; but after condemnation he was not permitted. Taverini, who, for reasons which will hereafter appear, exulted most indecently over the fallen sufferer, was about to leave the court, and turning about for that purpose, found himself stopped by the entrance of several people, among whom was a lady close veiled. He then sat down again, till the bustle should be subsided. Roderigo was not withdrawn, and the place remained crowded, when, on a signal from the judge, the new-comers were placed directly in front: a solemn stillness ensued.

The Lady, slowly removing her veil, discovered the features of *Juliana* Countess of Vanzenza. Amazement struck every one present; yet no one's astonishment equalled Taverini's. But what was his confusion, when the Countess, addressing that monster of iniquity, asked him if he remembered *that* countenance? [pointing to a person with whom she entered] and then added—"Receive your *Friend*, Signor." So saying, she presented to his recollection a figure the most formidable to his imagination.

"Carlotti!" exclaimed Taverini, as he shrunk from this unwelcome appearance.

"*Carlotti—yes!*" returned the man. "You cannot have forgotten one to whom you have been so confessedly obliged!"

Taverini could not stand the taunting question; he trembled universally—hesitated—turned pale—and would have retired; but this was not permitted; and he had the mortification of hearing Carlotti interrogated respecting his business there.

"I am come," said the desperado, with a bold, undaunted air, "to clear the innocent—denounce the guilty—and render up to the laws of my country a life, which is now become hateful.—*I*," and he raised his voice to an awful pitch—"*I*, in conjunction with that villain, murdered the good Count Francis. Possessed of diabolical strength, *I* first gagged, then strangled him; but *he*," again looking at the sinking Taverini,—"*he* was my instigator to the bloody deed!—*he* promised to free me from a prosecution, which (now renewed) must involve my life, if I would assist him.—*I did assist him*—and he kept off the danger I hinted at, which is of a treasonable nature, till, on a late application to him for money, he laughed at my request, and has even threatened my destruction. Now let him ward off his own!"

The malignant aspect of Carlotti, as he pronounced these last words, expressed the triumph of an infernal; and when Taverini was seized, he readily resigned himself to the same guard, who led them off amidst the shouts of a rejoicing multitude.

Lady Juliana, on the departure of these culprits, advanced with a timid air to Vanzenza, who could scarcely support himself under the various conflicts of hope, surprise, horror, joy and doubt: a cold perspiration hung on his forehead, and he was sinking on the gaoler's shoulder; when, perceiving the Countess's intention, he struggled with his feelings, and strove to receive her with a forced tranquillity.

She gazed on his agitated features, caught the hand which trembled in her grasp, and burst into tears—"Forgive, oh, thou most injured of human beings!" apostrophized the poor Lady—"forgive the unintentional wrongs done you by a creature, who was made to believe you guilty of the worst and cruellest excesses!"

Here, overpowered by the keenness of self-condemnation, she stopt:—she could not articulate any thing more than her earnest desire to see him immediately upon his liberation, when she would explain the horrible arts by which her credulity had been worked upon, her judgment misled, and even her humanity made to appear as a criminal weakness, that militated against the purity of conjugal affection.

Vanzenza kissed the hand which retained his; and being called upon to attend the decision of the judges, summoned every remains of fortitude to hear a sentence, which even then he in some measure dreaded to receive, while his acquired composure, and the long course of suffering he had endured, gave him, in almost every one's estimation, the merit of a martyr.—

"You were brought hither, Signor Vanzenza," said the denouncer of his fate, "under a striking and probable impression of murdering your brother, Francis Count Vanzenza.—I, from a coalition of circumstances, unnecessary *now* to go over, found indispensible reason for your undergoing the ordinary question; and from the manner in which you bore it, I deduced on your part a criminal obstinacy, and felt myself justified in inflicting the second degree. It was soon after this event, that an application was made to me to extend your confinement, from the idea that although positive proof was wanting, yet there was little reason to doubt the reality of your crime; in consequence you were not liberated till the prosecution fell to the ground, by the disappearance of a material evidence: and after your departure from Naples, the remembrance of Count Vanzenza's affirmation remained upon the minds of those who were interested in the discovery of a transaction, for which no particular motive could be applied; till at length, wearied by wrong conjectures, those who were most eager for the developement gradually remitted every enquiry: but on a late application for a renewal of the prosecution of you, Roderigo Vanzenza, I referred Signor Taverini to the ecclesiastic powers for your seizure, reserving to myself the privilege of again trying this extraordinary cause.—It now appears that, in consequence of Carlotti Colci's self crimination, *you*, Roderigo, now Count Vanzenza, are fully and honourably acquitted—restored to the title and estates of the deceased Francis. And I have further to say, that it will be expected that you become an actual accuser of Taverini, as the heir of your late brother." So saying, the court broke up, amidst plaudits and whispering execrations of a splendid audience, for there were few present who did not condemn the unfeeling precipitation of Vanzenza's former sentence.

The news of their Lord's acquittal, and his expected arrival, reached the ancient domestics residing with Lady Juliana, and converted a most gloomy residence into the abode of peace and joy. Tancred was among the foremost to pay his duty, and conduct the Count to his sister's chamber; who (upon sight of a venerable and now beloved relative, returned, as she would hope, to forgive and allow for the dreadful mistakes of premature judgement) evinced the liveliest marks of unfeigned tenderness—*"My brother!"* exclaimed the Countess,—"you have pardoned—yes, I feel you have pardoned, the delusion which has cost you so dear, attainted[1] a noble character, and barbarously struck at your life; yet if any natural reluctance remain, listen, I entreat you, to my exculpation."

"Cease, dear and respectable Juliana," answered Roderigo: "the exemplary retribution you have forwarded proves your innocence respecting *my* calamity. Do not, then, mix with the information I most eagerly wish to receive any invective against a conduct, which, I am *sure*, your motives will justify."

Delighted with this generous assurance, she bowed her gratitude; and while refreshments of every delicate nature were preparing for the exhausted sufferer, she entered upon the following detail of horrible facts.

[*To be concluded in our next.*]

———————

[Concluded from page 279.]

THE ascendency which Giovanni Taverini obtained in our family, certainly originated in that listlessness which marked the character of Count Francis, who sacrificed to his own temporary ease the quiet, the safety, and I fear his life. Left either to the dissipated society of a certain Cassino, or the yet more fascinating conversation of my cousin, no wonder I ceased to regret the lassitude of a husband, who seldom indulged me with the company which I should have undoubtedly preferred; and the death of a dear infant adding a forcible motive for my avoiding retirement, I became yet more indebted to Giovanni for his attention.

"Soon after my child's demise that base incendiary began to poison my mind against *you*. He urged the advantage Leonilla's

---

1 *attainted:* Corrupted, tainted (*OED*).

departure would prove, supposing I had no other offspring; spoke of the Count's declining health as a cause of the dreadfullest suspicion of *your* rectitude; and even insinuated a possibility—O, my Lord, I tremble to say—that the uncle of my lost babe was obliquely accused of *her* destruction, and her father's ill health!"

"Monster of impiety!" groaned the indignant Vanzenza.—Lady Juliana would have waved a farther explanation of the pernicious business, but he entreated her to proceed, which she did, and declared her abhorrence and disbelief of such a diabolical hint, till, by various means too tedious to develope, at that period, he so far obtained her credence as to induce doubts of Roderigo's innocence, which the assassination of her unhappy Lord confirmed.—

"No wonder, then," added she, weeping bitterly, "that I countenanced those barbarous proceedings against you—No wonder I joined in the renewed prosecution, after so many years had elapsed. In pursuing such a fratricide I thought myself completely justified, nor imagined myself otherwise than truly just in thus endeavouring to rid the world of one so criminal. But, oh, what a shock did the intelligence of Carlotti produce this eventful morning! Maddening with rage, pierced with grief for the evils I had caused, and indignant at my own credulity, I could scarce hear the murderer's story to an end.—'He will be lost!' I cried: 'fly, Carlotti—accuse the barbarian—defend the noble Count—But I will go myself, and defy the wretch.' Pleased with my proposal, Colci accompanied me with a wild and savage eagerness; telling me, as I almost flew, that Taverini had begun his terrible career of infamy by spiriting away my child from the woman to whom she was entrusted."

"At what time was this deed of cruelty performed?"

"About fourteen years since."

"And Lucia is now fifteen."

"Lucia?" exclaimed the Countess.

"Pardon me, Lady Juliana—I was rather absent."

Vanzenza's agitation could not be concealed from his sister; and she entreated him to explain what he meant by such a strange observation. Perceiving he had raised suspicions not easily to be done away, he went into a detail of the occurrences at St. Marino, not forgetting the ring he had seen in Lucia's possession.

This *was* to be, indeed, a day of wonders, for before Vanzenza concluded his little story, the sudden appearance of that very object, about whom the Countess appeared so very anxious, rushed in, followed by the honest Jacques;[1] and, careless of consequences, threw herself upon the astonished Vanzenza's bosom, expressing at the same time her joy at his deliverance, and this in terms so wild, yet artless, calling him by the most endearing titles, that Lady Juliana, overcome by her own feelings, approached with trembling feet to take a part in the ecstatic scene.

Lucia, raising her eyes, now felt somewhat abashed at the dignified appearance before her, and would have retreated, but the Count catching her hand, and addressing his sister—"*This*, dear Lady—*this*," he cried, "is the sweet girl, the mention of whose name gave rise to——."

He could say no more, for the Countess had caught a view of Lucia's ring.—

"That ring," she tremulously observed, "was—yes—it was my husband's. Who, then, can this lovely creature belong to?"

Jacques then, at Vanzenza's request, came forward, and related the following particulars respecting his young charge, whom he found in a superb tent belonging to a Turkish officer, the ornaments of which had attracted his notice, and induced the party to which he belonged to enter, in hope of plunder; that when their business was almost completed, a heavy groan, proceeding from the sofa, alarmed him. Turning, to see from whence it came, he perceived the figure of a man, apparently dying, who beckoned him with convulsive eagerness; and then pointing to the weeping little creature, clasped his hands as if to implore protection for it. As Jacques advanced, he perceived the sinking form respire with difficulty, and, unable to breathe another syllable, immediately expired. Struck with the scene, our soldier drew away the distressed child, and interested by her extreme grief, he determined not to abandon her; but, although inconveniently situated, contrived to keep her till the campaign ceased, after which period he returned to St. Marino; when, uncertain how far his generosity might be allowed for among his friends, Mingotli chose to announce her as the orphan of an English soldier, who had left property sufficient to

---

1 Previously spelled "Jaques," but "Jacques" is used for the concluding section.

maintain her sparingly, which the sale of those ornaments he found in the tent enabled him to do.

This was all Jacques could ascertain respecting his young favourite, and with this Vanzenza and Lady Juliana were obliged to be satisfied, although the wishes and half formed hopes of both pointed to an elucidation still more satisfactory.

Delighted with their cordial reception, Mingotli and his foster-child saw several days pass with unusual rapidity, nor once repented the eagerness with which they had quitted Marino to learn the fate of their valued friend.

The time soon arrived when Taverini and his iniquitous assistant were to receive the reward of their crimes; and on the morning after their condemnation, a memoir from Giovanni was received by the Countess, which accounted for the full revival of her long protracted felicity. It was couched in the following terms:—

MEMOIR OF GIOVANNI TAVERINI.

THE FIRST PART WRITTEN BEFORE HIS CONDEMNATION.

At a moment when the treachery and baseness of a conduct, which has brought about destruction to all my prospects, can no longer further the views I am constrained to abandon, this confession can claim no merit; nor is it extorted so much by justice, as a means of checking the triumph my fall has occasioned. Know, then, Lady Juliana, that, in default of a nearer claim, *I*, the despised Giovanni, am heir to Vanzenza's possessions; nor wonder if I strove to obtain it by what the cold-blooded man would denominate unlawful methods. Yes, Lady, I glory in the mischief I have wrought; and have the consolation to know, there is another dart in store to wound your peace—Your child, the little Leonilla, *I* sent to England; where she soon died. *I* fabricated the trumpery tale of my Cousin's apparition; and *I*—mark well the policy—imitated with exactitude a voice not easily to be copied. But what am I about?—Ah! how different are the sentiments which now actuated the wretched Taverini— my fate is decided—I must die!—Horrible!—No recompence can be made—Murdered Francis!—lost Leonilla!—Tortured Roderigo! When I began to write, it was under the influence of raging passion:—now reflection, aided by the representation of a worthy Monk, supersedes the reign of malice, and I am constrained to say—*I repent!* Forgive, then, oh ye remaining victims of my infernal malice, forgive a wretch who cannot forgive himself!—Ha! what says Carlotti?—'Lady Juliana, your child lives—She is at St. Marino.—Claim her, Lady;—She is at Marino, I repeat.' But first hear Carlotti's confession, which you would have known before, but for reasons he chuses not to explain; although I imagine they originated in the hope of again seeing you, and expecting, on that confession, to claim your interference for his release. Those hopes are done away, and this is what he says—"That, in consequence of *my* orders, he conveyed the child and her nurse to England, where they were hospitably received. The horrid business I meant him to transact inducing him to return, he hastened hither, after appointing a means of correspondence with Leonilla's attendant, for whom he professed a great attachment. In consequence of which he was soon informed that the Countess of Salisbury, attracted by the child's beauty, took her into the family, and afterwards leaving England with the Earl, she was permitted to take the little girl and her nurse with her, who informed them of its origin, which procured Leonilla an attention equal to what a child of their own would have received. It was long after this, he was informed, that the Earl had been taken by the Turks, his family scattered, and himself numbered with the dead;—and about two years since, business calling him to Marino, he saw a lovely creature, who was reported to be brought from Syria. The sight of this young girl immediately called to mind Leonilla, and his treachery: not that he could retain any knowledge of her features, but Leonilla *had* been taken to Palestine, and there was a possibility of her being captured with the Earl."

"It must be so," cried the weeping Countess. "Blessed Jacques, thou hast preserved my child, and Leonilla shall reward thee!"

The memoir then concluded with reiterated petitions for pardon to those he had so grievously offended; who, struck by the evident sincerity of Taverini, joined in a full and free forgiveness of both the unhappy men. From a concomitance of every circumstance relating to Lucia's history, her consanguinity to the noble family was established beyond a doubt; herself remembering something of a

voyage to Palestine—of seeing Lord Salisbury dying in the tent;—
and she thought the Countess died on her passage to Palestine. Of
the nurse she knew nothing after their arrival, nor was that of much
consequence to those who had been so much injured by her treachery. But what fixed the idea of Lucia's affinity to Lady Juliana still
more strongly, was the evidence of the ring, which, upon opening
a spring, discovered the initials J. V. under a very small miniature,
where that Lady's features were exactly delineated.

To Count Vanzenza, who daily approached to convalescence,
this developement was particularly delightful. His paternal affections were Leonilla's before her origin was ascertained; and he now
thanked heaven for the society his soul loved. Of his own family
nothing ever transpired, and the secret anguish he nourished for
their loss proved the insufficiency of mortal enjoyments.

It is hardly necessary to add, that Jacques and Marian withstood
the very liberal offers of their noble friends, who wished them to
reside at the castle, and passed the residue of their peaceful days in
their favourite republic.

M.[1]

---

[1] See Pitcher (150-156). Pitcher attributes other works to this "M," under the iden-
tifier "by the author of 'The Maid of St. Marino' and 'Macleod of Dunvegan, a
Scottish Trait'" (Nov. 1798, 343-353), such as (perhaps) "The Two Monks" (Sept.
1798, 207-213).

Thurston, Del.   Chapman, Sculp.

But mark, Young Man, I have yet a Dagger!

Published Aug.ᵗ 1ˢᵗ 1798, by Verner & Hood, Poultry.

Engraving for "Schabraco" from the August 1798 issue of *LMM*. The
caption reads: "But mark, Young Man, I have yet a Dagger!"

SCHABRACO.[1]

A ROMANCE.[2]

ENCHANTED with the gay and magnificent appearance of a Sicilian masquerade, Rinaldo Piozzi[3] contemplated his emancipation from college with the liveliest delight.—Confined to a species of study the most inimical to the buoyant spirit of youth, he entered into the amusements of Messina[4] with a rapture known only to one, who, in a few weeks, was about to forfeit them for ever (being designed by his father for a member of a society distinguished in the church as the severest in its pale): but in the full possession of present enjoyments, Rinaldo adverted not to their speedy termination; and while his ear was turned to the full swell of harmony, or the sweet and tender notes which Sicilian art can so well improve, his eye was caught by the fascinating beauty that blazed around him. Rinaldo was a stranger to the company, but their politeness did away that objection; and he soon found himself sufficiently emboldened to ask the name of a figure, whose solemn step and uncouth appearance, added to a scrutinizing manner, seemed to denounce him as

---

1 Vol. I (1798): Aug., 85-93; Sept., 179-185; Oct., 263-274; Nov., 362-372.

2 See Pitcher regarding the unidentified but female "The Author of Schabraco" (40). Mayo discusses the controversial role of "Schabraco" as a representative of the *Lady's Monthly Museum's* "program of Gothic fiction" (264). "Schabraco" was republished at least twice: in *The Amusing Chronicle: A Repository for Miscellaneous Literature* (1817) and in *Blackwood's* (1849) and subtitled "A Romance in Real Life".

3 Pitcher notes that aside from Schabraco, "the principal character is Rinaldo Piozzi, a college graduate whose enjoyment of Messina is interrupted [*sic*] by meeting the antagonist and learning of his grievance against Rinaldo's father. It seems extraordinary that an English writer would use the Piozzi name in this year and in this magazine (unless one were a Piozzi?). Hester Lynch Piozzi was published in *LMM* in April 1800" (40).

4 A city located on the northeast coast of Sicily at the edge of the Straits of Messina across from the toe of the Italian boot and facing Reggio Calabria.

an enemy to the gallantry of the place. To this question he received an equivocal answer.

The Signor was called Schabraco. He was seen wherever business or pleasure convened a crowd. If he spoke, it was to satirize. His smile was the smile of spleen. His frown, that of a dark revenge. But as to his origin, residence, or means of subsistence, no one knew, nor did any one seem desirous of investigating.

Our youth's curiosity was of a different stamp. Ardent in the pursuit of mystery, he seldom considered its object; and the purpose he sought to elucidate was defeated by want of caution. At the first approach of dawn Schabraco retreated; and before Piozzi could reach the portico, he was no where to be seen. The crowd of carriages, which nearly filled the street, made this very probable.

For several days nothing further occurred respecting this extraordinary personage, and Rinaldo felt his hope suspended, if not wholly extinct; till, on his taking the air on the noble quay which fronts the Calabrian shore, he beheld, in a felucca[1] that was making from the port, the figure of him he so recently gave up. His dress, which was that worn at the masquerade, his fierce air, and abstracted manner, convinced our young man of his identity; who, immediately stepping into another boat, directed the rowers to follow that ahead of them. This they did for two hours; when, crossing the strait, Schabraco coasted the shore, till a small inlet appearing, overshadowed by some vast trees, the felucca made towards it, and was soon hidden by the shady covering. To follow any farther, was dangerous; at least so argued the boatmen. Rinaldo entreated,—commanded,—but in vain. They would wait, if he chose to land; and with this argument he was obliged to comply.

A few stepping stones soon delivered him on the shore; and, mounting a small eminence, he perceived the gothic points of an irregular edifice upon the horizon, which the mild ray of a setting sun rendered tolerably conspicuous. To the north and west end of his situation all was wild and dreary. Vast woods, deep and dangerous dales, with barren hills, formed a comfortless prospect; when the sight of Schabraco, in a sort of rude path leading from the

---

1 *felucca*: A small vessel propelled by oars or lateen sails, or both, used, chiefly in the Mediterranean, for coasting voyages (*OED*).

water, quickened his curiosity as he watched him making towards the building in question.

Determined, then, to gratify the desire he had conceived to develope the mystery of Schabraco, he hastily descended, and making a lucrative bargain with the men to stay for him till midnight, which they unwillingly promised, once more ascended to his station, to look for a path that might lead towards the house, which he now supposed to be the Signor's habitation, but no track could be discerned that might favor his intention; and it was evident, from the encreasing gloom, that he should not only lose all traces of the edifice, but of its inhabitant, for so his fancy had decided the Signor, whom he could dimly notice as he slowly drew towards his home. To pursue him immediately, argued the most incautious conduct; but caution, at that moment, formed no part of Rinaldo's character, and he hazarded the safety of his person with very little reluctance.

Taking, then, the most probable direction, he walked swiftly onward, and, by the time Schabraco totally disappeared, found himself in a path skirted with oak, that led to a ruined pavilion: beyond this he caught a glimpse of the building; and looking up, observed a light stream from one of its windows. Rinaldo paused, to ask himself a very necessary question—"To what purpose had he plunged into danger? (for danger there certainly was in the experiment he was making) What motive could he urge in favor of the intrusion, should he encounter the Signor?" A faint groan interrupted his cogitation, but it accelerated his resolution to retire; and turning round, he cast an apprehensive glance upon the dilapidated walls that surrounded a kind of court, and was rendered, by the partial gleam of light that fell on them from the window, an object of no very agreeable import. A second groan quickened his steps, while a thrilling desire to know from whence it arose checked them.—He stopped again—listened—all was silent. Again he retreated, and again lingered, when the shadow of some person near him decided all. The pavilion was already in sight, and the sound of pursuit closely behind. It was in vain he sought the path by which he had entered the court. The wild and trackless scene about him prevented all hope of escape; and well he knew that part of Calabria was infested by the most ferocious banditti.

But he had not long to hesitate. The voice of Schabraco broke like thunder on his bewildered meditations; and to the stern enquiry of "What had brought him to that spot?" he could only oppose a considered silence.

"Speak," cried Schabraco, "dost thou come to torment with that detested similitude, a wretch, over whose secrets thou hast no power? I marked thy rudeness at the masquerade, and fled. Say, then, who art thou? I would have avoided thee, for there is death in that aspect, destruction in thy voice." Rinaldo had begun an awkward excuse, for he felt himself irresistibly awed. "Speak not again—plead not so like Sabrina.—But I rave.—Begone, nor tempt me to commit another murder."

"Murder!" echoed Rinaldo (who felt his native ardor rouse at this horrible implication); "dost thou own a crime of the greatest magnitude, and yet—" "Hark! she reproaches me!—*It is herself!—But mark, young man, I have yet a dagger!*"—An address so horrible—so broken—so inapplicable, and inconsistent—while it almost overwhelmed Rinaldo, carried to his heart the pungent reflection, that he had nearly deserved the consequences of his temerity. His situation became more critical, and not less dangerous. It was plain this mysterious mortal adverted to some epoch in his own fate of a horrible nature. The groans which yet thrilled our young hero's soul (if hero he may be stiled), although they yet seemed to accuse Schabraco as the inflicter of some lingering punishment.

These flying suspicions were speedily interrupted by his awful companion, who, awakening as from a painful reverie, commanded Piozzi instantly to depart. "I have," cried that unhappy being, "committed myself too much, in thus giving vent to the tortures which rack a restless bosom; but I charge you, give my words no place in your mind, but as remembrancers of these injunctions: never, if your life be of any consequence, breathe a syllable of what you have heard or seen. Nor, should you chance to meet, in a future hour, the man on whom you have so rudely, if not villainously, intruded, dare, by word or look, betray a knowledge of Schabraco. Yet stop—" (for the astonished youth was availing himself of this permission, after solemnly giving his oath never to reveal what he had witnessed) "first say, what is your family—your origin—your expectations?"

"My country is Sicily; I came from Syracuse. My father—" "Ay, your father—speak," urged Schabraco, "I would have the name of him whom I suspect." Rinaldo, as he announced the title of Count Piozzi, viewed with horror the blazing eye, pallid cheek, and trembling lip of his interrogator; whose face, being turned to the brightening east, revealed features working with a variety of contending passions. Still more was his surprise encreased, to be thus interrupted—"Yes, I knew it. Thou hast been employed as an active agent in—but begone, young Sir; nor stay to witness the weakness of thy superior." Rinaldo waited not a second bidding, but hastily retreated, lest his departure should again be interdicted. The path through the pavilion was clearly visible, and he entered, deeply musing on all he saw and heard. That Schabraco had traced on his countenance a striking similitude to a female called Sabrina, was beyond a doubt; but the name was totally beyond his knowledge.

The females of his family consisted only of an aged aunt, and a young sister. His mother deceased during his childhood; since which period, Count Piozzi was never seen to smile. Her death, as hinted to him by Count Piozzi's aunt, was attended with circumstances peculiarly terrible; but none of them could apply to the case in question.

While thus employed, he adverted not to the path directly leading forward, but, in descended to the right of it, entered a sort of wilderness, whose intricate mazes diverged imperceptibly from the shore; and after several hours' fatigue, the tremenduous edifice he had left, again appeared. Faint with long abstinence, unusual toil, and a bewildered mind, the energy of what at first might have been deemed curiosity, again gave way, and nature's claims could no longer be disputed. Once more he strongly condemned the motives that influenced his conduct, and induced a visit to that desolate shore. But while eagerly looking in the most probable direction, Messina caught his ardent gaze, as it arose indistinctly upon the blue horizon; but its distance checked every tide to exaltation, and he could only bend his steps, towards the point that distinguished it, with but an heartless hope of reaching the opposite shore; while Schabraco's residence still attracted his attention, as he travelled parallel to its site.—The morning was calm—the prospect sublime. A bright sun tinted Calabria's mountainous tracks;

even Messina's lofty buildings caught a faint but mellow lustre. The most transcendent feature in a scenery so grand, when it first remotely caught his astonished eye, was scarcely visible;—Mount Ætna[1] yet veiled her majestic figure in the fog that hung about her lower sides. Her towering head, indeed, was illumined with the brilliant ray, which shone with a radiance uninjured by the mist that enveloped its lower sides; which even as he looked, drew up like a vast curtain, and gradually discovered a wild confused mass of picturesque imagery.—The demands of nature had been some-what allayed by the juice berries that grew on all sides; and Rinaldo felt himself at liberty to indulge that romantic enthusiasm, which expands the ideas, almost the limits, of mortal enjoyments.

But this mental feast was quickly interrupted, and prudence whispered how necessary it was to effect his escape from a place, which independent of his recent surprises, was remarkable for the ferocity of its native spoilers.

Taking, then, another observation of the edifice, he was about to descend the hill, along which he was wandering, when the sound of an instrument, rising, as it were, beneath his feet, acted like electricity upon Rinaldo's faculties; and, half suspending the breath which threatened to interrupt this gratification that stole upon his enraptured feelings, our adventurer stood the image of Attention, personified; for added to the refined tones of an excellent lute, was a voice which sung the sweetest notes, and produced a melody so touching, so mournful, so enchantingly expressive, as put to flight every lively emotion. From whence arose the mysterious harmony Rinaldo could not ascertain, although the following stanzas were easily understood.

I.

Orient Moon, whose livid beams
Tremble o'er Sicilian streams;
Golden orb, whose ardent blaze,
Darts around refulgent rays;
Darkling I sit, and sigh in vain,
Or pour the sad, desponding strain.

1 Mount Ætna (Etna), located on the island of Sicily. The highest volcano in Europe, it has erupted many times, including in 1669 and 1775, both recorded in various accounts and emblematic of sublime images in nature.

II.

Sober Eve, whose softened shades,
With grateful change the air invades;
Silent Night, and silver Moon,
That well supplies the place of noon;
No more your sweetness lulls my cares,
Here Sadness wounds, and Sorrow wears!

The distance from Schabraco's dwelling prevented all suspicion of its originating from any subterranean apartment; and the ground beneath him was of a texture totally unfavourable to the supposition of any rocky caverns, as it was soft and rich; too remote from the shore for any communication with its indented cliffs. While perplexed, to a degree superior even to the terrors of the past night, Rinaldo again heard music; it passed on the air; and to his situation, when the first strains caught his ear, he attributed the notion of its being beneath him. However, to wait for any further elucidation was useless, and he slowly pursued a path which brought him to a part of the shore much nearer Messina. The straits opened in front, but no boats came within call; and Rinaldo rested upon a stone patiently, hoping the arrival of several which he beheld advancing. While thus employed, he was alarmed by the paddling of oars, to the left of a projection that concealed whatever might be the cause; and in a few minutes he was gratified by the sight of his own boatmen, who, on being hailed, directly made for the shore. From them he learnt, that, after waiting two hours beyond the time prescribed, they rowed to a sheltered cave, fastened their small vessel, and slept till the sun awakened them.

It was lucky for Rinaldo that the land tended so as to make that part of the shore convenient for crossing, and he stepped on board with a grateful heart, while new surmises, respecting the invisible music, occupied his mind. To account for an absence so unexpected, was Rinaldo's next business. Count Piozzi had that morning arrived at a villa, where his son was received. More vexed than alarmed at an incident not uncommon, he received the confused enterpriser with a countenance of severity. Rinaldo's sentiments, unfortunately, were reflected in his features; they spoke a mystery, which his words denied. The Count saw their confutation in an ingenuous blush, and the alarm became serious: his eyes were rivetted on the poor youth, who could scarcely bear a scrutiny so terrible. It was evening, and in a public promenade, when Rinaldo was thus situated. He would have drawn from his father's arm the hand he had just passed through it; and, starting suddenly back, fixed a wild and horrific look upon a figure who glided by them. The Count's astonishment encreased; there was something so strange in this perplexity, so suspicious in the fearful attention of Rinaldo to the stranger's steps, that his father determined, if possible, to force an explanation of this extraordinary business.—"You know something of that person, I presume, Rinaldo?" cried he. "That person!" "Yes, him, who is just now leaving the place." "The place!" "Amazing! What means this absence? Do you recollect with whom you are trifling?" "Pardon me, my lord; my ideas are so confused!" Schabraco (for it was him) again returned; and, passing at that moment, glanced a look of such stern import at the youth, as once more deranged even his speech.

The Count was almost tempted to seize the cause of his son's incoherence, but Schabraco was gone; and Rinaldo, gazing after him, exclaimed—"I am bound, fatally bound, by a promise, which even now is, in some measure, violated. Pity my agitation, and let it suffice, that curiosity has led me into a dangerous, and awful dilemma. My lord, I can say no more." "I understand you, Rinaldo; the Signor, who has occasioned your confusion by some unknown art, obtains an undue power over you." So saying, he rushed towards the spot from whence Schabraco retreated, but in vain, and he returned to his trembling son, with a countenance exhibiting marks of half-concealed agony. He saw the struggle of Rinaldo's soul; and, while he could not condemn the dictates of that integrity he had ever encouraged, felt determined to watch his steps, hoping to gain by that means the intelligence which seemed essential to his peace.

[*To be continued.*]

[Continued from page 93.]

As several days were now elapsed, during which Rinaldo had not exhibited the smallest inclination to quit his usual pursuits, the desire of Count Piozzi to develope this mystery gradually declined. He saw the youth apparently free from any anxiety, but that originating in his regret to quit Messina, and Sicilian honour would not permit him to tamper with Rinaldo's. Matters were thus situated, when the Count's wishes were again inflamed, and every painful suspicion revived, by the appearance of two obscure looking men in conversation with his son. They were on the quay, and, by their motions, appeared to be making some arrangements for a voyage; now looking down the straits, and now pointing to a boat which was fastened near them. Eager to understand the subject of their discourse, though unwilling to be observed, he resolved to watch the men, he now began to imagine were, in some degree, connected with the object of his uneasiness, and waited with considerable impatience for their separation, which was no sooner effected, than he cautiously followed one, who seemed to be dispatched as if with a message.

From him the Count, by proper management, obtained a full explanation of Rinaldo's conduct; as much of it as belonged to his visit to the Calabrian coast, his discovery of Schabraco's residence, and his return with them on the following morning; confessing himself, also, to be one of the men who had conveyed him thither.

With every advantage superior years and wisdom could give, Count Piozzi possessed also discrimination; and, added to all, had a secret, yet unaccountable, presentiment of evil respecting this Schabraco, which he could neither fully admit, or discharge. Impelled, therefore, by a very rational desire to come at the motive for such extraordinary secrecy, he ventured to engage this man, with his fellows, to do the same office for him that they had before executed for Rinaldo, whose business, Marco[1] frankly owned, was to settle some additional demand for the trouble they met with during that night, which had damaged their boat. Satisfied with this explanation the Count proceeded to a proper arrangement of his

---

1 Marco is referred to interchangeably hereafter as "Marco" and "Mercutio."

intended expedition. Signor Mercutio, a man of talents and probity, readily engaged to accompany him.

Ever distinguished for an ardent spirit, which in some instances might be denominated daring, he was suitably contrasted by Piozzi, who, with equal intrepidity, felt no want of critical courage.

It was thought impolitic to demand assistance of the police, as there was no certainty of its being at all necessary; and, with the closing evening, our gallant pair set out for the Calabrian coast, accompanied only by their boatmen, who were ordered to wait for them at the little cove, near which they had been discovered by Rinaldo. As this enterprize was carefully concealed from him, it made their intended excursion more difficult, and less certain of success; for none of the company could tell the path to Schabraco's residence from the place of landing, and Piozzi chose not to advance farther through the straits, lest they should be endangered by the effects of a storm, which hung above the eastern horizon, and had already roused the rippling waves, that began to roll in irregular succession. At the suggestion of Marco, they sought a secure situation for their boat, and, jumping on shore, left the men to provide for their own shelter, while they proceeded on this hazardous journey.

The astonishing perseverence of Piozzi, evinced on an occasion so inexplicable to Mercutio, induced that gentleman, while descending the first eminence, to express a laudable curiosity to know his motive for such exertions.

"I will tell you, my friend," he replied; "as much, at least, of my inducements, as may countenance my present eagerness to explore this extraordinary business. The person of Schabraco is not wholly unknown to me. The dark and lowering aspect; the ill-conceived malignancy of his sullen eye; that piercing, yet shy glance, which marked his notice of my son, apparently belong to a man, who, many years since, was amenable to the laws for an atrocious act. I was in a court of justice when he was brought forward to answer a terrible charge. I heard his artful defence; I beheld his stern, collected attitude; a countenance expressive of what I have now described, and a figure the very counterpart of Schabraco's. Should he, *indeed*, be released to curse mankind by similar practices, I will exterminate the villain from a world he has so long disgraced. Oh,

my friend, to him—to him I owe the death of my angelic Leonora!—To this monstrous impiety the peace of a happy family is
sacrificed! More than this I cannot say, lest in Schabraco his person
should not be identified. Indeed, my chiefest doubt arises from
his daring to frequent the haunts of mankind, as well as from the
certainty I once encouraged, that crimes so vast as his, and so fully
proved, could never escape condign punishment. A severe illness
which detained me at Florence prevented the satisfaction I sought
of his conviction. It commenced on the second day of his trial,
owing to some yet undecided cause; and when I recovered, neither
culprit nor witnesses were to be ascertained or discovered. No minutes of the event could be procured. I had but few friends in that
city, and from those few I could obtain no information; but they
unanimously joined in advising me to leave that part of Italy.——
Syracuse had its attractions, and I hastened thither. In a future hour
you shall know the whole of——."

The Count's obscure hints were suddenly interrupted by an
awful burst of thunder. It bellowed among the mountains with
re-iterated strength. The valley before them was wrapt in obscurity, relieved only by successive flashes, which served but to render
the scene more horrible. No trace of Schabraco's asylum could be
discerned: all was gloomy, desolate, and unpropitious. To descend
the path before them, promised no hope. They stopped, and, in an
interval of the storm, Mercutio, looking up, pointed out to Piozzi,
a sulphureous track, which, arising from the south-east, poured a
prodigious column of smoak, in a horizontal direction, along the
upper grounds. It had a tremendous appearance, and served rather
to confuse than elucidate their path.

"Surely," cried the Count, "that cannot proceed from Ætna?"

"Undoubtedly not, my friend; from such a distance it must be
impossible."

While they were puzzled to ascertain its cause, the light it emitted
became somewhat clearer, and Mercutio suddenly exclaimed—"I
see an edifice to the right of us." "And that must be Schabraco's,"
rejoined the Count. "The storm abates; yonder flame, which I
now perceive to arise from some vast trees, sired as is most likely
by the lightning, will guide us. Come on, my intrepid friend; my
heart beats high; I have a presentiment that some strange event is

at hand. Certainly it will now be in my power to exonerate Rinaldo from the burthen of retention."

They now proceeded with tolerable chearfulness. The clouds rolled off in heavy volumes; a yellow streak, which every moment brightened into a purer lustre, illumined the east, and with pleasure they observed a waning moon slowly unfolding its useful disk; still the valley, along whose upper side they were travelling, appeared dangerous to be explored; yet they must pass through it, as the ancient building in question almost hung over the opposite side. No time remained for consideration, and they rushed precipitately forward.——The vast trees which shaded that awful recess entirely shut out the softened rays; no path could be traced towards the house, and they wandered for some time in almost palpable darkness, while torrents of water from the higher grounds streamed on all sides. But Piozzi, who headed Mercutio, suddenly finding an abrupt ascent, joyfully availed himself of it, and in ten minutes regained a view of his journey's termination.

The solemn silence which hung over this scene; the dilapidated building breaking, by its inequalities, the moon's placid beams; the vast and varied prospect around, partially discovered by that orb; and the importance of his errand, gave a sublimity to his ideas, mixed with the tenderest melancholy. He looked back; Signor Mercutio was not in sight: this was peculiarly unlucky, as he dared not exert his voice. While considering what plan to adopt for the information of his friend, a sudden light, passing swiftly along the middle floor, illuminating irregularly the windows of that story, called Piozzi's attention, while a piercing shriek aroused him to the highest pitch of agony. He forgot his friend—his own danger— every thing, but the hope of giving assistance to an object in distress. The shriek was repeated—the light returned—and several shadows of undistinguished figures flitted along. Piozzi darted up a short avenue of cypress that skirted the great entrance; but all was fast, beyond the possibility of mortal exertion to conquer.

"Death," cried the agonized nobleman, "is busy in this infernal habitation. Ha! I see a door——perhaps of admission."

It was in another part of the edifice, attached to the main body only by a half-ruined covered way. The Count easily found a passage into this part of a place, ill calculated to inspire chearful ideas—half choaked with rubbish, the windows fallen from their situation, the furniture as equally ruinous—all seemed to point out its general disuse. But Piozzi gave not an instant to examination: he immediately explored the covered way, which his agitated spirit scarcely permitted him to do with effect. However, after repeated trials, and several times being upon the point of returning, to aim at some more probable method of admittance, a door, which had escaped his eager research, as it stood on the shaded part of a small recess, gave way to the strong yet cautious effort he made to open it. This conducted him to a room in the main edifice, apparently deserted, as being unconnected with others on the same floor. He could but faintly discern at one end a flight of stone steps, which led to the upper parts of the building. Silently, then, and somewhat intimidated, Count Piozzi passed up them, and stopped at a heavy door, that stood nearly closed, the hinges of which were so much rusted, as scarcely to yield to our adventurer's attempts to force them. This was no sooner effected than his soul was appalled by the voice of one pleading for pity—even for life. It came from a distant apartment, but distinct enough to be understood; and Piozzi could now perceive a ray of light stream from the spot where he supposed some dreadful tragedy was to be performed. He was alone, but well armed. It did not appear that there were many perpetrators of a deed he trembled to think was to be immediately executed; even the voice which struck him as being a female's, was a further inducement. He would go——Piozzi then darted forwards——But, oh, tremendous!——what a scene opened to his bewildered senses——Rinaldo!—his beloved, generous spirited, his noble Rinaldo——with eyes expressive of maniac's rage——his countenance enflamed almost to blackness——his attitude that of a furious murderer——one hand grasping a drawn sword, the other holding the dishevelled locks of an interesting female figure, whose hands, uplifted and unconfined, were raised to implore that pity which his heart seemed to disdain.

The Count could just perceive she was not young; when, advancing hastily, his eye was arrested by another figure in the group— Schabraco!——the detestable Schabraco!——*He*, to whom Piozzi had been indebted for so many years' anguish! *He* stood exulting in the scene before him——Malice, revenge, and rage triumphed on his livid countenance. The smile which distorted his features was composed of the above diabolical passions.——

"Strike!" cried Schabraco——"Strike, and clear your sullied fame!"

Piozzi rushed on his son, and caught the blow that he imagined was aimed at the prostrate sacrifice; his other hand, sustaining a sword which pointed at Schabraco, seemed to mark him as his certain prey——

"Ha! monster!——monster!"——exclaimed the furious Count—"See you not, in this helpless woman, the——."

"Author of his being!" added Schabraco:—"and you—poor, disgraced——."

"Disgrace back to thy heart, villain—with the degrading title!"

[*To be continued.*]

[Continued from page 185.]

DISTRACTED by a coincidence of wonders (for the present scene seemed to owe its existence to somewhat bordering on the marvellous), Rinaldo quitted the object of his seeming rage, for him on whom his direst resentment should have fallen, not adverting, in that cruel moment, to the dictates of honour, which forbid the unequal contest; when his father, darting a phrenzied look upon the miserable youth, bade him retire, nor dare to interfere with a just revenge——"*My* cause," he added, "must prevail——Begone, then, matricide!—my soul disdains thy presence!"

Trembling with the conflict of different passions, Rinaldo was retiring, when the entrance of several domestics gave instantaneous employment for his sword. The combat then became terrible; yet, from a superiority of number, he could derive but little chance of success, and his weapon dropt useless at the very instant when Schabraco sunk beneath a tremendous stroke. Still firmly vigorous, his strength unimpaired, his fury unabated, Count Piozzi turned his rage upon the other assailants, who quickly shrunk from his victorious arm, and became an easy conquest. Durandor (the chief of

four servants, who were neither of them possessed of an extraordinary share of courage,—weakened, too, as they might be, from the
badness of their cause) threw himself at Piozzi's feet, entreating for
mercy. This was the more readily granted, as his attention immediately fell on the helpless victim to an inexplicable cause. She had
fainted on a stone window seat, happily insensible to the present
commotion.

Schabraco still lay, weak and bleeding, on the floor; yet his closing eye gleamed with fallen malice, while half uttered execrations
burst from his parched and pallid lips against Rinaldo, who stood
over him ready to finish the awful business, had he offered to stir.

At the command of Piozzi, Durandor hastened for a female
attendant, who brought with her some useful restoratives; and the
languid creature, slowly reviving, cast a look of terror upon her
persecutor, which then settled with such a mournful expression
upon Rinaldo, as conveyed to his sick heart a sad and painful conviction that he had been dreadfully misled;—but when he heard his
father salute her by the endearing name of his suffering sister, he
could scarce bear the turbulent emotions of his soul. Durandor's
obedience to a nobleman, so lately his master's antagonist, would
have been a matter of wonder, if he had not been recognized by
that gentleman as one who had acted a considerable part in those
events which had embittered so much of his existence; and his
readiness to procure accommodations for the lady and her protectors, evinced, as least so Piozzi would hope, a wish to obliterate his
sense of former injuries.

To a scene so painful to the Count and his son, the arrival of
Mercutio gave some relief. In him Rinaldo saw a mediator; and
the Count welcomed his friend as an assistant, should Schabraco's
domestics again make head against them. Astonished at all he saw
and heard, the Signor could only ask for an explanation, which no
one seemed able to give. Piozzi was busily employed in soothing
and encouraging his unhappy sister, while Rinaldo stood gazing on
the almost expiring wretch, whose respiration was marked by convulsive sobbings, till perceiving he was past opposition, he quitted
the dreadful object to Durandor's care.

Day was now so far advanced as to render the winking lamps
of no effect, although they doubled, by their pale and melan-

choly gleam, the horrors of the place. Sabrina, for so, to his son's encreasing amazement, Piozzi stiled the relapsing Lady, entreated to be taken from a prison so justly hated by her——"For, ah! my brother," she cried, "the sweet approach of morn, the vivid and refreshing sun, these eyes for years have never witnessed. Even now," and she cast a heavy look about the room—"even already I feel the powerful influence of day. At present I cannot bear the long wished for light of heaven. Oh, God!——is it possible I shall again be———." Overcome by various emotions she suddenly became silent.

Durandor, who had been attempting to restore his wretched master, now resigned him to the care of two servants, one of whom was summoned to attend the Lady. He then offered to conduct her and her protectors to the water-side, and immediately leading the way, was followed by Mercutio and the Count, who supported his sister, whilst Rinaldo, almost petrified with a sense of the recent transaction, slowly accompanied them.

Before Piozzi quitted Schabraco, he conjured Durandor, if he meant to prove the sincerity of his repentance, to omit no means that might conduce to that monster's recovery—"I have reasons," added he, to Mercutio, "to wish him a longer existence. There are incidents in this dear creature's history which he only can eluci-date." And then turning to Rinaldo——"*You*, perhaps—*you*, the base abettor, as it seems, of crimes truly diabolical, may—But, oh, Rinaldo—your conduct wants a better defender than him."

"Hear me, Sir," cried the distressed youth:—"you are mistaken. I have been unhappily deceived; and from my observance of a com-pulsive oath have been drawn into—."

"No more, Sir.—If you can exculpate yourself from the black stigma that hangs upon your character, Signor Mercutio will, when we are all at Messina, take your confession."

Rinaldo bowed in silence, for his agonized bosom could give no further vent to his sorrows; and, from the account he gave to that gentleman, after their arrival, it appeared that, on the preceding morning, he had seen Schabraco, who, contrary to his usual custom of shunning any conversation with him, evidently sought to engage his notice. Surprised, but not displeased, at a change from which Rinaldo deduced the hope of elucidating incidents so uncommon,

he readily adjourned to a spot, solitary enough to elude the observation of any acquaintance, where, with an artfulness peculiar to
Schabraco, he prevailed on this impetuous young man to meet
him, at night, near the pavilion before noticed, when he promised
a solution of every circumstance attached to the house in Calabria,
and the cause of his own situation there.—Rinaldo owned himself
somewhat embarrassed at the arrangement, yet was determined to
try the event.

It may here be necessary to remark, that Marco, in his account to
Piozzi respecting the business with his son, had very much deviated
from the truth; for the fact was, that they were settling the mode of
this second expedition; but, confused by the Count's penetrating
questions, he evaded a just answer—agreed to *his* proposal—and,
in consequence, Rinaldo hired another conveyance, which landed
him about two hours before his father arrived.

He then went on to say, that, tired of waiting at the pavilion, and
disgusted with the gloomy air of the place, he ventured near the
edifice, round which he slowly and uneasily paced, till driven by the
fearful tempest he regained his former shelter. Still no Schabraco
appeared, nor could he observe any vestige of inhabitants about the
house. For more than an hour he submitted to his uncomfortable
fate; but, more than ever displeased with the scene around him, he
again left his refuge. All was now silent: the thunder ceased to roar
but at a distance; the lightning flashed feebly and horizontally, and
he was about to depart, when his ear was struck by a sound of lamentation, in a style calculated to rouse every feeling of humanity.
At that very instant Schabraco appeared at a side door, and upon
seeing Rinaldo beckoned him forwards. It was in vain to contend,
and equally so to smother the agony of his soul!——

"You are come in good time," cried this tremendous deceiver.
"The tempest prevented my seeking you at the pavilion; but it is
not too late; follow me."

With a trembling heart our agitated hero obeyed the summons:
there was no alternative, and he entered a vast and gloomy hall,
almost unconscious that he did so. The hollow echo of their steps,
which ran along the walls, seemed to whisper sounds of horror.
A superstitious dread defied every courageous exertion, and he
followed into a room at the farther end of the hall with the expec-

tations of a criminal.——Hardly could his bewildered sense permit him to observe a wretched female, who, on Schabraco's entrance, darted out of the apartment with astonishing rapidity towards the great door; but, upon being pursued, turned back, and attempted the grand stair-case. Rinaldo's blood was chilled. Her exclamations were fraught with anguish——"Save me!" she cried: "oh, for pity's sake, deliver me from hands stained with the blood of the innocent!" At these words the aspect of Schabraco defied description——"Ah! is it so, tigress!" was all indignation would permit him to utter as he caught the wretched victim; who, exhausted and almost breathless, sunk at his feet in the beforementioned apartment, while he deliberately unsheathed a weapon intended for the most horrible purpose.

"Guess," cried Rinaldo, "at my feelings at a moment like that! Caution, self-defence, even the certainty of my own dreadful fate sunk to nothing. A female—an imploring, pleading, helpless female—holding up her clasped fingers for mercy!——a furious monster, contemplating, with a grin so ghastly, the agonies he enjoyed, and ready every instant to seal her eternal destiny—— Wonder not that I threw myself before this intended victim!—— that I grasped her tangled locks, with a design to drag her from the vile wretch!——But, oh, Signor, how vain were my attempts, had not my unjustly offended parent so miraculously interfered. Schabraco saw my purpose, and smiled at the futility of it. I have no doubt but his address to my father proceeded from the savage delight he took in endeavouring, at least, to create in his bosom a detestation of his injured son; for did not the Count acknowledge Sabrina as his sister? What, then, could that detested deceiver mean by an insinuation so unnatural?"

To this statement of an affair so intricate, Mercutio could only give a wondering yet strict attention. Ignorant as he yet was of Sabrina's history, he could give no clue to Rinaldo respecting her connections with and sufferings from Schabraco; yet eager to exonerate the poor youth from a crime so heinous, he hastened to his friend, and in the Lady's presence gave a clear and simple detail of the young man's conduct.

"Oh, he is right, indeed," she faintly exclaimed. "I should, but for him, have fallen beneath the assassin's stroke.——Noble youth, accept my warmest thanks." She then, feebly raising herself from a sofa, where (in consideration of her extreme weakness) Piozzi had placed her, and shading with one hand her half-closed eyes, she extended the other to Rinaldo, who just then appeared before her.

"Ah," said the Count, "this is what I wished for:—his innocence is proved, and a wonderful————But I do wrong—Rest, my injured love:—we will quit this apartment. I see Signor Mercutio is impatient for a solution of our story. I will blend the account you have just now given with mine, and convince him of our sufferings, our disappointments, and our hope of future felicity."

The recollection, or rather recapitulation, of such mournful events as had distinguished the early part of Piozzi's life, generally awakens dormant sensations, composed of a painful regret; with that nobleman it was exactly so; but it was a sacrifice to friendship, and he paid it willingly. The fierceness of a Sicilian sun was abated: its lingering beams hung on a cool portico which commanded the straights of Messina, its opposite shore, tufted with a part of those woods so terrible to our travellers on the preceding evening, and an extensive track of the Mediterranean, on whose calm and brilliant surface the distant sail glittered to the declining ray, which as it gradually stole from observation seemed to melt into the blue horizon.

"I am charmed," cried Mercutio, as he seated himself between the columns of the portico: "I am always charmed with yonder scenery;—it unites the sublime and awful with the beautiful and magnificent."

Piozzi sighed, and turned to look towards the Calabrian shore, as if he could have wished to have avoided even the outlines of a place so horribly distinguished. The look and sigh was not unobserved by Mercutio, who, willing to evade a subject which must strengthen the sorrows of reflection, would have carried his attention from objects calculated to produce it. The Count saw, and was pleased, with his design; but well knowing that both him and Rinaldo ardently wished a solution of such wonderful mysteries, he turned affectionately to the youth; and after warmly expressing his regret for encouraging a suspicion of his humanity in the late horrible transaction, and placing him on a marble seat, addressed his auditors as follows.——

"You have already understood the nature of my attachment to the dear sister of my heart; and, from what you have seen of her in the hour of persecution and distress, will readily believe my assertion, that she was once a most lovely woman. Those charming tresses, that delicate complexion, and expressive features, now so worn—so faded—so dishevelled—were universally admired. Her mind was well informed, her temper sweet, her disposition friendly. Her spirit occasionally took a melancholy turn, which was generally attributed to an enthusiasm bordering on superstition. In this she was encouraged by Stephano, a Monk of the Dominican order, whose gloomy air and forbidding manner disgusted every one but the gentle Sabrina. His occasional penances were strictly observed, and she would fast for sins of which her pure soul had but a faint conception. The addresses of Signor Leoni, a brave and worthy character, were received by Sabrina with that chaste diffidence which rendered her so interesting: not the shadow of an objection could be raised against such an union, and for two years Leoni was one of the happiest of beings. The birth of Rinaldo (for thou art indeed the son of that invaluable woman) could not increase (although it was of consequence to) such felicity as theirs. And I well remember Sabrina's spirits were visibly enlivened by the acquisition; but how was this serene and rational enjoyment of domestic harmony over-clouded—not suddenly, yet unaccount-ably!——it betrayed itself on the part of Sabrina in a mournful silence; or, if obliged to speak, her answers were short, chilling, and unsatisfactory. The sight of her infant rather disgusted than amused. Lonely walks, long frequent absences from her husband, sighs, tears, and short ejaculations, were the general effects of this awful change. At first we hoped it might proceed from a defect in constitution; but her health was pronounced as convalescent. The only person whose visits seemed acceptable, was Father Steph-ano; and the only person whose attendance she permitted, when abroad, was Durandor. Yes, Mercutio, that Durandor—and—but I will not anticipate—Distracted by a change so terrible, Signor Leoni came to my palace, near Leghora[1] (his own residence was

---

1 Misspelling of "Leghorn," which is used on subsequent mentions. "Leghorn" is an Anglicisation of "Livorno," a city on the west coast of the Italian mainland.

at Florence), and entreated my company back with him; as the evident partiality his Lady had ever shewn me might, he hoped, on this occasion, be an inducement with her to commit to a beloved brother the subject of her anguish. Happy to soothe the Signor by my hearty concurrence with his wishes, I directly hastened our departure, and had scarcely entered upon the journey, when a servant of Leoni's abruptly stopped us. His haste, countenance, and whole appearance denounced something fatal. Never can I forget the unfortunate husband's distress, when told, his wife had—eloped!—That Durandor was her companion; and that the following note, confessedly meant for concealment, was found in an escritoir belonging to Durandor; which note criminated Father Stephano as being an accomplice in the treachery of spiriting her away.

TO DURANDOR

"You do right to discharge from your conscience all sense of shame or evil in the present business. I will from time to time, as occasions may arise, furnish you with the fullest absolution.—Fear not, then.—Be resolute—speedy—and impenetrable!"

"Leoni, who, in an attitude of indescribable agony, had ran over the infernal scrawl, immediately exclaimed—" 'Tis him—the diabolical Stephano, who has torn from my heart its sweetest comfort. But I will be revenged!—enthusiastic villain—*He* has poisoned her mind—*He* has insinuated (I know it) the pretended impiety of a conjugal life.—Artful monster!—The mask shall be torn from a hypocrite so detested!" It was easy to guess at what my brother's suspicions pointed; and that he dreaded Sabrina was intended for a sacrifice of an illicit nature: but in this sentiment I could not join. His character, his manners, his conversation, all forbade a thought disgraceful to a member of the church; and I employed those hours dedicated to our journey in favour of Stephano. But when we arrived at Florence, the truth burst upon us from all quarters. Signora Leoni was fled with Durandor. Stephano was absent: he had, previous to her departure, been shut up part of the day with my sister, whose melancholy encreased to the most heart-piercing grief, as she hung over her infant before she quitted her husband's hospitable mansion. Irritated almost to madness, and denouncing every punishment against the supposed author of his calamity, the Signor set on foot a strict search of such Convents as most readily occurred to him of a character to admit females without the strictest enquiry into the motives of their seclusion; and this he did from a presumption that Sabrina might be confined there till the fury of Leoni's pursuit might be abated. But he never saw her afterwards;—and, oh, my Rinaldo, what will you feel when I tell you, that respectable, unhappy gentleman, after three weeks absence upon an expedition, in which he permitted me not to accompany him, was reported to be murdered in a wood at some distance from Florence. His assassins were taken near the spot; and one of them, I am now confident, was the detestable Schabraco,—in other words, *Father Stephano*—Restrain, my dear nephew, this torrent of grief, and let it be remembered, if it were so, he has at last been overtaken."

"Impious monster!" exclaimed the poor youth.—"Oh, that he may survive long enough to endure——."

"Silence, Rinaldo;—your rage is impotent; nor can be gratified in that way. Schabraco may yet feel the extent of mortal suffering;—should life be spared, he shall be produced to answer for his enormous crimes in a legal manner. I have now only to add, that, in consequence of the illness I hinted at, the ground of his accusation could never be ascertained to me, nor the event of that accusation; though I have now every reason to think that the church stirred most effectually in that dark business; and I returned to Leghorn, with the precious charge my sister had left, with a determination to adopt him for my own. Not many weeks after my return, Leonora, the comfort and support of my wounded heart, too much attached to the lost Sabrina, and too delicate to bear its consequences, added by her death a dreadful increase to my miseries. Ah! had we known the nature of a beloved sister's sorrows, distraction must have ensued. But I will now, if my Rinaldo can bear the recital of those sorrows, follow up my melancholy account with her's."

Rinaldo bowed, in sad submission, to the question; while his heart floated in anguish for the fate of his almost unknown parents.

From Count Piozzi's relation they gathered, that Stephano,

taking advantage of Sabrina's naturally enthusiastic turn, omitted no opportunity of giving her a disgust to the laudable pleasures of society. Religion was represented as exacting a positive observance of its strictest tenets. Domestic, friendly, and even conjugal duties, were reprobated as sensual; and, for some time, his insinuations failed in their effect. Indeed, he thought proper to relax in some degree, lest her love and obedience to the husband of her choice might lead to a discovery, not altogether suitable to his views. Delighted to find the path of duty a path to happiness, Sabrina's chearfulness became an additional pleasure to those about her; and Stephano, from her confession, found no reason to suppose she would ever name him as an adviser or promoter of a contrary conduct. The birth of Rinaldo seemed to her as the very climax of felicity; but, shocking to say, it proved a stimulus for villany to exercise its horrid talents upon. Gradually, and by the practice of infernal cunning, the Monk again renewed the terrors of Sabrina's mind. Her tenderness to her infant was a criminal weakness. Her husband, he plainly understood, had rivalled the holy saint to whom she owed the humblest adoration. The innocent gaiety of an untainted heart, he denounced as perfectly incompatible with a religious spirit. In short, such was his power, and so fully did he exert it, that it soon produced the melancholy so much deplored by her friends.

When a mind so effectually becomes a prey to the slavery of superstition, it loses all firmness; a common invention can govern it; the slightest events encrease it. What chance, then, had the unfortunate Sabrina (given up, as she was, to the influence of diabolical art, and without the privilege of claiming the advice of friends) to escape its destructive influence? Stephano saw his advantage, and availed himself accordingly. A convent was the resource he pointed out as a positive cure for sins like her's. It was true her resolution, if taken publicly, would be combated by a thousand opposers—within—without—relations—acquaintances. All who knew not, or felt not, the importance of such a vocation, would set their faces against the pious resolution. Sabrina trembled; her salvation was at stake. What was the world—its pleasures—even the purest of its gratifications—when put in competition with her soul's welfare! Sabrina hesitated—shrunk from the compari-

son; but—*Stephano conquered!* It was then Durandor's assistance
was thought necessary. His Lady could not depart alone, and her
spiritual father chose not to give his sanction to the step she was
to take. Her agonies at quitting the asylum of her virtue may be
better imagined than described; but there was no alternative; and,
accompanied by Durandor, she went to a convent at some little
distance from Florence. The civilities of her superiors mitigated, in
a trifling degree, her excrutiating sorrow; while Stephano, who had
privately followed, contrived by his denunciations to silence the
pleadings of nature in behalf of her child; but he could not conquer
them. Her tears flowed incessantly, nor could she derive any consolation for his assurances, that her salvation would now be secure.

[*To be continued.*]

[Concluded from page 274.]

THE anguish which Signora Leoni could not overcome was a
bar to Stephano's intention. The abbess, who little imagined his
motives were otherwise than conducive to the honour of their
church, added all her rhetoric to his; and between both, Sabrina
found her fears encreased, and her resolution to quit the world
decidedly strengthened: but it was no part of her spiritual director's
purpose to let her remain at that Convent. The black design, so
artfully covered, must for ever lie concealed while she was under
such protection. Revenge for the distance he had been held at by
Leoni, the infamous passion he had long indulged for Sabrina, and
the gratification of an avaritious disposition, goaded him eventually to his own destruction. There was no time to lose; her abode
would soon be traced; yet some delicacy, as well as caution, was
necessary in her removal, to prevent suspicion. *How* it was effected
Sabrina could not tell with respect to the Lady Abbess; but certainly
she parted from the poor victim with an indifference bordering on
contempt; and on the fourteenth day from her first elopement she
found herself in the house in Calabria.

To describe the various methods practised on her superstitious turn, and her natural gentleness, would characterize a duplicity and baseness which may hereafter be more fully elucidated, it is sufficient to say, that, from the moment she discovered his horrible designs, her detestation of the man, and the reproaches of an enlightened mind, were extreme. The imbecility which had favoured Stephano's execrable art was no more. She could perceive the extent of her hopeless situation, but that perception was cursed with all the terrors incident to such a discovery. Torn from, or rather impelled by the conjunctive effects of villanous sophistry and a credulous belief, the sweet association of maternal and conjugal duties—plunged into irremediable disgrace—and completely in the power of one who dared to veil his impious motives under the sacred cover of religion (a dreadful proof of his flagitious[1] spirit), how was she to escape the mischief already closing about her, especially as the sincerity of her expostulations had already produced the cruellest threatenings of severe confinement.

For some months succeeding her flight from Leghorn she was permitted the liberty of wandering about the environs of her prison, but never till night had shrouded every distant object from her view. To account even for this liberty, it is proper to observe, that Stephano had suddenly withdrawn himself, leaving Durandor as no improper substitute. However, although perpetually watched by the treacherous delegate, she felt some satisfaction in gaining a considerable suspension from the tortures of Stephano's brutish address, whose dreaded return produced an immediate renewal of his former conduct. Irritated at treatment so indignant, her once gentle spirit no longer submitted in silence to the degrading proposals she was condemned to hear. She freely and pointedly reproached his sacriligious views, placed in the most glaring light his vile, deceptious method of poisoning a ductile and innocent mind, tearing her from the bosom of a family who properly appreciated those qualities they were fond of encouraging. She was going on, when, seizing her arm with a violence she could not withstand, while his eyes gleamed with vindictive rage from beneath the rugged brow, he forcibly drew her to a flight of stairs that descended beneath the pavement of the great hall, and stopping a

---

1 *flagitious*: Extremely wicked or criminal (*OED*).

moment, as if to gather breath (for Sabrina did not easily submit to be thus cruelly dragged), he pointed to the dark and ruined steps, as if to warn her of some shocking evil yet to come. She trembled, and the more, when, in an hollow under tone, he told her those stairs led to her *grave*, unless she complied with the terms he had so often held out. "Determine, then," cried the monster. "Behold yon softened twilight shedding its mild influence around; enjoy the reviving evening breeze that gently waves those golden orange blossoms before yon opened casement; but, *remember*—" and he paused, as if to give his denunciation greater weight—"remember, unless your decision is in my favour, all the beauties of creation will from this hour be eternally shut from your senses—Deep—deep in the bowels of the earth shall be your abode.——Fool, dost thou hesitate? Is the alternative so unconsequential?"—

Sabrina *did* look into the horrible disclosure—she *did* cast an eager eye upon the lingering shades of evening—The golden blossoms perfumed with a grateful scent the extensive apartment; and again she dropped a frightened gaze upon the scene below.

"Speak," cried the wretch, shaking her shoulder with unfeeling roughness—"Will you comply?"

"*Never!*" answered Sabrina——"*Never!*"—and her tears began to stream—"But hear me, Stephano—*Father* I would say—once thou wast my spiritual father—commissioned from the Most High with messages of grace and peace—I thought—but—nay, hear me—How, how have I deserved this? Nay—force me not below the confines of—Ah, monster!—monster! tear me not thus from light, and life, and hope!"

Deaf to the unconnected petition, he loosened her hands from the wall to which she clung, and, maugre[1] her strong attempts to resist the unmanly treatment, dragged her to the bottom of the steps which was dimly illumined by the evening ray. Exhausted by her violent endeavours, she now submitted to be carried along a gloomy passage, till arriving at a sort of niche in the wall, he placed her on a seat, where she sunk insensible of her wrongs, nor recovered, till, by a feeble light streaming from a lamp suspended from above, she perceived herself in a recess, but whether below the

1 Despite.

foundation of the house or not, she could not ascertain. On a table, near the mattress designed for her bed, lay refreshments of different sorts; and, had it not been for an earthy dampness that arose about her, she could have fancied herself as well accomodated as before.

It seemed as if her resolute denial had entirely changed the course of Stephano's intentions. His visits were seldom, and marked with a sullenness bordering on hatred. She was regularly served with provisions; and in a tedious illness that succeeded this horrible usage, which was attended with almost continual insensibility, she faintly remembered the appearance of female figures; but, upon addressing one of them in a reasonable interval, she could not obtain a single monosyllable in answer; nor could she ever understand to what was owing her emancipation from her supposed dungeon, unless it might be owing to the representation of the women she recollected to have seen; but, as if the restless passions of her monkish persecutor had found other sources of gratification, she once more so far provoked him, by her spirited conduct, as to bring upon herself the dreadful consequences of his revenge; and again was forcibly compelled to take up her abode in another subterranean prison, where (notwithstanding the cheering light of day was totally excluded) she was comforted by sometimes hearing sounds descending from above her head—the braying of mules, the gingling of their bells, the voices of their drivers, and those of such creatures as were to be met with in that dreary spot. Even the roaring thunder and whistling wind carried a gleam of consolation to a heart thus torn from its dearest claims. But what afforded a superior pleasure, was the possession of a guitar, which, next to the exercise of rational (not enthusiastic) piety, cheated the weary hours of half their anxiety; and thus passed eleven years of almost unintermitted solitude.

Her diet was spare, and scantily supplied, but it was equal to the demand of nature. She had the satisfaction of knowing it was regularly brought by a female, whose decent attention to personal inconveniences was grateful to the distressed Sabrina; but her kindness extended not to speech, and our poor captive was obliged to content herself with such limited enjoyments.

It was now her positive opinion that Father Stephano's revenge would end but with her existence, and that she should endure it in no other shape than that of perpetual confinement. She would sigh, and weep, when agonising retrospection brought the idea of her dear, deserted relatives before her; and years had elapsed before she could think of them with christian resignation. But there were moments, when even the tenderest recollections discomposed not the calm and pious frame she was sedulous to obtain; and in those moments her triumph was complete.

It was impossible for Sabrina to account for her sudden liberation from her prison, which only happened on the day, or rather evening, previous to Piozzi's visit; when, to her utter amazement, Stephano presented himself at the door of her cavern, and, offering his hand, led her through a long arched vault which opened into passages of a low, narrow construction. Sabrina conjectured, from the time they were passing through them, that her abode was at some distance from the house; and this well accounts for the mysterious music Rinaldo had so recently heard. The appearance of Durandor, who met her at the trap door through which she had formerly been conveyed, contributed not to calm the emotions Stephano excited. In *his* countenance she traced the dark and gloomy features of unsatisfied vengeance;——in Durandor's, expression of fear, servility, and confusion. She was conducted into an apartment on the ground floor, when Durandor retired, and her heart throbbed with agony inexpressible; when Stephano, again catching her hand, and pushing her as it were from him, fixed an eye so terrible,—so malignant,—so indicative of murder upon her death-like features, that she sunk intuitively upon her knee before him, while he uttered, in tremendous, yet half smothered accents—*"Sabrina, thou must die!"*—At the same instant drawing a weapon from his bosom, which he was upon the point of plunging into her's, when, impelled by that nameless something which clings to a desire of life, she started from him, and fled.

What followed this eventful moment has already been described, and we shall now return to the wretched Schabraco, who owed the prolongation of a pernicious life to the care of Durandor. Revived by the administration of volatile essences, that miserable victim to depraved and villanous principles, expressed, in terms the most diabolical, his hatred of Piozzi, Sabrina, and those whom he had so deeply injured.—"I tell you, Durandor," he cried, "my soul will never know peace till the whole of that race is abolished! They have gone before me in every great and noble purpose. But for the birth of him whom I detest, Stephano would have inherited the honors of Piozzi. The plea of illegitimacy was incompetent to my dispossession of them. Ah! little knows the poltroon that Father Stephano and Hernando Piozzi are one and the same person. But am I not talking to an enemy? Yes;—thou basely gavest up the cause of thy master."—A slight convulsion checked the sad ebullition of unrestrained passion. His wounds again poured forth torrents; impelled by the turbulent emotions of his mind strong spasms succeeded; but not without some intervals, in one of which he beckoned to Durandor, and then pointing to a small chest—"If ever you obeyed me," urged the unhappy sufferer—"If you would make amends for your treachery—destroy, I charge you—but, I cannot—Durandor —Revenge,——Sweet—desireable—Durandor—burn—Oh!——" another convulsion prevented what he had further to say; and Durandor soon after beheld him cease to breathe. The contest was over; and his attendant shuddered at the shocking close of a life *he* so well knew to be fraught with almost every vice that can disgrace mortality.

Desirous of making every restitution the case would admit, Durandor no sooner recovered from the shock Stephano's sudden demise had induced, than he hastened to Messina with the chest so strongly insisted upon by his master to be destroyed. Count Piozzi hastily forced the lid, and an icy horror crept through his veins upon discovering the insignia of an order which Signor Leoni constantly wore, as also several rings of value, well remembered by the Count to belong to that unhappy gentleman. These were covered by several papers, which proved, upon examination, to be a sort of memoir, written from time to time, and horribly expressive of the mind that could dictate its infernal contents. From what could be gathered from these, and the confession of Durandor, who had been deeply concerned in all the guilty secrets, Piozzi became fully possessed of those motives which had produced such terrible consequences; we shall therefore give the whole of the events as connected in point of time.

It appeared, then, that Hernando Piozzi, an illegitimate branch of that house, had received an education to fit him for the church at Rome. His existence was unknown to the Count; but Hernando knowing himself to be that nobleman's half cousin, and son to the then possessor of the title, conceived a design to become his legal heir, should the Count die unmarried. This happened exactly as he wished; but there was still an insuperable bar to his inheritance:— Piozzi, the present Count, whose father was also deceased, immediately claimed the honours of his house, and was duly established in them. From that period Hernando, who was inconveniently situated in respect to pecuniary matters, determined to give full scope to his intriguing powers; and quitting his convent journeyed to Leghorn, and in consequence of those powers became invested with the advantage of Confessor to Piozzi's house.

With-held by no moral ties, and laughing at the denunciation of a religious system, whose thunders he secretly defied, Father Stephano (no longer Hernando) viewed the gentle Sabrina as a proper object to gratify his criminal passions. It would be a glorious revenge for the disappointment they had innocently occasioned, to corrupt the purity of a guileless heart, and make her the primary cause of much misery to a family he detested. Besides, her person was charming, and would suit his voluptuous propensities. How far he triumphed is already seen, in respect to that unfortunate Lady; but the Signor, whose death Piozzi had long lamented, was equally detested by their most dangerous enemy. His attempts to dissuade Sabrina from an acceptance of Leoni's offers was not so completely shrouded under a religious mask as to evade the suspicion of an ardent lover. He saw, and exposed, the sophistry of Stephano, but he could not trace to its source the infernal motive. Enough, however, of his dislike to this conduct appeared, to convince the Monk he must adopt another plan, and Leoni was marked as an additional victim to his baseness.

About this time Durandor was introduced by his subtle friend to Piozzi's service, and by the humility of his manners obtained a considerable degree of notice in his station. We have before observed, that Stephano possessed by a scanty share of Fortune's favours, but it was in consequence of his misbehaviour to his father, who saw his wretched propensity to evil, and stinted him accordingly. The assassination of Leoni, in which he was deeply concerned, opened to him a source of affluence. It was brought about by his contrivance; for Father Stephano, although confessedly a member of the church of Rome, was connected with the most dangerous depredators in Calabria, and occasionally used the old house, where Sabrina had been confined, as a place of meeting. To them he committed as much of his intentions respecting Leoni as was sufficient to the sacrifice of that injured man, whom they robbed and murdered. His personal effects were extremely valuable, and Stephano was so excessively rapacious, that this rapacity had nearly proved his ruin; for one of the gang, displeased at what *he* conceived to be an unjust appropriation, contrived to accuse, without being seen in it, the man whom he had jointly sworn to stand by; and after seeing him in the hands of the police, the vile fraternity flew from Florence, and reached Calabria in safety. Stephano's deliverance, and the management antecedent to it, was a sure conviction that the church had exerted its endeavours for that purpose, and he was again at liberty to persecute the helpless Sabrina.

Soon after these events another occurred, which was productive of real joy to his wicked heart. True, he had once escaped the hands of justice, but the rod was still suspended. His companions were still in the habit of raising contributions, of which he shared an ample part, for the link which held them together was their joint interest, and he knew not that his former imprisonment was owing to one of them; but still there was a possibility of discovery, and his transport was indescribable, upon hearing that the whole posse had quitted not only Calabria and Italy, but Europe, owing to a daring robbery they had committed, attended with circumstances of almost unexampled cruelty.

It was then thought convenient for Stephano to quit the old building for a time, and he accordingly assumed the profession of a merchant, under the name of Schabraco de Mendozi, appearing wherever business or pleasure convened society, and this purposely to avoid suspicion. But as no one shewed any curiosity about him he soon returned to his Calabrian shelter, where he continued to reside amidst the agonies of an unsatisfied revenge (which nothing but Sabrina's entire destruction could complete) and the hourly dread of a full discovery.

The appearance of Rinaldo at the masquerade, and his subsequent visit to Calabria, with his striking resemblance of Sabrina, roused every dormant terror; yet the idea of another murder, added to that of the unhappy Leoni, was just then insupportable; feelings which, till then, held no place in his bosom, and took the likeness of compassion, and saved Rinaldo from his fury; and tolerably contented with the vow he had extorted from the amazed youth, he suffered him to escape. But as Schabraco's business was to detect the bare possibility of danger, his chief employment was to watch Rinaldo, whose embarrassed countenance, while thus scrutinized, encouraged suspicions in Schabraco's guilty bosom, which nothing less than his death could satisfy.

It was then the business of that bad man to contrive the likeliest method to ensure his own safety; determining at the same time that the innocent Sabrina should be another victim to his infernal motives. No wonder then, that, disappointed in the very instant his dearest purposes were about to be effected, the malevolence of his heart, unmollified by the danger of his situation, should operate even to the hastening of the awful moment.

It appeared, from his incoherent expressions relative to Sabrina, that it was *her* murder he alluded to when surprised by Rinaldo at Calabria. The youth now became convinced it was his lamented father's assassination which passed with such horror through Schabraco's mind, forcing, as it were, those obscure hints that so much alarmed the youthful Piozzi; who likewise attributed to the wretched man himself the groans he had heard on that solemn night.

When Signora Leoni was cautiously informed of her beloved husband's fate, her grief more than kept pace with her joy at finding in Rinaldo her son, and in part her deliverer. Languid from long confinement and the trials she had met with, Happiness, although possessed of so many unexpected blessings, seemed to reject her suit, and she almost despaired of obtaining that fleeting good: but she was resigned, and forgiving. To Durandor she accorded a ready pardon, nor would hear of Schabraco's emissaries in the Calabrian mansion being brought to justice: agreeably, therefore, to her wishes they were suffered to depart, and the house, with all its intricate and subterranean apartments totally destroyed. It was the chief desire of her widowed heart to reside with her son at Florence, where Sig. Leoni's estates were situated. Count Piozzi had no choice as to place of abode, therefore readily accompanied the Signora to that noble city, where he saw Rinaldo Leoni (no more Piozzi) invested with the rich possessions of his murdered father, and took a melancholy pleasure in soothing his unhappy sister. Sabrina was thankful for his fraternal attention, but her chiefest consolation arose from the hope of being re-united to the beloved husband of her tenderest affections. "I have reason," she would say, "to know that trouble is the lot of humanity!——but I also know, that patience and resignation will smooth the asperities of that rugged path; and I trust my submission will be acceptable to *Him*, who thus prepares his children for a blessed eternity."

Her conduct justified those sentiments, and in a few months she left a world (to her) so full of sorrow, in the full assurance, that all her pious expectations would be verified; nor could the Count and his nephew mourn for her emancipation from griefs, so complicated, so lasting, and (as to this earth) so irremediable.

The friendship of Mercutio now shone forth in its fullest radiance: he was the friend, the companion, (and the consoler in such moments as would sometimes occur) of Rinaldo and his valuable uncle; proving, by his attention, that friendship is, indeed, the

True balm and rich sweetner of life!

LETTERS CONCERNING "SCHABRACO"[1]

The Proprietors of this work have it much at heart to render it worthy of public approbation and patronage. And for this end they invite and solicit the impartial opinion of all their correspondents, that, from various tastes, they may learn what is best, for the benefit of the whole. They have no hesitation to acknowledge the censure, conveyed by the following masterly paper, in many respects well founded, and mean to incur it as little as they can for the future; though they take the liberty of saying, it might have been tendered in less unqualified terms, as there is always more of sentiment than reason in strong language. They insert it, as a proof of their impartiality, and that the utility of their publication is with them paramount to every other motive. With this concession, however, they must be allowed to think the papers, specified by this ingenious and critical Lady, not so destitute of a moral tendency as she would alledge. They exhibit the extravagance of vice as an antidote to the excess of passion. Schabraco, for example, paints hypocrisy, cupidity, sensuality, the ruin of innocence and premeditated murder, in all that ugliness and horror which are the natural colours of these detestable crimes. Nor is the picture less impressive, that spectators are entirely left to the guidance of their own feelings and intelligence. The other articles on which our witty correspondent comments, are all more or less susceptible of a similar apology. Our honour is already as strongly pledged as it can be, that nothing shall be wanting on our part to avoid the extremes to which she alludes; and if our lovely readers will only give us credit a little longer for a sincere desire to please them, we have not a doubt but that they will soon find the Lady's Monthly Museum *whatever they or their parents would wish it to be.*

———

1 Vol. 1 (1798): Nov., 388-389, 389-393, and 420; Dec., 467-471 and 471-473.

TO THE PROPRIETORS OF THE LADY'S MONTHLY MUSEUM.[1]

GENTLEMEN,

THIS letter comes from one of the first boarding schools in the kingdom, and is fraught with intelligence of great importance. Know, then, we take in not less than a dozen of your Lady's Monthly Museum. It was agreed among us, the moment we saw your proposals, and sanctioned by our governess, who had long wished, she said, for something of the sort, that every half dozen of us should subscribe for one, as it costs each only twopence a month.—Whenever we receive a number, our custom is to retire by ourselves, in so many separate companies, and read it by portions at a time till we have completed the whole. Then, on some day afterwards, our governess calls each of us to account, and makes every one tell, in presence of the whole school, what we have read, and state such remarks as have occurred to us on any particular passage or story. This task generally falls, as it ought to do, on those young ladies who have nearly finished their education, and who now spend more time in reading than in any thing else. One of our school mates, who reads from morning till night, and sometimes nearly all night long, was directed by our governess, but a few days ago, to ascend the desk where our parson reads prayers and delivers to us his weekly lectures, and read what she had written at her leisure on your work. We were summoned to attend on this occasion with more than usual earnestness, and required to listen respectfully to what we should hear. The consequence has flung us all in the dumps, and our half dozen have ordered me to lodge our appeal with you, as you only can redress the grievance we state. We sent you a copy of the young lady's remarks, some parts of which made most of us shed tears. And we shall have such a row, when they appear in your next number, as must finally decide whether we take it in for the future or not. It shall then, at least, come to the vote of the whole; and you may rest assured we are now canvassing for it as much as we can. Be not you wanting to yourselves or us in suppressing this our manifesto, for we are all your inviolable friends, as well as constant readers.

1 Vol. I (Nov. 1798): 389-393.

"My sisters, and fellow pupils;

"You know my father has the character of being a good man, a man of taste—and our worthy and much respected governess pays the utmost deference to his opinion in all literary matters. A few days ago he called to ask for me, and found me reading the Lady's Museum. What passed on the occasion he communicated to our governess, who has desired me to take this opportunity of laying it before you, as she is pleased to think that his observations to me may likewise be of use to you.

"Mary," said he, "we must have a few minutes' talk about this Museum you seem to devour with so much eagerness.—The taste of a young woman, at a much earlier age than your's, is generally a pretty strong specimen of what she will afterwards prove to be. You remember this stipulation in the plan of the work much pleased me:—to give ardour to virtue, to warn from the approach of vice, to paint the social, moral, and religious duties in colours calculated to allure, to form the amiable temper and correct the manners of the blooming maid, to add energy to the resolution of the good wife and the tender mother, are objects inseparable from the design of this publication.

"Ah, Mary," added my father, "a performance in which these principles have their full effect were above all praise. But, indeed, from the sordid taste and depraved morals of the times, it were madness to expect it. But all proposals for subscriptions to books are nothing better than quack bills, as I then told you; and in general to be suspected in proportion to their pretentions. Not one in an hundred are ever faithful to their engagements.

"You must yourself be perfectly aware, the great objects all good parents have at heart, in the education of their daughters, are not likely to be answered by the monstrous and confused jargon which distinguish Schabraco, the Knight of Jerusalem, Edric of the Forest, the Two Monks, &c——These appear to me no better than the genuine ebullitions of insanity; and it would be quite as satisfactory to me to surprise you listening with rapture, by Bedlam or St. Luke's hospital for Incurables, to the ravings of their miserable inhabitants, as poring over such frantic productions as these."

"Oh, father," said I, "these are the very things we like best. And you cannot think how much we are delighted when some of the young ladies are quite frightened at this horrid Schabraco. The school was all in an uproar at the fate of the poor lady he had in chains. Both the Miss Feelings actually fainted, and one of them has been very poorly ever since. Only think, that a parson should turn out such a villain! Is it any wonder, dear papa, we should detest all black coats and canonicals as long as we live?

"He looked very grave at all this, and observed, with a sigh—he had rather have found me in a fever, than in such a humour. "It is very plain you prefer what you ought to abhor, Mary; and that is a very heavy concern to me. These unnatural stories have the worst possible effect on your minds. The imagination that can produce such things must be extremely gross and barbarous; they mark the Gothicism of the rudest ages, and not only divert your study and attention from real life, but embarrass your affections with fictions and ideas not only of no use, but seriously pernicious, as they inflame the passions, and tincture both the fancy and the heart with extravagance and romance. What do you imagine makes so many creatures in high life, particularly, so irresolute and giddy, but that their minds have been fermented, and in some degree deranged, by the perusal of such exaggerated fables as these. To perceive any fondness for them in you, after all you have heard from me, sorely affects me, indeed. Publishers find it their interest to feed this diseased appetite; as pampering a bad taste may be more profitable than exemplifying a good one. But it is, surely, my duty to correct a propensity so big with mischief, and which a great deal of experience authorises me to assure you must prove, to all who indulge it, a prolific fund of sad regret."

"Do forgive me, dear father," said I; for now he became so serious, that he even made me cry. "I will never read any thing again my father dislikes or forbids. But, as you often say we must have amusement, and cultivate an habit of reading, here are great variety. The contents show we have many nice verses, charades, riddles, enigmas, &c. and these do puzzle us so charmingly!"

"There again, Mary," replied he, "you talk very wildly. No wise man ever puts such ridiculous compositions in the hands of his daughters. They are calculated for nothing but to nurse that constitutional flutter, or nervous kind of palsey, which seems the radical disorder of your sex. Physicians tell us, the feminine frame ought, especially in its early stages, to be kept as free as may be from all agitation. It has not firmness enough to suffer much, without deriving from it the most essential injury; and health is not, surely, to be thus foolishly hazarded. But this is the smallest mischief that ensues from such reading. It cherishes prying, inquisitive dispositions, which give young minds such a bias to intrigue, as they seldom or never lose; and all the education in the world which corrects not this, is useless. The whole class of these mystical conceits is but a species of conjuration, perfectly beneath the attention of a rational, not to say a cultivated, mind. And it really hurts me, after all my pains and expence, that your taste should be still so grovelling and vulgar. Accompanied by their respective solutions, the only pleasure these trifles can yield is anticipated; and to find them out occasions a shocking waste of time. For what, then, are they calculated, but merely to excite and strengthen the silly and vicious curiosity of the idle and impertinent?"

"All this frightened, perhaps more than convinced, me; but it became me nevertheless to bow with silence and acquiescence. Our governess, who heard the whole, coincided implicitly with every thing he said. You will excuse my having done a duty imposed upon me by an authority, which, on my part, allows of no hesitation."

This speech alarmed and agitated us very much. But, gentlemen, your editor only is to blame. You may possibly recover the influence you have lost among us, by giving the directions no longer to an *Old Woman*,[1] but a young man. For nothing our own sex can say is half so acceptable to us, as what comes from the other. Now, do you not trifle with us. It has occasioned us a world of pains to lay the case before you precisely as it is; and if you do not wish to do us justice, there are others who will.

So your humble servant,

TELL-TALE.[2]

Harrowby House, Hammersmith,
    Oct. 15th.

---

1 "Old Woman" was the pen name of the resident advice columnist for *The Lady's Monthly Museum.*

2 An unidentified correspondent.

ACKNOWLEDGEMENTS TO CORRESPONDENTS.[1]

Tell-Tale *and her* half dozen *of female critics will accept of our thanks for her candid relation, as we might not otherwise have known aught of the matter. We comply the readier with their request, as it shews our aptness to improve by every hint, favourable or unfavourable, and that, though our labours be imperfect, we are not incorrigible.*

Old Lady Wrinkle, *as she calls herself, from the* Haunted House, *will excuse our inserting her* Midnight Tale. *We know not what possible pleasure such a series of monstrous fabrications can afford one of her years, but are well aware of the imminent danger there is, in impressing young imaginations with gross improbabilities, unnatural horrors, and mysterious nonsense.*

TO THE PROPRIETORS OF THE LADY'S MONTHLY MUSEUM.[2]

GENTLEMEN,

It is with the truest concern that an obliged Correspondent is reduced to the necessity of making your valuable Museum the vehicle of an attempt at self-vindication. She would much rather suppress every hint of an expostulating nature, than tax your indulgence in this way; but stimulated by an earnest desire to recover the ground she may possibly have endangered in *your* estimation, as well as in that of a discerning public, by being the subject of unprovoked calumny, she trusts you will not refuse a generous suffrage to her request; and upon this presumption will venture a few remonstrances in reply to Tell-Tale of *Harrowby House*, and this with all the sober sadness of simple reasoning, untinctured by the *genuine ebullitions of insanity;* pledging herself to observe the boundaries of decency, and guarding that real delicacy which belongs exclusively

---

1 Vol. 1 (Nov. 1798): 420.
2 Vol. 1 (Dec. 1798): 467-471.

to her sex, with equal, perhaps greater, care than even Tell-Tale herself has evinced.

To TELL-TALE.

"My dear young Lady,

As a being (perhaps unintentionally, but) deeply injured, the Author of Schabraco claims from your candour, that exculpation which she is conscious you will not refuse to grant, in consequence of the following defence; a defence, excited by the duty she owes her character as a female, a matron, and a tender adviser of the young and inexperienced.—The case before us is extremely serious: the censures, so unjustly incurred, are of awful import; and to submit implicitly to sarcasms so plainly implied, and so extensive in their consequences, would fix an indelible stigma on every future endeavour of mine to obtain the countenance of the worthy in favour of any future composition: for do they not attack the principles, the feelings, the understanding, and even strike at the *peace* of a fellow-creature? Do they not tacitly accuse her of fabricating tales positively calculated for the destruction of the purity of the unconscious reader? *Destruction* is a word of unlimited tendency; but what other can so justly convey the painful sense I entertain of this dreadful accusation? To corrupt the mind, to pervert the disposition, to vitiate the taste, to spoil the temper, and give a wrong bias to the sensibility of innocence, are shocking charges!—and those who justly incur them are the vilest of destroyers!

These charges are brought against the Author of Schabraco; drawn in colours of the deepest hue, and confessedly by a parent, who *would rather visit his daughter in a fever, than in a humour to be pleased with works of such a description.* The governess, too, throws in *her* mite of condemnation; and if these censures obtain among those who patronize the Museum, my apprehensions are justified.

But Tell-Tale will observe—"It is the romance, not *you*, we seek to expose." Ah! Madam; your severe strictures involve the Author equally with her production; for in what light can she be viewed, whose *ideas are barbarous*, and whose *horrid, monstrous,* and *confused jargon*, is imposed on the public, and has already produced in your seminary such serious consequences? It remains, therefore, that I should drop a word in defence of this vilified work, and analyse its influence of the female mind. Will the question imply too much confidence, if I ask, "Whether it inculcates notions of disobedience to parents, or grants either in its progress or conclusion an indulgence to vicious passions, or even weak propensities?" Is not the miscreant condignly punished? Are not the timid recovered from the effects of a blind superstition? And is not innocence rewarded? Can Chastity itself detect a sentiment against her purest dictates that is not properly exploded? and does the condemnation of a monk (a character, in those days, too often justified by example) reflect upon the sacred institutions of the present times?

If the *jargon* be *confused, monstrous*, and *horrid*; how is it that your fellow pupils were affected, even to tears and faintings, by the sufferings of Sabrina? And what a reflection upon their understandings, to permit the working of a perturbed brain to obtain such power! Have we not a toleration from the greatest and most enlightened of profane authors for this kind of writing; and are they not made use of in schools of the highest character? Do they not abound with pictures of Vice and Virtue personified? What are the Arabian Nights, the Persian Tales, the extracts and abstracts of various romances, which are not only permitted, but commanded, to be read in boarding schools? It may certainly be objected; that the vices and conduct of Schabraco are unnecessarily delineated as objects of avoidance to young ladies: Granted.—But are there not degrees in wickedness? If hypocrisy, infidelity, ambition, are touched with a strong hand, still it shews to what excess such vile propensities may be carried; and she who nourishes in her disposition the seeds of such destructive faults, may be brought to shudder at the exemplification, and its attendant miseries. Again: has not Schabraco an equal right with Sindbad the sailor, Aladdin, the Three Calenders,[1] &c. to a perusal? And who ever thought of

1 The tales of Sindbad (Sinbad) the sailor, Aladdin and his magic lamp, and the Three Calenders (sons of sultans) are featured in the *Thousand and One Nights*, also known as *Arabian Nights*, popularized in eighteenth-century translations from Arabic and French.

setting up those wonderful beings, and their actions, as examples of imitation?

To the paternal, the tender, the virtuous anxiety of a father, I give the highest praise: his remonstrances, if well grounded, do him honour; and if the disposition of his child warrant the reluctance he shews for her perusal of the *Monthly Museum*, I could weep with him for the sorrows he so justly depreciates.

In addressing Tell-Tale as one of my censurers, I only follow the dictates of a suspicion that points her out as secretly enjoying the severity of my condemnation; she will, therefore, excuse me for observing, that *my* language and subject, at least, are free from every shade of ribaldry and licentiousness. And here I own myself at a loss for expression; I would not offend; but, surely, one of the *first boarding schools in the kingdom* has no reason to complain of that governess's strictness, who can indulge them occasionally with a *Row*; and whose precepts and example produce no better effect than encouraging them to confess, in a public appeal, their preference of a *young man* to an *Old woman!* From this view, there is much reason to fear, that the parents of those who can make such an open confession, have an heavy task before them! May their cares be rewarded in the way most grateful to paternal hopes, feelings, and wishes.

As to the restricting caution respecting charades, &c. I have only to say, from an attentive perusal of the Monthly Museum, that you can read nothing there inimical to virtue in its most comprehensive meaning.

My true reluctance to what is called a paper war, has rendered the task of self-defence by no means an easy one. But I trust its evident tendency will be sufficient to exculpate me from the supposition of such an intention. If my youthful opponent can allow for the warmth of expressions, dictated by a heart deeply affected with a sense of undeserved severity, she will be entitled to the grateful thanks of

THE AUTHOR OF SCHABRACO.

To my contemporaries, whose little effusions are implicated with SCHABRACO, I have only to observe, that, nowithstanding the odium we have justly incurred, there is every reason to believe, that while Virtue and Prudence hold the Reins of Fancy, she will never outrun the Public Suffrage.

TO THE EDITOR OF THE MONTHLY MUSEUM.[1]

SIR,

If I understood rightly, you requested the opinion of your Correspondents upon a paper in your last Museum, signed "Tell-Tale." I hope I shall not be deemed presumptuous for offering mine upon a subject which ought, for the benefit of my sex, to be thoroughly investigated. With respect to the immorality of modern romances, much has been already advanced, and the severest censures passed upon them by those who have not only read them with avidity, but have even themselves been the authors of similar productions. The perversity of our nature is such, that whatever is administered medicinally, in general disgusts, and we are obliged to have recourse to such palliatives as destroy the nauseous properties of the dose;—so it is with morality, unless embellished with the flowers of fiction. The Ancients had recourse to similar methods when they wished to inculcate the principles of virtue: can the most extravagant sallies of romance be more absurd than the fables of former days? in which not only animals of every species are endowed with the faculties allowed only to man, but even inanimate substances are equally enlightened! Yet these are works which the most careful father would put into the hands of his children. It is true, their improbability is their security: it is therefore obvious, that the stronger the romantic colouring is heightened, the smaller will the danger be. I have great reason to believe that a piece entitled *"Patience Rewarded, A Moral Tale,"* would not have half so many readers as *"The Mysterious Wanderer, A Romance."*— The former is overlooked; all the fine sentiments and religious tenets disregarded; and the unfortunate book, that contains a most elaborate eulogium upon the cardinal virtues, torn up, leaf by leaf, to curl the auburn locks of a beauty for an approaching ball,— while the romance is perused with rapture. The variety of incident

1 Vol. I (Dec. 1798): 471-473.

excites attention, and the virtues and vices of the particular characters are regarded with admiration or abhorrence as we take an
increasing interest in their fate, till we find a real benefit accrues
from a pleasing employment. Women are no longer considered
as irrational creatures, but are permitted to hold a rank in society
from which they were formerly excluded: it is not, therefore, to be
supposed their understandings can be so easily deluded with that
they know to be merely works of invention; and that may, in general, be safely allowed the use of those *terrible stories*, if not absolutely of a vicious tendency; neither do I think a moderate quantity
of the light sort of reading a *dangerous* relaxation from more useful
studies.

There is also another subject upon which the father of "Tell-
Tale"[1] expressed himself with much severity; and which, with all
due deference to his experience, I would attempt to defend;—this
is the encouragement given to Enigmas, Rebusses, and Charades,
which he both morally and physically condemns, and which
appear, to my weak judgment, still less offensive than the former
object of his disapprobation. There is a pleasant emulation among
youth in the solution of those puzzles, that exercises the genius,
quickens the intellect, and gives an acuteness to the fancy deserving of cultivation, besides inspiring them with an eagerness of
enquiry into the various and abstruse qualities of things highly necessary in an intercourse in the polite world. It is not probable the
gentleman in question would send his daughter to a fashionable
boarding-school, unless he wished her to become an accomplished
woman; and this cannot easily be effected without a knowledge
of Polite Literature, which is greatly promoted by an attention to
such "*Jeux d'Esprits.*" They are of service in recalling to the memory
lessons almost forgotten, and give an intelligible mind opportunities of shining, at once productive of satisfaction to themselves and
their friends. If I have advanced any thing impertinent or errone-
ous, I shall be patient of conviction; as my intention was merely
to plead an excuse for those who have undertaken the amusement

---

1 Presumably the father of "Mary," whose letter "Tell-Tale" forwarded to the
LMM.

of the public without any design to pervert the *morals* or injure the *constitution* of youth.

ELIZA.[1]

---

1 Pitcher postulates that Eliza could be "Eliza Andrews" and/or "E.A." (Pitcher 32-34). An E.A. contributed a number of essays and poems in 1798 and 1799.

THE JOURNALIST, OR DEBUT OF A FEMALE AUTHOR.[1]

Monday.—Arose this morning in better spirits than usual—No wonder—My novel is finished, and I have only to present it to some bookseller of celebrity to secure a gratuity equal to its merits; since I may be allowed to say, that, for language, sentiment, genius, and taste, it is beyond comparison; and then my mountains, valleys, torrents, castles, and gloomy forests, are so admirably described, so geographically defined, that I am certain they must produce a wonderful effect; copied, too, as they are, not from nature, (for I never was in Switzerland) but from the travels of those who have, and this is done almost verbatim; although my poor William assures me I shall be deemed a plagiarist: no matter; it is a common error among us writers.

Now then for a title—Let me consider—*The Apparition of the Castle*[2]—No, that wont do—Flat, common, and insipid.—*Infernal Mysteries of the Bloody Banquet, a Tale from the German.*[3]—Delightful to a degree—what a daring flight of the imagination—and how suitable to the subject—for my dungeons are so deep—my skeletons so disgusting—and their wounds so dreadful: another of William's objections—he absolutely scouts[4] the idea of *wounds* upon a skeleton. Dear creature, his helpless situation renders him too much alive to contradiction. However, I shall not give him his way in this instance; for the more marvellous the description, the more interesting to those readers who greedily swallow nonsense, when ornamented with the stamp of fashion!

---

1 Vol. 1 (Aug. 1798): 113-119.
2 Title recalls that of *The Sicilian Romance; or, The Apparition of the Cliffs* (1794), an opera by Henry Siddons.
3 Several years later *The Monthly Mirror* (Oct. 1801) published a one-paragraph parody titled "Extract from the MS Romance of The Bloody Mysteries of the Infernal Banquet" by "Mrs. Gloomly" in which the ghost is a scarecrow.
4 *scouts*: To treat an idea as absurd (*OED*).

Mem.—Mean to dash into the world with eclat[1]—nothing like it. One may abate, when one cannot raise one's price; and, truly, all I hope for, will come short of our present wants.—Little Robert's new suit (which I bespoke upon the strength of my expectations) must be paid for—Mary and Eliza, too, are extremely shabby—My afflicted husband, likewise, requires a thousand little attentions, which his scanty stipend forbids—Alas! when I look upon that loved, emaciated countenance—that enervated frame, so long confined to a hard, uncomfortable couch, my heart sinks beyond the power of buoyant hope to raise.

Tuesday.—Just returned from Mr. Shuffle—Oh, how my hand trembled, when I offered the important work! He took it, glanced an eye of astonishment at the title, and (yet, to be sure, it must be a mistake) I could not help fancying that somewhat of ridicule informed his voice, while he asked me, 'if the work was as *wonderful* as that title seemed to denote?' A tear was my answer, as I turned away from the penetrating look, which appeared, to my busy mind, as hunting for a confirmation of a suspicion he might have taken up respecting the poverty of my appearance. Alas! the scene was painfully new to one, whose life, till the birth of her youngest infant, had only been distinguished for its serenity. But there was little time for reflection, for my gentleman, after professing his utter inability to give more than five guineas for the best novel extant, turned carelessly upon his heel, and left me to the comfortable enjoyment of unavailing retrospection.

Mem.—Since the *size* of a MS. determines its merit, I hereby resolve, that my next work shall contain 1800 pages, at least.

Wednesday.—Disappointed again—for again I have been to Mr. S. He returned my book, nor would attend to any terms but those of printing it myself. No—no—my dear husband suffered enough by publishing a medical book, part of which he received again from the pastry-cooks, St. Paul's Church-yard, enclosing tarts for the children.[2]

Still I attempted to soften his hard heart; but, alas! the trial was

1 *éclat*: Brilliancy, radiance, dazzling effect (*OED*).
2 An allusion to the practice of using the pages of old or unused printed works for practical purposes—like wrapping up tarts.

pronounced, and he even smiled at the very liberal offer I had made, of three tragedies, and as many farces, to be thrown into the scale.

Mem.—If every dramatic piece which now obtains were as perfect as mine, the stage would speedily recover its long lost celebrity.

Thursday.—Now, then, I have scarcely any hope remaining, and poor William entreats me to give up what *he* terms a wild and improbable expectation. "For what" (he asks) "can you, who are without friends, without name, without even the assistance of a prior publication, propose, by engaging in a line so uncertain, and in which so many of your superiors have miserably failed?"— "*Superiors!* —my love, I cannot accede to the word; for till there is a competition established, how can a superiority be claimed?" [Twelve at night.] While we were discoursing upon this ungrateful theme, Mary ran into our little back room, to say, "She had seen our landlord pass the window;" and his arrival was that moment announced, with a violence that shook the debilitated frame of my husband. I ran to the door; when, O horrible!—Mr. Sharp made his appearance, followed by two strange men; and the words arrest—rent—arrears, &c. soon deprived me of every degree of fortitude, and I sunk nearly insensible; but the exclamation of my children, added to those of their languid father, awoke me to the pain of reflection, and I perceived Mr. Sharp was gone—the bailiffs impatient—and Pelham, with tears in his eyes, petitioning them to wait till he could send to a friend, who possibly would bail him. I understood his meaning, and flew to the gentleman; but he was absent; and before my return, the harpies had torn my beloved from his children, one of whom ran to tell me—"The naughty men had taken him to prison;—that Mary was in fits;—and little Robert struck down by a wretch, who was left in care of our miserable furniture, for teasing him to assist his sister."

Mem. —Mr. S. had only a *legal* right to afflict us thus.—What a sad and melancholy difference between law and justice!

Friday.—What a miserable night have I passed!—unable to leave my sweet children with an unfeeling mortal, who grumbles at the scanty fare which I had with difficulty procured for my little family, and dreadfully anxious for Pelham's situation. However, as I have reconciled Mary to my absence, by procuring a neighbour to supply my place, I will go to Carey-street—and, perhaps——yes, I will once more try the success of my unfortunate book. Great Heaven, in pity to our sufferings, incline some gentle heart to accede to my request! Seven—five—two—even *one* guinea—would be a blessed acquisition!

Carey-street, Friday noon.—Fatigued almost beyond bearing, and with spirits oppressed by grief, mortified love, and cruel disappointment, I have sat me down by my sleeping husband, to arrange and compose, if possible, my distracted thoughts. Dear soul! he cannot long survive such accumulated distresses. How can I tell him, that I have run the gantelope[1] of eleven booksellers, even from Leadenhall-street[2] to Pall Mall, and Bond-street, endured the cold denial—the pettish rebukes—the pompous advice, and from more than one?——That tender pity that breaks the heart it would wish to soothe—such a heart at least as mine—whose pride is more than equal to the task imposed on it; how can I relate to him my peregrination through the Mall,[3] where grandeur, gaiety, and ill-concealed distress, often mix in heterogeneous confusion? And, oh! how cruel to recollect the vexation of my soul, as I sat upon the only vacant seat, (for, indeed, I was both faint and hungry) when a party approached, who appeared to consider me as an unnecessary interruption to their intention. Seeing this, I arose, and dropped my papers, which were immediately caught up by a——; but I will not describe him; such animals are best characterised by their words and actions. With a loud exclamation, he expressed his astonishment, as the unfortunate title met his eye; and calling me his sweet Parnassean[4] votary, asked "When the world would be favored with the charming produce of my lucubrations?[5] Only

---

1 *"run the gantelope," "gantlope," or "gauntlet"*: A figurative version of the military (occas. also naval) punishment in which the culprit had to run stripped to the waist between two rows of men who struck at him with a stick or a knotted cord (*OED*).

2 Leadenhall Street was the address of William Lane's Minerva Press, one of the most prolific and best-known purveyors of Gothic novels and other popular fiction at the time.

3 A road running from Buckingham Palace (west) to Trafalgar Square (east).

4 *Parnassian*: Of or relating to Parnassus, as the source of literary (esp. poetic) inspiration; (hence) of or belonging to poetry, poetic (*OED*).

5 *lucubration*: The product of nocturnal study and meditation; hence, a literary work showing signs of careful elaboration (*OED*).

think," he cried, "what spirit, what taste, must be employed in a composition distinguished by a title so sublime! *Infernal Mysteries!* how grand!"——He was interrupted by an elderly gentleman, who sharply reproved him for his insensibility; and, seeing me ready to sink, offered to assist me as far as Spring-garden Gate[1]. I shrunk from his touch, and burst into tears (for the rest of the party to which he belonged appeared to have taken up a cruel opinion of my situation).—"O Pelham!" I cried, "if *you* were present, I should not be thus insulted."—"Pelham!" exclaimed my disappointed protector. "Great God! did I understand aright!"—Without stopping to hear more, I hastened away, and at the bottom of the walk just ventured to look behind me. The party had turned a contrary way; but I saw the beforementioned person.——Ha!—somebody enquires!——

Saturday.—No—I could not write yesterday; but my heart is yet too full to leave this little sketch of human disappointment unclosed; and if one sad, desponding heart should be comforted, by a brief relation of the following event; or one too sanguine author find her hopes and expectations moderated by a perusal of this true copy of literary deception, my purposes will be fully answered.

Astonished to hear the name of Pelham most anxiously announced in Carey-street, I crept softly into the passage, and beheld the very man from whom I had so recently fled. He saw me,—and springing forward, was at my husband's bed side before I could prepare the surprised William for a scene, to us most interesting; for he opened his weakened eyes upon—a father! To paint the various emotions of pity, tenderness, doubtful joy, and fearful hopes, which this interview occasioned, would be impossible. In the stranger, my husband beheld a justly offended parent, who had long disclaimed him, for forming an alliance with the offspring of an hereditary enemy; for, indeed, that was all the objection he could have to one who had never before seen him. In my dear William, Mr. Pelham beheld a son he had left to all the difficulties annexed to his station, who, while Surgeon of a man of war, contrived to support me and my little ones in peace, and a tolerable independency: but when, induced by unthinking advisers, he quitted the navy to follow his profession, we soon were reduced to live upon his half

---

1 Near the east end of the Mall.

pay, and even that became inadequate to the expences of a tedious illness, and a rising family.

Mem.—It was in the hope of realizing something considerable for the poor sufferer, that I was induced to quit the more useful and domestic occupations, for an employment, which I now begin to think ought never to be taken up, but by those whose connections, genius, and education, are calculated for such a disposition of their time.

It may now be sufficient to observe, that sickness, penury, and unhappiness, soon fled before this benevolent visitor, who confessed, that, alarmed by my apostrophe to the name of Pelham, he had followed me to Carey-street, and from some confused intelligence of the preceding day, derived a suspicion of the truth. Thank heaven! it came not too late.—With what rapture shall we take possession of the comfortable cottage designed for us by this dear reconciled parent, to whom I have already presented my sweet infants! And he has not only recognized them as his own, but settled a sufficiency on their father, equal to his most sanguine expectation.

MARY PELHAM.

Brומley. Del.   Chapman. Sculp.

Edric of the Forest. page.254

Engraving for "Edric of the Forest" from the Oct. 1798 issue of *LMM*.

EDRIC OF THE FOREST.[1]

A ROMANCE. IN TWO PARTS.

BY E.F.[2]

PART I.

> Th' humblest, simplest habit clad,
> Nor wealth, nor power had he:
> Wisdom and worth were all he had;
> But these were all to me.
>
> GOLDSMITH.[3]

HIS person was well formed, tall, and elegant; his manners graceful, and countenance lovely; the bright rays of intellectual spirit shone from his large hazel eyes, and beamed with benevolence, truth, and honour. Such were the endowments of Edric the Orphan, when received into the family of Lord Dunferne, a dependant upon the Earl's bounty; and while his soul revolted against the state of dependance he was submitting to live in, love, gratitude, and his native sweetness of disposition, prevented his departure from the Castle.

It had been his fortune, while fishing one day in his early years, to save the life of the lady Eleanor, who, passing incautiously over the natural bridge that was formed by interwoven branches of trees

1 Vol. I (Sept. 1798): 219-226 (Part I); Oct. 1798: 253-258 (Part II).
2 See Pitcher 96-98, who notes many contributions from "E.F." and indicates that this author is a woman who may have married in 1807 and become "E.T." "Edric of the Forest" and "The Cave of St. Sidwell" in this collection may have been written by the same "E.F."
3 From "The Hermit" by Oliver Goldsmith; see, e.g., *Poems by Oliver Goldsmith, Containing The Deserted Village, The Traveller, The Hermit, Retaliation, Songs, Elegies, Epitaphes, &c. With the Life of the Author* (c. 1798).

across the brook, missed her footing, and was plunged into the stream. Edric bore her from the water to Dunferne Castle, where, from that period, he became a welcome visitant. The death of his father, an aged peasant, now threw Edric upon the wide world, at the tender, inexperienced age of fifteen. The Earl, remindful of his former service, offered his protection; an offer which the grateful tenderness of Lady Eleanor induced him to accept, and he became an inmate of the Castle.

Previous to his death, Walter, the peasant, gave into the hands of Edric a small dirk,[1] the hilt of which was embossed in a curious manner. "My dear boy," said he, throwing his feeble arms around him, "this is all I have to bequest you:——pray Heaven you may never make use of it for the dreadful purpose by which it came into my possession. Edric, you are not my son! Years have dissolved all my tender connections, and the remnant of my days were devoted to this solitude, when chance threw you in my way. Wandering one day through the deepest recesses of a neighbouring forest, I heard a faint cry of distress. As I never walked unarmed, I hastened, without apprehension, to the spot, and found a soldier of no mean appearance, yet with the ferocity of the most savage ruffian, piercing the helpless bosom of an infant with this dirk. I instantly fired; the wretch fell; and snatching the child, weltering as it was in blood, from the ground, fled with it to my hut. By applying healing herbs I soon mitigated the anguish of the wound, and had the happiness to see a fine boy thrive beneath my care. Need I say, my Edric lived to repay me for the trifling trouble, by his tender, his affectionate attentions!"

The youth, affected, fell on the bosom of his more than father,[2] and sobbed his thanks. The old man continued—

"Nature shudders to repeat the surmises I formed. The mystery of your fate is yet unravelled, and it will be most prudent in you to avoid an investigation, which Providence, for the wisest purposes, may endeavour to conceal. This dirk, and the deep scar you still bear upon your breast, may one day discover you to your parents:

1 *dirk*: A kind of dagger or poniard. Interestingly, given Edric's later military service, a dirk was commonly considered a weapon used by Highland Scots (*OED*).
2 *more than father*: One who nurses and brings up (a child); a nurse, foster-parent; *esp.* with reference to the custom of fosterage (*OED*).

'till then, the blessing of an old man hovers over you. Persevere in the paths of virtue, and you will one day receive your reward."

He sighed deeply, and, falling back on his pillow, expired.—In the sincerity of undissembled grief, Edric mourned his loss; but the greeting smiles of Lady Eleanor, after a while, dispersed his melancholy reflections, and the kindness of the Earl soothed him to tranquillity. The refined manners of the former tempered the wild hardiness he had acquired in his secluded education, and the Earl's fund of knowledge, literary and practical, was imparted to the wondering Edric, who found a new world of science burst upon him at once; yet his emulation increased in proportion to the difficulties that seemed likely to obstruct his progress; and the Earl found it much easier to excite ardour in a sensible mind, than to repress it when excited. In proportion as his understanding expanded his impatience of dependance increased, and one only consideration detained him at the Castle; this was a passion, which had daily acquired additional force in his mind, for the beauteous Lady Eleanor, and which was returned on her side with equal warmth, kindled by gratitude, and cherished by the merit of the object in her heart. The Earl perceived it, and condemned his own want of caution for mutually exposing them to the dangerous society of each other. His niece was scarce less dear to him than his orphan protegée; but a fatal promise obliged him to frustrate all their enthusiastic and romantic dreams of happiness. He sent for the youth, and extending his hand to him, while tears of tenderness started to his eyes, he told him he must no longer consider Dunferne Castle as his home. "I know," he continued, "you love my Eleanor; and it pains me to state the objections I am unwillingly forced to make. Her father, the Baron Villency, was a man of high pride and ancestry. At his death he committed this child to my care, with a solemn injunction never to unite her fate with one of inferior rank or fortune. This promise I must fulfil; but my Edric shall not be abandoned; she owes you her life, and it would be but a poor return to send you an outcast from those gates which have so long, to the satisfaction of their owner, inclosed you. Your country calls for your services: I will send you out a soldier of fortune, and heaven send your arm may be successful, when raised in defence of your sovereign."

Edric stood some time mute with astonishment, grief, and indignation. At length he replied—"My Lord, your words have cut me to the soul: they seem to reproach me with a treachery, which I would abhor. I own, hitherto ignorant of your engagements, and unthinking of the distinction fortune has made between us, I have dared aspire to the lovely Eleanor, as the only blessing this world could afford:—that denied me, I scorn all further aid. I am not a mercenary; no bribe could tempt me to act otherwise than my innate sense of rectitude dictates or make me more assiduous in the performance of my duty. I am already more your debtor than I can support, and the weight of accumulated obligation presses heavy upon my spirits. I will depart, my Lord. Suffer me only one farewell view of her I must ever adore, and I bid adieu to Dunferne Castle for ever."

Lord Dunferne embraced him tenderly, and felt himself unable to oppose any of his resolutions: he granted his request, and at the feet of Eleanor, Edric poured forth his uninterrupted vows of unshaken fidelity, which were reiterated by her, who vowed to live for him alone. The interview becoming at length too painful on all sides, they were obliged to part. Edric buckled on his dirk, and after being prevailed on to accept a sword of considerable value, from the armory of the Earl, departed.

He wandered to the borders, and was readily received a volunteer into the forces of Sir John Cope, who had then the command of a large body, attempting to subdue the Scottish rebels, who, in the year 1745, gave England so much alarm.[1] He signalized himself with the greatest bravery in several skirmishes, when the unfortunate defeat of the forces, in which that brave commander lost his life, threatened him with a similar fate. He fought with a desperation that baffled all the efforts of the enemy to subdue him; till, exhausted by fatigue and want of rest, he sunk, insensible to all

---

1 Sir John Cope was blamed for a disastrous defeat at the Battle of Prestonpans on 21 September 1745, but he didn't die during the battle; instead he lived to be acquitted in a court of enquiry in 1746 and would die in 1760. Edric's valour during the battle shows how much greater a soldier he is despite his lowly origins, even greater than Lieutenant General Cope, who was also a Knight of the Bath. In 1745, Charles Stuart returned to Scotland, prompting the rebellion defeated in the Battle of Culloden the following year.

around him, upon the earth, and was left for dead among the slain. A lethargic stupor succeeded his fainting fit, from which he awoke refreshed, but weak and famished. The shades of night were falling fast, and he roused himself to escape from such a scene of horror as was presented to his opening eyes. His clothes were wet with the blood of those who had fallen beside him, and the groans of the dying were heard from every corner of this desolated spot.

A light, glimmering through some distant trees, kindled a faint ray of hope in his cheerless breast, and, as well as his feeble strength would admit, he crawled towards it. Upon a nearer approach, he found it proceeded from the turrets of a Castle; but the darkness of the night deceived him, and made the distance appear much less that it was in reality.—Knowing his life depended upon his reaching the destined spot, he exerted himself to the utmost, and arrived at the gates just as he felt a cold faintness come over him, and he had but just time to sound the large bell ere he relapsed into insensibility. Upon reviving, he found himself in a magnificent bed, surrounded by a number of well dressed domesticks, who attended him with the utmost assiduity.

As soon as he was a little recovered from his extreme illness, Edric begged to be acquainted with the name of his hospitable entertainer, and learned from the servants that he was now in the castle of the Baron Waldeck, a foreigner of distinction, who had resided for many years in a remote castle in Cumberland. An ill state of health under which the Baron laboured, had, they said, hitherto prevented his personal attendance, but hoped soon the amendment of the invalid would give him an opportunity of making his congratulations. Edric longed impatiently to be introduced to one, who had with so much politeness discharged the offices of humanity; and, as soon as returning convalescence permitted, waited on the Baron in his apartment.

Upon being first conducted into the room, Waldeck half rose, but the debilitated state of his limbs obliged him again to reseat himself, and he pointed, with an air of complacency, to a chair beside his own. His countenance was pale and emaciated, but his features were regular, and possessed a look of mild benevolence, suffering under an accumulation of misfortune, that strongly interested Edric, whose sympathizing heart was ever open to distress.

This first interview was so mutually pleasing, that they agreed frequently to repeat it; and in a short time they became most intimate friends. The Baron expressing some curiosity concerning him, Edric, as far as he could with prudence, gratified him; and Waldeck, in his turn, seemed desirous to place a reciprocal confidence in him.—

"The present infirmities I labour under," said he to him, one day, "are not those incident to age, or an impaired constitution; they are the effects of acute sufferings; miseries that admit of no alleviation——." He paused and sighed; then continued—"This spot is endeared to me by a variety of tender recollections, yet I have not resolution to abandon it, though environed by injustice and unmerited ignominy. I am persecuted by unknown malice, and the most heinous crimes are imputed to me by calumniators, with whom I am now, and shall probably ever remain, unacquainted."

Thus encouraged, Edric urged to be further acquainted with the story of his new friend. The Baron grasped his hand—"Spare me," he cried, "a recital so painful to my feelings:—yet you may essentially serve me, if you are so willing:—have you courage?"—Edric blushed at this unseemly question, but replied, with firmness—"If you have any occasion for my services, I think I may promise you shall never find me deficient."

"You may, probably, defy mortal prowess," said Waldeck; "but are you so wholly divested of weak prejudices as to dare to cope with supernatural powers?"

Edric, unacquainted with superstition, otherwise than by name, readily assented to do whatever he might deem necessary; at the same time a faint doubt arose in his mind, that some treachery might be intended: yet the apparent openness of the Baron, and the consciousness of his own insignificance, soon eradicated all his scruples; and the hope of benefiting one who had been so generous towards him, at once determined him, and he renewed his offers of assistance with encreasing warmth.

"You have to learn, then," said the Baron, "that the west wing of the castle is reported to be haunted; noises and uncommon appearances have certainly been witnessed by my servants; in consequence of which, and some domestic troubles, my reputation has been materially injured. I have myself watched repeatedly at night, but have never been able to discover any thing satisfactory; and however contrary to my judgment, I am obliged to coincide in the general opinion. I labour under a stigma the most distressing to a mind really innocent, and am almost inclined to wish for death as a relief to my unmerited misfortune."

His voice faltered as he spoke, and he leaned his head, for support, against the shoulder of Edric, who fervently sympathized with him, and reassured him of his readiness to watch that night in the west tower. The Baron overwhelmed him with acknowledgments; and at the hour of ten Edric stationed himself in the chosen spot. The room in which he was appointed to watch, was large, gloomy, and ill furnished. It had been the Baron's sleeping chamber, at the time of his first residence in the castle; but having been obliged, from the uncommon sounds continually heard there, to abandon it, the furniture had been gradually stripped from it, and the whole so mutilated and defaced, as scarcely to retain any traces of its former magnificence. The casement had long deserted the lofty grated windows, and swallows, as well as spiders, had begun to claim it as their right. A blazing fire now re-illumed the long deserted chimney, by which Edric seated himself, and the old decayed hangings waved to and fro with the draught it occasioned; the wind sighed in dismal blasts through the battlements, and the clock struck eleven. Edric now tasted some of the refreshments set before him by the Baron, who had been obliged himself to bring them hither, no servant being willing to approach that side of the building. His spirits, in spite of his efforts to prevent it, began to sink, and he indulged himself in mournful reflections on his beloved Eleanor, when a faint groan, not many paces from him, caught his ear: he started, listened; but all was still. Attributing it to his own lowness of spirits, he swallowed another glass of wine; examined the locks of two pistols, which lay on the table before him; replenished his lamp, and again betook himself to meditation; when a second groan effectually roused him. He sprang from his seat, and scrupulously examined every part of the apartment; but his search was fruitless, and he again returned to his chair.

[*To be concluded in our next.*]

[Concluded from page 226.]

Part II.

For Virtue can itself advance
To what the favorite sons of Chance
   By Fortune seem'd design'd:
Virtue can gain the odds of Fate,
And from itself shake off the weight
   Upon th' unworthy mind.

FAIRY TALE.[1]

THE deep and awful sound of the Castle bell, tolling the midnight hour, reverberated through every vaulted roof and dreary passage of the venerable building; yet the heart of Edric remained unappalled, all his present thoughts centering in his own adverse fortunes; till at length, almost stupified by the impetuous working of his imagination, he fell into a perturbed slumber; his mind, harrassed by the preceding events, still conjured up disturbing images: he fancied he beheld his guardian falling beneath the sword of an assassin, and in a moment, by his superior agility, he rescued him.—Again, he believed himself in possession of vast domains; his Eleanor came to welcome him; his arms expanded to embrace her, and he felt he grasped a substantial being!—Awaking with a sudden start, he found himself encircled in the embrace of a figure, whose hideous form at first appalled his scattered senses. His blood chilled for an instant, but returning courage soon animated him, and seizing his dirk, would have plunged it into the heart of the stranger; who, perceiving his intention, hastily drew back, and displayed his bosom already weltering in gore. The unnerved arm of Edric dropped the weapon, which the other as hastily snatched from the ground, and, surveying it attentively, uttered a wild cry of surprise and horror, and fainted away. Edric did not call

---

1 From *A Fairy Tale, in the Ancient English Style* (c. 1714) by Dr. Parnell (Rev. Thomas Parnell), published posthumously by Alexander Pope in 1722.

for assistance, lest there should be a party of ruffians concealed, whom his noise might alarm, but alone endeavoured all he could to bring the stranger to recollection, when, with a look of despair, he exclaimed—"I am dying: let the Baron Waldeck be summoned, that I may, before my death, confess to him a piece of villany, in which he is nearly concerned."

Losing all other apprehension of danger in his fear of the poor wretch dying without assistance, Edric laid him on the bed, and instantly sought the Baron, who, with two domestics, tremblingly repaired to the haunted chamber. They advanced to the bedside: the stranger raised his head, and, with a deep sigh, gazed around him.

"Orlando!" exclaimed the Baron, starting with affright—"are you, then, my hidden foe?"

"I was," replied Orlando, in a mournful tone:—"but the hour of retribution is arrived. Listen—oh, listen, while I have yet strength to relate a tale of guilt!"

All were profoundly attentive; and he proceeded.

"Fifteen years of estrangement cannot have obliterated from your remembrance our former friendship. I had a sister, beautiful in form as odious in disposition: her passion for you was violent, and you disregarded her: you married one of inferior fortune, of superior endowments. I beheld her with eyes of desire, and the revengeful machinations of the slighted Miranda taught my soul to glow with equal thirst of vengeance. The chaste Editha disdained my overtures, but her fear of giving grief to you restrained her accusation of your friend. Miranda, inspired with the hope, that the hated bar to her happiness once removed, she should secure you, entered with avidity into the most diabolical plot ever formed in the mind of man; which was, the forcibly carrying away your wife, and the destruction of your infant! Fearing to trust another with our scheme, I undertook the infernal office—I plunged that dirk in the bosom of the helpless babe; but from an unseen hand received a pistol-shot that levelled me to the earth."

Here the exclamation of Edric interrupted the narrator, who, baring his breast, displayed the scar; and, falling at the feet of the Baron, cried in an ecstasy of transport—"I am your son!"

New life seemed to rush through every vein of the Baron, as he strained him to his breast; but the Count Orlando waving his hand again, expressed his wish of proceeding—"Your wife was conveyed to a gloomy fortress, some miles distant, where I tried by every art I was master of to win her to my purpose, in vain. Miranda was equally unsuccessful in inspiring you with the sentiments she wished; when, in a paroxysm of rage she raised the dagger against you, which you detected, she fled to me for refuge: but, alas! I shudder to repeat the horrid catastrophe! Unsatiated vengeance will find vent; and the injured, angelic Editha fell a victim to the infernal passion of her own sex!—she perished by poison, which this guilty hand administered. Into what a sea of blood was I plunged! Remorseless conscience still haunted me, and I turned my vengeance against her who had instigated me to perpetrate crimes, at the bare mention of which my soul once revolted. Again were my hands imbrued in blood!—I fled the fortress, as though I would fly from myself, and joined a party of murderers who forage the country. Knowing all the avenues to this Castle, I recommended them to a subterraneous pass adjoining it, as a place of safe concealment; but, to ensure all in greater perfection, it was judged expedient, by odd sounds and dreadful noises, to intimidate the inhabitants of the castle from occupying that part of it adjoining the passages leading to our cave. The report of its being haunted gained but too ready credibility among a set of ignorant, superstitious people; and the disappearance of your wife, murder of your child, and extraordinary conduct of Miranda, gave a horrid colouring to the suspicions excited against you. Little remains to be said:—in consequence of some plunder, about which we disputed, a battle among our party ensued; and after a most horrid slaughter part of the set fled, and I was left wounded as you see. A faint hope of yet making atonement for my transgressions inspired me, and I crawled hither; and, oh, may my guilty career prove, that happiness is never to be obtained by treachery or a vain attempt to counteract the intentions of our Supreme Guide. I die a repentant sinner; but I feel my crimes have been too great!"

Strong convulsions choaked his utterance, and, in spite of all medical assistance, which was immediately procured, after suffering three hours of unspeakable torture, he expired.—As soon as they could with decency after the interment of Orlando, which was done as secret as possible, the remains of the Baroness were brought from the fortress, and deposited in consecrated ground. This melancholy rite for a while revived the grief of Waldeck, but the pious and soothing consolations of his son taught him a proper estimation of the blessing he possessed, and he was soon restored to happiness.

Edric, now every obstacle was removed likely to impede his union with Eleanor, entreated his father's permission to seek her, to try whether she still loved him: a trial he had too great consciousness of her virtue to fear would turn out to his advantage. This obtained, he hastened to the castle. The Count received him with open arms; told him that many noble, illustrious suiters had presented themselves to Eleanor, but, for Edric, she had refused all. He led him to her. She received him with transports of chaste love; and when he unfolded to them the discovered mystery, the Count, taking the hand of his niece, joined it with that of Edric; assuring them, that his happiness was complete, now that he could, with honor to himself, confer it upon them. "But, my dear child," he added, turning to Edric, "let me suggest one idea to you:—the inglorious event of the service you were lately in, renders it highly necessary that you should again exert your arm against the rebels, nor secure your own private ease, when your country is in trouble. I would have my Edric shine no less splendid in public than in private life."

"You have anticipated my wishes," cried Edric, glowing with heroic ardor. "I wished only to secure the prize, for the obtaining of which life was alone to me valuable. In the expectation of this sweet reward, my courage will be invincible: and as I expect my father hourly hither, an uninvited visitor, to see and confirm my choice, I wait only his consent to fly to the performance of my duty."

Sentiments so congenial to his own filled the Count with unconcealed admiration, which the approving presence of Waldeck confirmed. He beheld the lovely, blushing Lady Eleanor, with the partiality of a father, and longed ardently for the hour she would be secured to his Edric; on whom he bestowed, at his departure, his fondest blessing.

No more an obscure wanderer, did the now happy son of the Baron seek to rush into the arms of death, under the banners of the

Duke of Cumberland. He raised his name in the annals of fame, and the country rung with just praises of the youthful warrior. On the happy termination of the rebellion he was presented to royalty; from whose hands, in token of gratitude for his signal services, he received the honor of Knighthood, and returned a happy victor to his Eleanor's arms. Their union was now no longer deferred; the humblest peasantry for miles round partook of the general festivity; and the wonderful history of Sir Edric became the chaunt of the village mothers to their infant sons; shewing them, how courage, fortitude, and virtue, were rewarded! Age, instead of destroying, added lustre to the beauty of the fond couple. Calm serenity and virtuous innocence sat on their brow; and when the evening of life closed in upon them, they sunk as into the slumbers of a peaceful sleep, till their spotless souls waked into a happy futurity!

ADVENTURE AT NETLEY ABBEY.[1]

BY T. P.[2]

How still is the evening! The vessel's white sail
Loosely flags at the mast, as it droop'd for the gale;
  The sailor-boy whistles in vain:
The bark scarcely moves as upborne by the tide,
Whose waters in silence salute its bright side,
  Where Netley looks down on the main.

I see the sun's last rays illumine its wall:
From ivy, o'erhanging, the hoarse raven's call
  Comes fearful and deep on the air!
But mark the strange accent! Ah! what can it mean?
Hark! Echo repeats it!————repeats it again!
  And bids me for wonder prepare.

I relinquish my bark, and thrice round the Pile
I traverse. I enter the wood-shaded aisle.
  I stumble:————a skull!————no, a stone.—
What shadow enormous reclines near yon door?
Retire!————ah, no————apprehension is o'er:—
  How simple;————the shadow's my own!

Here once stood the altar. These steps are unsound;
They lead to the roof————what a prospect around!
  But what should yon dark vault contain?
Its arches are fallen————how spacious the room!

1 Vol. 3 (Sept. 1799): 241-242. Netley Abbey, located in the village of Netley near Southhampton in Hampshire, was a popular literary gothic location as early as 1764 in George Keate's poem "The Ruins of Netley Abbey."
2 According to Pitcher (199-201), a "T. P." contributed poems from 1799 to 1801. See also "The Abbey."

Are those coffin nails that I see thro' the gloom,
   Or glist'rings of late-fallen rain?

This door stops my progress——Oh, Heav'n, a key!
It opens—and Fate seems to point me the way
   That leads to yon Ruin's drear shade.
How sable within! Yet methinks now I see
One niche still entire——But, ah! what is he
   That prostrate before it is laid?

How heavy that sigh! Be firm, oh, my heart;—
Some tale of foul murder he means to impart:—
   I pity his sorrows, alas!——
He rises!—he beckons!——I follow——Go on!——
The duty my Fate has enjoin'd shall be done:—
   'Tis done——and I follow an———Ass!

THE ABBEY.[1]

BY T. P.[2]

The placid Moon her silver light
    Shed on yon ruin'd Abbey's tow'r,
When two fair lasses of their loves
    Took leave, at midnight's solemn hour.

Maria's form, of tender mould,
    Contain'd a gentle, constant mind;
But Mary's, airy, free, and bold,
    Betray'd the spirit unconfin'd.

Often, when Mirth possess'd the hour,
    Maria left the board, to stray
Midst the lone Abbey's solemn shade,
    To think on William, far away.

But Mary join'd the dance, the song,
    Or on the knee of some fond swain
Would laughing sit, nor think of him
    Who thought of her upon the main.

It chanc'd, one eve, the storm grew loud,
    Maria to the Ruin came,
And, as the wind rav'd thro' its aisle,
    She sighing call'd on William's name.

---

1 Vol. 4 (Feb. 1800): 161-162.
2 See Pitcher (199-200). Possibly the same "T. P." as the author of "Adventure at Netley Abbey."

When, to bless her longing sight—
  To sooth her bosom's fond alarms—
William, returning, met her view,
  And clasp'd her with a lover's arms:

And vow'd the next day's sun should see
  His lovely lass a joyful bride——.
"Shall see me, too, a joyful wife,"
  Cry'd Mary: "Good or ill betide.—

"But lest my sex my purpose blame,
  "I'll seek yon ruin'd Abbey's wall,
"And see if Henry, too, will come,
  "Like William, at his mistress' call.

"If not, young Thomas takes my hand,
  "And, lo! to-morrow's golden sun
"Shall Mary see a joyful wife:—
  "Not by a sighing maid out-done!"

Boldly she seeks the Abbey's shade,
  And loudly on her Henry raves——
When, ah! her Henry's ghost appears,
  All pale and shiv'ring from the waves!

She shrieks——she falls!——alas! the day
  That saw her friend a bride so meet,
That very day beheld, a corpse,
  Poor Mary in her winding-sheet!!

THE COMPLAINT OF A GHOST.[1]

Written by Himself, Herself, or Itself.
Published from the Original MS. (with Notes) by *Sam Scribble*,[2]
author of "Thespian Mania," &c. &c. &c.

———

> In various shapes I oft the town delight,
> But ne'er before did I attempt to *write;*
> And yet I'm tortur'd by no maiden fears—
> I claim the right of *trial by my peers.*

SPECTRE.

NOVELTY being, in the present dearth of genius, the most admired ingredient in the composition of literary beverage, the effusions of a *supernatural* scribe (from the portion which they contain of that favourite article), aided by the infusion of a sufficient quantity of extravagance and absurdity, would, without doubt, prove a delicious treat for modern amateurs, and gain me no small degree of celebrity in my new character of author. But I deprecate the idea of mounting to fame on the wings of Folly. Mine is a tale of oppression and woe; harsh and discordant to the refined ear of a fashionable reader; and merely designed to render humid the eye of genuine Sensibility, and to nerve the arm of offended Justice.

Torn by the irresistible incantations of a literary coxcomb[3] from

---

1 Vol. 4 (May 1800): 365-370.

2 Pitcher suggests that "S.B.," "S. Baker, Pentonville," "Samuel Baker," and "Sam Scribble" are the same person and ascribes the following to this author: "Thespian Mania" *LMM* 4 (March 1800): 195-196; "Ali: An Oriental Tale. By S. Baker" *LMM* 2 (Jan. 1799): 19-21; "The Fatal Effects of Curiosity, Exemplified in a Narrative Founded on Facts" *LMM* 1 (Oct. 1798): 302-304; and "To Eliza" [poem] *LMM* 8 (Jan. 1802): 68 (see Pitcher 49, 54-55, 234).

3 This title has been aptly conferred, by an impartial Critic, on the late Horace Walpole, Earl of Orford, to whose "Castle of Otranto" we owe the introduction of the fantastic herd of Ghosts, Goblins, &c. into novels and romances. [Author's note.]

my peaceful abode at the bottom of the Red Sea, where I enjoyed
the calm sweets of oblivious repose, I have for several years been
doomed to the most odious and abject slavery, in a land character-
ized as the favourite residence of the fair Goddess of Freedom.

The jetty Negro, inhabiting the torrid zone of Africa, whose
oft-recounted woes rend the heart of Humanity, never experienced
the minutest particle of drudgery, compared with that imposed
upon me by the irascible tyrants whom I serve.

The dingy African, after his daily toil, is permitted to recruit his
exhausted strength in the arms of Somnus, until the radiant sun
re-cheers the earth; but hapless I am denied even the benefit of
that necessary vacation from fatigue. Every paltry scribbler usurps
the right of dragging me from my bed, and of forcing me to obey
the capricious mandates of his fantastic imagination. Sometimes
I am constrained to perform penance, arrayed in a sheet, on some
frozen heath or dreary wild, amid the howling wind and boisterous
tempest; at other times, to march bare-foot, with majestic gravity,
in a damp vault or decayed cellarage, rigged out in rusty armour
as old as Adam's breeches; or, according to the poet's whim, to
sneak across a crazy draw-bridge, glide along a rotten wall, tremble
behind worm-eaten arras,[1] dance in a belfry, chaunt "lullaby" in a
deserted bed-chamber, stand tip-toe on a tombstone, crack nuts in
a church-porch, pinch the tail of a favourite cat, pop through a key-
hole, rap my knuckles against the wainscot, or sport my figure in a
cock-loft![2]

Shakspeare, that darling child of Nature, regarded me as an
useful auxiliary, not an abject slave. When he availed himself of my
assistance, he adorned me with the blooming flowers of genius,
and rewarded me with a participation of his immortal fame; but
modern play-wrights bribe gazing stupidity to applaud the most
disgusting nonsense, by allowing it a peep at poor me, divested of
every grace, and awkwardly decorated with gaudy (though worth-
less) weeds; nurtured by the sun-shine of modern *taste*, on the prolific hot-bed of arrogant folly!

---

1   *arras*: A hanging screen of [rich tapestry fabric] formerly placed round the walls
of household apartments, often at such a distance from them as to allow of people
being concealed in the space between (*OED*).
2   A loft or attic.

In one of the theatrical vehicles of my disgrace and torment[1] I was constrained to possess the person of a tall and buxom dame (whose sturdy limbs did not bear much resemblance to the ærial form of a *spirit*), and after *piously* imparting a dumb blessing to Mrs. Jordan, amid the harmonious strains of a choir of *play-house saints and angels*, in one scene, was most barbarously obliged, in a subsequent one, to make my exit in a terrific volume of sulphureous flame, like (if I may be allowed the metaphor) a filthy soul, sinking into the scouring-tub yclept[2] purgatory!

The barbarity of my treatment, instead of rousing the indignation and exciting the vengeance of the spectators, evidently afforded them much pleasure and satisfaction, which they expressed by loud and repeated bursts of applause!—This flattering encouragement completely absorbed the small remains of sense and propriety in the breast of the elated playmaker; and, with the heroism of a Quixote, he determined to eclipse all other dramatic maniacs, and out-Herod Herod in absurdity: for this purpose, he transformed me into *Queen Betty*, and forced me, against my conscience, to relate a stupid falsehood, in order to save the *immoral* effusion of a *boy* from the fate it deserved.[3]

Another of my persecutors, with consummate ingenuity, devised a new mode of tormenting me, by hoisting me into the air,

1 "The Castle Spectre." From the singular coincidence between the structure of this play and that of the German drama of the "Robbers," there is great reason to suspect that it is a plagiarism. This will not excite surprise, when it is known that the author of the "Castle Spectre" is indebted to that popular work the "Spectator" for a passage in his highly praised tragedy. [Author's note.] *The Castle Spectre* was a popular Gothic play by Matthew Gregory Lewis, author of *The Monk*, first performed in 1797.

2 *yclept*: As past participle: called (so-and-so), named, styled (*OED*).

3 The Epilogue to the "East Indian," (which play is said by its author, or *compiler*, to have been written by him at the age of 16) was spoken by Mr. Bannister, Jun., in the character of *Queen Elizabeth*, who ascends from a trap in the middle of the stage, and who is supposed to have obtained the permission of Pluto to revisit her kingdom, in order to witness——*the representation of the "East Indian"!!!* Old Bess gravely tells the audience, that, unless they give it their encouragement, she and the author must descend, and be d——d together! In pity to the brains of the audience (or rather to its deficiency in that scarce article) I feel much compunction in relating, that this paltry subterfuge had the desired effect; and that the play was suffered, *for a few evenings*, to disgrace the stage. [Author's note.]

to the no small hazard of my neck, but to the infinite amusement of the omnipotent gallery-gods, who were hugely delighted with the novelty of the idea; conceiving, perhaps, that the ancient mode of getting rid of a ghost favoured rather strongly of *Old Bailey stage-trick!*

The *writers*[1] of dumb spectacles, called *ballets*, and *pantomimes*, in imitation of their brethren the play-wrights, have added, in a considerable degree, to my torments. One of these inhuman purveyors of stupidity, with refined cruelty, metamorphosed me into a *lanthorn*, and nightly crammed my tortured body with burning candles!

I shall not adduce any more instances of the tyranny exercised on me by my dramatic foes. I shall proceed to a more pleasing task,—that of paying a tribute of gratitude to the renowned *finisher* of "Pizarro," for the holidays[2] that I enjoyed at his *unfinished* theatre, during the exhibition of that superb spectacle. The author of the *"School for Scandal,"* conscious of the strength of his own and of his German ally's abilities, disdained to be indebted to supernatural assistance for the applause of the public; and his well-grounded confidence was fully substantiated by the applause of the public. Splendid scenery, glittering dresses, common-place rant, clever tricks, and a pantomimic bridge, pleased the unruly deities of the galleries, sage critics of the pit, and patrons of genius in the boxes, as well as I should have done myself.

It gives me infinite pain to be under the necessity of adding a large portion of the fair sex to the list of my persecutors; but the stern demands of Justice must be obeyed, and they must participate in the odium attached to the oppression of innocence.

The exquisite delicacy of the female character no longer revolts at scenes of horror. Sepulchres are violated, charnel-houses are ransacked, and Deformity itself rendered more hideous, to gratify the *refined taste* of the *soft* sex. Formerly, ghosts were as much an

---

1 The Spectre is perfectly correct; Gentlemen now *write* their *pantomimes*, and *ballets of action*. Vide modern play-bills. [Author's note.]

2 The Spectre's *holidays*, probably, afforded him as much gratification as the fond mother experiences in the enjoyment of those so *ludicrously* described by Mr. Sheridan in his sublime production. Vide a *pretty* dialogue between Mrs. Jordan and Mr. C. Kemble; "Pizarro," page 18, *twentieth edition!* [Author's note.]

object of terror to the ladies as gray hairs; but now, a lady's book (a novel), destitute of barbarous murders, and dreadful apparitions, is as rare a phenomenon as an author entirely free from vanity.

Next among the strong host of my foes, may be ranked the caricaturists, or *scratchers;* the generality of whom *exist* by calumniating the great and the good, and holding up to ridicule every thing sacred and valuable. These mercenary time-servers find laborious employment for me: sometimes they make me a stumbling-block, over which some harmless old virgin breaks her neck; at other times they oblige me to terrify some of the *venerable* and *equally harmless* tribe, called "*Guardians* of the night;" or ride behind a timid boor across a solitary common, merely for the purpose of keeping him *in spirits!* By these, and various other pretty jokes, I generally gain a violent cold, or fit of the rheumatism; and all to pamper those *gentlemen*'s voracious stomachs with sheep's-heads and hog's-puddings.

I must not here omit the haggard tribe of antiquated beldams,[1] that use me by way of succedaneum[2] for *Messrs. Rawhead and Bloodybones*, two gentlemen of great notoriety in the country, for the enviable purpose of keeping squalling brats in awe. Alas! to what misery am I reduced!——the prey of knaves——the amusement of fools——and the bug-bear of children!

Were I to relate the thousandth part of the inconceivable sufferings imposed upon me by the before-mentioned knot of persecutors, and many others equally tyrannical and cruel, Credulity itself would stop its ears, and brand me with the odious appellation of liar; and Humanity would pack up her property, and decamp, even to the blessed land of liberty itself, where—

> Revolt, from gloomy Chaos, rear'd its hydra-head,
> With Murder leagu'd, fell desolation spread;
> Exulting wav'd its bloody banners high,
> And broke, with giant force, each social tie.——[3]

---

1 *beldam*: An ancient woman, grandmother, or remote ancestress (*OED*).
2 *succedaneum*: A thing which (*rarely*, a person who) replaces or serves in the place of another; a substitute (*OED*).
3 Both this quotation and the epigraph have been attributed to the complaining ghost.

in preference to remaining in a nation, whose members are capable of perpetrating and encouraging such glaring enormities on the person of a poor, harmless ghost!

The redress of my unparalleled grievances remains with the Public alone: to it I submit the decision of my fate; and when I reflect that my appeal is made to BRITONS (who are well acquainted with the blessings of freedom), hope and confidence assume, in my breast, the place of despondency; and I anticipate the joyful period of my emancipation from a state of most degrading and abject slavery.

S. B.

A FRAGMENT.[1]

. . . . THE gates of his kinsman were closed upon him. Sir Edward[2] raised his eyes to the driving clouds; and while he smote his breast at the recollection of man's ingratitude, his horse moved slowly on. The winds seemed to burst in fury from every point of the threatening heavens; the thunder followed each fitful gust in long, loud, and tremendous peals; the cataracts which rolled from steep to steep, swollen by the rains, appeared to rush in deluges, as they roared through the devoted valley; the lightning flashed incessantly from the black curtain which surrounded the hemisphere, at one moment discovering all the horrors of the scene, and in the next leaving him to utter darkness, with peril menacing his every motion. Sir Edwin drew his cloak closer around him, and, sighing heavily the name of his distant Guralanda, his horse plunged forward, and he found himself immersed in a mass of waters, which the descending torrents from the sky had swollen to a mighty pitch. The waves dashed against the sides of his steed, and the driving rain, beating in his face, flowed down the polished steel of his casque, and dropped from the hem of his mantle in soaking abundance!

Emerged from the flood, he pursued his way over a wide tract of uncultivated country, where no light, save the flashes from the clouds, served to direct his wandering steps. The road narrowed, the high trees which avenued the path closed around him, and he found himself lost in the mazes of a deep wood.

Sir Edwin paused:—a soft gleam of radiance streamed before him. He alighted, and, pursuing the direction, a hand suddenly grasped his. The winds howled over his head, and the trees, bowing their august diadems, swept with their heavy umbrage the satu-

---

1 Vol. 5 (Sept. 1800): 228-230.
2 After this initial identification as "Sir Edward," the knight-protagonist is called "Sir Edwin."

rated earth.——He looked up with terror, when a majestic female form, wrapped in a long white veil, holding a crystal lamp to his face, saluted him by his name——"Sir Edwin!—follow me!"

He silently obeyed the soft pressure of the maid, and led by her through the groaning forest, entered a long, deep, and winding cavern. Sir Edwin hesitated, but stopped not, until he saw himself within the depths of a vast dungeon.

"Why am I here?" cried the Knight.

"Still follow me,—and have faith!"

He did; but, laying his hand upon his sword, and half drawing it, with caution pursued her steps, still fearful that the villanous Llanidlos might be again renewing his treachery. A flight of mould-ering stairs, which his conductress rapidly ascended, led them to an iron door. She opened it, and stretched forth her hand to Sir Edwin, who, dreading that he was a second time to be immured within the walls of his rightful heritage, fell a few steps back; but the Lady, by a gentle violence, drew him within the threshold, and he beheld— not the glazy walls of a dripping dungeon, but the magnificent banqueting-hall in the castle of his kinsman!——He shuddered.

"Am I again in his power!"

"You are in mine, Edwin!" cried the seraphic Guralanda (casting her disguise from her, and throwing herself on his bosom).—— "The base Lord Llanidlos died this night, by a stroke of lightning; and I am here, my beloved, after having been near thy prison for eight long months, at liberty to kneel at thy feet, and thus declare, that thou art my betrothed husband!"

——"How is this?" cried the weeping Lady Llanidlos (advancing from the pall of her Lord, which nodded its sable plumes as high as the ceiling).——"Explain, Guralanda!—Would not my cruel Llanidlos have repudiated me, to have wedded thee?—And how, mysterious maid, canst thou be the wife of his nephew?"

Guralanda smiled sweetly, as she seated herself beside the Lady; and, while the fond Edwin yet grasped her hand in his, she thus began . . . .

E——.[1]

---

1 Pitcher (84) lists three ascriptions to "E" but disparate subjects, forms, and publi-cation years suggest they aren't the same author.

CASTLE WALSTENFORTH:[1]

A Dramatic Romance,

IN THREE ACTS.

———

Dramatis Personæ.

Count Walstenforth,	a German Nobleman,
Fredrique,	his natural Son,
Marquis di Valmontan,	an Italian, Friend to the Count,
Osric,	an old Peasant,
Orlando,	his supposed Son,
Hubert,	a Servant of the Count's,
Baron Steinhault,	confined in a dungeon by Walstenforth,
Baroness Steinhault,	his Wife, Sister to the Count,
Ellinor,	her adopted Daughter,
Lisette,	her foster Sister,
Countess Walstenforth.	

———

Act I. Scene I.

A magnificent apartment in the Castle of Count Walstenforth.

Enter Hubert.

Hubert. What a poor half-witted paradoxical fellow I am! With all my honesty, I am a sad rogue; and though courageous enough to do deeds that terrify myself in the recollection, too pusillanimous to make one bold effort to free myself from this thraldom. They

———

1 Vol. 6 (Jan.-March 1801): 13-23, 97-102, 181-191.

say 'love makes a man:'—faith, it has unmade me; for, were I not bribed to secrecy with the prospect of my dear Lisette's future happiness, and a little squeaking wrangler called Honour, this tongue should tell tales; that——Ha!———my Governor approaches. Now, Hubert, one mean action more, to add to thy list of transgressions.—Thou must convert evil into good, and *listen*, for the sake of easing thy *conscience*.   [*Retires.*

Enter the Count, *followed by his Son.*

Fredrique. Emboldened by your condescension, my Lord, I will impart to you the cause of this cherished sadness. You well know the affection I have ever borne towards my amiable aunt, and with how much eagerness I covet her society; but, though at most times anxious to give me pleasure and instruction, there are hours when she seems desirous to shake me off, and indulge, uninterruptedly, in solitary rambles through the forest that skirts these demesnes. Alarmed for her safety, I have presumed to follow her, unperceived, into its gloomy recesses; and urged, perhaps too far, by curiosity, have seen her enter a small hut, from which she returned accompanied by such a lovely pair, as seem only calculated for the celestial regions!

Count. A male and female, were they not? Have you ever overheard their conversation?

Hubert (*aside*). So, so——this is pretty work——our secret is revealed.

Fred. Never, my Lord. The Baroness loads them with caresses, and seems reluctant to forego the pleasure of their society; and when I afterwards accost her, she starts, and trembles at my every glance [*the* Count *appears lost in thought*]. Why, how is this?——even you, my Lord, seem interested.

Count. I am, most deeply. Oh! Fredrique, this refreshens in my memory scenes I would, vainly, strive to forget. But, proceed: I will attend. How say you——does this account for your depression of spirits? What can all this be to you?

Fred. Ah! my Lord, bear with my weakness, while I confess, that this lovely mysterious girl has made an impression on my heart never to be erased.

Count (*angrily*). Has your prying curiosity led you to visit those peasants without my knowledge?

Fred. I scorn prevarication——Once, and once only, did I enter their humble dwelling, and saw the peaceful inmates; virtuous and happy! I was delighted with their innocent gaiety; for you know, father, the inhabitants of this Castle are never disposed to mirth——(*the* Count *starts;* Hubert *shakes his head significantly*)——Dare I say, I envied their pleasures, which seem unknown to pomp?

Count. You are sarcastic, Sir.

Fred. Unknowingly, my Lord. I mean not to offend.——You seem affected! Dearest father!——oh, why this agitation?

Count (with much emotion). I will confide in you, my only child——(*falls on his neck: recovering*).—I was left, in early youth, possessor of this magnificent estate. My marriage with the lovely Clementina ensured my happiness. The establishment of my sister remained my only care; and with satisfaction I received proposals from a man of rank and fortune; my earliest friend—the Marquis de Valmont. What was my consternation, when Julia not only positively rejected the suit of my friend, but shamefully avowed a passion for a man who was indigent and obscure—an alien from his country! Affection overcoming pride, I pardoned their stolen marriage; and, importuned by the generous Marquis, suffered them to reside within these walls.

Fred. 'Twas like yourself, Sir,——humane and noble.

Count. Oh, hear the rest and wonder how I live!—Young and licentious, the Baron soon beheld my wife with eyes of admiration, and treated Julia with indifference. I watched with a keen, mistrustful eye, and every day brought stronger proofs. At length, disgusted with the tears of my much-injured sister, the Baron left the Castle, on a pretence of visiting his native country. Jealousy, once awakened, seldom sleeps: I guessed his purpose; and the Marquis, wrung to the heart by treachery so base, assisted my design, and soon apprized me of a plot, that worked my soul to frenzy. A letter, intercepted by my friend, evinced the guilt of the abandoned woman whom I called my wife. In it——oh! God!——she breathed her brutal passion——invited him at midnight to her chamber; and urged, in the warmest terms, her wish to fly with him to France.

Fred. Oh! most horrible!

Count. Yet hear me out——now let one gleam of softness

dart across my heart, to quell my rage. Such was the woman I had loved!——had wedded!——who promised soon to make me a *father!* Sooner should some distorted, poisonous reptile spring from unwholesome ground, and foster in my bosom, than I would call that unnatural object——*child!* I was revenged. Concealed behind the arras, I, with my friend, beheld their meeting; lighted only by the rising moon: she clasped him in her arms, as he, enraptured, hung upon her charms, which racked my soul with torture. Oh! what a moment *that* of struggling nature!——I plunged my poniard in her faithless bosom, and sunk, myself, insensible of the surrounding horrors.—You weep, Fredrique!——My eyes are dry!—the fever of my rage has drunk up all my tears——my heart is scorched!!——

Fred. Oh! say no more——you cannot bear it now.

Count. Yes, yes, I can——you know not how my mind is strengthened by vengeance——deep, justifiable vengeance!

Fred. Did the Countess expire, my Lord?

Count (softened). She did! I was incapable of taking any further measures; and, by the Marquis's orders, the Baron was confined in a dungeon beneath this Castle, where he now remains.

Fred. ——And the unfortunate Julia——

Count. ——Involved in the deepest distress! I pitied her misfortunes; but her attachment to the spot which contains her husband induces her to remain here. His child I removed far from my sight; and though the separation cost my sister dear, it was a sacrifice due to my wrongs.—One of those two you mentioned is her child; which, I know not; the other is the peasant Osric's.

Fred. Then, indeed, despair is mine!

Count. Not so——Justice forbids the innocent to suffer. Fourteen years of gloomy sadness have wrought strange changes in my temper: my resentment is less violent. Your interest, Fredrique, is dearest to my heart; you may hope, should this object of your love prove, in other respects, a proper match for you, my misfortunes shall never be a bar to your happiness.

Fred. (kneeling) Words but feebly speak my gratitude and joy.

Count. Leave me, Fredrique——I feel much agitated. [*Exit* Fredrique.] Ah! could I but forget my wrongs, I might be happy, and make others so; but that can never be: the Marquis has acquired a power over me that binds me to his will. I love him not. What binds me, then?—'tis guilt, and fear!

Enter Servant.

Servant. My Lord, a courier has this moment announced the approach of the Marquis di Valmont.

Count. 'Tis well——make ready for his reception.——[*Exit* Servant.]——He knows my weakness, and dreads to leave me long without his counsel. I almost fear to meet his scowling eye.   [*Exit.*

Hubert. I'm sure I do, I must seek courage from the mild looks of the sweet Baroness.   [*Exeunt.*

SCENE II. *A pavilion.*

The Baroness *discovered in earnest conversation with* Hubert.

Baroness. But, why this deception, good Hubert? I know you to be my friend, and think you have no cause to doubt my honour.

Hubert. To say truly, Madam, it has been ever my maxim,—that the surest way to keep a woman from telling a secret, is not to trust her with one.

Baroness. You are gay, Hubert:—my mind is little fitted to partake of its cheerfulness.

Hubert. Lord bless you, Lady!—my head is light, but my heart is heavy enough sometimes. But, pray, now, take my advice in this instance; the terms may, perhaps, seem hard, but, believe me, it will in the end prove of the utmost service; and, if I thought you could be bribed, there is a reward!

Baroness (eagerly). Oh!——name it.

Hubert. Your *husband!*——

Baroness (catching his arm). Will you give him his liberty!—— Oh! Hubert!!

Hubert (withdrawing). Alas! Madam, I cannot. Attached as I am by duty and gratitude to the Count, to whom I owe my life, the preservation of my aged parents, dare I be the villain who would abuse the trust he places in me!——Oh! Madam, employ not the voice of Virtue in a cause so base!

Baroness. Far be it from me to tempt you to the commission of an unworthy act; but, think, Hubert——.

Hubert (waving his hand with an air of sadness). I share his confidence. Would to Heaven 'twere in a cause more virtuous!——I do my best to serve my master, without injuring my own conscience. Should I depart from my integrity, would not the world point at me as the base wretch who betrayed his benefactor?

Baroness. True!—true!

Hubert. All I can do, I will.——Wish you to see your husband?

Baroness. It is my only wish—would be my only happiness!

Hubert. So far you shall be gratified. Meet me this night, in the stone gallery, at twelve. I will conduct you to his arms.

Baroness. Thanks!—a thousand thanks! (*embracing his hand.*)

Hubert (*aside, and wiping the tears from his eyes*). Poor soul! her gratitude almost chokes me!——Madam, your brother is in sight: he comes this way. I must not be seen with you.——Heaven protect us!   [*Exit.*

(*The* Baroness *turns her head away in gloomy silence, as the* Count *advances and takes her hand.*)

Count. Good morrow, my dear sister!—See how lovely and smiling all Nature seems around! Must I never hope to see your features enlivened by a ray of pleasure?—and are you determined that your looks shall ever wear the reproachful remembrance of past offences?

Baroness. Can you expect, Count, that I shall welcome with smiles the man who keeps my husband in a dungeon!——Restore him to my arms——to liberty; then shall my lips once more pronounce the fond, the tender appellation——*brother!*

Count (*melted almost to tears; after a pause, aside*). No!—no!—it must not be.——Tear not my soul, all-powerful Nature: it shall not be!——Julia, revenge is sweet:——your husband tore from this beating bosom all it loved!——Curse on the hour! Recall it not to memory, lest destruction fall on all around——hurled by my hand!

Baroness. And is it possible that your heart is still so callous, still so dead to feeling!——The innocent——.

Count. Shall not suffer. Your child, whom, in remembrance of the various crimes, I banished, now shall be restored.

Baroness. My child!——Ah!—no!

Count. I say, it shall.——A daughter, was it not?

Baroness (*pausing*). It was! And, oh! could her artless looks move

pity in your breast, how would our prayers, united, rise for blessings on you!

Count. Recall her while my humour serves!—Time may do
wonders. The Marquis, too, is coming. Let the apartments in the
northern wing be ready for him.

Baroness. That hateful wretch!——

Count (sternly). Forbear!

Enter Fredrique. *Bows to the* Baroness, *who gives him her hand.*

Fred. (aside, to the Count) Are there hopes, my Lord?

Count. Yes! *(aloud)* We soon shall introduce a lovely cousin to
you, the daughter of my Julia! Do all within your power to render
her abode among us pleasant.

Fred. Indeed, my Lord, I will exert myself *(to the Baroness)*; and
may I, Madam, bespeak the favour of your good report?

Baroness. Yes, dear Fredrique! I would have you feel a brother's
fondness for the lovely girl.

Fred. I'm sure my heart already bounds to meet her!

Enter Servant.

Servant. My Lord,—the Marquis di Valmont.

Count. I fly to welcome him. [*Exit* Servant.] Julia, wait here,
and give my friend a kind reception.   [*Exit.*

Fred. This guest seems not to please you, aunt?

Baroness. Fredrique, he is a villain!

Enter Marquis *and* Count. *The* Baroness *turns her eyes upon him with
a look of dignity and scorn.*

Marquis (obsequiously). My charming Julia! has not the length of
time I have, at distance, sighed, for my hopes wrought any change?

Baroness. If you wish me, Marquis, to preserve the *appearance* of
politeness, refrain!

Marquis. Still the same haughty beauty! [*Enter* Hubert.]—So,
Count, you still retain this worthy domestic?

Count. A trusty servant is a valuable acquisition, my Lord Marquis. Such I have hitherto found Hubert.

Hubert. And ever will, my Lord.

Marquis (sneeringly). I doubt it not *(aside)*. Your services are of
no small importance.

Baroness (to the Count). Permit me to retire.

Count. Go!—go!

[*Exit* Baroness. *The* Marquis *snatches her hand, and kisses it as she passes.*

Marquis. No alteration has as yet taken place, I presume?

Count. None. I would to Heaven there were!——Leave us Fredrique.   [*Exit* Fredrique.

Marquis. Pshaw!—mere baby weakness!——Hubert, be faithful to your trust: you shall not be without reward.

Hubert (*superciliously*). I seek no lucrative advantage, Marquis: the approbation of my own heart would give me greater pleasure.

Marquis. I trust you have that also (*significantly*).

Hubert (*looking earnestly at him*). I have!

Count. Come—come—no parley: the day wears away.——Let's to the banquet.

Marquis. Excuse me: I feel indisposed. Hubert will shew me to my chamber.

Hubert (*aside*). So, now for my examination!——This way, my Lord.

Count. Farewell, Di Valmont:—we'll discourse tomorrow.

[*Exeunt.*

SCENE III. *A bed-chamber.*

A couch, table with lights and wine, on one side; the portrait of a lady, half-concealed by a crape,[1] *on the other.*

Enter Hubert, *followed by the* Marquis.

Marquis. The Baron, you say, still languishes in prison?

Hubert. He does.

Marquis. So I would have it. Years of cold indifference and scorn have not diminished aught of my passion for his wife: her charms— faded, not withered—still inspire me with the fondest passion; while, yet, her modesty and virtue awes me. By these alone women are sure to conquer.

Hubert. You seem disposed to moralize, my Lord. Does it bespeak good or evil?

(*The* Marquis *turns to give an angry answer, and his eye catches the picture.*)

---

1 *crape*: A thin transparent gauze-like fabric (*OED*).

Marquis. Damnation!—Must that figure ever blast my sight?——Take it down.

Hubert (trembling). I cannot—on my soul, I cannot!

Marquis. Cowardly villain, obey me!

Hubert (resentfully). Pardon me, Marquis: a man may be a coward, yet no villain; but, I believe, there are few villains not cowardly. (*Takes the picture down, and discovers a sliding partition, which he opens.*)——Know you not this passage, my Lord?—it leads to the blood-stained chamber of the murdered Clementina!

Marquis (hiding his face). Oh!—oh!

Hubert (shaking his head). She was a charming lady; and, from my soul, I think her innocent!

Marquis (in a hurried manner). It could not be:—the letter—all——all proves her guilt.

Hubert. Alas!—she suffered for it.

Marquis. 'Tis fit she should. The Marquis thinks the wound he gave her proved mortal.—We are better informed, you know.

Hubert. I do—I do.

Marquis. By Heaven, your fear will betray us!——But, hark, I have more occasion for your service:—Julia must be mine.

Hubert (with a look of horror). While her husband lives!

Marquis. No, fool!—his life need not be long an obstacle——You understand me.

Hubert. I do, unwillingly. But mark, my Lord; though thus far bounden in each other's power, no persuasion nor menace shall induce me to do what you require; nor will I even connive at a deed so horrible.   [*Exit.*

Marquis (securing all the doors). That villain shakes my soul: yet he is young in his iniquity, and but the creature of my will. Still do I tremble in his presence, and every look of dawning honesty breathes daggers to my heart: every creaking motion of the wainscot gives me fresh alarm. This place is hell to me, yet it contains a charm that courts me to the torture. (*Throws himself on the couch——starting*) Sure, I heard a step!—Di Valmont, this is dastardly!——A glass of wine will raise my spirits. (*Drinks.*) Hubert may play me false: I'll not take off my clothes (*spitting*).——Perhaps there's poison in the wine: I'll drink no more, for guilt is never safe.——Hark! they are laughing: 'tis the servants. Curse on their mirth!—the screeching owl would yield me better music.

End of ACT I.

[To be continued.]

━━━━━━━━

[Continued from page 23.]

ACT II. SCENE I.

A dungeon in the Castle. The Baron *seated at a table, with books, lamp, and an hour-glass.*

Baron. These are comforts Hubert has provided me hitherto; they have afforded me solace and amusement; for I had ceased to hope, and long exclusion from all social intercourse had cramped my mental faculties. But, now, the sickening pangs of expectation rack my soul; each tardy minute seems an hour—for Julia is coming!——Hark!—'tis her step! Ethereal music could not sound more sweet to me!——Julia!—my faithful, tender wife!
    (*The gate is unlocked.*) Hubert *leads the* Baroness, *who faints in the arms of her husband.*
Baron. Ah! sorrow has wasted all her bloom!—'tis but the shadow of my beauteous wife!——Julia! my love, look up!—Our time is short. Life will afford too few such hours as this!
Hubert. Your conference must last but just ten minutes. [*The* Baroness *revives.*] I will retire, and watch without the gate. Should any alarm be spread, I will give you timely notice. [*Retires.*]
Baron. Oh, Julia!—lose thee again!——It must not be. Years of imprisonment have left me little wish for life, unless enjoyed with thee.——Canst thou still think me faithless? Our deadly foe, I learn, still lords it in this Castle: his power is absolute. But here, again, I call on Heaven to witness, I never sought, in thought or deed, to wrong the Count.——How came the Countess in your chamber?
Julia. I know not. When you departed, the Marquis grew importunate. No longer awed by fear, he dared to utter wishes,

which I blush to name. I knew my brother's weak infatuation, and penned a parting line to you with notice of my danger. The illness that ensued, as sudden as severe, could not be natural. A strange sensation, such as I never felt before, came over me at table. They laid me on the couch, from which I was but roused to such a scene of horror as makes my soul turn sick! Had but the Countess lived, you might have proved your innocence; but now, alas!——

Baron. Despair is all! Your letter reached me at the port from which I was to sail. Joyed that, at length, you yielded to my wishes, I hastened back, to press you to my doating heart.——'twas all a base delusion! We have but one way left to set all right. [*Wildly.*]

Julia. Ah!——What!

Baron. To die together! [*Draws a dagger from beneath his robe.*] ——I saved this weapon for the purpose, determining, should I hold you once more in these arms, to lose you but with life!—— One last embrace!——Now, Julia, follow my example! [*Raises the dagger to stab himself.*]

Julia (shrieking). Oh, stay!——Our child!!

Baron (starting back). Have we one living?

Julia. We have. One who will soon obtain redress for all its father's wrongs.

Enter Hubert.

Hubert. This moment, separate; day breaks through the grated windows, and may betray us. Perhaps you soon may meet again. No matter.——Oblige me now.

Baron. You are our dearest friend!—To you I give up more than life. Yet do not tempt me longer with the blessing.——Go!—go!

Julia. Farewell! Perhaps we soon may meet again. Let that rejoice you.——Embrace! [*She follows Hubert out.*]

SCENE II.

Orlando, Ellinor, Lisette, and Osric. *The door of a cottage. A rustic wedding.*

(Lisette *presents* Louisa *a wreath of flowers, with which she entwines the young couple. The villagers dance and sing.*)

ORLANDO.

Happy ever be the youth,
   Who, by love and honour bound,
At the altar plights his truth;
   Ever there may bliss be found!

LISETTE, *and Chorus.*

Let the sprightly tabour sound,
   Mirth and glee be our's;
While we trip the mazy round,
   Heedless pass the hours!

ELLINOR.

See the modest, blushing fair,
   Child of Innocence and Truth,
Still may she be Virtue's care,
   And honor'd age crown happy youth!

OSRIC, *and Chorus.*

Let the sprightly, &c.

Enter Hubert *at the back of the scene.*

Hubert. Sweet innocents!—their guileless hearts know no evil. How soon I shall spoil their sport! I wish any other ill-looking dog had been the messenger. [*Approaches.*]——Good morrow, friends! The day begins merrily with you!

Osric. Ay, my lad! We have deserved no sorrow.

Hubert. True, father; but evil spirits, sometimes, work mischief, and prove the test of Virtue.

Orlando. You seem to augur evil: perhaps you slept unsoundly last night. Good Hubert! your dreams have made you hippish.[1]

Hubert. My waking dreams have not been pleasant.

Lisette. What might they be?

Hubert. Such as you will not like, my pert one. A truce with raillery: I dreamed that this happy group were separated! [*Wiping his eyes with unfeigned sorrow.*]

All. How!—how!

Hubert. Concealment, now, will work no good.——You,

---

1 *hippish*: Somewhat hypochondriacal; low-spirited (*OED*).

Ellinor, are daughter to the lovely Baroness, who now can proudly claim you.

Ellinor. Astonishment!——Ah! this is but a jest of your's, to try me, Hubert.

Orlando. No, no, I see it by his eyes; and I must lose you!

Ellinor. Why so, Orlando? Am I not still the same; nay,—better, richer, and fitter for your love?

Orlando. Simple child of Nature!—your heart deceives you;—— but I must lose you!

Ellinor. Ah! you are much mistaken; but, no matter. Have your own wayward will, and——break my heart!

Hubert. See!—the Baroness approaches. She comes to take you with her to the Castle.

Enter Julia. Ellinor *runs towards her in tears.*

Ellinor. Are you, in truth, my mother?

Julia. Would you I were *not?*

Ellinor. No!—for most fondly do I love you!——But poor Orlando!

Julia. What!—is he jealous of my love?

Hubert. No;—but he fears you'll frown on his.

Julia. Dismiss this subject till another time. You, Ellinor, must win the favour of the Count, my brother; and all may then be well. Till then————*I am your mother!* [*Embraces* Ellinor.]

Orlando (sullenly). And that implies, you claim *obedience!*

Julia. The implication is but just, and *necessary.* And are not you my son——both, both, the children of my *heart!*——What are all other ties?

Orlando (running into her extended arms). I am assured! How could I doubt your tenderness and care?——I will rejoice in Ellen's[1] exaltation!

Julia. Come, then, my love; and, if you please, Lisette shall go with us. Osric, I think, will spare her.

Osric. Ay—ay—take all! Now, I may lay me down, and die!

Ellinor. Then, farewell, dear Orlando! And you, dear Osric! still let me call you father. Expect me soon again.——Farewell!

Osric. May Heaven bless thee, child! [*Enters the cottage.*]

---

1 Diminutive for "Ellinor."

Julia. Orlando, conduct us to the carriage. Nay, tremble not: our welfare is but part of thine; thy woe a heavy grief to us! [*Exeunt.*]

SCENE III.

An apartment in the Castle. Enter Count Walstenforth, *followed by* Fredrique.

Fredrique. And you promise, my Lord, that Ellinor shall be mine?

Count. As far as mortal man dare vouch for, I do; and, for the Baroness, I know well how to bribe her.

Fred. But, ah! my Lord, you have not yet beheld the object of my choice. Should you disapprove her!

Count. Nature, for once, speaks to my heart. The daughter of my Julia can never be unlovely; besides, Fredrique, your happiness must be my constant care.——But, hush!——my sister comes.

Enter Julia, *leading* Ellinor, *who, tremblingly, approaches the* Count, *as he extends his hand to welcome her.* Fredrique *retires to the back scene, and surveys the group attentively.*

Count. To what may I attribute this timidity?—aversion, fear, or joy?

Ellinor. Indeed, my Lord, the simple words I know would ill express my gratitude for all this goodness. These clothes, though fine, please but the eye awhile; an humble roof, perhaps, might suit me better. But, can my heart know aught but love and reverence, when I reflect that you gave me to a mother? [*Falls on the neck of* Julia.]

Count (affected). This foolish child will give us all the vapours.[1]—— Julia, attend me to my study, while Fredrique conducts his pretty cousin through the magnificent apartments of the Castle. [*Exeunt.*]

Fred. (*approaching* Ellinor). This is a welcome office! May I hope the pleasure will be mutual?

Ellinor. This is a gay illusion to my eyes! So many years to live

---

1 *vapours*: A morbid condition supposed to be caused by the presence of such exhalations; depression of spirits, hypochondria, hysteria, or other nervous disorder (*OED*).

obscure, and now to dwell midst scenes of affluence and splendor, seems magic to my mind.

Fred. What would you say, were I to tell you, that, in me, you find the sage magician?

Ellinor. This the enchanted Castle! You, of course, the rightful heir!

Fred. And you the destined mistress! Jest often treads upon the heels of Truth.——Speak, Ellinor! Wish you this fiction to be realized?

Ellinor. Indeed, I do not understand you.

Fred. Has not the Baroness told you the reason of your being so suddenly acknowledged?

Ellinor (hesitating). No.——Can you tell me?

Fred. I could; but fear!

Ellinor. Nay, speak! Pray, tell me!

Fred. Your want of penetration chains my tongue: were you but conscious of your power, my task would be less difficult.——Look on me, Ellinor!—Think what I would say!

Ellinor. Let go my hand!——Fredrique, your words, your looks, distress me! Was it for this they brought me to the Castle?

Fred. It was! Yet, do not hate me for the deed!

Ellinor. How little can I love you! You knew the situation of my heart; nor could I have expected this from you.

Fred. Yet, hear me but a moment:—your's was an infantile attachment; you are of noble birth; and might I not expect ambition might have stronger power than love?

Ellinor. You knew me little, when you thought so; but, even so, could you accept my hand on terms like those?

Fred. You probe me to the soul!——No, Ellinor!—your heart is chiefly what I covet; nor need you fear compulsion on my part. Cheer up your drooping spirits, and believe me all you wish—your friend—your brother!

Ellinor. Pray, leave me! Your words have raised strange doubts within my mind: another time I'll view the chambers. Pray, leave me now!

Fred. Think favourably of me, and I'll die to serve you! [*Exit.*]

Ellinor. Orlando was a prophet——pray, Heaven, he prove a false one! He shall not long have cause to doubt my constancy.

[*Enter* Baroness, *with a thoughtful air.*] Did you, too, mother, sport with my feelings, and bring me here to try my truth?

Julia. Fredrique has been abrupt in his disclosure; but, since he has begun, I must unwillingly proceed.——You must resign Orlando!

Ellinor. Never!!

Baroness (*aside*). Noble, faithful girl! why is this task imposed on me?——Stay, Ellinor!—make no rash determination. Obscurity, indigence, perpetual estrangement from the splendor to which you were born, must be the consequence of your refusing Fredrique!

Ellinor. Then, let me go! Grandeur cannot allure me from my truth.——My vows are registered in Heaven!

Baroness. 'Tis well. Vows are sacred things; but there are duties which may justify the breach of them.

Ellinor. In my situation, I know of none.

Baroness. Much as it hurts me, Ellinor, to counteract sentiments so virtuous, painful circumstances render it a necessity. I am not just now at liberty to relate to you the complicated sufferings which I have endured; suffice it, you have a father!——he lives within these walls. Do you not tremble, Ellinor? The life of the Baron De Steinhault is in your hands. Your marriage with your cousin will, in one moment, release him from a fifteen years' imprisonment.

Ellinor (*falling on her knees*). Inspire me, Heavens, with fortitude to bear this stroke of horror!——Orlando, where are you—dear Orlando! Oh! why will not insensibility release me from this heart-rending conflict!

Baroness. Dear child! I know the conflict of thy soul. Forgive me, Ellinor!————A dear husband's life!——Oh! pity and forgive me! [*Kneels.*]

Ellinor (*in distraction*). A parent at my feet!————Oh, Heaven! this is too much! [*Faints.*]

Baroness. Sure, this is Nature's hardest conflict; and I, wretch as I am, must urge her on!——Yet, Hubert is my friend; but for his assurances, worlds would not bribe me to this cruelty. No, dearest Steinhault! death with thee would be far better than an act of such injustice!——Dear, suffering girl! how can I mitigate your anguish?

Ellinor. Reason can scarcely hold her seat. Was it a dream; or am I such a wretched, perjured being?——No——no! Who talks of perjury? Orlando will be faithful; and so will Ellinor! [*Starting at the sight of* Julia.]——Ah! I remember——Horrible!——My father's life——

Julia. Is in your power. This paper is the contract of his release, if you consent to what I mentioned.——See the Count's signature.

Ellinor. Let me collect my scattered senses. I will be all you wish—my father's life!——Oh! if my blood could purchase it, 'twould be less dearly bought!

Julia. Ellinor, spare me these reproaches! [*Hiding her face.*]

Ellinor. Give me a little time.——Hush!—hush!—we are observed.——This way, dear Madam! Let me support you; my heart seems strengthened by my laudable endeavours.

(*As they go out, the* Baroness *drops the paper in putting it up.*)
Enter Marquis.

Marquis. So, the wheel of fortune turns again! This minion holds the sway in every heart, and Julia triumphs as I sink. Less anxious for my friendly presence, Walstenforth holds familiar conversation with his sister; and every sneering vassal taunts me to my face. Let them beware:—love may with patient tameness creep and fawn; but hate is quick and deadly in its work. [*Perceiving the paper.*]——A love scroll, too! Letters are precious things, and give assistance to ingenious heads: I found them so. [*Reads.*]——Ha! the Count give Steinhault life and liberty, without my acquiescence!——No! — that will never do. His hag-rid conscience kicks and starts, perhaps. I will find means to quiet it. Ah! he comes. [*Enter* Count.]——Why so gloomy, FRIEND?

Count. Mean you to taunt me, Marquis?

Marquis. A treacherous mind might seek concealment: I scorn such artifice.——See, here; all friendship cancelled. [*Shews the paper.*] You would betray me!

Count (confused.) Believe it not——an artifice merely to work my purpose! This cottage girl, full of romantic notions, scorns my son, who loves her as his life. I know her milky[1] nature, and have little doubt, by stratagem, to gain our end.—You must assist us.

Marquis (dissembling). Oh, charming!—you learned your skill in management from me. I am quite reconciled. [*Extending his hand.*]

---

1 *milky*: Of a person, or a person's action, attribute, etc.: soft, gentle; (with unfavourable connotation) timorous, weak, compliant; effeminate (*OED*).

Count. You see your error. This once effected, Julia shall prove my gratitude and friendship for the Marquis. [*Aside.*] I fear his power, and thus must silence him.

Marquis. We'll talk that over in the garden.——Come, Count—my friend, indeed! [*Aside.*] I'll take good care you shall not play me false! [*Exeunt.*]

SCENE IV.

The Forest.

Enter Orlando.

Orlando. I think I heard the voice of Hubert.——Three tedious nights have passed, since I beheld my Ellinor. My harassed spirits seek for rest in vain: a secret fear of danger haunts my soul, and superstition seems to enervate my faculties.

Enter Hubert.

Hubert. Well, my young Knight!——still vigilant and watchful.

Orlando. Say, my good fellow!—how fare our friends within the Castle?

Hubert. Badly enough! This is a crisis of some moment. Patience and resolution are all the weapons you, as yet, have need for. Be ever ready at my call, and you shall find me faithful to your interest: be fortified against contingencies, and trust your fate to me. My time is precious.——Fare you well!

Orlando. Hubert is still mysterious; his very looks are fraught with meaning; yet, my senses are too dull to guess their import: some important duty only thus could chain his tongue. In such eternal silence he still exhorts me to be watchful: What if he means me mischief?—Orlando never was a coward: this sword will do me right.——Hist!—Sure, I heard a gentle step! Some aerial figure glides between the trees.——Should it be Ellinor!——It is!—it is!

Enter Ellinor: *he rushes to meet her.*

Ellinor. What!—can you hold me to your heart——a faithless wretch like me!

Orlando. What means my Ellinor?

Ellinor. Do not look so fondly on me—I am not worthy of your love!——Oh! I can tell you such a tale!

Orlando. Your senses wander, love.

Ellinor. Alas! that would be happiness to what I feel. But, come this way; your eyes would vainly seek to read the meaning of a heart, which throbs with anguish, love, and virtue. Let us retire among the trees. I fear we are observed. [*They retire.*]

Enter Fredrique.

Fred. Forgive me, Honour, if this once I disobey thy mandate: I think this heart of mine beats with a nobler sentiment than mere self-love. Ellinor shall never be compelled to yield her hand against her inclination; but, if this sylvan youth should seek his own aggrandizement in her debasement, it is but fit that I should guard her from the wily snare.——They come: this tree assists my purpose. [*Retires behind a tree.*]

Enter Orlando *supporting* Ellinor, *who reclines on his shoulder.*

Orlando. Bear up, my love—my virtuous Ellinor!——This is a noble effort! Thine upright conscience will applaud thee, and be sweeter than all my praises.

Ellinor. I know not which is sweetest; yet, think not I shall long survive this hated marriage! Fredrique is worthy of a better bride; he made a foolish choice in chusing me. I cannot but esteem him, although he proves my ruin: I shall not be his trouble long, Orlando.——Will you strew my grave with flowers, and moisten the hard earth with tears of love?

Orlando. Each look, each accent, bribes me to dishonour. Oh! leave me, Ellinor, while I am worthy of thee!——Can I behold thy tenderness, and bear to lose thee?

Fred. Nor need you, honest youth!—Believe me, from this day, your sworn friend. Forgive me, if, mistrustful of your worth, I listened to your conversation, and heard sentiments which at once confirms your hopes, and seals my doom to fixed despair! Appearances must be preserved as yet: meanwhile, accept my hand, and with it take my faith, never to do you wrong.——Can you believe me?

Orlando. How could we doubt it, generous friend!

Ellinor (*kissing his hand*). Thou dearest—best of men!

Fred. Your gratitude moves me to womanish weakness. Reserve your thanks till I have proved my trust!——Ellinor, your absence will be marked: trust yourself with me to the Castle.

Orlando. Not with a brother would I sooner trust her.—— Adieu, my love!—despair is changed to joy. Oh! I will glad the aged Osric with this news!

Fred. Farewell!—you soon shall hear from me again.——Come, dearest Ellinor! [*Exeunt.*]

(Orlando *retires through the trees, but returns hastily, upon hearing the report of pistols.*)

Orlando. The voice of distress!——That way the sound!—— Oh, Heaven, preserve my Ellinor! [*Exit.*]

Re-enters, bearing the Count, *wounded, in his arms.*

Count. Thanks, brave deliverer!—I fear your succour came too late!——But, has the wretch escaped?

Orlando. He has; but not unhurt. This weapon pierced him, and he fled, howling with rage and vengeance!

Count. My sense of your kind assistance shall not be spent in words.

Enter Hubert.

Hubert. My master safe!—and you, Orlando!——What does this mean?

Orlando (astonished). Is this the Count?

Count. Hubert, some base assassins sought my life: this gallant youth most bravely interposed, and conquered!——I feel very faint! Assist me to the Castle. [*They bear him out.*]

End of Act II.

———————

[Continued from page 109.]

ACT III. SCENE I.

The apartment of the Count, *who is discovered reclining on a couch;* Ellinor *reading by his side.*

Ellinor (reads). "What an infernal monster is Prejudice! that depraves the best of hearts, and puts the voice of Nature every moment to silence."[1]——[*The* Count *starts.*] What makes you uneasy, my Lord? Shall I move your pillow?

Count. No, Ellinor! You have moved my soul.—The words of Rousseau are applicable to my circumstances: I shall not forget them.——Your gentleness, my sweet girl, has calmed all the rougher passions in my mind. I have not merited your tender attentions.

Ellinor (embracing his hand). Do not speak thus, my Lord!—indeed, you wrong yourself. To me your kind indulgence has been manifest.

Count. But your father, Ellinor!

Ellinor (kneeling). Oh! could I move compassion in your breast—!

Count. Rise, child! You know how far I have already condescended in your favour. What even a sister's tears could not effect——You tremble, girl! Are the terms hard?

Ellinor. Ah! good, my Lord, forgive me: your will shall be my law. Bred in obscurity and ignorance, my heart, perhaps too easily, was given to one whose only requisites were birth and fortune; gifts which, in my misjudging eyes, avail but little——'twas he who saved my uncle's life. He loved me truly; but his generous soul disdained to keep me while my fatal preference abridged the existence of a parent! [*Weeps.*]

Count. Nor shall it, Ellinor!

Enter Fredrique.

Fredrique. Ah! what is this I hear! Have you anticipated my desire, by giving me *unconditional* liberty to the father of my lovely cousin?—for to all other titles, here, my Lord, I solemnly resign all hope or claim!

Ellinor. Generous youth!

Count. Shall I learn virtue from these children, who ought to follow my example? This is hard; but, come—it shall be so: the task is greater than you may suppose.——Leave me awhile, and send the Marquis hither. [*Exeunt* Ellinor *and* Fredrique.] I dread his presence, poor misguided man! His zealous friendship makes him

---

1 From *Eloisa: or, A Series of Original Letters Collected and Published by J. J. Rousseau* (trans. 1761) by Jean-Jacques Rousseau.

think he does me service; but well I know, by sad experience, that my bitterest foe could not afflict me half so bad as a disapproving conscience.

Enter Marquis, *with his arm in a sling.*

Marquis. I congratulate you, dear friend, upon your fortunate escape. The youth has done himself no evil in being your preserver.

Count. I have just learned that he is the lover of my niece, and am well satisfied with the intelligence, since it affords me opportunity of paying a debt of gratitude, while I perform an act of justice.——But, you are hurt! How came you by the accident?

Marquis (confused). Alarmed by the rumour of your danger, I ran with too much eagerness, in the hope of affording you assistance; and, missing a step, fell down the great staircase. But, 'tis a mere trifle: proceed, I pray you.——What magnanimous act of justice is it you meditate?

Count. One, the omission of which has lately oppressed my mind:——it is the release of Steinhault. Julia will never willingly listen to you, and violence is what I cannot suffer.

Marquis (enraged). Base villain! So, you would betray me!

Count. Be cool, dear Marquis; I have no such thought. Danger brings grave reflections, and Nature pleads within me; yet, hear me patiently. My sister still bears some affection towards me, and would not overwhelm my declining years with shame: she and her family may depart the kingdom without molesting us; and we shall soon be satisfied with approbation of our own hearts.

Marquis. A coward's consolation! However, take the consequence.——You know me, Count. One act of your's may draw destruction on your head.

Count. My life would make you poor amends—'tis scarcely worth the taking; and let me tell you, Marquis, I had far better die, than live in guilt.

Marquis. These are your doting thoughts, weak fool! But, be it so. Here ends our friendship.   [*Exit, hastily.*

Enter Julia.

Julia. Oh! Count, what new evil have I cause to dread! The Marquis passed me in the corridor: his looks spoke vengeance!——Save us, save us from his malice!

Count. Julia, the spell is broken that enchanted me: my eyes seem opened to new life, and you shall share it with me. I have a long account to settle with the Marquis; you must not interfere: if I should fail, remember that the Marquis is your most inveterate foe.——Here, take this key: at midnight free your husband from his prison; depart this Castle; and leave me unmolested.

Julia. Then let me bathe your hand with tears of love and joy. Live, live, my brother, and witness all our happiness!

Count. No, Julia; my hands are dipped in blood. The murderer finds no peace.

Julia. Dispel these thoughts: let us all live in amity.

Count. It must not be. You are not safe within the reach of that impetuous man.

Julia. I fear him not: my husband will protect me.

Enter Fredrique, Ellinor, Orlando, *and* Hubert, *who keeps back.*

Fred. Complete the work you have begun, my Lord: reward your brave preserver.

Count. My noble-minded boy, wait but a little while, and all shall be adjusted to your wish: and you, young man, accept my warmest thanks.

Hubert (aside). My turn will come anon!—(*Aloud.*) Why is the Marquis absent at this joyful period?

Count. Pray, name him not: his heart is callous to the call of sensibility; he would not share our joy. He just now left the room in high displeasure. I fear there is more mischief in his mind.

Hubert (aside). And so do I, or wrong I read his looks. I'll watch him closely. [*Exit.*]

Count. Withdraw a little while, dear friends: my weakened spirits scarce can bear this agitation. You, Ellinor, may stay: your kindness soothes the hours of pain.   [*Exeunt* Orlando *and* Julia.

Scene II.

The court yard.

Enter Marquis *and* Hubert.

Hubert. And so, my Lord, you leave the Castle?
Marquis. I do; but not alone.

Hubert. Whom do you mean to bear you company?

Marquis. Yourself and Julia.

Hubert. The Baroness!——Impossible!

Marquis (seizing him, and drawing a dagger). Not so, villain! I fear you mean me harm.——Now, swear by all that's sacred that you will assist in what I shall propose; or expiate the injury you design me with your life!

Hubert. Oh! let me go, or else your knuckles will leave no business for your dagger.——Fie, my Lord!—why should you use me thus? Have I deserved it of you? In all these years have you not proved my faith? I am a man, and have the feelings of a man; and, though I firmly wish your genius was exerted in a better cause, I am the last you need to fear: I know my duty, painful as it is to act against one's nature. Be satisfied; I will not counteract your plans.

Marquis. I know not what to think. However, meet me here within two hours: meanwhile, prepare a chaise and horses; let them be stationed in the wood; and keep a watchful eye upon that meddling rustic. Be punctual in obeying my commands.—So, fare it well with you. [*Exit.*]

Hubert. I know you well enough to dread you: hypocrisy, for once, must prove my friend. I must learn his plans; but how to act I know not.——Ha!—who comes here?——[*Enter* Orlando.] Oh! Lord, Sir, I thought you had reached the cottage by this time? I am glad you are here, though, for————Oh, my foolish head!——I shall do mischief now!

Orlando. Why, Hubert, are you mad? You look pale——you are in a tremor. Are you ill?

Hubert (frightened, lest his looks should betray him). No!——Yes!——That is, my Lord——Sir, I am not well!

Orlando. Something has terrified you——one of Lisette's cold superstitious legends. Let me conduct you to your room.

Hubert (aside). A lucky thought! Faith, you are right!——Hist!—let me see. There's no one nigh——Such a cheating story, Sir!—Lisette says, that every night, at twelve, a spectre, tall, and wrapped in costly clothes, walks through this court yard, and enters by that door——mark, Sir, that door!

Orlando. Enough of this nonsense. It grows late: I have no time for such vagaries.

Hubert. But, hark, Sir! That door leads to the dungeon of the Baron; and 'tis a certain sign that his death is meditated.

Orlando (starts). May I not see the Baron? Now, perhaps, he may depart without my knowledge; and I feel interested in his favour: perhaps, you can indulge me.——[*Aside.*] Something prophetic seems to warn me of impending danger.

Hubert. Not for worlds could I do that; but you may stay. Perhaps, the ghost may be more civil.——Conceal yourself, and act as Heaven directs you. [*Exit.*

Orlando. This is strange! Hubert has ever seemed my friend: his honest joy has caused him to make free with drink.——My presence is required within the Castle. This night gives Ellen to my arms——a welcome guest! [*Exit.*

Enter Marquis, *with dagger, cords, and lantern.*

Marquis (looks cautiously around). This tardy fellow always makes me wait. Were he no——[*A noise is heard.*]

Hubert (without). Hist!—hist!——Are you there?

Marquis. To be sure; I have been waiting.

Hubert. Ay, I warrant; I thought you would not go. But, hide yourself behind that tree. [*Entering, looks aghast at the sight of the* Marquis, *instead of* Orlando.]

Marquis. Fool! why are you so slow? What means this panic? What am I to hide from?

Hubert. Oh! my Lord—I thought——I thought I saw some one coming along the Castle walk!——It was old Nick, perhaps! [*The Castle clock strikes twelve.*]

Marquis. Peace, idiot! Take these.——[*Gives cord and lantern.*] Now, follow me! [*Enters by a small door in the wall.*]

Hubert (holding up the lantern). Orlando! Orlando!—Plague on the fellow! I thought his curiosity would have kept him here.—— Oh! had it been a woman!——Now, all is lost!—I am a ruined man!

Marquis (re-enters). Villain! why this delay?——Follow me instantly! [*They both enter.*]

SCENE III.

The prison. Steinhault *sleeping.*

Enter Julia.

Julia. Steinhault!—Awake, my love! I come to give you liberty!
——Steinhault!

Baron. Ha!—is this a vision!——Julia, my guardian angel, what
brings thee hither?

Julia. Fate has ceased to persecute us. Let me lead you from this
place to scenes of happiness!——Hark!—Did you not hear a noise?
                Enter Marquis *and* Hubert *by a secret door.*

Marquis. Now is the time! They are unarmed!——Bind the trai-
tress down!——Obey me!

(Hubert *reluctantly binds* Julia's *arms with cords, while the* Marquis
                seizes Steinhault, *and holds a dagger to his breast.*)

Julia (shrieking). Oh! spare my husband!

Marquis. Now is my hour of triumph, haughty fair one!

Baron. A brutal triumph, monster!

Marquis. Your taunting words will cost you dear! Your wife shall
pay the cost of my insulted honour, and she shall learn to feel and
dread my power!

(*At the moment he raises the dagger to stab the* Baron, Orlando *rushes
through the door which the* Marquis *left unclosed, and pierces his breast
                with his sword. The* Marquis *falls.*)

Julia. Eternal Providence, this is thy hand!——Orlando, you
have saved a father!

Baron. Is this my son? [*Embracing him.*]
                        (*They unbind the* Baroness.)

Hubert. It is your son, and worthy of you!——Oh! what joy to
have the fond filial embrace unmixed with guilt—to have a father
he may proudly own!——Yonder is mine! [*Pointing to the* Marquis,
and averting his face.]

All. Your father!

Marquis. Yes, harpies——tear me piecemeal!——he is the
natural son of an unnatural father!——What but the sovereign
uncontroulable ties of Nature could bind a virtuous man to such

a villain!—See! see! the murdered Countess!——for that my SON must curse me!——Oh! bring a thousand daggers!—The tortures of the rack are slight to mine!——Hubert, I sold thy soul!

Hubert. I cannot bear this sight! I must procure assistance! [*Goes out.*]

Orlando (*supporting the* Marquis). Unhappy man!—I know not all your guilt, which must be great, to bring you to a state like this!——Live, and repent your crimes!

Marquis. Yes!—life must be most dear to me!——See how I scorn your pity! [*Stabs himself with his own dagger, and expires.*]

Enter Count, *supported by* Ellinor *and* Hubert, Fredrique, Lisette, *and attendants, with lights.*

Orlando. Behold, my Lord, the man who basely sought your life! These lights reveal to me the countenance of him I once pursued, after affording you such fortunate assistance.

Count. Base wretch!——Did I receive these wounds from him I thought my friend?

Julia. You are too late for his confession. Hubert must explain all this.

Hubert. I am prepared. And now, my Lord, take comfort to yourself, for you were not the murderer of your wife.

Count. How so?——Oh! ease me from that weight of guilt, and I will bless you!

Hubert. Of my own ignominious birth suffer me to say but little. Your friendship—blind friendship—for the Marquis made you readily accept my services upon his recommendation; your kindness kindled a glow of gratitude in my mind never to be extinguished. The Marquis ruled me with severity, made me impose upon you with a fictitious tale; and Osric, out of pity, owned for his son the base-born son of his most guilty wife. I knew the claim the Marquis had upon me, and early learned to fear and hate him: his passion for your sister was confided to me in trust; and, though I dared not openly proclaim his guilt, I secretly determined to act, in every respect, conformable to the dictates of my own conscience.——Mine was an arduous task!—I kept a watchful eye upon his actions, and, eager to prevent mischief, fraudulently obtained the knowledge of that diabolical plot which was so fatally effected. In his bureau I found papers, which acquainted me that he had intercepted letters from the Baroness, and substituted others, which, if produced, would prove equivocal, and suit his purpose; and one of these it was which wrought such jealous frenzy in your mind, so fatal in its consequence to all. Suspicions once admitted eagerly repel conviction. The Marquis worked you to his will; opiates were administered by him to the Countess and Julia, by which means the former was easily placed in the apartment of the latter, while each were ignorant of the transaction. My mother, who was then servant to the Baroness, alone was privy to this dark transaction; and she has paid the forfeit of her crimes!

Orlando. Oh! what a tale of blood and guilt!

Hubert. The Baron returned, was detected by the light of the moon with the sleeping Countess in his arms, at whom, my Lord, you aimed a blow; and I received her, senseless and bleeding, in my arms!

Count. Did she not die?

Hubert. Not of that wound. A victim to credulity, you permitted the Marquis to confine the Baron, as if by your own desire, without once hearing his justification. Fearful of my explanation, the Marquis commanded me to finish the work you had begun. My life, my all, was in his hands; I dared not dispute his order, but by stratagem saved my own soul. I conveyed the hapless Countess to a safe asylum:—she recovered; but, faithful to the vow she made me, never revealed the place of her abode, nor even made her existence known; for her heart abjured the weak man who could so readily admit unjust suspicions.

Count. Oh! spare me this!——But I deserve it!

Hubert. She lived three months, and brought that lovely creature into a wretched world; and lived but to welcome its existence with a smile! [*Pointing to* Ellinor.]

Count. This is a day of wonders!——Come to my heart, my injured girl! Well might my heart beat with a strong and secret impulse in her presence.

Fred. Mysterious Heaven!——Ellinor! my sister!

Julia. Here let me explain the deception so long practised, and suggested by Hubert for purposes then unknown to me.—— Orlando is my son!——the child of Steinhault!——When Fredrique owned his passion for Ellinor, Hubert, with eagerness,

entreated that I would claim her as my child. Fearful of the consequences, I consented, on his solemn promise to prevent all harm,
should we be driven to extremities by an open declaration; and I
beheld their virtuous struggles with equal pain and admiration.
Forgive me, Fredrique—Ellinor, forgive me, if depending on your
virtues, I gave you for a while some pangs. I know it was in my
power to reward them; but Providence has more effectually repaid
your merits!

Ellinor. How many claims have this dear circle on my love!——
Father!—brother!——To Hubert we owe all!

Hubert. Ill I deserve your thanks. Let me proceed: mine is a
tedious tale, and badly told.——The child of Julia was, in your
first rage, expelled for ever from the Castle; nor would you hear
it named. Poor Osric took the charge of both the infants, and they
throve beneath his care. Attached by every tie of love and virtue, I
trusted that the charms of Ellinor would, if once known, soon win
your heart; and I was not mistaken. Had it not been so, in spite of
every mortal power, this hand had placed a sword within Orlando's; and, armed by justice, he had never ceased till he had brought
destruction on his foes, and gained a parent's liberty. I have little
more to add: where I did wrong, I acted through the strong impulse
of fear; where I did right, I owe the deed to some innate virtue,
and the mild counsels of Osric, whose honest soul cherished the
dawning shoots of worth, and warmed them into action.

Julia. You claim our thanks; nor shall it be confined to words.
Lisette shall not be portionless; and with her may you long enjoy
the blissful serenity of conscious rectitude.

Count. Let us quit this gloomy scene.——Bear out the lifeless
body of the Marquis; and let us all unite in gratitude to that Omnip-
otence which has so justly proved its retributive powers!   [*Exeunt.*

DE VALCOUR AND BERTHA:

or,

The Prediction Fulfilled.

A Romance.[1]

CHAP. I.

But while he measur'd o'er life's painful race,
In Fortune's wild illimitable chace,
Adversity, companion of his way,
Still o'er the victim hung with iron sway;
Bade new distresses every moment grow,
Marking each change of scene with change of woe.

FALCONER.[2]

THE inhabitants of the Castle de Montalpine had retired to their respective apartments, ere the ponderous bell tolled the midnight hour. Bertha counted the heavy lengthened notes, and then, with palpitating heart, stole from her chamber; first ascertaining, that her attendant, Rose, was in a profound sleep. Anxious to meet her expecting husband, she descended the spiral stair-case with a light and cautious step, unfastened the postern gate, and entered the wood. Looking back over the gloomy pile she had passed, she had the satisfaction to find that every light was extinguished within the castle. The moon emerged from her obscurity with splendor, and lighted the agitated Bertha on her way to the hovel where De Valcour awaited her. "You must be almost frozen in this

---

1 Vol. 10 (Jan.-June 1803): 13-20, 84-89, 154-158, 229-233, 301-304, 378-382.
2 From *The Shipwreck: A Poem. In Three Cantos. By a Sailor* (1762), Canto 1, by William Falconer.

place," said Bertha. "I am already shivering: I have a comfortable fire in my apartment, you may safely venture." De Valcour threw his arm round her waist, and accompanied her back to the castle. As they passed the grand portal, a gleam of light shone through one of the upper casements. Bertha started. "I thought all were in repose for the night. That gallery leads to my father's apartment; what can induce any one to go thither at this hour?" The bell at that moment struck one, and the light was extinguished. Bertha smiled, and endeavoured to seem gay, thereby to re-assure her lover, who would have returned to his miserable hovel, rather than expose her to the risk of detection. "We have nothing to fear," cried she, with encreasing chearfulness. "The Baroness is indisposed, and sleeps in a distant apartment: perhaps my father has been to enquire how she is. At any rate, that suite of rooms is so remote from those I occupy, that we need feel no alarm." She had scarcely spoken, when a shadow passed along the wall which both distinctly perceived; though uncertain whether it was that of man or woman. They halted in breathless trepidation. De Valcour placed his hand upon his sword; but a motion from Bertha checked his impetuosity, as she pointed to the tall trees on the other side of their path, where the shade slowly glided in a distant avenue, and then totally disappeared. The moon-beams fell full upon the face of Bertha: her cheek was pale with terror, her lip quivered, and her icy hand fell motionless by her side. "Bertha, my love, look up," cried the agonized youth: "strive against this weakness. A moment's delay now may prove our ruin. Let me leave you in security, before I go to explore this mystery." "Leave me, Julian!" exclaimed Bertha: "Ah, could you leave me in this dreadful state of alarm? rather let us brave our fate. I shall die of terror, if you abandon me now." They had by this time reached Bertha's apartment: the lamp was burning on the table: Rosa still slept soundly; and the chearful fire blazing in the chimney, revived their sinking spirits, enabling them to discourse tranquilly of their present situation and future prospects.

"I fear, Julian, we have done very wrong," said Bertha, dejectedly, "in marrying without my father's consent. Should I never succeed in removing his cruel prejudices, not even your love will preserve me from wretchedness. Hope, and your ardent assurances, may flatter my senses, but reason chills my glowing fancy with the recollection of my *disobedience*."

"Call not our conduct by so harsh a name, my lovely bride," said Julian, pressing her to his heart. "Surely, in the sight of heaven, you are not disobedient. Your father encouraged and sanctioned our love. He took me an orphan into his protection; gratitude to him, and love for his beauteous daughter, were the first sensations which gave value to my existence. He beheld our affection with apparent delight."

"You have often promised to tell me your story, Julian. Suppose you amuse me with it now: it will serve to beguile us from melancholy thoughts."

"The recital will poorly repay your curiosity, Bertha: your affection for me can alone render it interesting. A slight recollection remains in my mind, of a venerable looking woman, whom I used to call mother. Our habitation was indifferently furnished; yet we enjoyed all the comforts, and sometimes the luxuries, of life. The transactions of one day, as the most important of my little history, is also the freshest in my memory. My mother had desired me to amuse myself with my toys till she returned from market, and on no account to stir from the bed on which she placed me. She had not been gone many minutes, when two strange-looking men entered: one of them caught me in his arms; and when I endeavoured to cry out, stifled my cries, by grasping my throat brutally: the other opened every drawer and closet, uttering exclamations which I did not understand; and at length having concluded his search, covered me with his cloak, and carried me away in his arms. My little frame was convulsed with agony, and his threats alone made me stifle my fears. He had placed me before him on a horse, which fled with great swiftness. The unusual fatigue rendered me almost insensible. The man who carried me, often spoke to his companion in a complaining tone, which the other answered with reproaches. A fierce quarrel ensued. At length I distinguished the following words in rotation, which was the only part of their conversation I understood. 'Place the brat on the ground, and let us settle this dispute at the sword's point. The Chevalier shall see who serves him best.' 'I want not to fight,' replied the other sullenly: 'I only wish the reward to be shared equally.' While they were debating, a party of horsemen approached: the villains appeared dismayed. 'It would be useless to return,' said one of them; 'we should be overtaken: let us hide the boy; and let us give them battle.' He immediately dismounted; and placing me behind a hedge, applied a whistle to his lips, the sound of which echoed through the forest; and soon a fresh party of horsemen appeared. He then threw a parcel of papers into my lap. 'Take care of these,' said he, 'and keep yourself concealed till I come to you.' By this time a brisk firing was commenced: the sound terrified me, and I vainly tried to shield my ears from the dreadful noise. Disregarding his injunctions, I ran with all my strength from the spot where death seemed to menace me. What few papers my little hands could grasp, I still held fast, nor stopped till, exhausted with fatigue and terror, I sunk down in a public road. It was there I was found by your father, who, passing with his domestics, formed the benevolent design of protecting me, in compassion for my wretched helpless state." "But the papers," said Bertha: "what did they contain?" "They were letters without any signature. Here they are." Bertha took them, and in the first read these words:

"Good Maud, be careful of our dear Julian. Every supply necessary for your pleasures and comfort shall be punctually remitted: he must as yet remain with you; but be cautious, as usual; for should he be discovered, his life will be the forfeit. This will be delivered by a trusty messenger, by whom you may send word if you have any wants or wishes ungratified."

The second ran thus:

"Fernando, you must set out directly. I cannot join the party to-night: but I can depend on your punctuality. Leon may attend you. Tell Maud to resign her charge immediately into your hands; but be careful not to delay an unnecessary moment. Should she refuse, force must settle the business."

"This mystery is impenetrable," said Bertha, "and conjecture is bewildered." "It is indeed," replied Julian; "for it seems by the contents of those letters, that my very life depends on secrecy; and to the Baron only have I revealed the events I have just related. His kindness has hitherto prevented my feeling the want of parental love. But now, Bertha, how changed are my prospects! Fatal to us was the hour in which he first beheld the beauteous, the haughty Valeria: she first taught him to treat my humble suit with disdain: for though the Baron, strictly honourable, has never acquainted her with my real story, my being poor and obscure are sufficient crimes in her eyes. Our love was then forbidden. *Caprice*, not justice, dictated the mandate, which turned me a friendless wanderer from the hitherto hospitable Castle di Montalpine. Disdaining this unmerited ignominy, we dared to ratify our vows of love, by holy, though secret union; and surely, my Bertha, no sin attends on the transgression. Cruel necessity alone compelled us to do it; and though awhile we part, heaven will prosper virtuous affection, and crown our re-union with peace and honor."

Bertha shook her head prophetically: a tear stole down her cheek. "A heavy apprehension at my heart," said she, "tells me, that day is far distant. Your profession is full of danger; you may fall: or should my father not live to retract his fatal prohibition—Oh, Julian, a thousand dreadful suggestions fill my fancy. Forgive my fears, and do not doubt my affection: but, indeed, I am very wretched."—She leaned her head on his shoulder, and wept bitterly. De Valcour would have consoled her; but a deep groan caught his attention; and Bertha, too, started at the sound. "Heaven protect us," she exclaimed; "what was that?" "Nothing, but the wind," said Julian, forcing a smile. "Your nerves are weak, and you yield yourself a prey to superstition. Come, rally; you would make a coward of a soldier. See how the clouds gather; we shall have a tempest: believe me it was only the wind." "Well, then," said Bertha, "you had better return to the abbey. I will awaken Rosa; her prattle will divert me. Go, go." He plainly perceived that she was fearful of his being discovered in the castle; and, to quiet her, departed. As soon as he was beyond hearing, and her listening ear counted every retreating step, Bertha roused her domestic. The thunder rattled in tremendous peals round the castle; and the vivid lightning gleamed in through every crevice of the dilapidated building. Rosa was even more terrified than her mistress, and clung round her for protection. A loud shriek was presently heard; but drowned by such a terrific crash as threatened total destruction to the fabric. Bertha fell on her knees; Rosa sunk beside her; and both remained in fervent prayer, till called to active exertions by the sound of the alarm-bell, which soon roused every servant in the castle. Bertha hastened to her father's chamber, where she beheld him lifeless, disfigured, and bloody; while the Baroness franticly shrieked, tore her hair, and called aloud for vengeance on the murderer. The castle was ineffectually searched; no assassin could be discovered. Bertha was carried senseless to her apartment, and the Baroness shut herself up from the sight of every one. Father Ambrose, the confessor of the neighbouring convent, was sent for: his pious exhortations were the only means of restoring tranquillity to the distracted family: the sanctity of his manners, his active benovelence, humanity, and piety, created him many admirers, among whom the Baroness was not the least zealous.

Bertha, by some unaccountable prejudice, did not feel for the father that enthusiastic veneration professed by the rest of the family; but his subsequent good offices, and friendly advice, to herself and Julian, soon taught her to condem her former Scepticism; and to him she unburthened every secret care: To him only was the Lady Valeria accessible, and he succeeded in regulating her deportment to the observance of decent grief.

Valeria was the illegitimate daughter of an Italian Noble, dissipated and profligate; her earliest days had been passed in gaiety and luxury; and the love of pleasure, pomp, and power, were her leading principles. Her father's affluence, and high favor in the cabinet, had occasioned her to be received into the first company; but an early attachment between her and one of rank far beneath her father's ambitious views, had drawn on her his displeasure. Valeria was too mercenary to give up her expectations, and had sufficient art to calculate every probable advantage; therefore, doubting the stability of her lover's affection, should she be abandoned by her wealthy father, she contrived to gratify her own passion without offending him. And Antonio Adimeni, soon satiated by indulgence, released the lady from her vows of fidelity by withdrawing from Naples. Valeria was not too constant for her peace. Chance led her into the presence of the Baron di Montalpine: he was captivated by her beauty, and the wily Valeria neglected no lure to secure her conquest. Age has its follies; nor are they inferior to those of youth.

The Baron, delighted with the blandishments of a young and lovely girl, in a short time made her his wife. Valeria no sooner beheld the blooming artless Bertha, than envious hate filled her malignant bosom. She beheld, too, the fondness of the Baron for his adopted son, the orphan Julian, with equal aversion; and the hopes of benefit to her future offspring, made her resolve to ruin the views of the young couple. By slow degrees she rekindled the sparks of family pride in the mind of the Baron; ridiculed his weakness, or chid his injustice to his own children; bade him look forward to the providing for a natural heir, and not impoverish him by bestowing his fortune on a beggar. These arguments had the desired effect on the weak Baron, and he soon grew cold in his behaviour to Julian. The spirited youth could ill bear unmerited slight; and his resentful deportment increased the evil. Unmindful of all his former promises, the Baron thought he acted full generously, when he gave De Valcour a commission in the army, and dismissed him from the castle, with a peremptory command to think no more of Bertha, unless he would draw on his head a parent's curse. Love was too deeply engraven on the hearts of Julian and Bertha to be erased by this cruel mandate; and, thoughtless of consequences, the impetuous youth succeeded in persuading the yielding girl to a private marriage, lest fraud or force should throw her into the arms of another, before fortune should enable him to return, and claim her with a father's blessing. Father Ambrose performed the ceremony, and Bertha sacrificed her *obedience* to her *love*. De Valcour, then half blest, retired indignantly from the castle, and found a temporary asylum at the Monastry of St. Francis, where he could sometimes hear of Bertha; and, by the friendly aid of Father Ambrose, occasionally wandered to the castle, and obtained a private interview with his beloved wife. Such was the state of affairs in the Castle di Montalpine, on the night of the shocking incident before related. Bertha remained in a lethargy of grief till the succeeding evening, when the sound of the vesper-bell at the monastry reminded her, that in a few hours she must prepare to see Julian. It was their last promised interview; but it was her intention to desire he would not leave the abbey till her father's will had been read.

[To be continued.]

[Continued from Page 13.]

CHAP. II.

Ah! what will not that woman do who loves?
What means will she refuse to keep that heart
Where all her joys are placed?

SAVAGE.[1]

ON the following day the Baron's will was examined: it was by the peremptory command of Valeria, who suggested the idea, that it might contain some particular directions as to the manner of his interment. Bertha was too ill to attend minutely to the contents; but when the whole was perused, and she found herself left entirely dependent on the haughty Valeria, she shrieked with anguish, and was conveyed to her chamber in strong convulsions. Hope was entirely crushed, and she fully felt all the horrors of her situation. It was with difficulty she roused herself sufficiently to meet De Valcour at the appointed hour; and as she stole softly down the staircase, her own footsteps appalled her. Julian was ready at the usual signal: his loved presence dispelled her fears; and, after reaching her apartment in safety, they passed the first hours of the night in uninterrupted conversation. Bertha failed not to make known to her husband the unjust neglect of her father, deplored her own poverty, which now left her no prospect, but the success of his exertions; "and, alas!" added Bertha, "should I become a mother in your absence, what have I not to dread from the persecutions of the Baroness?" Julian vainly sought to calm her fears: he projected a thousand vague schemes for their future advantage, till at length, exhausted by the fatigue and cares of the two preceding days, and seized with an unusual stupor, he fell into a deep slumber on the couch beside the fire. Bertha gazed with tender emotion on his beloved features: her tears flowed fast, and wetted his cheek. The lamp emitted but feeble rays, which conspired, with the gloomy

1 From Cleopatra's speech in Act IV, Scene 1, of *All for Love: or, The World Well Lost* (1678) by John Dryden. The "Savage" attributed here is Cleopatra.

solemnity of the hour, to fill her with a variety of apprehensions, till, harrassed by watchfulness and afflicting thoughts, she yielded to the drowsiness which stole over her senses; and throwing her arm round Julian, she sunk to repose. Her eyes were scarcely closed to sleep, when a rustling noise near her caused her to start up, and, to her extreme terror, she found the lamp extinguished; but a gleam of light shot across the wainscot, and then disappeared. Bertha gazed fearfully around: she shook the arm of Julian; he was in a profound sleep, and a low murmur of, "Hush, hush," sounded through the apartment. Bertha would have called aloud on De Valcour: but, before she could articulate a syllable, a hollow sepulchral voice exclaimed, "Can Bertha sleep in peace upon the bosom of a murderer?" A loud crash, as of distant thunder, succeeded, which awakened Julian; when the pallid cheeks, and quivering lips, of his wife, called his attention, and drew forth his tenderest endearments. In vain did he reach for his unknown accuser. The morning began to dawn; Bertha, half dead with affright, entreated him to leave the castle. Julian unwillingly departed. "I will consult Father Ambrose," said he; "and to-morrow night I will endeavour to detect this midnight intruder. Fear not, my love; I will bring proper arms for my defence: this mystery must be cleared up before I leave you."

De Valcour failed not on the following night to keep his promise. He carefully secured every entrance, and placing his pistols on the table before them, anxiously awaited the slightest noise. To divert Bertha, who was almost sinking with terror, he drew from his pocket a volume of poems, and began to read to her. She had become deeply interested in the fate of Prior's "Nut Brown Maid,"[1] when the turret-clock struck one. Her eye fearfully wandered round the room, but no unusual object was visible; and again she listened with attention to Julian. A noise, similar to the rattling of keys, gave them instantaneous alarm. Julian seized a pistol, and pointed it towards the door, when a violent creaking, in a distant part of the room, diverted his attention to the spot. The apartment was so large, that the solitary lamp burning on the table, scarcely

1 Matthew Prior's *Henry and Emma* (1708), based on a Middle English poem, *Nut-brown Maid*, by an anonymous poet, which Prior also included in his *Poems on Several Occasions* (1709).

illumined half of it, leaving the arched recesses in total obscurity.
Julian would have proceeded to examine them, but Bertha, frantic with terror, clung to his cloak, and prevented his advancing.
Soon, however, she relinquished her hold, when she beheld on
the opposite pannel, written in letters of blood, encompassed by a
blue flame, *"Bertha shall know no Peace till her Hand has slain the
Murderer of her Father."* "God of Heaven! what can this horrible
prediction mean?" exclaimed De Valcour. "Bertha! my wife! look
up. Let the earth open, and entomb me; let the lightning of Heaven
direct its misplaced vengeance on my devoted head, but do not
thou believe me guilty." Bertha shuddered; her whole frame was
convulsed; she pointed to the terrific spot; her lips moved, yet no
sound proceeded, but her agonised groans. Julian laid her on the
couch. He then took the lamp, and carefully inspected the pannel:
the writing had vanished, but many traces of blood remained; and
there was not the least appearance of door, or aperture, by which
any human being could have entered, except that on which his eyes
had been stedfastly fixed. He returned to his wife. "Bertha," said he,
"this affair is still inexplicable. Some malicious fiend wishes to effect
our ruin. I will return—" "Oh, no, no!" shrieked Bertha wildly: "you
must never return. A father's curse attends me.—Fly, while yet my
reason holds." "Fly you, Bertha, under this vile opprobrium! Oh,
no; rather let thy hand now complete the work of fate. Had nought
but poverty assailed us, these arms, unaided by ought but virtue,
should have protected thee from every ill: we would have sought
some retired spot, where cheerful industry would have supported
us in love and confidence: but now, aspersed[1] by some unknown
calumniator, suspected by Bertha, life is valueless." He bent his
knee before her; his air and accent were solemnly impressive, as
he took her cold hand; and, after pressing it fervently to his bosom,
placed within it a pistol. "Here," said he, "satisfy the enemy who
persecutes me; annihilate the heart which hitherto never throbbed
with a passion that could disgrace it. But why do I meanly seek to
plead my innocence? Bertha, be resolute; this is the hour when
justice must triumph over every tender sentiment: the blood of a
murdered father calls for vengeance!"—Bertha gazed on him with

---

1 *aspersed*: Calumniated, slandered, defamed (*OED*).

horror. The fire which flashed from his dark eyes betrayed his desperation; she dashed the pistol to the ground. "No, Julian, I cannot be thy executioner. Justice cannot be awarded by my hand. Fly, fly!" De Valcour rose with dignity: "O, cruel Bertha, you know that while life remains, I will not leave you. This hour must terminate my miseries:—this hand must execute the awful purpose of fate." He raised the pistol to his head, and would have fired. Bertha sunk upon her knees, exclaiming, "Power infinite, pardon my involuntary crime if I am guilty! Julian, whatever *were* my duties, I am now thy wife. I will go with thee from this hateful place; we are not safe within its walls. I will never, never leave thee." He received her in his arms, and they mingled tears of love and sorrow. "To-morrow night," said Bertha, "I will in disguise meet you at the hut in the wood. We will repair to my good old nurse at D——, where I shall find a safe asylum till some eligible plan occurs to us. I feel inspired with fresh confidence; let us now separate." Julian departed with reluctance, after insisting on her taking some repose, and promising to consult the venerable Father Ambrose, who would be their best adviser. When De Valcour left her, Bertha secured the door, and passed an hour in fervent prayer; then, rather more tranquillized, sought that rest of which she stood so much in need.

The following day was appointed for the interment of the Baron; and, to the great surprise of Bertha and Valeria, Father Ambrose did not appear. Great rewards had been offered by the Baroness for the apprehension of the assassin, but no discovery had yet been made; and the *pious* Ambrose had in person visited several of the surrounding towns and villages, in the hope of gathering some satisfactory knowledge. On the morning of the day he left the abbey at an early hour, for the purpose of visiting a sick man, whose dwelling was at the distance of five miles, and was not expected till the vesper service, after which the funeral rites of the Baron were to be solemnized. Still Ambrose did not appear; and the holy brothers were filled with alarm. De Valcour found an opportunity of speaking to Bertha unobserved; he begged her to delay their departure another day, or at least till the return of Ambrose, for whom messengers were dispatched in every direction; but their conference was scarcely ended, when two of the laymen returned with horror in their looks, and displayed the hood and vestment of Father Ambrose, rent and stained with blood, which had been found in a deep pit near the high road; but all search after his body had been fruitless. That he had suffered a violent death, was probable, and the whole abbey was thrown into consternation. The ceremony of the Baron's funeral was, however, concluded; and the Baroness returned dismayed and afflicted to the castle. Her deportment towards Bertha was haughty and reserved. She reminded her of her dependent situation, and pompously assured her, that while she conducted herself as a dutiful child towards her, she should find her a liberal and indulgent mother. Bertha shrunk from her offers with unconcealed disgust; but respect to her father's memory sealed her lips from uttering the sentiments with which the conduct of Valeria inspired her, and she now determined to lose no time in quitting the inhospitable mansion, which she could no longer hope to call her own. She hastily secreted all her valuable jewels, the gift of her once indulgent father, and arrayed herself in a habit of Julian's, he wore when he first declared his love to her. He was then sixteen, caressed by all, beloved by her father, and to her the first, the only object of affection. Her faithful Rosa was her confidant and assistant; and but for her kind attentions, Bertha would have sunk beneath her emotions. A few select articles of dress Bertha desired Rosa to send to her the first opportunity; the rest she was to appropriate to her own use. She then took an affectionate leave of her long-valued domestic, and bade a sad adieu to the scene of her earliest joys, her severest calamities; and, with an aching heart, and faltering step, hastened to meet De Valcour at the hut in the wood.

[To be continued.]

[Continued from Page 89.]

CHAP. III.

BERTHA reached the centre of the wood in safety, but not without alarm: the hut was still at some distance, and the darkness of the night rendered every object indistinguishable; Bertha listened anxiously, in the hope that De Valcour would come to meet her; and, after a considerable interval of expectation, she heard footsteps approaching: but there seemed more than one person, of which voices soon convinced her. Bertha was lost in conjecture, till, as the sound drew nearer, she was terrified to find that both were strangers. They passed on without observing her; but near enough for her to perceive that they were armed. She stole cautiously forward, and, with trembling steps, reached the door of the hut. It was open: she softly called on De Valcour, but no answer was returned. Fearful lest the strangers should surprise her, she entered, and groped about in search of a secure corner, where she might conceal herself till the arrival of Julian, when her hand fell on an object which chilled her with horror. It was the cold face of a man, who was extended on the ground. She faintly shrieked, when a sigh from her suffering companion convinced her he was still living. Ignorant whether it was a friend or an enemy, humanity induced her to raise him in her arms: He breathed with difficulty; and, endeavoring to open his collar, she felt the chain of hair which was suspended round the neck of Julian. This was a most horrible conviction; yet a fortunate exertion of mind enabled her to preserve herself from sinking under the shock. De Valcour revived sufficiently to articulate a few sentences; and informed Bertha, that he had been wounded in endeavoring to defend himself against some ruffians who attempted to seize him; and that they were then in search of her. Scarcely had he spoken, when two men entered, and, by the light of a torch, discovered Bertha supporting her lover. Her terrified looks, and shrill scream, instantly betrayed her sex. The foremost advanced on; tore her from De Valcour, who fell with a deep groan on the ground; then grasping her round the waist, bore her from the hut. Total insensibility succeeded, from which she was only aroused to a scene of new alarm. A number of masked men surrounded the couch on which she was reposing; their eyes were earnestly bent on her, as if watching each motion; their dress was such as she had never beheld before; and the sable plumes which waved in their hats, made her imagine them persons of distinction. She eagerly enquired for Julian. "Do not distress yourself, lovely maid," said one with a dignified air: "he is taken care of. Your meeting cannot take place yet; but you shall meet with every attention here your situation and sex demands." Fearful of provoking resentment, Bertha forbore to make any further enquiries. Every thing round her seemed to wear an air of mystery: the person who addressed her appeared superior to the rest, who obeyed his motions; and he alone watched beside her couch. When he first spoke, she thought the voice familiar to her; but when he raised his tone to address those who attended, she was again at a loss to recollect it. Several hours passed on without any change, and Bertha began to be anxious for daylight to appear. "It will be long before you see the sun rise," said her companion: "the place were are in precludes all possibility of a visit from the sun: but if you are of a good and cheerful temper, you will find enough here to make you happy. We have sumptuous fare, soft beds, and merry hearts. What say you, Lady, have we cause to complain?" "Heaven defend me!" exclaimed Bertha, "where am I? Among whom has my evil destiny thrown me?" "Among those," said her companion, with a more serious tone, "who love you too well to see you thrown away upon a needy adventurer. Bertha, I have long loved you, long envied a boy the happiness of possessing your affection. The farcical ceremony of marriage which passed between you is not valid. Be mine; and every luxury, every pleasure of life, shall be yours." Bertha rose indignantly from the couch; she surveyed him with a scrutinizing glance; his person was totally unknown to her; and she vainly endeavored to discover one motion by which she might recognize him for a former acquaintance. A few moments elapsed in silence. Bertha again addressed him. "By whose authority am I detained here? Where is De Valcour?" "De Valcour is confined in a cell at some distance from this spot: he is beyond hearing of your voice, Lady, should you raise it to its utmost pitch: and should it reach his ear, a strong iron door would preserve us from impertinent interruption. It is by my order all this is done; for no one else has authority here: but, fear not; no violence shall be offered you; neither shall you be made a prisoner here. I have provided a commodious and pleasant retreat for you. I would not be your tyrant, Bertha; I would win by gentle means." Bertha gave him but a smile of contempt for answer; and finding resistance vain, put up a secret prayer to heaven for preservation. For some time she refused any refreshment, till, finding herself completely exhausted by grief and fear, she consented to take a glass of wine and some bread. The whole party, consisting of about ten martial looking men, sat down to an elegant repast. They remained masked, and conversed on general topics: every one behaved to her with marked respect, and retired soon after the meal was concluded, except one, who seemed to wait some orders from the chief. "Tyrault," said he, "conduct this lady to the apartments designed for her in the fortress. Perez is centinel this watch; is not he?" "He is," said Tyrault; "and every thing is prepared for the lady's accommodation: she shall want nothing." "That is right," returned the chief. He then added with a sigh, "I hope she will soon be reconciled to her situation, and not feel a wish to leave us." Bertha's tears flowed fast during this conversation. The chief took her hand, and bowing respectfully over it, said, "Farewell, Bertha, for the present. Calm your apprehensions; you need not dread molestation. I will see you to-morrow, and explain circumstances more minutely." He then bowed slightly to Tyrault, who led her away. They passed through several arched passages, till they came to a spiral flight of stairs. Bertha was too much absorbed by her own reflections, to speak to her conductor, who lighted her along with polite attention. He at last stopped against a large grated door, when he requested her to hold the lamp, while he removed he padlock by which it was secured. Bertha complied: hope was lost, and she determined patiently to wait the event. It opened into a spacious gallery, encircled by iron railings: from this they passed to a suite of rooms, light, and well furnished. Tyrault lighted a lamp which was suspended from the ceiling of the last apartment, observing, that as he should not return for twelve hours, she might find it necessary.—"Merciful powers!" cried Bertha, "am I to remain for ever in this captivity? What have I done, tell me, I intreat you, who are my persecutors?" "I am forbidden, Madam, to answer any questions," returned Tyrault; "but my admiration of you prompts me to transgress. Your captivity will be lengthened according to circumstances. The gentleman who detains you here is the head of an honorable society, known by the title of Independants, who are chiefly men of rank and fortune. I am in his confidence; and think I can promise you the most respectful treatment. A female servant will attend you here; and you will be furnished at stated periods with what refreshments you wish. A change of dress is also in readiness for you. But let me remind you, Madam, that while the Seigneur is thus provident for your accommodation, any attempt to seduce his attendants from their fidelity will be punished with the utmost severity. Farewell, Madam. Judith[1] will wait on you presently." He then bowed, and retired, fastening the door after him. Shortly after which Bertha heard him say without, "Perez, this is your station. I consign this key to you; no one must be admitted, except bearing the signet of our Seigneur." Bertha flung herself on the bed in an agony of grief. Her own lot she could have borne with composure, could she but know the fate of Julian; but now every prospect of communication was cut off, and she was filled with the most dreadful apprehension that he had fallen a victim to the vengeance of her persecutors. In this state of painful suspense she remained, till an impulse of curiosity induced her to take a survey of the apartments allotted her before night-fall should prevent investigation.

[To be continued.]

[Continued from Page 158.]

CHAP. IV.

THE suite of apartments allotted to the use of Bertha, were furnished in a style of splendor which surprised her, and, from the appearance of every thing she saw, she concluded that they must have been recently inhabited; but there seemed to be no outlet or passage of communication with any other part of the building, except the iron door by which she had entered. One large window (and the only one which was not secured by a strong iron grating) commanded a view of a most beautiful and extensive lake, the calm bosom of which reflected the glowing tints of the setting sun, whose radiant beams illuminated a large track of land on the opposite shore. The scene would have had many beauties in the

---

1 After this first instance "Judith" becomes "Maud."

eye of Bertha in happier days; but now confinement, and reflections on her uncertain fate, sickened her heart, and made even the
charms of nature an aggravation of her misery. Yet she found food
for hope, in the idea that her melancholy fate, and peculiar delicacy
of situation, might inspire the breast of her female attendant with
compassion. A few minutes terminated her suspense, and drove
her back to despair; for, in the long-expected, wished-for Maud, she
beheld a figure uncouth, ill-featured, old, and apparently insensible
to all she uttered. Imagining her to be deaf, Bertha addressed her
by signs; but all her effects seemed unheeded by the inexorable
Maud, who silently placed some provisions before her, trimmed
the lamp, added fuel to the fire which had been kindled to air the
rooms, and retired without a single look of feeling or kindness.
Bertha had little rest that night. The first object which met her eye
in the morning, was a complete suit of black, to which was affixed
a ticket: on it was written, *"A Mourning Dress for the Widow of Julian
de Valcour."* Bertha started up: it hung across a chair by her bedside: she surveyed it again and again, imagining she was but in a
fearful dream, but soon found the reality too true. Maud entered
soon after: the unhappy girl grasped her withered hand, and, with
streaming eyes, entreated to know if her Julian had been murdered.
The old woman shook her head as if ignorant of her meaning, and
every attempt to make her comprehend seemed vain. Bertha lost
all composure; she paced the room with irregular steps, tore her
hair, and gave way to the most alarming wildness. In this state she
continued several days, during which Maud never left her, but continued to preserve the same forbidding cast of features as before.
One day, when Bertha was more tranquil than usual, Maud retired
for a few hours, and returned with a note, which she presented very
respectfully: it was addressed to *"The Lady Bertha,"* and contained
these words: "The Chief requests a short audience of the Lady
Bertha; to which privilege he hopes his long attention to her wishes
has entitled him. Every thing in his power shall be done that can
contribute to her comfort or pleasure." Bertha hastily snatched a
pen, and wrote, "Bertha de Valcour has *now* no wish, but for death
or liberty." This she delivered to her attendant, who received it
silently, as usual; but with an expression of countenance, such as
Bertha had never observed before, and which now filled her with

horror. Maud had not been gone many minutes, when a gentle knocking at the outer door gave her a momentary alarm. She listened in trembling anxiety; it was repeated. Convinced that it was no one who had allowed access to the apartments, she approached the door, when some one said, in a low voice, "Madam, Madam! your destruction is certain, if you do not escape within two hours. Trust neither to appearances nor promises; you are not safe." The friendly voice ceased. Thinking it was the centinel who had thus warned her, she eagerly demanded of him the means by which she could escape, and whether he would assist her; when the gruff tones, and rude reply, of the guard, convinced her of her mistake. He tauntingly asked, if "she was mad enough to think he would betray his trust for the whimpering of a woman?" Adding, "No, no, Signora; you are not the first bird that has fluttered in the cage; but if you escape from it without leave from our Signor, you will be a rare bird indeed." Disgusted by his inhumanity, and severely disappointed, Bertha retired from the door to devise some plan for her escape, each of which, as it occurred, she soon found impracticable. An hour elapsed by the glass[1] which stood on the table, and no one came near to assist or comfort her. She turned her eyes despondently to the window. "Surely," she exclaimed, "this is my only alternative—death or dishonor. The height is fearful; and my fate seems certain, should I leap from hence; yet it is in the power of a benign Providence to assist me, to preserve me; to that alone will I trust." As she was thus reflecting, the clouds began to darken, the wind rose with considerable violence, and the vivid lightning dazzled the eyes of Bertha. With the agitation of the elements her mind seemed roused to energy, and she gazed with awful expectation on the foaming waves beneath her, which seemed swelling to meet and bear her to her destined grave. A distant cry of distress vibrated on the air. Bertha stretched herself from the window, and looked anxiously around. A small fishing-vessel seemed driven by the tempest towards the building, but the mariners appeared exerting their efforts to keep her clear. The heart of Bertha bounded with joy: heaven seemed working a miracle in her favor; for should they be brought near enough to distinguish her signals of distress,

1 Hourglass.

she might yet escape in safety. Filled with this hope, she took a knife, and cut the sheets into strips, which she joined, and made a line almost long enough to effect her design. Again she approached the window: the vessel was within sight; she suspended her line, waved her handkerchief, and was at length successful in attracting the notice of some of the crew. Two or three, more venturous than the rest, hoisted out a boat, and rowed towards the tower where Bertha was confined, and which had long been a beacon to mariners. Finding the men below ready to receive her, Bertha secured her line to a large bar which crossed the window. She sprang nimbly on a chair; and was preparing to descend, when she felt her arm rudely grasped, and turning, beheld her masked persecutor. This was a moment not to be neglected. Desperate in her determination to escape from the horrid fate which his presence seemed to menace, she madly plunged the knife she held into his bosom. He gave a cry of rage, and grasped her yet more firmly. In vain the sailors below called to her to hasten her descent; every faculty was suspended by the dreadful sight of her enemy's blood streaming on the ground! streaming from the wound inflicted by her hand! She saw him stagger; she endeavoured to support him; but he groaned, and fell! Bertha shrieked aloud for assistance: the centinel rushed in; fired his piece; and in a few moments the room was filled with armed men, who surrounded their dying chief. One among them attended with assiduous care to Bertha: it was the kind Tyrault, who bore her from the curious crowd, and laid her upon a couch insensible to all that passed.

Meanwhile the ill-fated Julian had languished ten days in a noisome dungeon: all the misery which a malicious foe and a jealous rival could inflict, was his lot. He was made to believe his wife was faithless, and dishonored; and at length, by incessant persuasion, and in the dear hope of obtaining health and liberty, he was induced to take the formal oath of fidelity to the society, and became one of the Independants, whose offences were chiefly of a political nature, and who seldom committed such depredations as could occasion them to be classed with robbers; yet each was sworn to espouse the private interest, and revenge the wrongs, of each other; and the breach of this promise was punished with death. Tyrault, who pitied his undeserved sufferings, yet dared not violate his oath, sought every opportunity of enquiring into the situation of Bertha, with the generous design of bringing the unfortunate faithful couple together; but the vigilance of the Chief gave him no opportunity of effecting his benevolent purpose. Julian became one of the society; and Tyrault learnt that it was the intention of the Signor to make Bertha his by force. All he could then do was, to warn her secretly of her danger, which he did, and hastened the solution of the mystery in which the fate of the unfortunate lovers had been so long involved.

[To be continued.]

[Continued from Page 233.]

CHAP. V.

THE agonised groans of the expiring Chief roused Bertha from her temporary stupor: she broke from the arms of Tyrault, and at the same moment beheld the altered form of her loved Julian: his eyes gazed on her with melancholy wildness, while she shrieked with surprise at the unexpected rencontre. But a new object of astonishment presented itself, when, approaching the bed, she beheld the distorted features of Father Ambrose. He beckoned her to his side: she advanced fearfully, supported by the anxious De Valcour. Ambrose took her trembling hand, and placed it within that of De Valcour; gazed earnestly at them; and a tear of remorse stole down his pale cheek. "The Prediction is, indeed, fulfilled," said he, gasping with mental and bodily agony. "I was thy father's murderer. Pray for me, suffering angel! for thy looks beam mercy to the despairing sinner. My crimes have been many. Let the Baroness Valeria be secured; she has been my instigator to the basest acts: a paper in my cabinet will explain all. Julian, you are my son." The horror and astonishment of this discovery was suspended by the last convulsion which seized Ambrose; and his kneeling children ventured to address a prayer for his forgiveness, to the Power who had terminated his guilty career. But all the joy which would otherwise have attended the re-union of De Valcour and Bertha, was destroyed by the dreadful recollection, that she had also been a murderer; nor could all the persuasions of Julian chase the horrid idea from her mind. Pursuant to the last direction of Ambrose, Julian secured the important paper, and read the contents to Bertha and his friend Tyrault; the rest of the party having retired at his command; some to secure the person of Valeria; others to their respective avocations. The confession of Father Ambrose ran thus.

"Born of indigent and obscure parents, the annals of my early days would be unimportant to those for whom this packet is intended. It has been written in moments of bitter remorse; for, amidst all the scenes of dissipation, such moments will occur to the soul labouring with guilt. I was intended for the service of the church; but as much interest was requisite to obtain an advantageous situation, I was forced to submit to such menial offices in the convent where I was placed, as gave me a violent disgust to the calling. I quitted the convent; and being a lad of spirit and ingenuity, went through a variety of changes in my pursuit of wealth and pleasure. The person and reputed fortune of the Lady Valeria was a dazzling bait, and my natural vanity led me to imagine the prize within my reach; but I had to deal with one more ambitious and artful than myself, and the consequence was, that I became entangled in a fruitless amour. Aware of the danger attending a discovery, and cured of the passion which at first actuated me, I quitted the city where she resided, having previously directed her as to the disposal of the infant to which she must shortly give birth. By a few well-connected measures, I contrived to pass for a man of some consequence, and formed acquaintance with youths of distinction, who, in pursuit of pleasure, sacrificed prudence and fame. By some of these I was introduced to the society of Independents. Their principles were readily adopted by me; but the strong suspicion, and strict regulations of government, obliging us to disperse awhile, I obtained, under plausible pretences, admission to the Convent of St. Clare. The holy habit covers many a depraved heart. I was an adept in hypocrisy, and succeeded in making my brethren believe me a man of the strictest piety. It was there, to my infinite surprise, I was sent to by the Baroness Valeria, to officiate as confessor to the family. Her infidelity gave me little pain: but the loss of my child, whom I had sent for at the commencement of my league with the Independents, had occasioned me much pain, and now revived in my mind, with a degree of tenderness (towards the mother) which I imagined I had long been incapable of feeling. I made myself known to her: she heard me with astonishment; professed undiminished regard; and laid open to my view such ambitious schemes, as soon engaged me completely in her diabolical plans. The daughter of the credulous Baron to whom Valeria was united, equally beauteous and innocent, was marked for destruction by the designing Valeria; and I engaged in her cause with views little less criminal than those which actuated the female fiend. But, to effect my purpose more completely, much dissimulation was necessary; and I became, in fact, the dupe of my own artifice. To complete the ruin of the young couple, (Bertha having formed an attachment to an orphan lad under the protection of the Baron), I favored a secret marriage, to which Valeria prompted me. By assurances that it was the only method of crushing the youth's aspiring hopes, as she had the entire sway of the doting Baron, who would thereby be induced to disinherit them entirely, and make a will in her favor. This plan succeeded: De Valcour and Bertha were united, and long carried on a clandestine correspondence. The unsuspecting Julian confided every thing to me, except the circumstances of his first introduction to the Baron, which, had I known, innumerable crimes might have been avoided; as I should have thereby learnt that he was the son whose loss I had ever lamented. To hurry over a painful recital, the death of the Baron was determined, and effected by my hand. I had easy access to the castle, and found little difficulty of escaping from the convent when the pious brotherhood imagined me reposing in my cell. That suspicion might be averted from me, it was necessary to prevent too strict investigation, by attaching it to another; and as I was well acquainted with the hours when Julian was admitted to a private interview with his wife, I judged it an easy matter to work on her credulity, and terrify her from the castle. For this I had a double purpose: her beauty had inspired me with a criminal passion; and I resolved to get her into my power. My intimacy with the confederate Independents had been recently renewed; and temporary concealment with them I judged my best expedient, till the Baroness completed her promise of bestowing on me wealth and independence. The only difficulty attending my scheme, was that of breaking the strict oath of the society; but as I should thereby have the whole band in my power, I resolved, at all events, to brave the consequences, and prefer my own advantage to any consideration of honor or justice."

"Alas, Julian!" said Bertha, laying her hand on his arm, "we are now taught cruelly the consequence of disobedience. Our own rashness has undone us, and made us the dupes of an artful unrelenting enemy." "Perhaps we may be able to avert the dreaded evil," returned Julian. "We have erred without being criminal; may our present punishment be the expiation."

[To be continued.]

[Concluded from Page 304.]

CHAP. VI.

DE VALCOUR was prevented from continuing the narrative by the return of Tyrault. He had succeeded beyond their most sanguine expectations; the Baroness had expressed the keenest remorse for her late conduct; affected to throw the whole blame on the criminal Ambrose; and waited only for the presence of Julian, and her injured daughter-in-law, to make ample restitution, explain several interesting particulars, and then throw herself penitent and unprotected on their mercy. This was a favourable moment, not to be neglected. Julian had attached the band to him by his gentle manners, and manly endurance of calamity. They agreed unanimously on dissolving his oath of association; substituting only one, by which he was bound not to betray any of their secrets; and he then obtained an honourable discharge. Tyrault conducted them by subterraneous passes to the hut in the wood; and Bertha, with astonishment, discovered that she had been confined within a mile of the Castle de Montalpine. Tyrault, who was now the chief of the Independents, selected a few, on whose fidelity he could depend, to escort his friends to the castle, at the gates of which he took an affectionate leave; assuring De Valcour, that, in any hour of distress or peril, they should ever find assistance and refuge where he was. The lady Valeria, in sable robes, hastened to meet them: her countenance was marked with deep despondency; her eye alternately glistened with a tear of despair, or brightened with a gleam of kindling hope. The deportment of Bertha was neither exulting nor servile: she returned the salutation of the Baroness with civility, but shrunk from her extended hand, and rested for support on the ready arm of Julian, who cheered her with encouraging looks. In the spacious saloon a collation was prepared; every thing seemed to wear an air of awful preparation; for the chair of the late Baron was placed beneath a small canopy, over which waved a vast plume of black feathers: his banqueting robe was thrown across the seat, and his sword suspended across by an embroidered scarf. The Baroness placed herself in a seat on one side, while she motioned to Bertha to take that on the other; and Julian placed himself opposite to the Baroness. For some moments a mournful silence prevailed. Bertha was too deeply affected to speak, and Valeria seemed absorbed in gloomy meditation. Breaking silence at length, she pledged Julian in a goblet of wine. "It is of no use," said she, sighing, "to waste our time thus. I have much to say; and though the subject is painful, it must be entered on. Refresh yourselves, and we will proceed to business.—Alice," continued she, turning to the person who waited behind her chair, "on the table in my chamber you will find a sealed paper: bring it hither." The heart of Bertha was too full to permit her to taste the sumptuous fare set before her. Julian selected the choicest dishes for her; but her efforts to eat were ineffectual. Alice returned with the paper, which the Baroness delivered to Julian, and then addressed him with much solemnity, after ordering the attendants to withdraw. "The implacable hatred I have hitherto ever entertained for you, Julian, I know not how to account for." (Julian turned pale with horror.) "It seemed interwoven in my nature, and has led me on to the commission of acts, at the remembrance of which I now shudder. That paper you will find to be the true will of the unfortunate Baron, entrusted by him to my care soon after our marriage. Bertha is thereby his sole heiress, though an ample jointure has been allowed for me." Bertha leaned over Julian to peruse it. The Baroness called for more wine; the attendants were withdrawn; she rose, brought some from the sideboard, and filled the goblets. "Bertha," said she, raising her voice, " your father never cursed you. That will was his only one; he died pronouncing his forgiveness and blessing on you." "Eternal Providence be praised," exclaimed Bertha: "I may yet be happy." She sunk on her knees in the fervency of rapture, while imagination pictured the spirit of her father regarding her with pity and pardon.

"But," said Julian, "how are we to account for the mysterious threatenings by which our fate was accelerated?" "By the chemical skill of Father Ambrose," said Valeria, with a forced smile, "they were all effected. His voice was that which menaced you; and his hand traced with phosphoric characters the prediction which accident has since fulfilled. Early superstition, which is seldom eradicated, aided by concurrent circumstances, and your own consciousness of misconduct, all conspired to make our plan succeed. The pannel on which the terrific words were written, turned on a swivel; and in my apartment, where the whole plan was contrived and executed, you may behold and examine the apparatus. It was necessary you should quit the castle, that Ambrose might escape detection, while his association with the Independents rendered it an easy matter to keep you still within our power. Upon considering the whole of our proceedings, you will find how much you have been the dupes of your own credulity; though that consideration does not lessen our crime." The Baroness paused; she seemed yet struggling with some secret. She gazed alternately at De Valcour and Bertha; then rose from her seat, and walked precipitately about the room. The wildness of her looks terrified Bertha: she besought her to be pacified, and, after much entreaty, she returned to the table. "I know," said she, in an altered tone, " what I have to expect from your generosity. I injured you; was accessary to the murder of your father; for that you owe me vengeance. You are restored to your rights, have avenged yourself on your persecutor, have repaid blood with blood; and now satiated, may in pity for a repenting, defenceless woman, connive at her escape from justice; allow her an annuity; and bid her linger out her days in obscurity, a prey to the horrors of a guilty conscience. This will be your mercy, if I submit. But know, foolish pair! I disdain such pity. You are in my power; not I in thine. In the book of destiny it was written, that

Valeria should live infamous, and die triumphant in revenge." "For heaven's sake, what mean you!" cried Julian, rising, and seizing her arm, while his heart seemed to sicken with dreadful forebodings: "we mean not to exult over or to insult you." Valeria burst into a convulsive laugh. "I know it, I know it!" cried she. "You have little time for exultation. Summon the attendants; let me be seized, bound, and carried to the place of execution: I have more murders than one to answer for. Fools! to think Valeria penitent. Nay, nay; embrace once more; you have not long for such endearments. Your drink was poisoned!" Bertha shrieked with horror, "I have not tasted it! O, Julian! my Julian! Inhuman woman, you have killed your son!" De Valcour began to feel the effects of the baneful drink: he grasped the hand of Bertha with agony, thanked heaven for her preservation, and confirmed to the distracted Valeria the dreadful truth which Bertha had just uttered. Words cannot describe the feelings of the wretched woman whose malice had recoiled on herself. She tore her hair in phrenzy, and would have plunged a knife in her own bosom, but that the attendants at that moment rushed in, and wrested the weapon from her hand. The zealous Tyrault was amongst them: he supported his dying friend, whose last moment was hastily approaching. "I feel," said he, "mortal aid would now be vain. I die the victim of the most diabolical treachery. Protect my lovely wife; her only fault was that of being too tenderly attached to one, who has but brought her into endless misery. Bertha, my beloved, farewell. We may meet in happier regions; for we are guiltless, and our earthly disobedience has met an earthly punishment. Unhappy mother! I forgive thee!" Bertha clung round him till forcibly dragged from his lifeless body. The Baroness yielded herself up to justice, and suffered the due punishment of her crimes with that insensibility which is often mistaken for heroism, but is too frequently the last refuge of a turbulent spirit, and an impious soul. Bertha found a zealous and active friend in Tyrault: he arranged her affairs with fidelity, and gave her every consolation in his power. But her heart had received too deep a wound to admit of future happiness; and resolving on retirement, she devoted the greater part of her fortune to the endowment of a convent, in which she passed the remainder of her days. In commemoration of her own sad story, she founded the order of Disobedients, enjoining a life of the strictest piety and severest penance. Of this order she remained superior some years; and at her death was laid beside her dear Julian in the family vault; and a simple marble tablet in the convent chapel bears record of the fate of the two faithful and unfortunate lovers. By the will of the Lady Bertha, Tyrault, who was an orphan, succeeded to the estate; and his heirs for many centuries were possessors of the Castle di Montalpine, while gratitude has perpetuated in their hearts the virtues of the unhappy pair.

HENRY'S SHADE.[1]

Oh, heard you that deep hollow sound,
That seem'd to shake the troubled ground?
And heard you that low rust'ling sweep,
Which seem'd across the grass to creep?
'Tis hapless Henry's restless shade,
Which nightly walks the silent glade.

Unhappy youth! a maid he lov'd
Who false to his affection prov'd;
The morn she promis'd him to wed,
That morn she with another fled:
'Twas then that Henry, on this heath,
His God forgot—and rush'd on death.[2]

Unhallow'd here, his body's laid;
O'er him no burial prayer was said;
But on his grave the rank weeds grow,
And o'er the place the loud winds blow;
Whilst on the stake the rav'nous bird
The long drear night is screaming heard.

Soon as arrives the evening grey,
No peasant dares to pass this way;
Yet, as they take their lengthen'd round,
They mourn his fate with sighs profound;
And offer up a prayer to heaven,
That his rash crime may be forgiven.

1 Vol. 13 (Oct. 1804): 285.
2 That is, he committed suicide.

Still o'er the wild and dreary waste,
With hurried footsteps on they haste,
Nor check their pace till past the wood
Which leads to where his cottage stood.
For till morn dissipates their fears,
Amid the gloom his shade appears.

SUSAN.[1]

---

1 Pitcher (see 243-245), in the note for "The Orphan Girl's Tale" (Vol. 12, May 1804, 349-350) comments that "Susan" is a regular contributor of occasional and patriotic poems (from May 1804 to March 1806; Pitcher's survey ends in 1806), but the author remains unidentified.

ENIGMA.[1]

In some dark cave, as dark as ten-fold night,
Immur'd beyond the reach of cheerful light,
Devoid of cooling breeze, or sunny rays,
Such is my case, and such the place I hold,
Secure from summer's heat, or winter's cold.
But when the page of knowledge lies in view,
And science bids the skilful sage pursue,
Like Hamlet's ghost, from my dark cell I rise;
As thin my form—as ghastly are my eyes.
Perhaps from this you'll treat me with abuse,
And call me frightful, and of little use.
If that's the case, it soon revers'd shall be,
And all shall know what fame belongs to me.
I've led the ancient bards, in days of yore,
Through paths of learning unexplor'd before;
Have giv'n assistance to the hoary sage,
And guided him through many a tedious page,
And you, ye fair, fresh, blooming, young, and gay,
Whose charms, tho' beauteous, must in time decay,
See that ye don't that usefulness despise,
Which one day ye may know, and highly prize.
Perhaps, too, while these mystic lines ye view,
I may be seen attach'd to some of you.
Sublime I sit, while you the theme explore,
I then dismount, and soon am seen no more.
Like some poor hermit, fled from care and pain,
I clasp my arms, and to my cave again.

N. H., Sneydgreen.[2]

SOLUTION OF THE ENIGMA.[3]

A Pair of Spectacles.

1 Vol. 14 (Jan. 1805): 72.
2 "N. H., Sneydgreen" also contributed "The Nocturnal Visit to the Grave of a
Lamented Wife," Vol. 14 (May 1805): 358 (see Pitcher 117-118).
3 Vol. 14 (Feb. 1805): 144.

Craig Del.   Lester Sc.

'Tis she, the Lady all in white,
  The taper glimmering in her hand.

Page 278.

Published Oct.ʳ 1. 1805 by Vernor and Hood, Poultry

Engraving for "The Lady of Elfinglen" from the Oct. 1805 issue of *LMM*.

THE LADY OF ELFINGLEN.[1]

[With an elegant Engraving.]

WHEN the cold North unlocks his store,
    And fast descends the pelting rain,
And midnight hangs her deepest shade
    Around the towers of Elfinglen,

Who has not heard a faltering step,
    And mark'd a lady all in white,
High on the northern turret stand,
    And brave the horrors of the night?

Ev'n now the shades of midnight fall,
    And fast descends the pelting rain;
And the tempestuous whirlwind rocks
    The battlements of Elfinglen.

Her faltering step dost thou not hear?
    And dost thou not behold her stand?
'Tis she—the lady all in white,
    The taper glimmering in her hand.

So stood she on the turret's height,
    So her step falter'd on the floor,
What time her lord spurr'd his best steed,
    O, spurr'd him to Culloden Moor![2]

---

1 Vol. 15 (Oct. 1805): 278-279. Previously published, also anonymously, with this
title under "Legends of the North. No. III." in *The Poetical Magazine; or, Temple of
the Muses*, Vol. II (1804): 61-63.
2 The brutal Battle of Culloden in Scotland on 16 April 1745 was the final defeat of
the Jacobite uprising by the British army.

Culloden Moor is red with blood—
 Red with the current of the slain:
Call, call, thy mountain heroes round,
 And wave thy banners, Elfinglen!

From heathy hill, and forest deep,
 The *Pibroch*[1] calls the clans afar;
They leave their native solitudes,
 And plunge into the thickest war.

The Highland sword is flaming bright,
 A meteor on the darken'd plain;
Call all thy martial prowess forth,
 And wave thy banners, Elfinglen!

Oft have thy country's boastful foes
 Been taught thy vengeful wrath to feel:
Oft have they shunn'd thy warlike arm,
 And fled before thy burnish'd steel.

The spirits of your fathers view,
 They bend from yon ethereal plain:
O! wield thy trusty weapon, wield,
 And wade to glory, Elfinglen!

Why do the elements contend?
 Why do the Boreal whirlwinds sweep;
Drifting the everlasting snow
 From mountain wild, and valley deep?

Yet, on the battlements sublime,
 Still beauty braves the wind and rain;
And still, in Fancy's eye, pursues
 Thy dancing crest from Elfinglen.

---

1 Ceremonial or martial music for Scottish bagpipes.

O! hie thee, Lady, to thy bower,
　And God be with thee, Lady fair;
For nought avail'd the Highland sword,
　That blaz'd with meteor gleam in air.

In vain he rais'd his nervous arm;
　In vain his trusty clans combin'd;
And bade the *Pibroch* sound to war,
　And gave their banners to the wind.

Well may'st thou wander up and down,
　And thy step falter on the floor:
For never shall the chief return;
　He perish'd on Culloden Moor.

This is the tale the stranger hears
　On neighb'ring hill, and heath, and plain;
And this the Lady all in white,
　Seen on the towers of Elfinglen.

THE CAVE OF ST. SIDWELL:

A ROMANCE.[1]

"Whoever has been so unhappy as to have felt the miseries of long-continued hatred, will be able to relate how the passions are kept in continual irritation by the recollection of injury and meditations of revenge." HAWKESWORTH.[2]

IT was in a gloomy recess, hollowed by the hand of nature, and decorated only by her rudest ornaments, that the misanthropic Reginald sought to bury the remembrance of his early woes: penitence and remorse were his only companions, and his self-inflicted mortifications, the only variety which his situation afforded. He possessed the means of affluence, but his heart was deadened to sensations of social comfort, and abhorring himself, he also abhorred mankind. Deep in the gloom of an extensive forest, he remained secure from observation; the only human countenance he had beheld during his voluntary seclusion from the world, was that of a simple but honest wood-cutter, who occasionally ventured to visit the cave, when its austere inhabitant relaxed from his usual ferocity, and would endeavour, with artless good-nature, to amuse the recluse with details of rustic diversions, and pictures of the blessings which society afforded; but on this theme Reginald was obdurate, and any persuasion to quit his solitude never failed to excite his wrath to a degree almost bordering on phrenzy. His countenance, which could once boast lineaments of beauty, was now pale, haggard, and stamped with the expression of malign horror; his figure had been graceful and majestic, but now, emaciated with suffering, and distorted from its natural symmetry by the

---

1 Vol. 2, n.s. (1807): Jan., 26-31; Feb., 80-88; April, 171-176; May, 218-222; Vol. 3, n.s. (1807): July, 34-39; August, 55-57.
2 From John Hawkesworth's *The Adventurer* (1753) Vol. 3, No. XCV. 177-183 (180-181).

rude manner of living to which he had accustomed himself, was terrific and disgusting to the beholder; the skins of wild animals served him for raiment; his food was coarse, and scantily provided; his bed the withered leaves which winter's chill blasts had scattered through the forest. The only vestiges which within his cell marked civilization, were a flute and an escritoire;[1] on the former he indulged himself very rarely, and only at those intervals when his mind was tranquillized, or exhausted by the intenseness of anguish, and at those periods the indulgence was most precious; but his escritoire was periodically visited: the wild suggestions of imagination were committed to paper. Arnold[2] had frequently found scattered fragments, but he possessed not sufficient erudition to decypher the contents, and Reginald checked every inquiry with such vehemence as made the rustic tremble. In this state had Reginald remained five years, when wandering one night through the mazes of the forest, his ears were assailed by a sound to which they had long been unaccustomed; an unaccountable sensation thrilled in his bosom—the ferocity of his temper was in an instant subdued: it was the cry of an infant which had caused this momentary change; yet recollection soon returned, and with desperate obduracy he fled from the spot. In the confusion of ideas which assailed him, he mistook the path; once more he was necessitated to retrace his footsteps, and again the infant's lamentation was distinctly heard. Reginald gazed fearfully around—one step more brought him close to the object of his alarm and agitation: it was a female child, apparently about six years of age, reclining on the damp earth, and unsheltered from the inclement season. Reginald could not leave her to perish; with a rude grasp he seized her in his arms—she shrieked with horror, and struggled to disengage herself from a being so terrific; his voice had been long unaccustomed to tones of soothing tenderness; all he could articulate was hush! hush! and his broken discordant voice augmented the terror of the child. With swift steps he reached the cave: he placed the little trembler on his bed, and kindled his lamp to gaze on the features of his infant charge: he beheld them lovely beyond description; her dress

1 Although typically a writing desk, the *OED* notes that earlier escritoires were portable, likely the case here.
2 The wood-cutter.

was neat but simple, and it was evident she was no peasant's child; but if her appearance softened his heart, and filled his breast with tenderness long unfelt, his had a far different effect on her he had preserved. To his rough question—"Who are you?" she replied, with tears and clasped hands—"Oh! do not kill me!—I am little Rosa!"—"Kill you, child!" he exclaimed, starting from her with horror;—"Is *murderer* stamped on my brow, that even this babe can trace its marks!" The convulsion of his features was terrific, and Rosa hid her face among the leaves, sobbing fearfully: again he approached her—"Who are your parents, Rosa?" she shook her head.—"She is perhaps an orphan," he thought.—"Have you a mamma?"—"Oh, dear mamma! take me to poor mamma—she is very sick."—"What is her name?"—"Madam Windenbourn." —"Enough, child—you shall see her to-morrow; but now go to sleep."—"I am very hungry."—Reginald started; he had nothing fit for a child to eat, and he feared she would perish; but a moment's recollection obviated the diffficulty: Arnold had once with difficulty prevailed on him to accept a young goat, whose milk was the only luxury he indulged in, and a delicious draught was presented to his famished guest, who assured by his gentleness, soon after fell into a sound sleep. Arnold, engaged in his own occupations, did not come near the cave during the three following days; Rosa was for a long time inconsoleable; she wept, she called on her dear mamma, and exertions to pacify her were vainly used by Reginald, who became insensibly interested for the lovely child: by degrees, her regret and terror wore away; she seemed much delighted when Reginald, to divert her, played several tunes on his flute; and as her apprehension subsided, she gradually became more familiar with him; she would at times attempt a description of some very terrible transaction; she spoke of horsemen with swords and guns, and frequently mentioned the name of Madeline, but was incapable of giving any distinct account of the connection that subsisted between them. The simple fare which she had at first rejected indignantly, was soon rendered palatable by hunger, and her infantile prattle unbending the gloom which had heretofore clouded the brow of the wretched recluse, he assumed innumerable gay airs to divert his youthful charge. At length Arnold visited the cave, and his astonishment was extreme at perceiving it had acquired a fresh inmate. Reginald related his adventure, and desired Arnold to make inquiry in the village and its environs for the parents of the child. Arnold did so, but his inquiries were unattended by success; and after several days passed in perplexing incertitude and fruitless researches, he returned to the cave. Reginald, instead of expressing disappointment, seemed much gratified; habit had reconciled him to the innocent intruder, and her endearing ways had beguiled him of many sad hours. His imagination extended not to the future: Rosa as a child delighted him, and it never for a moment entered his thoughts, that Rosa would ever be other than a child; he therefore returned an obstinate denial to the generous offer which the wood-cutter made of taking the child home with him, but readily agreed that he should occasionally supply her with better fare than what the cave afforded. All the ferocious passions which had before agitated the breast of Reginald, were now suspended; if his counte-nance for a moment assumed its wild disordered expression, the undisguised terror and aversion of Rosa instantly subdued him; he would then clasp her fondly to his bosom, entreat her not to hate him, and as his scalding tears fell on her lovely face, kiss them away with affection almost paternal. Rosa, gentle and timid, shrunk equally from these extremes of sensibility, and as advanced age gave expansion to intellect, frequently wondered at her peculiar situation. The past events seemed faded from her memory; but an impression of dread had been stamped on her mind by the singu-larly uncouth form and manners of Reginald, which no subsequent kindness could wholly eradicate. Before him she wholly suppressed the curiosity she felt, but to Arnold she expressed it in the most inquisitive terms, when the wanderings of Reginald afforded her opportunity; and his information, instead of affording her satisfac-tion, seemed but to increase her anxiety. One day Arnold men-tioned inadvertently, that he had a son and daughter at home about her own age—"Are they like me?" asked Rosa. Arnold smiled: "No, my dear, they are poor rustic children."—"And what am I?"—"It is very easy to perceive that you are belonging to some great family, if we could but find them out."—"And what should I be the better for that?"—"Oh, a vast deal; you would have fine cloaths instead of that coarse camblet[1] dress; and you would sleep on a soft bed, hung

1 Variant of "camlet," a type of woollen cloth.

round with beautiful furniture; and you would have delicious food."—"What then," cried Rosa, clasping her hands with delight and wonder, "do other people live in that way? I thought every body lived in the same manner as ourselves."—"Bless you, my pretty innocent, it was a very natural mistake; but, indeed, nobody lives like the strange man you are with."—"I am sorry for that," said Rosa, shaking her head; "I should like to see how other people live."—"But the hermit will think it unkind of you to wish to leave him."—"I would not leave him for any thing," cried Rosa; "for when he is good-natured, I love him dearly; but cannot you bring your children to see me?"—"I dare not."—"Then I will go to them."—"That I cannot promise: you must ask the hermit." Rosa entertained not a doubt of success, and instantly, on the return of Reginald, assailed him with intreaties to permit her to visit, for a short time, the cottage of Arnold. Reginald started with dismay: her presence was now his only solace; and fearing that the pleasing contrast which the cottage might present, would fill her mind with dissatisfaction at her present situation, he gave a stern refusal. The spirit of Rosa sunk under his harshness; she spent the remainder of the day in tears, and rejected, with repellent disgust, all his endearments. Fearful of wholly alienating her regard, Reginald at length was induced to yield a reluctant acquiescence, and on the following day, after affectionately embracing her guardian, Rosa tripped lightly through the forest, led by the hand of the honest, guileless Arnold. Every object had the charm of novelty, and Rosa expressed the most lively rapture: the hovel in which the woodman's family resided was a palace to the inexperienced orphan; she examined minutely every article of furniture, the uses of which she could with difficulty comprehend, and embraced the young rustics with fond familiarity. A small looking-glass at length caught her attention: the animated object it presented, gave her unspeakable pleasure; she gazed at her own resemblance with mingled surprise and admiration: when informed that it was herself, she played a thousand antic gestures, and throwing her arm around the neck of Julette, cried—"Ah, now I see you are not like me; how brown your skin is! and your eyes, they are quite black!"—"I am not so pretty as you," said Julette, dejectedly.—"I am sure I think you are," replied the unconscious Rosa;—"but come here, Lucius, I think you are most like me." Lucius was a blooming boy, about twelve years of age; his glossy auburn hair curled in sportive ringlets round his dimpled cheeks, on which health had fixed her seat; his eyes were dark hazel, and beaming with expression; his features formed with beautiful regularity.—Rosa drew him towards her—their eyes met in the mirror—mutual admiration heightened the colour in their cheeks, and a smile of satisfaction played on the lips of each.— "What a pity it is," cried Lucius, "that you cannot live with us."— For the first time in her life, Rosa sighed.—"I will come to see you very often," said she; "for I am sure the cave is a dismal place compared with this; but I must not live with you."—"I should love you dearly," cried Julette; "we would play together and sleep together, and we should be so happy!" Rosa again embraced her young friend, and again expressed the joy it would afford her to be permitted to live with them. Arnold soon after hurried her away, and Rosa that night retired to rest with a discontented mind.

(To be continued.)

[Continued from page 31.]

"It has been said that he who retires to Solitude is either a beast or an angel; the censure is too severe and the praise unmerited; the discontented being who retires from society is commonly some good-natured man, who has begun life without experience, and knew not how to gain it in his intercourse with mankind."
GOLDSMITH.[1]

REGINALD, delighted with the winning graces of the lovely Rosa, grew daily more and more indulgent, and with the tenderness of an anxious parent, busied himself in the pleasing task of instruction; he made out a list of books, which Arnold procured from the neigh-

1 From Letter LXVII from William Goldsmith's series published under the title of "Chinese Letters" in the newspaper *Public Ledger* and later collected under the title *The Citizen of the World: or, Letters from a Chinese Philosopher Residing in London to His Friends in the East* (1762).

bouring town, and Rosa proved an apt scholar; he next instructed her in the use of the pen; and, to encourage her and reward her for her attention, he suffered Arnold to purchase a guitar, which proved a most gratifying present to the lively Rosa; thus the cave, from being a scene of gloomy horror, became gradually the abode of content and serenity. Rosa no longer shunned her protector with aversion, but became sensible of his superiority over the peasantry she had hitherto met with; she began to look up to him with reverence not unmixed with love. She was allowed occasionally to visit the children of the good woodcutter, and these amiable young people soon cherished towards each other a friendship pure as unalterable. One day, Reginald returned from his accustomed solitary ramble, with an altered countenance: he caught Rosa in his arms with extreme agitation, and pressing her to his bosom cried, "Dost thou love me, Rosa?" "Indeed, indeed I do," returned she, with affectionate ardour; "but why this unusual question, dear Sir?" "Ask me not now, Rosa," he returned, with increasing tenderness; "business of importance calls me from you for several days; only promise me that no persuasions shall induce you to quit the cave during my absence. I could not live without you, Rosa, and should you voluntarily abandon your unfortunate friend, oh! Rosa, terrible, most terrible would be the consequence;" he struck his forehead with his hand, and a look of desperation recalled to the memory of the appalled Rosa emotions which had once made an impression on her mind which no subsequent kindness could wholly obliterate. "Be not thus anxious," cried she, grasping his hand: "I would not quit the cave without your permission for the world; but indeed the time will hang heavy on my hands while you are away, solitude is so irksome." Reginald sighed; "To you, my sweet girl, it may seem so; you have not felt the sting of ingratitude; the just hatred of mankind, which fills my soul, is as yet a stranger to your gentle bosom; I would preserve you from these miseries, from sensations which must agonize thy feeling breast even to madness; but my language is incomprehensible to you, and your ignorance is your bliss. Should you want amusement while I am away, you may turn over the contents of an old chest, which you will find in the passage which branches to the left of the cave: there you will find some old music and books, which will no doubt afford you entertainment for a much longer period. Arnold will take care that you do not want for provisions. And now, Rosa, I have another surprise for you; retire awhile, my love, and return when I call you." Rosa, lost in astonishment, withdrew behind the curtain with which Reginald had of late divided their places of repose: she remained there but a short time ere she was again summoned into the presence of Reginald; and her surprise was augmented by the transformation which his person had undergone. He had thrown aside the uncouth garb which had so long been his only covering, and now, in the elegant habit of an Italian nobleman, displayed all the native grace of his form. Rosa gazed on him with unconcealed admiration, and he could not suppress a smile at the whimsical expression of her countenance. "What do you think of this transformation, Rosa? I trust you are not displeased to find that I am not entirely the savage you thought me." "Indeed," replied Rosa, affectionately pressing his hand, "I am delighted with the change, and hope you will never again resume those disgusting habiliments." "That must depend upon circumstances, my girl, which I cannot at present explain; at my return you shall know more; let it now suffice that, for your sake alone, have I entered upon an undertaking which will in all probability determine my future destiny. Ask no questions, but obey my injunctions implicitly; observe a profound secrecy as to what has passed between us, and shun the prying eye of curiosity. Should my stay exceed two days, and you find yourself dull, you may visit the cottage; but let your visits there be short, and observe the caution I have given you." Rosa promised willing obedience, and after embracing her tenderly, he departed. Rosa watched his progress from the mouth of the cave; he frequently looked back and waved his hand to her, till at length the gloom of the forest wholly obscured his figure. Rosa burst into tears; she felt as if left alone in the world, and terrible apprehensions filled her mind that her only protector and companion would be snatched from her. It was in vain she endeavoured to retrace the scenes of her infancy; confused ideas only floated in her imagination, which she found it impossible to connect or reduce to any certainty. The retiring sun now obliged her to light her lamp; sleep seemed banished from her aching eyes, and she took up her guitar to beguile the heavy hours, but her mind was agitated, and her favorite tunes had then no charm to sooth. Novelty must be tried: she recollected the old chest, and in a moment formed the determination of examining the contents. She accordingly took the lamp from the hook, and, with the impatience of curiosity, hastened into the recess: after turning over a number of things, which she considered mere rubbish, she perceived in one corner a packet of letters—the music was in an instant forgotten—she eagerly seized the prize, and returning to the habitable part of the cave, anxiously endeavoured to peruse the contents; it did not immediately occur to her, that the action was improper; a fair opportunity seemed to offer to discover mysteries which had long perplexed her, and she unfolded letter after letter in the hope of perceiving her own name; for Reginald, with his mistrustful caution, had never mentioned the total ignorance she was in, respecting her connections, but rather gave her to understand that she was particularly recommended to his protection. Yet still Rosa remained ungratified; the names were entirely unknown to her; but female curiosity still urged her to proceed, and every line increased her astonishment at a perfidy of which she had hitherto never formed an idea. Yet they in part revealed the cause of her unhappy guardian's retreat from the world, at an age when most men enter with avidity into all its pleasures. The letters were written in an elegant female hand, and the contents ran thus—

LETTER I.

"Your last, dear Julian, filled me with concern—your illness alarms me. Why am I condemned to this cruel separation, at a time when my tender affections might sooth the pains of disease, and calm the agitation of that too susceptible heart? yet doubt not that my whole soul is with you. It is in vain that Reginald would drag me from one scene of dissipation to another; I take no pleasure in his kindness; his fondness disgusts me; he seems astonished at the apathy with which I behold scenes to me so new to others so delightful;—he is full of a thousand tender apprehensions.—Troublesome creature! he pursues me like a shadow; even now I hear his steps, and the discordant omen grates on my ears!—It compels me to conclude this abruptly—it checks all the fond things I would have added.

"JULIA."

LETTER II.

"CALM your apprehensions, my beloved Julia: I am better, infinitely better; your sweet epistle was the healing balm which restored me to life and happiness.—And are you still faithful? has not the doating caresses of —— alienated your affection from your poor Julian?—Oh, no! the conviction brings rapture with it!—our very names denote our inseparable union!—But, dearest creature! how did it happen that you forgot my request?—can you think that I would have taxed your generosity without pressing necessity?—I am ashamed to repeat my request; it must have been inconvenient, or Julia would not have suffered it to pass unnoticed.—I am too weak to write long letters—my love must excuse me.——Adieu!

"JULIAN."

LETTER III.

"PARDON me, Julian; anxiety for your health banished every other consideration from my mind.—I enclose you a sum larger than you required; *he* gave it to me this morning to discharge some petty bills; but I can make a thousand excuses to get a fresh supply, so accept it without scruple.—But I have something still better to impart— Reginald is going from the Chateau for a week—there's tidings for you!—no doubt you will avail yourself of it.—Why should not my *brother* be as welcome as his *sister*—and my brother you must be. Reginald begins to entertain hopes of an heir!—We can laugh over that story when you come to the Chateau.——No more at present.

"JULIA."

Rosa, though incapable of comprehending the whole purport of these infamous letters, yet understood enough to convince her that the confidence of Reginald had been grossly abused, and she tossed them from her with indignation. The night was already far advanced; her mind, diverted from her own solitary situation by the wrongs of him who was now regarded by her with more tender esteem, gradually recovered its former serenity, and she soon composed herself sufficiently to enjoy the sweet sleep of innocence. In the morning Arnold paid her a visit; he was surprised at the absence of Reginald, and hazarded innumerable conjectures. Rosa was silent as to what had passed previous to his departure, as well as on the subject of the letters she had found; and Arnold in vain endeavoured to persuade her to accompany him home. On the following day, however, he was more successful; lively joy sparkled in the eyes of young Lucius at the sight of her, and the afternoon was spent in innocent hilarity. At an early hour Rosa returned to the cave, and could not but shudder at the gloomy contrast it presented when compared with the cheerful party and comfortable fire-side at the cottage.

Rosa was now sixteen, and though habit had reconciled her to the inconveniences of the cave, she could not but consider her situation irksome, though respect for Reginald prevented her from expressing the least dissatisfaction.—This night in particular, Rosa felt all the horrors of her situation; the loud wind whistled through the trees, and every appalling blast struck terror to the heart of the unprotected girl. It was to no purpose that she called music to her aid; the overpowering whirlwind silenced her feeble strains; and though safe from the fury of the tempest which raged without, her depressed spirits felt its full influence. For several hours Rosa remained in this uncomfortable state, when at length a calm succeeded, and she prepared to take that repose of which she stood so much in need, when a cry of distress assailed her ears, and again excited sensations of alarm. For some moments she listened attentively—the cry was repeated, succeeded by the trampling of horses.—Dreading any danger to her friend, Rosa rushed wildly from the cave, calling aloud on the name of Reginald: no answer was returned, and she ventured boldly onward, till her progress was impeded by some object on the ground. Not doubting but that it was Reginald, she raised the person in her arms, and in gentle accents inquired if he was hurt; but it was a stranger to whom she addressed herself, and she succeeded with difficulty in assisting to the cave a youth who had been wounded by some banditti in the forest. Rosa bound his wounds with some of her own linen, but restoratives she had none, and the stranger remained several hours insensible to her care; at length, opening his eyes, and fixing them on the interesting figure of Rosa, he exclaimed—"Sweet spirit! for in this dreary spot I can scarcely believe thee mortal, how have

I become the object of thy tender charity?" Rosa, unused to the refinement of language, knew not what to make of this speech: "Compose yourself, Signior," said she; "you have been much hurt; you are in friendly hands, and all I can do for you I will do with pleasure; perhaps to-morrow we may get better assistance."—"Are you alone in this dreary cave?" asked the stranger.—"At present, I am; but I have a very dear protector, who will soon return." At that moment it occurred to Rosa, that probably Reginald would be displeased at this new intruder; yet she thought him too good to condemn an act of humanity, and she eagerly wished for morning, which she doubted not would either bring him or Arnold to the cottage. Her hopes were confirmed by the early appearance of the wood-cutter: he listened to her account with surprise and pity, and assured the stranger, that if he found himself able to accompany him through the forest, he should be accommodated with respect and kindness at the cottage. To this the youth readily assented, and leaning on the arm of the benevolent Arnold, after expressing himself with all the energy of admiration and gratitude to Rosa, he departed. The artless girl, who had never before beheld a form so attractive, suffered her eyes to express the sentiment he had raised in her inexperienced bosom, and assured him in the simple accents of sincerity, that she should be happy to hear of his recovery.

About the middle of the day Reginald returned; Rosa flew to his arms with rapture, and welcomed him a thousand times;—delight sparkled in his eyes: "And are you really glad to see me, Rosa?"— "Can you doubt it, my only—my best friend!" was her reply.— "Then I have pleasing tidings to impart," returned he cheerfully; "you shall accompany me to Naples; we will live there in splendour and happiness, my girl!—you shall be my wife!"—"Wife!" repeated Rosa—"how is that? I do not understand you."—Reginald smiled: "I will explain it to you, my love.—In civilized society it is common for two people of different sexes, who feel the warmest attachment of friendship for each other, to be bound together in the most sacred manner, according to the form of the established religion. When two persons are thus united, the bond is indissoluble but by death; their property and interest become mutual; they are wholly dependent on each other; they live together by day and by night; their children are lawful, and can inherit their property; and they live happily and respectable in the eyes of the world; neither has the power to make another choice, but must behold every other object with indifference." Reginald paused—some unaccountable emotion choaked his utterance, and he anxiously awaited Rosa's answer.—She, too, hesitated: at length—"I think I understand you now," said she, innocently: "all you have told me is very desirable, except the last observation you made. I wish to know how it would be possible to behold every other object with indifference, if they happened to be more agreeable and amiable than the person one happened to be united to?" Reginald started: "So, so!" said he, "is this nature?"—"You do not reply, Sir," cried Rosa,—With some sternness Reginald answered—"By the power of virtue, girl! when once a person knows their duties to be sacred, the performance of them becomes easy and practicable." Reginald spoke not from conviction, nor could he convince Rosa, who, nevertheless, fearful of offending him, readily consented to accompany him to Naples. She then related to him, with the utmost candour, what had occurred during his absence: when she mentioned the letters his colour rose, and his agitation was extreme; but when she described the wounded cavalier, and dwelt on his interesting manners, his eyes flashed fire, and Rosa shrunk appalled from his angry glances!—Her terror recalled him to a sense of the impropriety of his conduct: he feared to disgust her, and changing his tone, said mildly—"I am not angry with you, dear Rosa; you have done but what is right; pardon the impetuosity of my feelings, and listen with attention to a recital which, though painful to myself to enter upon, is now fully necessary.—But tell me honestly, Rosa, do not you prefer this handsome stranger to your friend Reginald?"—"What a question!" replied Rosa, blushing: "he had, indeed, a most pleasing countenance, and a majestic figure; and then his voice is so soft and so persuasive, that—that—one cannot but admire him!—But, you know, my dear sir, I have loved you so many years, that I can never prefer a stranger to you."—Reginald sighed: "Well, well!" said he; "I will no urge you farther on this subject—but it grows late—we will retire for the night—to-morrow will be time enough for my story—at present I am exhausted, both in mind and body." Rosa kissed his hand, and they retired to rest.

On the following day they were visited at an early hour by

Arnold: he gave Rosa the most satisfactory assurance that his guest was in a fair way of doing well; and hinted to her, that his anxiety was great to see and thank once more his fair preserver. Rosa knew not what to reply; but she was spared the trouble by Reginald, who immediately disclosed to Arnold his intention of quitting the cave.—"This night," said he, "you must endeavour to procure us accommodation in the village, as your house is too small to admit of such an increase."—"You are mistaken, Sir," replied Arnold; "we can manage tolerably well.—Rosa, I dare say, will have no objection to partake of my daughter's bed; Lucius, since the strange gentleman has been among us, has slept with me, and our best bed is still at your service."—"I thank you," replied Reginald; "I prefer your offer to being thrown among strangers, therefore will accept it: to-morrow, if every thing can be properly arranged, we set out for Naples. I consider myself much indebted to you for past services, and will not forget the obligation; I have also many instructions to give you this night—at sun-set you may expect us." Arnold was full of wonder; but he was too much awed by the dignified manner of Reginald to express the least hint of what he thought; he therefore bowed respectfully, and soon after departed. After partaking their usual repast, which no longer was confined to hermits' fare, but consisted of palatable though plain food, and was furnished every day by the assiduous woodman at a moderate expence, Reginald drew his seat nearer to Rosa, and taking her hand fondly between his own, endeavoured to impress her mind with a sense of the strong affection he felt for her: "When you have heard my story, Rosa," said he, "you will be better able to judge of the strength of the regard which can induce me once more to enter into scenes which I once flew from with horror. My injuries, Rosa, will excite pity in your tender breast. I thank Heaven, the clouds which have so long obscured my prospects are now gradually dispersing—happiness may yet be mine, if blest with the confidence and affection of my Rosa!" He then proceeded to enter on the particulars of his life in the following words.—

(*To be continued.*)

[Continued from page 88.]

"She has beauty, which spreads and blooms
Like a fair opening flower;
But poisonous adders lurk beneath its root,
And from such briars springs this lovely rose;
It wounds the hand which it invites to pluck it."

DRYDEN.[1]

"AFFLUENCE and pleasure attended my early years," said Reginald, sighing. "The only male descendant of one of the noblest families in Naples, I was flattered and caressed wherever I went: indulged in every extravagant caprice by a doating father, whose liberality knew no bounds, I became vain and dissipated, and associated with men whose intriguing talents made me readily their dupe. My father saw his error too late; his remonstrances had little power to draw me from the alluring haunts of pleasure, or to counteract the insidious flattery which bewitched my senses, and deceived my understanding. I had one sister, amiable and attractive; her virtues and accomplishments won the admiration of many distinguished cavaliers; but an unhappy perversion of judgment fixed her affection on one of my most intimate associates, named Julian de Zoresti. I was imprudent enough to sanction the attachment, for I was myself enamoured of his lovely sister, and in this double union of the families expected the utmost felicity. My father, influenced by some reports which had reached his ear, to the disadvantage of Zoresti, and not deeming him a proper match in point of rank, positively rejected all his overtures; and my sister, too duteous and gentle to disobey a parent's injunctions, gave her hand to a gentleman on whom my father had fixed his choice. The concern and disappointment which Julian expressed, wounded my friendship, and in a fit of love and enthusiasm, I espoused the beauteous Julia. This daring transgression of his darling son, at first

---

1 From Sir Thomas Overbury's speech in *The Tragedy of Sir Thomas Overbury* (1724), Act I, Scene 1, by Richard Savage. Incorrectly attributed to Dryden here. A variant of the original, which reads: ". . . She has beauty, / Which spreads and blooms like a fresh-opening Flow'r! / But poisonous Adders lurk beneath its Shade; / And from such Briars shoots this lovely Rose, / It wounds the Touch which it invites to crop it."

afflicted my father severely; but fond partiality getting the better of his temporary resentment, he at length vouchsafed me his pardon and blessing. Nothing was now wanting to complete my happiness, but to see my sister's tranquillity restored; but secret regret preyed on her cheek, and all the attentions of a generous and affectionate husband, were unable to eradicate the unhappy passion which had unfortunately taken such deep root in her heart. The birth of an infant son at length seemed to restore her to her wonted serenity; and the delightful occupation of rearing her tender charge, gave new strength to the energies of her mind, and even rendered her husband more agreeable in her sight.

"The death of my father, the Count St. Osbert, which happened soon after, left me uncontrouled and independent. Influenced by the persuasions of my fascinating bride, I launched into every species of luxury, nor awakened to a sense of my own imprudence, till the dreadful discovery of my wife's infidelity shot through my brain like a thunderbolt, and hurled me from the pinnacle of imaginary felicity, into the deep abyss of despair. In short, Rosa! for I cannot be minute in relating this horrible transaction, I detected Julia in a correspondence with the base Zoresti. You have seen the infamous letters which passed between them, you may now form some idea of my distraction." "But, dear Sir," cried Rosa, "are you certain there was no mistake? Zoresti was Julia's brother." "It was all an imposition," returned Reginald; rage distorting every feature; "Julia was an abandoned woman, and Zoresti a needy sharper; no relationship subsisted between them. In the first paroxysm of my phrenzy, I meditated the destruction of Julia; but the dreadful recollection of her situation withheld my vengeful arm, and for the sake of the unknown babe, I spared the mother. She, however, found means to apprize Julian of what had happened, and he effectually secreted himself from my fury. The unfortunate Adeline[1] sunk beneath this shock; the gentle sensibility of her nature was unable to endure the agonizing conflicts of her mind; and in addition to my other calamities, I had to bewail the loss of a sister whom my own indiscretion had hurried to a premature grave. For several months I wandered about in an unsettled state of mind, till one

1 Reginald's sister.

night, passing through an obscure street, a villain sprung from behind a portico, and plunged a poniard in my side: guilt and fear had unnerved his arm, for I grasped it vigorously, and drawing my sword, pierced him to the heart. He fell, uttering vindictive curses, and in my fallen foe I recognized the detested Zoresti.—"Thy wife will not thank thee for this," said he, malignantly, "but I hope her next messenger will be more successful." These were the last words he uttered, for the agonies of death succeeded, and I fled from the spot with disgust and horror. After the insinuation of Zoresti that Julia had conspired against my life, I could expect neither peace nor safety in Naples; I therefore returned home, packed up all my valuables, and without again beholding the infamous wretch who had caused all my misery, quitted my native home. Heedless what became of me, I travelled many miles, till fatigue and hunger overpowered my exhausted frame, and I was obliged to solicit shelter in a woodcutter's hovel: the man was kind and hospitable, and I remained with the good Arnold several days. Listless and wretched, I shunned society, and to avoid the observation of the rustics who came occasionally to the cottage, I every day rambled with him into the forest, whither his laborious occupation obliged him to repair. His cheerful manners and obliging assiduities, drew me by degrees from my sorrows; yet solitude was my only wish, and the discovery of this cave promised me a retreat I had for some time unceasingly wished for. I intimated my design to Arnold; he at first opposed it with earnestness, but finding nothing would dissuade me from my purpose, he at length began to consider my proposals with attention, and exerted himself to the utmost to render my retreat as commodious as circumstances would admit: some of the furniture was removed from the cottage, and I supplied him with money to replace it with better; but every accommodation which might have bordered on indulgence, I strenuously refused. I buried what money I possessed in a corner of the cave, and in a short time I grew so misanthropic, that the sight of man was hateful to me. Arnold, however, brought me intelligence that my wife had quitted the chateau, and fled, no one knew whither; that the Marquis Veronia, my sister's husband, had taken possession of my estates, in trust for me, and that he had caused me to be searched for throughout the city. All this interested me very little; there was no remaining tie to attach me to society, and I cared not what became of my worldly property, as it was not my intention ever again to claim it, or mix again in a world so full of deceit and ingratitude. This was the state of my mind, my dear Rosa, when chance first threw you in my way a helpless infant. I cannot describe the various emotions of my mind at beholding your countenance, nor account for the extraordinary impulse which urged me to cherish you in my bosom; for know, dear girl, that but for me you would have perished in the forest, where you was left helpless and unsheltered."—Here Rosa expressed her surprize, and the Count related every particular.—Rosa, overcome with the sweet emotion of gratitude, flung herself into his arms, and wept on his bosom. Reginald thus proceeded: "For sixteen[1] years you have been my comfort and consolation; judge then if I can now endure the idea of a separation; I love you, Rosa, beyond every earthly thing; I have beheld the dawning virtues of your heart with proud delight; I have neither deceit nor guile to dread from you, and if my sweet girl will bless me by devoting her future life to my care and affection, peace and happiness may once more be the lot of Reginald." "My friend, my preserver!" exclaimed Rosa, "I am all your own, command me as you please; but pardon my apprehensions. Should the wretched woman —I will not call her your wife—should Julia even see me, would not she do some desperate act?—kill you perhaps." "Sweet innocent!" replied Reginald fondly, "I will calm your apprehension by a proper explanation: dear as you were to my heart, I could not think of making you mine, till every obstacle was removed. On this account I so lately repaired to Naples; I found my estates in good order, and the worthy Marquis ready and willing to restore them to me whenever I should make the claim; from him I learned that Julia has long since ceased to exist, and has left behind her no pledge of our union. I need not tell you that I rejoice at this, as doubt and suspicion would have filled my mind, and perhaps have alleviated my affection from an innocent child. You will now be every thing to me, and by your kind decision, have spared me from the painful necessity of placing you in a convent for life." Reginald paused, and Rosa again

---

1 Probably closer to ten years, as Rosa "was apparently about six years of age" when Reginald first found her.

expressed her willingness to accompany him to Naples. As soon as nightfall screened them from observation, Reginald drew the arm of Rosa within his own, and conducted her safely to the cottage of the faithful Arnold, who received her with unfeigned pleasure; the young cottagers too were delighted with her being permitted to continue with them a few days, and the pallid countenance of the stranger lighted up with pleasure. Reginald threw off the reserve which had before been so chilling to the ingenuous ardor of the youth, and by revealing his own name and rank, afforded an opportunity to act with equal candour. "Sincerely do I congratulate you, Count," said he,[1] "on the happy change which seems to have taken place in your sentiments; a life of misanthropic seclusion is a manifest breach of the Divine will; and I trust you will, upon further acquaintance, do me the justice to believe that the happiness of your acquaintance, and if I may presume so far as to expect it, the honor of your friendship, will amply compensate for the loss of those advantages of which your restoration to society must necessarily deprive me." "I am at a loss to comprehend your meaning," said Reginald, gazing at him with surprize; "In what way can my return to the world affect your prospect in life?"—"You will not be long at a loss to understand my meaning," replied the youth, "when I inform you that I am Alphonso, the only son of the Marquis Veronia." "Is is possible!" exclaimed the Count, surveying the youth with a mixture of sensations which he could scarcely define; "do I behold in you the child of my beloved Adeline?" "It is true indeed," replied Alphonso, "and I hope neither you nor the amiable Rosa will be dissatisfied at the discovery." Rosa expressed her joy in the most unrestrained manner; but a frown clouded the brow of Reginald, though he embraced the youth with affection, and promised him his friendship. "Your father's noble disinterestedness is remembered by me with heart-felt gratitude," said he; "and if it is in my power to make any compensation for the deprivation of expected inheritance, be assured the will to serve you shall not be wanting; but I hope no such exertion can be necessary." Alphonso sighed.—"I am sorry," said he, "that my father's too liberal spirit has involved him in embarrassments of a most unpleasant nature. The commis-

1 The injured cavalier.

sion which I hold renders me independent, but it would grieve my heart to see his latter days clouded by adversity; on his account only have I taken the liberty to speak to you in this unreserved manner, for I know the pride and delicacy of his nature too well to imagine, for a moment, that he would even make you acquainted with the real state of his circumstances." "I am greatly obliged to you for the information," said Reginald; "it shall not escape my memory." When the rest of the family were assembled to supper, the Count mingled familiarly among them; he exerted himself to be cheerful, yet a secret anxiety preyed on his spirits, and he cautiously watched every look and motion of Rosa.—When he retired to his comfortable, though humble, chamber, he sought not repose, but pacing the floor with agitated steps, thus meditated within himself: "Am I doing right in endeavouring to attach this lively, artless girl to myself? have I a right thus to take advantage of that chance which threw her in my way, and confine her to duties of which, at present, she has no idea? I fear I do wrong—yet it shall be the whole study of my life to make her happy; to teach her to love me, and I have reason to believe it will be no difficult task. Yes, yes, Rosa must be mine; I feel I cannot exist without her." Rosa, on her side, passed not a better night; a thousand new ideas floated in her imagination; busy fancy alternately presented to her her guardian and his nephew, and every comparison ended in favour of the latter. The Count was finely formed and handsome, but his features were harsh and sometimes stern, while the more youthful charms of Alphonso suffered under no such disadvantage. Reginald was majestic—Alphonso graceful; the former possessed sense and spirit, but his temper was irritable, and his manners austere; while on the contrary the latter was unassuming, mild, and occasionally gay. This was a dangerous contrast for Reginald, and might have ended in her total rejection of his proposals, had not the peculiar circumstances of their acquaintance given him a pre-eminence in her estimation which nothing could remove.

[*To be continued.*]

[Continued from page 176.]

"What has she to fear who stamps with reverence and honour
every sentiment she inspires. Is there on earth a wretch base
enough to offer the least insult to such virtue?"   ROUSSEAU.[1]

ON the following day, as soon as every thing was satisfactorily
arranged, our travellers set out in hopes of reaching the chateau,
which was at the distance of thirty miles from the wood. Rosa
parted with reluctance from her young friends at the cottage; and
promised, that as soon as she was settled in her new residence, she
would send for Julette to live with her, not as a domestic, but as
a confidential friend. Lucius dejectedly hung his head, and could
scarcely restrain his tears, as she bade him adieu with the tenderness of sisterly affection. The party rode slowly, on account of
Alphonso's ill state of health; and their discourse took an interesting turn, till heavy falling drops gave them apprehension of
an approaching storm, and turned their thoughts awhile from
domestic arrangements to present convenience. They had reached
the skirts of the wood, an open plain lay before them, and heavy
gathering clouds warned them that shelter would be necessary. "I
think," said Alphonso, "that when I passed this track before, the
turrets of an abbey appeared somewhere to the right, at no great
distance. Could we retreat thither, as a temporary asylum, it
would save us the trouble of returning to the cottage." Reginald
thinking the advice good, turned his horse into the path pointed
out by Alphonso, and pursuing it at a brisk pace, soon reached the
postern gate. Rosa, who had never beheld an edifice of the kind,
declared she would rather continue the journey, notwithstanding
the torrents of rain which fell, than enter such a gloomy pile of
ruins. "This gate is fast, I find," said Reginald; "we must ride round
and try our luck at the grand entrance." Rosa timidly followed her
guardian, while Alphonso rallied her for her timidity, and strove
to excite her curiosity by a description of the various religious
institutions, the ingenuity of the nuns, and the spendour of their
devotional ceremonies. Reginald, however, could obtain no answer

1 From *Eloisa: or, A Series of Original Letters Collected and Published by J. J. Rousseau*
(trans. 1761) by Jean-Jacques Rousseau.

to his repeated sounding of the ponderous bell—all was wrapped in inhospitable silence. "These monks are very negligent of the offices of humanity," said Alphonso; "I fear my fair Rosa will not be gratified with the novelties I promised her." "Perhaps they are at their orisons,"[1] rejoined Reginald.—"But hark! did not you hear voices among the trees?—Travellers like ourselves, perhaps, hastening hither for shelter." He had scarcely finished the sentence before two cavaliers rode up to the gate, who seemed in merry converse. On perceiving the group already waiting for admission, they seemed a little embarrassed; and after speaking to each other in a low voice, one of them accosted Reginald—"May I presume to ask, sir," said he, "whether choice or necessity occasion you to seek admission here." "The latter, I can assure you, cavalier," replied Reginald: "I should unwillingly tax the hospitality of the holy fathers, but that I am anxious for the accommodation of this fair companion in distress." The stranger smiled courteously, and replied, "Our arrival is fortunate; we have some influence here, and can promise you a good reception.—Please to ride this way." Reginald was rather surprized by the familiar manners of the stranger; but followed, with many expressions of civility, to the postern gate they had before vainly tried to open. The stranger, putting aside some thick underwood, discovered the handle of a bell, which he sounded twice, and in a very short time the gate was opened by a tall hard featured monk, who, bowing low, with his hands crossed upon his breast in silence, permitted them to enter. The monk then cautiously fastened the portal, and preceded them into a large apartment, where he pointed to chairs, and then retired. "This is a strange reception," said Alphonso, looking at Reginald; "I should like to know the name of this monastery." "You are now in the abbey of St. Sidwell," rejoined one of the cavaliers; "and the oddity of the holy brotherhood is only equalled by their hospitality. I have often been entertained here, and always went away satisfied with my reception." Alphonso seemed rather better reconciled by this information, but he began to feel a little alarm, as he observed the encreasing interest with which the strangers appeared to view Rosa. In a few minutes the monk returned; his cowl was drawn

1 At prayer.

closer over his face, and in his hand he held a basket well stored with wine, cakes, cold tongues, and bread, which he promptly spread on the table before them. "Be not strange," said he, respectfully bowing, "but freely partake of this refreshment. If you will permit me, gentlemen, I will take your cloaks and outer garments to dry." Rosa threw off the large cloak which covered her, and displayed the lovely symmetry of her form; and again the strangers gazed on her with rapturous admiration. "Your swords will be rusted with the wet," said one of the strangers, delivering up his own; his comrade following his example, Reginald and Alphonso incautiously did the same, and they altogether sat down to the repast. The strangers took upon them as masters of the feast, and the wine circulated briskly. In about an hour's time Reginald rose.—"It is fit," said he, "that we pursue our journey—the atmosphere seems cleared, and we shall proceed with renovated vigour." "Stop," cried one of the strangers, "we must first return thanks to the holy fathers for this kind reception." He looked significantly at the monk, who hastily retired: after a short interval, approaching footsteps were heard—the door was thrown open, and a party of armed men entered:—Rosa shrieked with terror, and flew to the protecting arms of Reginald. "Ha! treachery!" cried Alphonso, "then we are lost." The chief, named Fernando, advanced with a resolute, yet respectful mien. "Gentlemen," said he, "we mean you no violence. It is true, your own credulity has assisted us in deceiving you as to the nature of this order, which is that of Independence and Universal Property, rather than Mercy and St. Sidwell; but, though free-booters, we are not assassins. Self-preservation may oblige us to be strict, but if you are not perverse, you will acknowledge that you might have fallen into worse hands. By a recent misadventure we have lost several brave men, and now make you the offer of filling their places, reserving this lady only as the hostage of your fidelity." Who can speak the anguish of Reginald, at this horrid proposal;—he beheld all his dearest hopes blasted, and dreading to exasperate the ruffian band by his expressions of abhorrence, he turned disdainfully away. Rosa, overcome with terror and dismay, fainted away; and was, by the peremptory command of Fernando, torn from Alphonso's arms, and conveyed to a separate apartment. "I will give you twenty-four hours to consider of my proposal," said Fernando, "and you will do well not to reject it; meanwhile, the lady shall be treated with respect, or if you will consent to yield her to my arms, you shall be suffered to depart unmolested, after taking a solemn oath of secrecy." The rage and indignation of Reginald now broke forth with unrestrained bitterness; but all his threats and invectives were listened to by Fernando with contemptuous indifference. "Exhaust your useless fury," said he, "and you will then be more reasonable. Know you not that your life is in our hands, and that we are not accustomed thus to temporize with our prisoners." He then haughtily retired, and secured the door with strong bars. Locked in each other's arms, Reginald and Alphonso bewailed the fate of their tenderly-beloved Rosa; they trembled at the idea of the insults which brutal power could inflict, and cursed their own credulity which had led them into such a snare.

Let us now return to the hapless Rosa, who, sunk on a miserable bed, in a gloomy apartment, remained a prey to the most agonizing suspense: with bitter cries she called on Alphonso and Reginald, but her cries were unheard, except by a withered old hag, who sat by her side, and muttered peevish execrations at her impatience, and threatened her with severe punishment if she remained so perverse. Rosa regarded the countenance of this wretch with shuddering antipathy; it was cadaverous, wrinkled, and unsoftened by any feminine trait. "Are you a woman?" cried she. "Is your heart dead to all humanity?—Merciful Heaven, for what a destiny am I reserved!" "For a very good one," replied the woman, "if you know how to deserve it.—Mercy on us! what an uproar is here about nothing." "Nothing! do you call it?" exclaimed the heartbroken Rosa, "Is it nothing to be torn from the dear protector of my infancy, to become the victim of inhuman outlaws? Oh, Reginald! unhappy friend! what will be thy destiny?—thou art surely doomed to be the sport of misery." "What Reginald is this of whom you so often speak?" asked the old woman, gazing curiously in her face. "Oh, he is the most noble—the most injured of men!" cried Rosa, clasping her hands, with a fervent ejaculation for his safety. "I want to know nothing of his goodness," replied Maud, peevishly; "What other name does he bear?" Rosa, fearing she might do wrong by incautiously betraying the name and rank of her friends, repulsed the curiosity of her attendant with some dignity, and the old woman, piqued by her behaviour, relapsed her usual ill-temper.

(*To be continued.*)

[Continued from Vol. II p. 222.]

REGINALD remained in his cell a prey to the most heart-rending apprehensions; rage, despair, and mortification alternately distracted his mind, yet he still determined on giving a positive denial to the persuasions of Fernance,[1] even though the idea of his beloved Rosa's being the victim wrought his mind to a state of phrenzy. Could he have seen her he would readily plunged a sword into her bosom, rather than have left her exposed to the indignities which he well knew awaited her, but as that was impossible, he could only pray that Heaven would inspire her with fortitude, and protect her innocence. Several hours elapsed in this state of mental anguish, when his meditations were interrupted by the entrance of the old woman: he eagerly enquired for Rosa. The woman surveyed him with scrutinizing attention.—"She is well, signor; but pray may I know if she is related to you?" "Your question is impertinent;" replied Reginald, turning from her. "Nay, signor, be not displeased; I may have more friendly intentions than you imagine." Reginald was surprized; a gleam of hope enlivened his heart. He regarded the old woman with an anxious air, and her countenance fell beneath his scrutiny. "Couldst thou serve us," he cried, "doubt not my gratitude—the most ample reward thy wishes could demand should be thine." "Answer my question," said the old woman, with a faultering voice, "How is this girl connected with thee,—by marriage, or is she thy daughter?" "Candidly, then," said Reginald, "she is my adopted child, and I design to make her my wife." The old woman trembled—a deep groan burst from her withered bosom, and she covered her face with her hands. "What means this emotion?" demanded Reginald. "You knew not her parents?"

---

1 "Fernance" on this mention is "Fernando" in the rest of the novelette.

rejoined the old woman. "I knew them not." "Suppose they were infamous?" "No matter, Rosa is virtuous!" "Can you swear this in the face of Heaven?" "I can." "Thank Heaven!" exclaimed the old woman, fervently. Her exclamation astonished Reginald, and he eagerly demanded why she seemed to deeply interested. "The child is mine!" Reginald started—"Horrible! it cannot be:—Who and what are you?" A ghastly smile played on the old woman's features;—"I am now servant to a band of robbers, but I was not always the wretch you see me—I dare not reveal more—another time—but pray tell me where and when did you meet with Rosa." Reginald related every circumstance. "In the forest, say you?" cried the woman; "how miraculous!" And when Reginald spoke of the desolate life he led in the cave, tears trickled down her furrowed cheeks. "Did she never mention Madam Winderbourn?"[1] "It was the first person she spoke of—her mother!—could it be you?" "You may believe it—but we must talk of things more important. I will release you from this place if you will permit me to accompany you." Reginald hesitated; he feared that the old woman's assertion might be a fabrication; but when she repeated to him every particular of the child's dress, and mentioned the mark on Rosa's arm; by which she had recognized her, his doubts were, in great measure, removed, and the desire of escaping surmounting every other consideration, he agreed to her proposal. Midnight was the time fixed on for their deliverance, and Reginald impatiently awaited her fulfilment of her promise. At the appointed hour, his prison door was thrown open, and Rosa threw herself into his arms; Alphonso too pressed forward to embrace him. "Oh, my dear sir!" cried Rosa, "What a discovery; but what are your sentiments now towards your poor girl?—can this woman be my mother?" "She asserts herself to be such," said Reginald, "and we cannot disprove it; but she has proved herself our friend, at least, and we have yet much to learn before we can decide." "I know not how it is," said Rosa, sighing; "but a secret antipathy which I cannot account for, checks the impulse of nature. Anxious as I was to know my parents, the discovery now gives me more pain than pleasure." In a few minutes they

---

1 Spelled "Winderbourn" in this section only and "Windenbourn" in the first and last sections.

were joined by Madam Winderbourn.—"All is well," said she, "we must now escape without delay. The robbers are all safe." Alphonso shuddered with horror: "Is it possible you can wear that calm and satisfied mien, after the perpetration of such a deed; though they are robbers my heart recoils at the idea of murder." "In the present case," said Madam Winderbourn, drawing her hood, which she always wore, closer over her eyes; "murder has not been necessary; at supper I mixed a powerful soporific in their wine, and the whole party are in a sleep, as deep almost as that of death. When we are safe beyond their reach it will be at your option, signor, whether you will deliver them up to the hands of justice, or suffer them to continue their depredations on the public." "Assuredly, I will," said Reginald, "but let us away while we are safe. I see you have been provident in securing our arms." "Whither are you bound?" asked Madam Winderbourn. "To a castle some leagues from hence, but I think it best now to return to the cottage." This being agreed on, Madam Winderbourn led them to the stable, from which they supplied themselves with horses, and without further delay departed.

The good Arnold and his family were surprised and delighted at the unexpected return of their friends. After they had related their adventure, Arnold was dispatched to the next town to give information to the police, and in a few days the forest was cleared of this infamous band of depredators; Reginald then proposed setting out for the chateau, and requested Madam Winderbourn to furnish herself with apparel suitable to the situation she must hold in his family. "Alas!" said she, "it is not possible for me to hold a respectable station in society; all I have to request of you is, that you will use your interest to procure me admission into a convent, where, in peace and penitence I may end my wretched life." Reginald and Rosa offered to oppose this resolution, and intreated her to relate the occurrences of her life. "You know not what you ask," said she. "The story I have to relate will prove, I fear, fatal to your peace; and, but that *it must be told*, it should be buried in my breast for ever: promise, however, that you will do as I require of you.—I must have your promise." Her features seemed convulsed with agony— her whole frame shook; and Rosa was obliged to support her, while Reginald promised most solemnly to comply with her request. She then rose slowly from her seat, tottered towards Reginald, and falling at his feet, threw back her hood—"Gaze on these features," she cried, "does not a trace remain of what was once beheld with rapture:—has infamy and misery so completely deformed my countenance that you know not Julia?" "Heaven and earth!" cried Reginald, "can this be?—When, when shall I find peace?" With a frantic arm he seized his sword, but was withheld by Alphonso, who restrained his fury, and used every gentle persuasion to con-troul his rage and indignation. The wretched cause of all his misery remained senseless on the ground: Arnold and Rosa assisted her to a bed, and soon succeeded in restoring her to recollection. "It is all over," said she, "I see deep-rooted abhorrence is fixed in his heart. Oh, shield me from his wrath, and hide me in the bowels of the earth! I will never see him more—the lightning of his eye would blast me. Yet still I have a consolation; Providence has brought us this once together, to prevent a most dreadful event—an union of sin and horror. Rosa, Rosa, fall on your knees and adore that mysterious power which has disclosed to you the secret of your birth.—That Reginald is your father!" Rosa clasped her hands with rapturous emotion, she rushed wildly from the chamber—she flew to Reginald, and clasping his knees, bedewed his hands with tears.—"I feel, I feel I am your child;" she cried. "Oh, my father! do not turn away from me with disgust.—Your frown will kill me. Though you hate her who gave me birth, I am innocent—you cannot hate your Rosa!" Reginald's rage was calmed. A soft sensa-tion of paternal love subdued the stronger passions; he caught her in his arms and wept over her. "How could I mistake my feelings?" said he, "Nature ever pleaded for you, my Rosa; ever welcome shalt thou be to a wretched father's heart: but thy mother, girl, let me not think of her—distraction would be the consequence."

"Oh, dreadful fate!" cried Rosa, "to shudder at the name of a mother. What can I say?—How can I dare to plead?"

"She surely cannot hope to be reconciled; she must not be so presumptuous."

"Ah, no!" replied Rosa, "she is now busy with her pen, to make you acquainted with the events of her past life; when that painful task is completed, she claims your promise to place her in a con-vent, and there, without daring to ask one parting look, it is her intention to quit you for ever." "It must be so," said Reginald, musing; "I will write immediately to the superieure of St. Sidwell's abbey, and procure her admission. Bring the paper to me when it is finished." Rosa returned to her mother's chamber; she found the guilty penitent in a state of nervous irritation, which gave symptoms of a fever. She called Rosa to her, with tenderness;—"Child," said she, "would thy pure soul shrink from an embrace? not all the pangs inflicted by remorse, shame, or a tormenting conscience, can equal the anguish of a mother who feels herself the object of abhorrence to her own offspring. My very heart's blood would I now voluntarily yield to obtain one kiss of affection; but it cannot be—I feel it cannot be." Rosa trembled almost to fainting, and fell into her mother's arms agonized beyond description. "Poor child!" cried Julia, "I have distressed thee too much; this parting embrace, and I will exert every faculty to act this last scene with becoming resolution. Go Rosa, sweet innocent! may Heaven's blessing be on thee, and the prayers of a wretched sinner avail!—Go, child, go; the scene will soon be too shocking—go, go, go——."

Rosa took the paper which her mother held towards her, and pressing her hand, as if with an assurance of pity and forgiveness, quitted the room, and returned to her father, repeating to him what had passed, and presenting the letter, he instantly unclosed it, and read as follows.

(*To be concluded in our next.*)

(Concluded from page 39.)

"In what language, most injured of men, shall I address you? I have transgressed against the laws of religion and morality, without one plea to mitigate the pangs of self-reproach. In the intoxicating round of vanity all is delusion, but the world now fades from my view, and I behold only the horrors attendant upon infamy. Woe unto the woman who deviates from the path of duty and virtue! But I must be brief: I have erred, I have suffered, and am now self-condemned. When I quitted that home, which your fond affection should have endeared to me beyond every thing, the vilest passions degraded my nature; and in my endeavour to shun the reproach of an indignant husband, I plunged into new crimes. I took refuge with the Chevalier Windenbourn; while under his protection Rosa was born; the first pang of remorse I had ever experienced, was occasioned by her infantile caresses. I considered that I had basely deprived her of birthright, and formed the determination of restoring her to your arms, with the most solemn asseveration that she was your child; I accordingly dispatched my attendant, Madeline, with proper directions: but, alas! my rashness exposed them to the most dreadful dangers, the carriage in which they travelled was surrounded by a banditti, the servants murdered, Madeline reserved for the most horrible fate, and my infant left to perish. Though I had not acted as a wife, I felt as a mother; and the unfeeling Windenbourn, disgusted by my sadness and incessant lamentations, left me, to pursue an object more capable of inspiring pleasure, than a heart-broken repentant wife. Destitute of fame, of fortune, and even of hope, I sunk into the most abject state of misery; and, to secure the very means of existence, became the abandoned creature you found me. Chance introduced me to Fernando; the remains of a beautiful person had still power to enchant him, and as he made me the welcome offer of entire seclusion from society, I accepted his proposals; necessity, not inclination, directed my choice, and for several years he treated me kindly, but new pursuits changed his inclinations, and I was at length degraded into a menial. Thus was I situated when your appearance at the Abbey roused all the dreadful tumults of my soul—how I adored you—how I abhorred myself——Oh, Reginald! I am punished, no human pang can inflict a torture equal to conscious guilt.—I Iad you been weak enough to have pardoned and received me to your arms, I should have despised you—but your indignant frown was annihilation to me—from that moment I resolved to rid the earth of a wretch beneath its pity, though above its scorn. The measure of my crimes is complete—the poison creeps through my veins— my words are incoherent—Reginald, do not include an innocent child in your maledictions on its mother—the cold earth will soon cover this frail form—let the remembrance of Julia's sins be buried with her—one tear, Reginald, is all I ask—adieu, for ever.

"JULIA."

Whatever were the feelings of Reginald on perusal of this letter, had he even felt inclined to pardon the transgressor, his sensibility was awakened too late for the guilty Julia, who expired in Rosa's absence. All the love he had once felt for his wife, while the bloom of innocence and beauty mantled on her cheek, was now transferred to the lovely Rosa, her happiness was his only care; and now that self-delusion was banished by the sacred feelings of paternal affection, he perceived, without regret, the bent of her inclinations. As soon as the funeral obsequies were performed, the party repaired to Reginald's Neapolitan estate; the Marquis Veronia received them with open arms, and gave a most willing assent to the proposals made by Reginald. Rosa was united to her adoring Alphonso; and the dreadful recollection of her mother's crimes and sufferings remained too deeply impressed upon her mind, to suffer any temptation to lead her from the faithful performance of her conjugal duty. The sorrows of her remaining parent were softened by her tender assiduities, she was his pride and delight—beloved by her husband, respected by her friends, and looked up to by her children as an object of tenderest veneration. Such is the happy prerogative of the faithful wife—the virtuous mother.

E. F.[1]

1 See Pitcher (96-98). Although his index stops in 1806, he notes that E.F. received the editor's thanks "for 'her valuable correspondence' in 1:168, so we know this signature belongs to a woman. She also contributes to the magazine after the period catalogued here, and seems to have become 'E.T.' (by marriage?) in 1807." E.F. is probably also the author of "Edric of the Forest."

THE RUIN OF THE ROCK;

A FRAGMENT.[1]

Fate sits on these dark battlements,
And, as the portals open to receive me,
Speaks of a nameless deed.[2]

"LOVERS, least of all people, ought to be dilatory," cried Don
Cavallo, yawning.—"I acknowledge it;" returned Don Pedro, "but
could I avoid the delay? could I help the death of the old grandee,
my uncle? and would you have had me left him and his doubloons
to disappear by themselves? I am sure you would have thought the
money at least worth looking after: and if you had sufficient
honesty, you would confess that, in a like situation, you would have
acted as I did. Then, could I foresee that the inclemency of the
weather would force us to stop by the way? which, by the bye, was
your own proposal." "Well, well," returned the other, "you need
say no more: for I have a notion that we shall arrive as soon as the
lady now; this stormy weather must have delayed her as well as
us.—But I would the wind did not drive these hail-stones against us
so; they are like cannon-balls, and upon the heath will take as much
effect upon us, I am afraid; without we can find some place to retire
to for shelter." "Travellers," interrupted Don Pedro, "must endure
all things;—for my part, I should neither care for my own welfare
or thine, could I be assured, that Elvira was in safety—but, in such
hurricanes as these, the vessel may be lost, or driven upon rocks,
and the passengers perish; and with them my long hoped for
happiness. While such reflections haunt me, every blast of wind

---

1 Vol. 2, n.s. (March 1807): 120-128. This story proved popular enough to be
reprinted a number of times over the next several decades, under slightly varying
titles, in collections such as *The Stanley Tales* (1826), *The Continental Landscape
Annual of European Scenery* (1835), and *The Literary and Pictorial Souvenir* (1848).
2 Title page motto to Ann Radcliffe's *The Mysteries of Udolpho* (1794), Vol. 1.

strikes more forcibly to my heart, than it can possibly do to your skin." "It will strike to my heart too, before long," replied Cavallo, "without I can get out of the way—would I had some strong Madeira to keep it out—nevertheless, I wish as much for the safety of Elvira as yourself: St. Nicholas preserve her—and I would that something would preserve me, before I am beaten to a mummy, by these plaguy hail-stones—could we but see an old castle now, such as we took shelter in before." "Wish and have," returned Don Pedro; "If I mistake not, there is one before us.—Now I see it again, as the lightning gleams against the battlements; therefore let us hasten to it." They now spurred their mules towards the place; but a thick underwood, which surrounded the castle, soon compelled them to alight, and pursue their way on foot. Having fastened their mules to a stake in the best manner that they could, they endeavoured to proceed; but, owing to the rough and uneven way, which entangled their feet, they made but a slow progress: and only by the lightning could they discover that they had not strayed from the place that they were in pursuit of. Perseverance, however, brought them to the court-yard of the castle; and time had overthrown many obstacles which, in the unmutilated state of the mansion, would have opposed an effectual barrier to their progress. "Are there any inhabitants of this place, I wonder," cried Don Cavallo, raising the massy knocker, "I will try." The loud and solemn report of the knocker, as it reverberated through the hollow passages of the building, impressed them with awe and dread. They waited some minutes in silence. "It is not reasonable," at length, cried Don Pedro, "to suppose that this desolated ruin contains any inhabitants, unless they are pirates or plunderers, in which case we may endanger our lives by gaining admission, even if it were possible; which I think is much to be doubted." "Hazardous or dangerous," returned Cavallo, "I am determined to make the attempt; but you may choose whether you will accompany me or not, for this dreadful weather I will not bear if I can avoid it." "I am determined not to forsake you," replied the other: "therefore let us draw our swords and prepare for the worst that may happen." They now endeavoured to force the door, but without effect; its strength defied their united efforts, and the attempt was productive only of lassitude and fatigue. In vain they surveyed the time-worn edifice—the windows were lofty, beyond their power to reach, and secured with bars of iron; nor did there appear to be any breaches in the walls sufficiently low for them to enter by. On one side of the castle was a long terrace, which overhung the sea; from whence, when the lightning permitted, they surveyed the building with the most scrutinizing attention, but in vain; no inlet appeared, through which they could possibly effect a passage. "Would I knew that Elvira were in safety," cried Pedro, sighing; "with what violence the waves dash against these walls; their hollow roaring appears to me as if it were to announce the destruction of my hopes, and I see in imagination the pale form of my Elvira calling on her lover to rescue her from a watery death."—"Hold," exclaimed Cavallo, "I am sure I saw a light on the west side of the building." The light was now distinctly visible to both. Inspired with fresh hopes, they halloed as loud as possible, in hopes to gain admittance; but the loud roaring of the winds rendered the sound inaudible long before it reached that part of the building, and they were again compelled to desist from their attempts. Wearied at length with their fruitless endeavours, they resolved to return to their mules, and try to pursue their journey in defiance of the storm; when in hastening along the terrace, Cavallo stumbled, and, in endeavouring to recover himself, fell against a small door, hitherto concealed by a thick ivy from their view, which burst open, and precipitated him upon the floor of a room in the castle. Fortunately he received no hurt from his fall, and Pedro hastening to join him, they surveyed the apartment with mingled sensations of satisfaction and dread. It appeared to have been a private way to the terrace from the suite of apartments which occupied that side of the building. They determined to proceed; and passing through the apartment, they entered an extensive room, which seemed formerly to have been a state bedchamber. The walls were hung with tapestry, which, now damp and decayed, hung in tatters round the room; the subject was a battle of a detachment of Spaniards against a Moorish banditti; and, as they passed along, the superstition which the gloom inspired seemed to give the figures animation as though they were starting from the walls to menace the intruders. The furniture and bed were fast falling to decay, and every part of the room, which displayed the most stately magnificence of former days, wore the appearance of desolation and destruction. They advanced cautiously, fearful of the sound even of their own steps, taking care to leave the doors open through which they passed, to favour their retreat in case of necessity. Light they had no means of obtaining, but the storm at times illuminated the apartments, and again plunged them into utter darkness. They now entered an ante-room, through which they passed into a grand saloon; but, like the other, its grandeur had fallen to decay. They trod lightly across it, and were preparing to pass into the next, when a violent burst from one part of the room which they were quitting, made them return as hastily as possible; but ere they gained the opposite door, a violent gust of wind, which flew along the passages, suddenly closed all the doors through which they had passed, with a tremendous noise, which seemed to shake the whole fabric to its foundation. In vain did they attempt to unclose the door; it resisted their utmost efforts, and they were obliged fearfully to relinquish their design. They therefore placed themselves with a desperate resolution against it, and determined to defend themselves against their concealed enemy. The noise still continued; Cavallo's heart sunk within him, and Don Pedro almost forgot Elvira under his present fears. It increased from the same corner of the room, and with it their alarms, till, by a violent flash of lightning, they beheld the draperies of a curtain gradually rise, after a violent flapping, and an owl flew across the apartment. "And is this all that has frightened us," cried Cavallo, "I protest I thought St. Nicholas had left me to the mercy of robbers; but I am glad to find that his saintship has been more merciful." "Do not be too sanguine;" rejoined Don Pedro, "we had much difficulty to get into the castle, and we may have as much difficulty to get out again; and of the two evils I should think that much the worst; we have therefore nothing to do but to proceed in search of a way out, and if St. Nicholas would but guide us in this emergency, I would ever after acknowledge my obligations to him." "Onward, then," cried Cavallo; "here is another state apartment, cousin german[1] to the last; but I hope it will not be

---

[1] "cousin german": a first cousin or near relative, "german" deriving from "germanus," Latin for "brother."

found to contain such uncivil inhabitants." "Behold another room of the same family," cried Pedro, "excepting that it is cloathed differently: its garments are of cedar, you perceive." "Yes," returned Cavallo, "and I doubt not but those pannels contain plenty of secret passages about this castle; would that we could find one that would lead us to the outside of these gloomy walls. I'll clink them, and try if they are hollow." "Hush," cried the other, "surely I heard a noise." They listened, and with equal astonishment and horror heard, distinctly, sounds at some distance, like the screaming of one in distress, which the fear of Cavallo interpreted into the yells of evil spirits. "Let us proceed;" said Pedro, undauntedly, "this mystery shall be unravelled, if human power can effect it; come on, then, my friend, the lightning will guide us, and I am determined to follow the direction of the noise, let the consequences be what they may." "St. Nicholas protect us;" cried Cavallo, following, "for I confess that I feel no desire to encounter either ghosts or assassins." With resolute courage Pedro rushed forwards, and was followed by his more lively, yet less undaunted companion, till they reached the great entrance hall. Here they paused, uncertain which way to pursue; besides the passage from which they had entered, three others presented themselves to their view, and a grand staircase; nor could they form any idea which of them could lead to the sounds which they had so recently heard. "My opinion is," cried Cavallo, "that we had better try to walk quietly out of this door, without setting out on a wild-goose chase we neither know where nor for what—perhaps after all to be frightened by an owl again." "I confess that I am much of your opinion," returned Don Pedro, "so let us proceed to draw back these bolts without loss of time." Like many other things, however, this was easier talked of than done— the bolts and locks, rusted by time and neglect, refused to move; and after exhausting their united strength upon the attempt, they were obliged to abandon it in despair. "My resolution is fled," cried Cavallo; "I will proceed no further this night, but stay here till the morning light shall have brightened these gloomy passages." "You may stay then by yourself," replied Pedro, "for, by St. Nicholas, this cold marble pavement chills my very heart; and I am convinced, that to stand here another hour, may be the death of us both: yet I confess that I cannot decide how to proceed." In vain did they endeavour to fix upon a plan for their future conduct. Irresolution had deprived them of half their courage, and they stood in a state of listless anxiety, till a dismal toll on the castle-bell roused them from their inactivity to a recollection of their dreadful situation. A violent noise similar to the former succeeded, but for a longer time: and the castle bell again tolled deeply at intervals for some minutes. With a desperate resolution they again rushed forward through one of the passages. All was silent, dark, and gloomy—the lightning had ceased, and the moon's feeble light scarcely illumined the dusky paths which they now explored. A grated door soon arrested their further progress, but yielded to their endeavours, and discovered a passage similar to the former. A piercing shriek, which reverberated through the echoing vaults of the ruin, fixed them horror-struck to their places—it was repeated faintly several times. Still undaunted, Pedro rushed forward, followed by his friend. Another passage succeeded—still they proceeded onwards—and still were their souls harrowed almost to distraction by the tolling of the dreadful bell.—"As I live there is a light," cried Cavallo. "Hush," returned the other; "tread softly." With light footsteps and beating hearts they pursued a lambent flame, which seemed to move along the distant extremity of the passage; when, as they were hoping to approach it, it suddenly disappeared, and left them in utter darkness. Groping their way with their swords they carefully proceeded, till the stumbling of Pedro, who was foremost, convinced them, that the passage terminated in a flight of steps. They hesitated a few moments, whether to proceed or to go back; but wonder and a strong impulse of contending passions, determined them to chuse the former. While descending the stairs the shrieks were succeeded by a loud laughing, which seemed more like the rejoicings of evil spirits than of any human beings; but the direction from which the sound proceeded, convinced them that they were approaching the object of their search. The steps were of considerable extent, but mutilated and broken, and terminated in one of the vaults of the castle. This vault seemed to lead to others of the same description, and with mingled wonder and dread they again beheld the reflection of a light against the side of the cavern.—They proceeded onwards to another; the light was more distinct, and they found that it beamed through a chasm from the adjoining cave. Some large masses of rock which were strewed on the floor, enabled Don Pedro to raise himself up so as to look into the adjoining cavern; but what could describe his terror and astonishment, when he beheld, by the faint and uncertain light of a lamp which was suspended from the ceiling, a newly dug grave, by the side of which was a spade and a mattock, and a shroud lay at a small distance. While yet he gazed, the castle bell again tolled—a faintness seized him, and he was obliged to lean against the side of the cave to prevent himself from falling. Cavallo, who perceived his disorder, was in but little better condition, although he was ignorant of the cause. Again Pedro raised himself up to behold the soul-harrowing scene, which was increased by the appearance of a figure moving along in the gloom of the dungeon. The shrieks were again renewed more violently than ever, and Pedro beheld the figure glide into some more distant apartment. "I will proceed," cried he to Cavallo, "to the unravelment of this mystery, though death should follow the attempt." They retreated to another cave towards the left, and to their astonishment discovered an outlet which led to the sea beach. "St. Nicholas, be praised," cried Cavallo, "let us hasten to escape; for never did my heart jump about so as it does at this moment." "Not so;" replied the other, solemnly, "my mind is roused up to a pitch, which will not permit me to leave this place ungratified; and I cannot resolve to quit this mysterious abode, without penetrating farther: a secret impulse, which I cannot account for, impels me to the search, and it shall be made. Yet let me go alone: never shall my rashness bring my friend into danger—remain, therefore, here; and if I live, I will return to you in half an hour." "Wrong not my friendship so much," returned Cavallo, earnestly, "as to believe me capable of deserting you in the hour of danger. Whatever may be the perils of the enterprise, yet I am determined to share them; nor shall persuasion induce me to rescind my resolution." "Arm yourself with courage then," cried Pedro, advancing, "and fear nothing." A brighter light gleamed on one side of the cave which they now entered, and they perceived an opening into the adjoining cavern. With cautious steps they crossed the vault, and placed themselves in a situation so as to observe the interior; nor could any sight have interested their feelings in a higher degree, than the one which they now beheld.—A lady on her knees before two ruffians, seemed to implore their pity. "I have already given you all that I am possessed of," cried she, in supplicating accents, "I have no more." "We know it, pretty lady," returned one of the villains, "but we must not leave you the power to hang us for our plunder—fortune seldom sends us such a booty, and we must guard against even possibilities, and not stand the chance of having it taken away from us again; you must therefore prepare to die—the grave is already dug, the bell has been tolled to answer a double purpose (since it would be sure to deter every one from approaching the place), and a shroud is ready at hand, so that you will have the satisfaction of being buried in a decent manner." "And have you then saved me from a watery grave," continued the lady, "to murder me on shore? better that I had perished with my companions, and that the sea had received me, than to be preserved only to die a more cruel death by the hands of ruffians." "We should have got nothing by that though," cried the villain; "but come, we have no time for parleying, so prepare for death. Sancho, count out those ducats, while I sharpen this sword a bit." "Oh, Pedro, Pedro," cried the lady, with streaming eyes, "where are you now?" "Who?" cried the ruffian, tearing off her veil. "Heavens! 'tis Elvira herself," cried Don Pedro, rushing forward, and springing upon the ruffian, while Cavallo at the same moment seized the other, and after a long struggle, as the ruffian was unarmed, succeeded in fastening him to the wall so effectually, as to deprive him of all further exertion, with some ropes which were lying on the ground. He then hastened to the assistance of Don Pedro, who maintained an obstinate battle with the other; and in consequence of his opponent being well armed, and desperate with rage and disappointment, had to support a skilful attack, which might have terminated fatally, had not the assassin's sword breaking, laid him at the mercy of the conqueror. "And is it Pedro then," cried Elvira, "who has thus rescued me; what fatality directed thee so opportunely to my assistance? O my good Cavallo too; but say what chance can have conducted you to this dreary abode." "You shall know all," cried Don Pedro, and proceeded thus. . . . . .

ARMINE.

THE PRINCE OF THE LAKE.[1]

From Miss Porter's interesting Novel, "The Lake of Killarney."[2]

"THE Princess Anne to her bower is gone,
　　"To watch, to weep, and pray,
"Where the yellow moon shining alone,
　　"Lights the traveller on his way.

"Her bower is high on that lonely hill,
　　"Where hoary ash trees shake,
"And down below, sublimely still,
　　"Lieth Killarney's Lake."

The warder ceas'd, and clos'd the gate,
　　And the man who ask'd rode on;
No word he said, but bow'd his head,
　　And heav'd a heavy groan.

The man was clad in a mantle red,
　　His bonnet was large and dark;
So musing still, he gain'd the hill,
　　The lady's bower to mark.

'Twas bleak and drear, the silent trees
　　Stood tall and still around;
The tall grass stirred not in the breeze,
　　The waters gave no sound.

---

1 Vol. 5, n.s. (Sept. 1808): 161-164.
2 *The Lake of Killarney* (3 vols., 1804) by Anna Maria Porter. Mayo (300) includes Porter in his list of "authors of signed novels and novelettes," that is, authors willing to put their names to their published works, who also contributed to "the miscellanies."

But the lady bright, on the battlement's height,
    He saw by the brilliant moon;
From her locks so light, and her garments white,
    The stranger knew her soon.

"Ho! Lady Anne, thou must come down,
    "Thy husband sends for thee;
"By the cross of stone, on the heath alone,
    "He waits to fly with thee.

"For the fight is o'er, and rebel power
    "Hath vanquished its lord;
"And now his store is nothing more
    "But only his good sword."

"Now tell me, knight, by a warrior's might,
    "I charge thee, tell me true:
"If from the fight, this fatal night,
    "My love unhurt withdrew?

"Ah! be my bed the leaves that are shed,
    "By autumn's hollow wind,
"If on his breast my head but rest,
    "The sweetest sleep I'll find."

"He waits for thee," the knight reply'd,
    "By the mould'ring cross of stone:"
"Thy sleep will be sweet," the lady sigh'd,
    "But never sweet alone."

"Come mount thee here, nay do not fear,
    "Though the clouds be gathering fast,
"My courser is swift, for his career
    "Is like the ocean's blast."

They rode o'er hill, they rode o'er vale,
    They rode through the groaning wood,
Till by the glare of the lightning pale,
    They saw the holy rood.

And near it lay a comely form,
 In dusky armour drest;
He lay in sleep, and the raging storm
 Could not break his rest.

The warrior slept, and the lady stepp'd,
 His well known form to fold;
She kiss'd his brow, but the nightly snow
 Is not so icy cold.

With piercing cries she rais'd her eyes,
 And the stranger stood by her side;
His mantle was gone, and his armour shone,
 And his dark plume floated wide.

His steed was form'd of the foaming surf,
 Which roars on Killarney's lake,
When the furious blasts its water casts,
 And rocking turrets shake.

"Behold your lord," the phantom said—
 "The fight indeed is o'er;
"And under this shade my corse is laid,
 "To sleep for evermore.

"But thou must with me, for the boundless sea
 "Is given us for our reign;
"And Killarney's lake each year shall shake,
 "For its prince and hero slain.

"Killarney's hills, and Killarney's caves,
 "Our lonely dwellings must be;
"Till this yearly hour, when its shudd'ring waves
 "My airy horse shall see.

"Then in angry pomp thro' the waters wide,
 "In lightning and thunder drest,
"Your prince shall ride, while the stormy tide
 "Shall break his vassals' rest.

"For three long days, and three long nights,
    "Must they tremble with guilt and fear,
"Till the whirlwind cease, and all be peace,
    "And I no longer there."

He spoke, and clasp'd his arms to grasp
    The form of his lady fair;
But she breath'd a groan,
And her spirit alone,
    Now wanders with his through the air.

MISS PORTER.

ESTABLISHED RULES FOR THE COMPOSITION OF A MODERN NOVEL, OR ROMANCE.[1]

In the first place, you must make a point of beginning in the middle of the story: as nothing can be more absurd and insipid than letting a person know who, or what, they are reading about, for four chapters at least; and moreover, be sure to let the first sentence be an exclamation of horror, astonishment, or apprehension.—In the next, take particular care to let the leading characters have foreign names, of at least three syllables; as the frequent repetition of them will be found, on calculation, to occupy a considerable number of pages in the course of the work.

Let the domestics be always faithful, and on the most familiar terms with their employers.

Let all handsome personages be amiable, and all that are plain or deformed must be vicious.

Make parents tyrannical, strangers disinterestedly benevolent, old maids envious and ridiculous, and children possessed of uncommon talents.

Select words from a good dictionary; such as these, "isolated" —"unsophisticated"—"contour"—"melange"—"machinations" —"analogous"—"energetical;" and let two at least be found in every page: they will give it an air of "sublimity" and "incomprehensibility."

Make a point of concluding the first volume with a dilemma, the second with a mystery, the third with a scene of confusion and dismay, and the fourth with four or five weddings; making marriage the sole reward of the good, the ultimatum of happiness, and the only object of female ambition.

This will undoubtedly have an amazing run for six weeks.

---

1 Vol. 5, n.s. (Dec. 1808): 279.

THE BANDITTI OF THE FOREST;

OR,

THE MYSTERIOUS DAGGER.[1]

CHAP. I.

> By my christendom,
> So I were out of prison and kept sheep,
> I should be merry as the day is long;
> . . . . but that I doubt
> My uncle practises more to harm me.
>
> *Shakespeare.*[2]

ALL was hushed in the solemn silence of night, when Gudolvo was roused from the dark machinations of his soul by a violent knocking at the portal of his ruined habitation. Thrice he essayed to rise from his seat before he came to a determination; till at length, summoned by louder and more obstinate clamours, he arose, and drawing back the rusty bolts, opened the sullen door. A manly figure entered, and with an eye of suspicion, which the place seemed well calculated to inspire, craved shelter from the inclemency of the weather and the beasts of the adjoining forest. Gudolvo silently nodded an assent; but what little conversation took place between them was soon interrupted by the sound of a horn from the exterior of the castle. Gudolvo immediately answered this signal, and closing fast the door, left his guest to amuse himself in drawing conclusions not the most agreeable to his feelings.

---

1 Vol. 11, n.s. (1811): July, 21-26; Aug., 76-82; Sept., 162-168; Oct., 204-211; Nov., 273-281; Dec., 317-323; Vol. 12, n.s. (1812): Jan., 20-23; Feb., 79-84.

2 From Arthur's speech in *King John* (1623), Act IV, Scene 1, by William Shakespeare.

Albert, the intruder, now turned round to view his asylum. The lofty ceilings, dilapidated groins, the broken pillars, and chasms in the walls, filled up with lumber, shewed very plainly that time had struck this fortress with no very lenient hand; and this did not in the least tend to alleviate his melancholy. He waited some time for the return of his host with anxiety; but not hearing the least sound of his footsteps, he proceeded in his researches, when casting his eyes to the further end of the room, to where the lamp's pale light barely reached, he espied a kind of bundle lying on the floor. He rushed forwards, in hopes of finding his unfavourable suspicions were groundless, when imagine his surprise and horror on discovering the body of a dead person, but so disfigured with blood as to make it doubtful whether it was a male or female.

By the corpse lay a dagger, clotted with the blood, as he firmly believed, of the unhappy victim. He had but just time, through some unaccountable presentiment, to conceal the weapon under his cloak, when Gudolvo hastily returned, and, with the look of a dæmon, demanded, with horrid imprecations, how he dared thus to infringe on the laws of hospitality, by prying about his apartments. "Dearly," added he, "shalt thou pay for thy temerity."—But suddenly softening his demeanor, with a horrid grin, he wished him "good night," and locking the door, again retired.

Albert, heart-broken with misfortunes and fatigue, had become petrified with this sudden change; he remained chained to the floor with surprise, and scarce heard the sullen echo of his gaoler's steps sound more and more distant, till they at last died away in the hollow whistling of the wind, which swept along the avenues of the castle. At length he recovered himself, and viewed every corner, in hopes to procure his emancipation. He could not forbear shuddering, notwithstanding his inherent courage, every time he passed the dead body; but his thoughts were too much bent on his own deliverance, and too much agitated by suspense, to think of taking a nearer view of it. He tried every door, but the cumbrous fastenings, and even the mouldering rubbish, resisted all his attempts to destroy them, till, becoming weary with disappointment, while the wounds which he had received in the forest, beginning to bleed afresh, and the embers of the faggots which composed the fire having emitted their last light, obliged him to give up all hopes of escape until the morning. Stopping the blood, which again oozed from the wound in his arm, he bound it with his sash, and throwing himself upon an ancient couch, the following soliloquy escaped his lips:—

"Oh, fortune! when wilt thou cease to persecute me! Torn from my Adelaide, and from every sharer of my affection, for what further am I reserved? To what am I to impute this further violence, this detention? Can it be possible that my uncle, however he may have been my persecutor, can wish to be my murderer?—No, surely he can never be so base." At the end of these thoughts his ideas became bewildered; nature could no longer support herself without repose; his memory was confused; he dozed, and at length resigned himself to a profound slumber.

Albert was the only son of Baron Bruhn, a nobleman of immense fortune, who, dying some years after his wife, and deceived by the hypocritical professions of his brother, Count Zittau, left his child to his care and guidance, till he should become of age to receive his patrimony; but the count, who was a man of desperate fortune, had for some time endeavoured to obtain possession of his nephew's, and had already converted a great part of it to his own advantage.

Albert had become enamoured of Adelaide, daughter of Baron Holstein, but his uncle, fearing a match would take place between them, and not choosing to refund what valuables he had already embezzled, he for some time used all his endeavours to prevent their union. For this purpose he had, under some plausible pretext, caused Albert to leave his father's castle, and reside with him; he also gave strict orders to a banditti, which he secretly favoured, either by fair or foul means, to rid him of this obstacle to his ambition. To these ruffians he had granted the use of one of his dismantled castles, which had been already the scene of many enormities, practised upon some poor defenceless creatures, who had, either by direct or indirect means, forfeited his favour. His purposes these men were too ready to perform; and in return they received the countenance of Count Zittau, and were allowed to commit their depredations unheeded on the unguarded traveller.

In consonance with their order they one day attacked Albert, while he was hunting on the domains of a friend. For some time he resisted the efforts of four of these myrmidons (for guilt is ever weak) but overcome by fresh numbers, he was obliged to submit. They bound and tied him on horseback behind one of their companions, and, pleased with their prize, continued on their way. Night had already begun to draw her mantle from the sky, when they had nearly reached the place of their destination. But as yet nature was wrapt in a sullen silence, which was only interrupted by the hollow grumbling of his conductors. When arriving on a barren heath, they perceived a company of soldiers, whose employment was to rid the country of these miscreants; they sounded their horns, and proceeded to engage with these well-known desperadoes.

Albert now felt a slight gleam of hope irradiate his bosom in the idea of escape; but this gleam was soon dispelled when the man with whom he rode clapped spurs to his horse, and left his companions to finish the rencounter. When they had travelled for some time in this manner, (Albert making promises of rewards and punishments, in order to make the fellow release him, and the man as steadily refusing his wishes) he recollected he had his purse about him; this, as an inducement, he also promised. His conductor seemed a little to relax, but after he had taken it from the place where Albert told him it was deposited, no sooner did he gain possession, than he refused what he had before promised, and with the most bitter taunts on Albert's credulity, declined either releasing him, or giving him any information regarding the cause of this outrage.

Worked up to desperation by this conduct, Albert made a violent struggle, and disengaging his right hand, he gave the fellow so violent a blow, that he sent him headlong to the earth, and putting his spurs to the horse, travelled across the country, unacquainted with his situation, and nearly exhausted by exertion. He now dismounted, and proceeeded to rifle the sumpter bags, which hung over the saddle, where he fortunately found some provision to satisfy the cravings of nature; but fearful of again falling into the hands of the banditti, he remounted, nor halted till he came to a thick grove of trees, where a spring, which ran gurgling from a fissure in the earth, invited him to quench his thirst, and the situation seemed to promise that here he might rest in perfect security.

This spot was shaded by thick rows of trees, which rendered it almost impervious to the sight of any human being, while the length of the grass below indicated that man seldom disturbed its verdure. He had ridden the whole of the day; he threw himself on a bank, and remained lost in thought. He was, however, soon disturbed by the roaring of beasts of prey, which the approach of evening had drawn from their holds. The sun had sunk in the distant horizon, leaving behind streaks of gold, fringing clouds of darkest purple, as the last gleam lighted the distant hills; but these tints soon subsided into a dusky blue; the air was hot and sulphurous; the pale lightning struck across his spurs, and glanced round the hilt of his sword; large drops of rain pattered on the branches, the trees sighed heavily, and the heavens became convulsed with thunder.

He arose to mount his horse, but alas! the animal had broken the branch to which he was fastened, and had escaped; at least he was not to be seen. "Perhaps," said Albert, "he is already devoured by wolves, and I may soon meet with the same fate." This idea chilled him; he attempted to look further, but the trees became more and more intricate. A wound which the man gave him in the scuffle still continued to bleed; he attempted to move further. At length, to his joy, a castle appeared in sight, and unconsciously he rushed into that danger which he had so long and so sedulously evaded.

(*To be continued.*)

CHAP. II.

"For faith 'twas strange, 'twas passing strange;
'Twas pitiful, 'twas wond'rous pitiful."

Shakespeare.[1]

WHEN Albert awoke the following morning, in the dwelling in which he had been withheld by Gudolvo, his first idea once more turned upon his emancipation, and to recommence that search which fatigue, the preceeding night, had obliged him to relinquish. It was very early in the middle of summer, the sun had risen and

---

1 From Othello's speech in *Othello* (1622), Act I, Scene 3, by William Shakespeare.

darted his beams through a casement, which was high beyond the captive's reach. Albert again viewed the dead body; and with attention, at least with that attention that imaginary sounds upon his ear often interrupted; the face was covered with a cloth, but he was arrested from removing it. On discovering clots of blood, which were near it, though they were dry, and on comparing them with the dagger, too dreadfully they told the murderous tale. Pausing in his search with his eyes fixed upon the floor, he discovered a crevice, through which light appeared, and striking it violently with his foot, it sprung up, and he fell, somewhat bruised, into an excavation beneath. Astonished at this sudden descent, he quickly arose, and inspired with the thoughts of liberty, made his way through a circuitous passage which yawned before him: it appeared cut through the solid rock, and from several irregular insterstices he perceived the distant ocean, and heard its irritated surges dash the yielding sand; this passage was terminated with a small door. Hope flushed his cheek; "doubtless," he cried, "this will release me;" but all his efforts to open this barrier were fruitless, and the agony of disappointment racked his frame; again he became calmer, and it was then that a flight, up irregular steps, caught his eye; he ascends them, a turret presents itself, he crosses from it (a long corridore) he forces a door from its hinges, on which time had already made no little impression, and it fell with a violent crash, which made him tremble for fear of a discovery. While he paused on the intricacy of the passages, doubtful of that which would prove most fortunate to his wishes, he chose that which led to the prison that he had left that morning; and he threw himself upon that ground, which, it appeared to him, fate was determined he should not escape from.

The noise of the falling door had indeed alarmed the inmates of the castle, and although they were ignorant from whence it proceeded, yet Albert, enervated as he was, heard their loud signals rive the air. His impatient soul became frenzied with passion; hope seemed cut off forever; and drawing the dagger he had secreted, he was about to put a period to an existence, now rendered a burden to him, when the word *forbear*, curiously engraved on the hilt, diverted his purpose, and in contemplating it in silence, he for a while forgot the horror of the action he was about to commit. The weapon was a remarkable one: its handle was ingeniously ornamented with diamonds; in the centre of it was an enamelled medallion, on which was painted those words[1] which had arrested his hand. But his surprise was awakened on perceiving, that after he had placed it in his girdle the words had disappeared, and the German eagle appeared in its place. He was, however, interrupted by sounds approaching; he returned the dagger under his cloak, and regained the intricate passages; fortunately he found one which brought him out under the ramparts of his dungeon.

The fickle goddess[2] for once here favoured him, for his escape took place at that hour when the banditti were about to commence their depredations. On hearing the noise occasioned by Albert's forcing the door, which vibrated along the passages, fear of his escape had got the better of their caution; they ran to the place which they conceived to be the scene of action, leaving their horses in the court-yard. Albert vaulted upon the fleetest, and escaped from them by a miracle, while they imagined they had him securely in their power, priding themselves in the intricacy of those corridores, from which they flattered themselves no one could escape undetected.

For several days did our wanderer travel, over deserts and through forests, unknowing and unknown, scarce existing on the food which his enemies had provided in the sumpter bags of the saddle; this was coarse, and now nearly exhausted, he continually dreaded again falling into the hands of his enemies; and scarce daring to rest his head, though many a downy pillow of greenest turf had invited him. Often had the sun risen and set upon his aching eyelids, when at length the majestic Rhine appeared in the distant landscape; but this river, in which he had so often laved after the fatigues of the chace, did not, as he approached its margin, seem to gladden at his approach. The golden hues of the sun did not, as heretofore, gild its bosom; but a dusky blue haze hovered over it, and, as it melted away in the horizon, displayed a broad expanse of a greenish gloom; numerous water-fowl skimmed its surface, and their screams only broke the silence which nature seemed wrapt in. For the first time he threw the bridle on his horse's neck, and

---

1 The only word appears to be *"forbear."*
2 Fortune.

as at length he saw his domestic spires glitter at a distance, all the woman[1] rushed into his soul. At the end of a few days he returned to a home, which, for several years, by the command of his uncle, he had long ceased to visit; although he had resisted his wish of having it dismantled, as an unnecessary expence; and to discharge those servants, who, though now grey-headed in the service of Baron Bruhl, had dedicated their youth to the service of him and his father.

Though still ignorant of the fate of his Adelaide, whom he loved with all the fervour of a young enthusiast, he forbade not those emotions of joy which rushed into his bosom as he approached his paternal roof; while memory of the days, those days that were past as a shadow, filled him with a pleasing melancholy. He anticipated meeting with some old domestic, wandering later than the rest; and he felt almost as much pleasure in that idea, as a father would on meeting with his children. But it was late when he arrived at Castle Bruhl, the sun had long sunk, rosy red, beneath the highest mountain top; and the darkness of eve had painted nature in one hue, by the time Albert arrived at the warden's gate. Yet the autumnal beetle flew round his head, as he sounded the horn at the portal: three times did Albert hear its deepening sound break the awful repose, answered only by the hollow of every neighbouring glen, when a presentiment, chilly cold, struck his bosom; he waited in dread suspense; the clouds now drove along in volumes, leaving part of a moon sometimes unveiled, at others apparently borne away by the elementary agitation. But in vain he sought for admission. He rode round to the draw-bridge, it was down; no impediment checked his progress; and now, indeed, he became convinced that all was not right. The portcullis was raised, every door was open. His hat was now displaced from his head, by the flirting of an owl, many of which had already taken up their abode in this house of almost desolation. He passed the servant's hall, where every thing was still and silent; no cheerful fire emblazoned the hearth, and the sounds of mirth no longer resounded through every passage; the story of the Grey Beard was no more, and the

---

1 *woman*: [Reference] to qualities traditionally attributed to the female sex, as weakness, fickleness, vanity, etc. (*OED*)

Minstrel's Tale had ceased. Tears of regret filled the eyes of Albert; and he, who was generally as brave as the enraged tyger, played the child. As he entered those rooms endeared to him from infancy, all, all were alike robbed of great part of their furniture; nought was left, save a few old couches, and the arms and portraits of his ancestors, which decked the walls; he returned to his horse, whom he led into the court-yard, and the grass, which had covered the pavement, afforded the beast many a fragrant mouthful. It was now too late to think of going farther; Albert was nearly broken hearted; he wrapped himself up in his cloak, fatigue lent him assistance, and he fell into a profound sleep. Unfortunate and persecuted youth, thou who hast so often revelled in all the luxuries of life; who hast, till now, drunk of the quick passing cup of happiness, little did ye expect so cold a welcome. At length he roused himself in thought, after this entire dereliction of his faculties: conjecture followed conjecture, but to no purpose, he was only bewildered with thinking. He hoped that his nurse, the old Urganda, might still be living; he lost no time in visiting her: when he did, the talisman was broken, and the dreadful truth burst upon him; he struck off a tear which had intruded, on leaving the dwelling of his ancestors, and mounted his fatigued beast.

The vapours of night had nearly dispersed, the dewdrops were waiting for the incense breathing morn, and he felt his heart somewhat lighter on entering the cottage of the helpmate of his infancy. She alone was left of all the train; and, when she received him with all the fondness of a mother, he forgot his grief, and nearly wept for joy upon her bosom. She welcomed him with a shriek of surprise; it was almost too much for her; and, notwithstanding Albert kept continually pressing her to relate what had passed during his absence, he could not for some time get a rational answer to a single inquiry. His horse was taken care of; refreshments were set before him, which he found himself obliged to partake of (if he had the least desire to hear of aught else but his own accommodation) and then in nearly breathless ejaculations, the old lady began to recover her speech: "Ah, lack-a-day, my lad! where have you been all this many a long day; nobody knew any thing of you but your uncle, and he is so snobbish, that there's no getting an answer from him. He is more gloomy than ever; and he said lately that he knew nothing of you. He gives it out that you were murdered in the forest; and I am sure it has cost me many a tear; and if you had been made away with, I know who———. Your goods are all sold, and Katherine and Walkmaer, and Wolf, and all the other servants, were discharged at a moment's warning, with tearful eyes and breaking hearts!—But pray, but pray, my lord, eat a little more: I'm sure you can eat another omlet."—"I cannot," interrupted the impatient Albert; "for God's sake go on with your story."—"Not a little bit more of that krout!"[1]—"If you have any regard for my welfare," reiterated he, "if you wish not to drive me mad, I conjure you to proceed."—"Ah! my lord, I warrant me you have passed many a sleepless night. Mercy! how your poor eyes are sunk in your head! and how pale!"—"I conjure you, my dear nurse, to proceed; you keep me on the rack," cried Albert, impatiently. "I rack you; Lord have mercy on you," replied his garrulous narrator; "I am sure I would be the last to torment you, poor soul!" Thus he found it was to no purpose to wish to hurry Urganda, she would proceed in her own way; and Albert, overcome with vexation, which the respect he had for her prevented being visible, and although suffering all the torments of suspense and agitation, determined to await her pleasure for the expected communication.

(*To be continued.*)

———————

CHAP. III.

"Oh! thou foul thief! where has thou stowed my daughter?
———————A maid so tender, fair, and happy."

Shakespeare.[2]

THE impatient soul of Albert would have little brooked the tedious garrulity of Urganda had not he been deeply concerned in her recital; beside, to her age he payed every indulgence, and where

1 *krout*: Cabbage (*OED*).
2 From Brabantio's speech in *Othello* (1622), Act I, Scene 2, by William Shakespeare.

else was he to gain that intelligence which he so much wished to attain? She had proceeded thus for some time, uninterrupted by Albert, and only his menacing brow or trembling lips betrayed the agitation which racked his frame. At length the much-loved name of Adelaide struck his ear; "what of her!" exclaimed the impatient youth. Alas! he now heard that she had been torn from her parental roof by some ruffians who had overcome her attendants, and fled with her no one knew where. His passion became fierce with revenge, his face was pale and cadaverous, he gnashed his teeth with agony, and with a hurried air he left the cottage, on foot, straying he knew not where. But he had not proceeded far, when the terrified nurse's cries saluted his ear, as she was hobbling with all her powers after him. She was nearly exhausted with calling out his name: her fears were so visible, and her pity for his sorrows so great, that Albert could not forbear being melted with her kindness, and, taking her hand, he told her he was about to repair to the castle of Adælmar, late the residence of his unfortunate Adelaide. "Alack! my lord," said the terrified Urganda, "is it not two long leagues? and are you not on foot? I beseech you return, your horse shall be got ready for you." This was but rational, he took her advice and gallopped off for the castle, where he was received by an awful, a dreadful chilliness, which indeed told him that misfortune had here taken up her abode. He was not received with a friendly bow of joy from the domestics, as heretofore, but he placed to grief what was in effect the lower of suspicion. The appearance of the countess was also not only that of grief but resentment had a great share in her demeanor. She was sitting at the further end of the room, to which he was introduced, pale, and in mourning: a handkerchief was held to her eyes, and when she attempted to speak passion checked her utterance. The frigidity of his reception occasioned him no little surprise; but grief he knew was to be respected, and he waited in silence till the countess recovered, and by the following words she increased, even if possible, the astonishment in which he was plunged. "It ill becomes the son of Baron Bruhl thus to insult the mother of Adelaide Holstein with the presence of the ravisher of her daughter's honour! Wast thou not content to take her in the presence of the holy church, without forcing her in this evasive way to thy polluted arms? Where is her father? Give me back my lord!—hence, murderer! to approach me nearer, lest I, 'tis true but a defenceless woman"——here her voice faltered, and she burst into a flood of tears.

Indignant as were the feelings of Albert on hearing an unjust accusation, these emotions disarmed him, and he replied, "madam, that you wrong me is most true; and that you can, for a moment, suppose me guilty of so base an action, can only be attributed to the machinations of one whose plans I fear will at length succeed too well, and render me miserable perhaps for ever. But know, lady, that Albert loves; yes, still loves with too pure a passion to insult any person connected with her he adores, and that he is ready to prove his loyalty with his life."

The firmness with which he made this asserveration somewhat staggered the countess, and when she put a packet into his hands the mystery was solved; the villany of his uncle appeared.—"And dost thou not really know aught," said the bereaved parent, "of my child."—"Alas! madam, no; I swear I will not rest until I have punished her accursed betrayer, and restore my Adelaide to your arms!" "Forgive me then," said the countess, "the horrid imputations you have suffered from me, after the many proofs of your honour, and place it to my too intemperate zeal for the loss of such a daughter. That packet was put into my hands but two days since by your uncle's steward; he informed me that Count Zittau was firmly persuaded that, aided by banditti, you had sought his life and my daughter's honour; and that his master had ordered him to deliver me these proofs of your baseness, while he hasted to throw himself at the feet of his sovereign, there to be permitted to throw down the gauntlet of revenge, and to challenge you to single combat. But, alas! Albert, you know not half my grief; in addition to the loss of my child I am a widow also. The baron, my husband, returning from attendance at court, was beset by robbers and only one domestic escaped, covered with blood, to tell the dismal tidings." As she said this she cast her eyes downwards, and beholding the dagger, whose hilt appeared under the cloak of Albert, she exclaimed, "merciful heavens! if then you are innocent of these allegations, where didst thou get that instrument." He informed her of every circumstance which had befallen him while hunting; the banditti, the discovery of the dead body, and, finally, his escape from Hereitzein castle. Fully convinced of his innocence, his kind hostess exchanged suspicion for certainty that her husband was murdered, but by other hands. Albert was to remain with her until the morning, at which time all the vassals were to be assembled; they swore to die for their dear mistress, and, enlisted under the commands of Albert, they proceeded to attack the castle from whence he had been emancipated, as the most likely place in which the joy of his soul was now immured.

The night preceding this expedition he in vain attempted to refresh himself with sleep; but, notwithstanding the many nights which he had scarcely enjoyed an uninterrupted repose, he disdained to rest his eye-lids, and he awaited in meditation for the morning light. That light, after many tedious hours, at length came, and he arose from his irksome pillow ere the sun had welcomed a new day. He blew a blast at the warder's gate; the hammering of armour was heard throughout the castle, with the cheerful neighing of horses, arrayed in all the glory of war; and the small party were eager for the fight. Albert, on his knees, bade the countess farewell, and her handkerchief waved from the turret, till it became as an atom in the air; and, after replacing his beaver, proceeded on his journey. He had sworn by the honour of a knight never to return until some part of the object of his search was accomplished, and in his mind he revolved on the plans most likely to further his intention. 'Tis true he paced along the road in sombre silence; but not so the party under his command, they enjoyed themselves, though at a respectful distance. At the head of this group was Sebastian, that faithful servant who only remained to tell of his lord's death, after he had forced his enemy, superior in numbers, to quit the field; he was of those kind of men who feel violently for a time, but in whom habitual gaiety, soon make them overcome melancholy emotions.

He had now long been in the service of Baron Holstein; his story he had said was remarkable; he had often promised to tell it, and the calls of his companions were now urgent to be gratified; these he obeyed in the following manner:—"My mother told me that the man she last lived with was my father, and that I was born somewhere in Africa, but I don't know in what part, for it was always a matter of indifference to me where I was born, I had no choice. My father was reckoned the greatest man of our tribe, and for very good reasons; he could run the fastest, climb the quickest, and bear the greatest pain; he was also reckoned very handsome; you may smile, gentlemen, but though we are blacks we have our beauties. From his nose was suspended a large brass ring, and his left ear was beautifully ornamented by the insertion of a knife, almost as large as the sword which I have now upon my thigh; my mother bore also the palm of beauty in her tribe, her head was always the most tastefully powdered with red ochre, and she washed and perfumed herself with the blubber of the whale oftener than other women: she was also accomplished, could assist at the Morai,[1] sing, dance, and cut herself with the fish tooth more severely than her companions. At the battle feast she ever presided, was the first to fill the bowl with the blood of our victims, and was the only one that was allowed to taste of it after my father, as chief of the warriors. I was early instilled in these orgies by my amiable parents, as they held me up as a pattern to all the Nugbaing[2] squaws, as a child who could bear the greatest pain without flinching. My upper lip as you may perceive has been split through, and I even bore the hot tattooing-iron without a cry. But, as our pastor says, the world is full of trouble; one day in a great battle that we had with Boto-Kiotto, king of Mucklandingo, while throwing the tomahawk, and animating my companions with the war-hoop, in which I particularly excelled, I was taken prisoner of war by the adverse party, and doomed to bear the greatest punishment they could inflict, that is to say, either to be roasted alive, as I had roasted others, or sold for a few bits of glass to the Europeans. This latter, supposed by them to be the least honourable, was determined on, though I conceived differently. My father was also made prisoner with me, but he dashed his brains out against a stone, and died, cursing our god, Hiloo, for deserting so zealous a devotee. I thank heaven that I was not arrived at such a pitch of greatness. I was sold to a merchant, where to be sure there was plenty of work for me to do, and plenty of nine-tails for reward: this so little suited my disposition, that I determined on the first opportunity to escape,

1 Morai (from marae): A central open space in a Polynesian village, esp. used as a forum or centre for ceremonies, social functions, debates, etc. (*OED*)
2 Nugbaing, Boto-Kiotto, Mucklandingo, Hiloo: fictional terms.

and this opportunity at length offered itself. One night when our driver lay on the ground, intoxicated, says I to myself, Zuco, here's now a fine chance for a runaway, and I immediately knocked out his brains, and ran for the wood, and made for the sea, in order to secrete myself on board a vessel, that I knew would sail as soon as the wind would permit. I could swim like a fish, thanks to my mother's tuition, and soon passed the ship's bow. I was hailed by the watch on deck, to whom I returned piteous signs, he hauled me up, and introduced me next morning to the crew, as a bargain of his own, here I remained in the most lively terror, till we sailed, which luckily was the next day, not doubting but my master would send for and demand me; in that case I should have suffered a cruel punishment. We had not long been out at sea before I soon understood their language sufficiently to excite a degree of compassion in the captain, to whom I related my ill usage, apprehensive that I had become the property of the boatswain who had taken me on board, and that again I might be sold as a slave. On my arrival in England, he informed me I was free, but without friends or money; what could I do, gratitude had also some place in my heart, and I resolved to remain with Captain Stedman, with whom I made three voyages; at the end of which, as a reward for discovering a mutiny which threatened his life, he made me a handsome present, and offered to carry me back to my own country, where I hope to meet my dear Yanka, a young girl of whom I was not a little fond. I thought her then a great beauty, for she had all the requisites for one of our country; her face was round, and flat as the war-shell, her teeth white as the cocoa milk, and her lip brown as the rind which covers it; her nose was flat, and she walked with a dignified straddle, peculiar to herself; but when I arrived; Yanka and all my friends were dead. And again I returned with my worthy captain. We had not been much more than a month at sea, when we were wrecked; and after suffering every deprivation, in which I should have been starved had it not been for Baron Holstein, on whose domains the waves had left me, heaven rest his soul; and now I am seeking after his murderers." The waters of gratitude visited his eyes, as he finished his tale, and a sad silence ensued, as this little band followed Albert; he was also engaged in thought, which he fully enjoyed, and had thrown his bridle carelessly on his horse's neck, in order fully to indulge his melancholy.

(*To be continued.*)

CHAP. IV.

The Gods to their dear shelter take ye maid.   *Shakespeare.*[1]

By this time the gloomy turrets of the castle in the forest appeared misty blue in the distant landscape; and Albert halted his little company, to inform them that the midnight hour would better suit the completion of his plan, begging them to watch every avenue of the forest, and to be upon their guard from ambuscade. He then proceeded in the same listless manner until he arrived at the place where he was first attacked, and every circumstance of this affair he revolved in his mind; it was here that he was first seized; 'twas there his horse took fright and threw him; and in this place he lay weltering in his blood. He was interrupted in his meditations by the appearance of Sebastian, who had been one of his out-posts, and now returned to inform him, that a party of horsemen had entered the thickest of the forest gloom, and that amongst their party he could discover some prisoner, who was wrapt up in a large cloak, and who evidently was not, to them, a willing companion. Albert's bosom fired with revenge; his horn blew defiance when he discovered his old enemies. He charged them to stand   on their peril to proceed, when a sound from the disguised person, whose mouth appeared to be gagged, made strong exertions to ejaculate for help; but the banditti proceeded to fly from the pursuers, and Albert received a shot from one of their pistols which penetrated his cloak: he clapped spurs to his horse, he pursued them; and notwithstanding their superiority of numbers, the ruffians were forced to seek their safety in flight. Three lay dead at Albert's feet:

1 From Kent's speech to Cordelia in *King Lear* (1608), Act I, Scene 1, by William Shakespeare. More commonly printed as "The Gods to their dear shelter take thee, maid."

but his grief was unbounded when he found that their victim and her conductor were no longer visible, for the fellow had thought it most prudent to leave the field with his fair charge, whose sex, in the commencement of the rencounter, had become visible.

Irritable as were always the feelings of Albert, at this disappointment he now foamed at the mouth—he raved with passion. "Fool that I was," he cried, "to be so much occupied with my own wrongs, as not to attempt to rescue her—to engage at first with the rascal who bore so precious a burden; some Adelaide, perhaps, like mine, torn by these assassins from a parent who loves her, and a lover who adores her. And you, ye dolts, why did you not stop those ravishers of beauty; you had no private wrongs to redress, you were not influenced by revenge, but had to wish for the death of the whole of them. A female in distress, and perhaps Adelaide herself."

It was some time ere he would hear reason, and his companions ventured to assert, it was little probable it could be the lady that they were in pursuit of, as she had disappeared before Albert's return, and was probably closely immured from that time. The gust of passion blew over, his bosom remained calm, but he had awakened the suspicions of the banditti, and now, of course, alarmed for their safety, would cause them to be on the alert. He feared that an attempt on the castle would for this night be impracticable; but they had arrived nearly under its rampart, and the impatience of Albert made him endeavour to fix upon some plan to surprize and conquer them.

Already had the clock struck eleven, and its last tone was dying away in the shades of night, when Sebastian and his master watched the movement of light through the dilapidated casements, as they shewed their chameleon hues through the painted glass. Something extraordinary seemed about to take place; and Albert was not wrong in supposing that it might be occasioned by the reception of the unfortunate Adelaide, who, owing to his negligence, was obliged to take up her abode in this inhospitable spot, without a friend to comfort her; "and I," said he, "suffered her to escape me." The idea of its being her whom he was in pursuit of, again struck him. "Peace, maddening thoughts," he exclaimed, "ye would drive me to despair. No one could dare to bind her lovely limbs." Sebastian was alarmed; he feared his master's intellects were wandering, and he used all his eloquence to calm his feelings; and again they directed their attention towards the castle. All was now wrapped in silence, naught was heard but the cricket, or the gentle glutter of some alarmed bird. At length Albert counted the hour of twelve stealing on the gale; that hour in which murder and devastation, with horrid strides, stain the earth with enormities; the hour when the midnight steel is bared by the assassin, and the unprotected female becomes a prey to the dissolute Tarquin.

Now was the time they seized their arms, the low murmurs of their plans were buzzed in each other's ear. Albert, with Sebastian, had determined to visit the trap-door, from which the former had made his escape; and should they become the slaves of the banditti, they were immediately to storm the castle, on hearing Albert give the preconcerted signal. When they arrived at the bottom, Albert groped about for the several doors; these he found; Sebastian followed at his heels. Not particularly partial to his situation, his fears did not decrease on being informed by Albert, that he had mistaken the passage; he besought him then to return, to leave the completion of his plan until another night; but Albert was inexorable, and he followed, while his frame trembled at every piece of earth which fell from the excavated corridor, expecting to be laid hold of by some dead hand, or froze by fear at a pair of large eyes, or a mouth vomiting fire and brimstone; he was somewhat cheered, when he was informed that they had at length gained the wished-for door, and they entered a circuitous passage. Chilly icicles dropped from the wall, teeming with humidity upon their heads, and seemed to impart their chilly nature even to Albert's heart. He was struck with horror and dread, the wind howled around him, nearly extinguished the glaring torch which made darkness more visible, and spite of all his efforts to avoid it, his feelings quite subdued his courage. A bat struck against Sebastian's forehead, it felled him with fear to the earth. Albert recovered himself, but sounds seemed approaching him; a heavy chain fell apparently over his head, its clank made his heart sicken, but he crossed himself, and darted forward. At the turn of a corner a strong glare met his sight; in a second he was environed by numbers, and before he could sound the expected charge, he was disarmed, and conveyed into a dungeon, he knew not where situated.

His faithful companions, who began, at length, to be uneasy at his stay, blew a gentle blast, as they lay upon the ground; but they were unanswered, and in vain they placed their ear to the earth—no sound approached. At length the welcome bugle's note was heard; they rushed forward, but they were opposed by the banditti: desperation contributed to their bravery, but overcome by numbers, some were content to sell their lives dearly; but finding that of no avail they at length were obliged to seek their safety in flight.

Albert's benumbed faculties were long in recovering their powers; at length he found patience to be his only resource; but he had heard the fatal bugle, and that, although it awoke him from stupor, soon plunged him deeper in nonentity. He feared that his faithful friends were all cut to pieces; but now, as he had in some measure recovered, he hoped some might have escaped, his sovereign would interfere, and it would not be long ere liberty would again be his. But for Adelaide—alas! said he, her name must be for ever banished from my lips. His meals were served him by the silent Gudolvo; and he had sunk into that kind of listlessness, that the banditti hoped would soon end his existence. A nervous fever preyed on his frame, and his appearance was consumptive. They had given his uncle these particulars; and Count Zittau had rather a natural death should rid him of his ill-starred relative, than that the discovery of another murder might too much blacken his character to the Emperor Leopold. Albert frequently walked out from his window into a small turret, and this was the only liberty allowed him; but not even this privilege was allowed until the shades of darkness had descended.

One night, when to cool a parching thirst he had crawled out for air, while he was offering his orisons to the moon, he heard the sound of a female singing a plaintive air, but he regarded it only as the effect of a disordered imagination; but again he heard it louder; it was silent; and again it recommenced; and again it died away upon the breeze, and all was silent; he approached nearer, and heard some words, and, at length, with much attention, this part of the end of a stanza—

"am torn!
While my lover he mourns my delay!"

A deep sigh followed—it was the voice of a female, and it was also the voice of illness and distress, and Albert knew it not; when at length it continued:—

"Then haste to my lover, ye cherubs, your flight,
    On the breeze bear my sorrows away;
And tell him I languish, I die for the sight
    Of a parent—who mourns my delay!"

The voice complained not again. Astonishment, rapture, and apprehensive dread, by turns, convulsed his thoughts, when he now fully discovered the voice, altered as it was from its once sweetness. Yes, it was his beloved Adelaide, whom he supposed had composed these words to sweeten the gloom of a prison. He calls Adelaide, but she hears him not, and the voice of one of the myrmidons cautioned him to retire. The man had brought his wonted refreshment; he took it, for the first time, with a degree of zest; and that Adelaide was near him roused all his dormant hopes. With his frugal meal in his hand, he climbed the circular staircase, and again appeared on the turret. Adelaide's name is resounded, but alas! he receives no answer. Again he sunk into melancholy upon his couch; he dozed—he slept.

The following morning he busied himself in contriving to escape, for several weeks had elapsed, and no return of his companions. Often had he strained his eyes over the immense waste, but to return them unsatisfied; his keepers, grown circumspect, left him now less at liberty. He had no prospect of emancipating himself with his life; he might have thrown himself over the battlements, but Adelaide lived and he would live for her, and his only pleasure was in singing aloud a verse to the same air as Adelaide, expressive of his situation; it was as follows:—

"Your lover, alas! is immur'd from the light,
    From the joy and the sight of the day;
Your cherubs in vain, then, will tell of our plight,
    To your parent who mourns far away."

This he frequently sung but he was unanswered; and of late her voice had ceased. Albert supposed her apartment had been changed, for he could not conceive that they could immolate such lovely innocence. Alas! he knew not, that when wretches discard the ties of humanity, how far their wickedness and interest will carry them. It was in vain he argued on the cause of his detention, he could gain no answer. At length a new attendant was somewhat more merciful; this fellow promised him a book; he conjured him if he was not divested of all pity to inform him if there was not a young lady immured in the same walls, the fellow began to be moved, he ran to fetch the book, he told Albert that there was a young lady, some little time since, but he believed she was there no longer. Gudolvo now interrupted the man, and choaking with passion, bade him retire: the hardened wretch smiled maliciously on him, and closed the door. Albert threw away the book in a fit of madness; and feared that the man would not be allowed to return. Had he been sure of this, no doubt he would again have proceeded to end his existence by the mysterious dagger, which remained concealed in his cloak; the German eagle[1] still appeared, but the other medallion was invisible, and Albert paused over its secret. "Yes," said he, drawing it from its sheath, "spite of thy ominous words I would use thee, and rid the world of so wretched a being." But the troubles of Adelaide made him, though they augmented, soon forget his own; he returned the dagger; he took up the book, and ran over the leaves insensibly. It consisted of provincial tales, but he read them not; he waited with impatience for the return of his friendly communicator. As night approached, the man came with the key of the turret, and his lamp; the latter he sat on the floor. In silence Albert would have enticed him to stop, but the man was resolute; he shrugged up his shoulders, significantly, as if he would have said, I dare not, and retired. Albert was now left to his only physician, patience, but this quality was nearly exhausted; he tried to recollect the face of this man, to know if he had seen him before, in the banditti party, but it was strange to him; whence then his seeming pity for his situation. Poor Sebastian, too, what had become of him? His murdered followers also sat heavy on his soul.

---

1 A black eagle with red claws featured on the coat of arms of Germany.

The breeze blew refreshing and he prepared for his usual walk in the turret.

(*To be continued.*)

―――――

(Continued from page 211.)

CHAP. V.

―――――"Thy currish spirit governed a wolf;
Even from the gallows did her fell soul fleet, and
While she lay in thy unhallowed dam,
Infused itself into thee, for thy desires
Are bloody, ravenous.   *King John.*[1]

In vain, like the perturbed spirit of a departed murderer, did the soul of Albert strive to gain repose. All was silent in the turret. He strove to recall those sweet tones which his dear Adelaide had once carolled; but they were scarce present to his imagination. He found not the refreshing breeze his soul sickened after, and he returned to his chamber. Days dragged heavily, deferred hope still mocked him. He accused the tardiness of his followers; and while he climbed the highest battlements to watch their return, alas! he little thought that only sufficient time had elapsed when their greatest speed could enable them to reach the countess. Often did he hear the sound of horses' hoofs pace over the hollow draw-bridge; but these were unfriendly ones; and every day found him regarding his dagger with a more gloomy satisfaction. One evening, however, he ventured to trim his, as yet, ever-neglected lamp. The book still lay open before him, which his compassionate attendant had borrowed; but now Gudolvo was his only purveyor. He caught it from

1 The attribution to *King John* is incorrect. From Gratiano's speech in *The Merchant of Venice* (1600), Act IV, Scene 1, by William Shakespeare, with notable changes: ". . . thy currish spirit / Governed a wolf, who, hanged for human slaughter; / Even from the gallows did his fell soul fleet, / And whilst thou lay in thy unhallowed dam, / Infused itself in thee, for thy desires / Are wolfish, bloody, starved, and ravenous."

the ground; his eyes wandered over the rude wood cuts with which
it was embellished; he glanced insensibly over the black German
letter with which it was printed, when his attention became a little
chained by the following exordium:—

"Mortal, whoever thou art, who beholdest these pages, attend to
the moral and be content. Though thou art assailed by concealed
enemies, who have murdered thy dearest reputation by stealth; if
those, whom thou thoughtest were thy friends, have left thee in
adversity; if she on whom thou hast gazed, and gazed till thou hast
loved, has, after breathing vows of constancy, left thee for another;
or, if from what cause else thou hast drunk of the cup of bitterness
even to the very dregs, let not despair suggest to thee suicide! let her
not darken thy soul with her suggestions, for these will only make
you miserable here, and in eternity. But put your trust in the Power
above; call on religion; her mild and celestial ray shall illumine thy
mind, shall take from thee thy load of care, and lead thee back to
happiness, if thou wilt but endeavour to deserve her assistance.

"Ægander was strong as the mountain eagle; the rosy finger of
health painted his cheeks, and danced jocund in his eyes. Wisdom
had instilled into him some of her precepts; and the birds and
beasts of the forest taught him piety and gratitude; he imitated
their morning carols to the Supreme, and their evening songs conveyed his gratitude to the Father of all. He saw the tygress fight for
her young, and the cravings of appetite satisfied, man might pass
by her unregarded.

"Ægander saw the modest Morvina, the pride of that canton in
which, from his youth, he had resided. Age had nearly classed them
together; and from a similarity of ideas, love stole imperceptibly
into their hearts. It was not breathed in the nonsensical rhapsodies
of the boy and girl taken with a pretty face, but it grew from an
instinctive desire of pleasing each other, by mutually disclosing the
wisdom of their thoughts, and encouraging each other in rectitude
of conduct. Their parents saw the growing passion with joy, and
wished but to live to bless their union.

"But envy, that self-corroding fury, who too often instils her
poison into the breast of human nature, now reigned tyrannic in
the bosom of Morvina's aunt; a wretch, who by the number of her
herds, fancied that she had a right to usurp a tyrannic sway over the

less wealthy than herself; and though an inhabitant of a sequestered vale, found miscreants whom bribery would force to her will. They seized Ægander; they forced him on board a vessel, and conveyed him to a house of hers, washed by Walga's[1] stream, where he was confined, and nearly hid from the face of day.

"'Twas not the gloomy pleasure of mischief only, yet this she dearly loved, but she was also prompted by jealousy. Yes! start not, gentle peruser of this tale, this wretch, disfigured by age and malevolent passions, thought herself a fit match for the youthful Ægander.

"Some time after he had been confined, his prison door was thrown open, and he discovers his Medusa: 'Now, foolish boy,' she exclaimed, 'now may you pine, unpitied and unknown, torn from that doll's face which thou hadst the effrontery to compare to mine. My majestic tread,' continued she, walking fantastically, 'was to be slighted for her childish trip; my auburn tresses, for her black curls, ah! ah! ah! But know, the daughter of Dionarbus never yet asked in vain, but for your smiles, and you have dared to treat me with contempt; yes, and you live to hear me say it.' Here her rage obliged her to pause, but she soon recovered. 'Once more,' she exclaimed, 'I make you an offer of my hand. Consider, upon your refusal here you are immured for ever; everlasting misery shall be your portion. Your friends have given you up as no more, and my fortune will always be sufficient to pay for every risk I shall run in your detention. To-morrow, then, I expect a decisive answwer.' She then bade him farewell; the guards resumed their posts, and she retired.

"The next morning, ere the orient sun had gilt the forest, she entered to him again, her face struggling with contending emotions. 'Wilt thou be mine, thou proud youth,' she said, affecting the bashfulness of virtue. 'No,' exclaimed Ægander, 'never! I hold the name of Morvina too dear ever to sacrifice its love to thee!'—'Who waits there,' cried the incensed aunt of his dearest. He is immediately surrounded, bound with cords, and again conveyed on board a vessel. To be thus treated with ingominy was too much for the

---

[1] A fictional location.

high spirited soul of Ægander to bear. In the night when all was still,

> "When the sweet winds did gently kiss the breeze,"[1]

he determined to end a life, now become a burthen to him, and from which he saw no possibility of escape. He burst his bonds—the watch has neglected his duty—he sleeps and Ægander's leaping in the sea, disturbed not the drowsy mariner.

"But, alas! for Ægander, he soon repents, when he finds the water flow in upon him. He now tries to recover a life, which but a minute before he had wished to lose. He dreads to meet an offended Deity, a sure punisher of suicide; and lastly he thinks of his Morvina, and that some chance might have occurred to effect a meeting. These thoughts give him strength; he continues to swim, invoking Providence to forgive him his temerity, and assist him to reform; but he has put himself upon an equality with his enemy, and punishment awaits him. The sea continues to break over his head; he is nearly exhausted—he thinks all over; he rises for the last time, and a pitying wave throws him motionless upon the beach. Here he remains for a time senseless; till, as from a dream, recollection dawns. What joy then, what happiness convulses his renovated frame, when he discovers the poplars, the curling smoke, and the distant thatch of the humble Morven, the father of his dear, beloved Morvina. How he kisses the earth; how he utters his grateful thanks; and weak as he is, love assists him to the dwelling of her he adores.

"The old man, her father, blind with age, is sitting at the door; he calls to him while at a distance, the organs are but dull; he yet hears, but cannot be persuaded that it is the voice of Ægander, until the scream of joy from his wife, makes this delightful truth no longer to be doubted. He embraces him, after satisfying his most earnest enquiries after Morvina, who had not left them long for the wood. 'Ah! my son,' exclaimed the venerable old man, 'what has happened to you; something very shocking, I am sure, to make you absent yourself from our cottage: the cottage also of your Morvina. She,

---

1 From Lorenzo's speech in *The Merchant of Venice* (1600), Act V, Scene 1, by William Shakespeare. More commonly printed, "When the sweet wind did gently kiss the trees."

poor girl, has been ill, very ill; 'tis true, she says, she is somewhat better, but if you leave her, I fear she will die broken-hearted. We have had not only to feel for your absence, but for the fate of an only child, sinking into an untimely grave. And could we long survive her? And your parents, run to comfort them, they have been inconsolable for your loss; yet I long to hear your story. Spare not the cheese; and the grapes are of the best vintage that Providence has favoured us with for years.' He quickly related his story, which was necessary to regain the confidence of the good old folk. At his narrow escape from the waves the old man's groans, with his wife's convulsive sobs, prevented his proceeding with his detail, which he soon finished, frequently casting his eyes to the door at which his Morvina now appears. They beseech him not to shock her by his sudden appearance, but scarce can he keep his seat, from the violence of his feelings. The rose which he had left on her cheek was vanished, and like the storm-stricken lily, her form bent in the tempest. She walked feebly, and scarce were her hands capable of bearing in her lap the few sticks that she held in her apron. She sees, in a darkened corner of the room, a young man, and hopes, yet fears, it cannot be Ægander. Her heart throbs violently, while she gently pushes open the half door. " 'Tis him!" she cries; the faggots drop from her hands, and like a corpse she staggers into the arms of the agitated Ægander. At length she opens her eyes, she fixes them upon him with tender regard, then relapses into a vacant stare.

"This tragedy is repeated for some time, till at length an hysteric fit, followed by a flood of tears, brings her to reason. What a scene for an amiable girl now presents itself; her aged father is wringing his hands, while ever and anon a tear steals down his furrowed cheeks; her mother is invoking, upon her knees, mercy, and wearying heaven with petitions for her daughter's recovery; and the youth that she adores gazing with stupid anguish over her agitated frame.

"Her father is now told she recovers. Her mother assists him to take his daughter's hand, which he gives to Ægander. Joy is diffused round the room. He conducts her to his parents. What delight do they not experience. They shudder at the behaviour of the aunt, and yet dread the consequence of her revenge. But Morvina bids them not to fear, that her father and the good pastor shall plead for them; 'and surely,' she cries, 'age and religion cannot plead in vain.' They knew not, that long ere this, passion had ended this woman's wretched existence, and that her riches must soon devolve to them. They seek this worthy pastor on the morrow; they will no longer be separated from each other, and with his blessings, and those of their parents, they are united—they are happy.

"Pause here, oh, reader, and ask thyself if thy despair was ever better founded than was the misery of these children of unadulterated nature. Let not then thy fortitude sink under thy cultivated understanding; and if thou wilt profit aright from this lesson, perhaps yet, like them, you may be happy!"

Albert threw down the book, for his eyes were heavy. He paced the room, cool and collected; no bursts of passion escaped his lips; and he pondered on the tale which he had just been perusing. "Surely," cried he, "my good genius has thrown this book purposely in my way, to comfort me in my affliction." The similarity of circumstances struck him most forcibly. Ægander was torn from her he loved, so was he! They were both persecuted, and both tempted to end their beings by their own hands. "Yes, merciful heaven!" he exclaimed, "I now own thy correcting power. Forgive me, and I swear solemnly to bow with resignation to thy will. I will summon more resolution than the uncultivated soul of Ægander could. Spare but my Adelaide!" Here he was interrupted by the clatter of horses' hoofs in the court-yard; but they were so familiar to him, that he loitered ere he essayed to view. He perceived with the banditti a man of superior mien. The horn blew, yet they were detained. At length the rattling chain proclaimed the portcullis was drawn up. The stranger looked upwards suspiciously, and Albert's strained vision now acknowledged the person of his uncle, to whom he waved his white feather. But Zittau saw him not, the draw-bridge fell, and all was again silent.

"Our fates are then decided," exclaimed the wretched Albert, "and Adelaide will become the sacrifice to this monster. Oh! merciful heavens!" he exclaimed, "this is more than I can bear;" and he paced the turret in agony. There was a butment[1] which projected far from the walls of the castle, and oft when Albert's impatient

---

1 *butment: Archit.* The supporter of an arch (*OED*).

looks would pervade the distant landscape, for the return of his followers, would the wretched lover cling. The place was dangerous; for had the niche, whose crumbling stones had once held the blazonry[1] of the castle, given way, death must have been the consequence. But Albert heeded it not. Oft when he would catch the bandit's words, did he cling, and bend over immensity. 'Twas to this place he repaired, when the moon had arose, pale-orbed, upon the landscape; he overlooked an immense terrace, and straining his ear, voices, as if disputing warmly, broke the silence of night. The wind was favourable to him, he heard his uncle threaten, yet he felt no alarm; but revenge swelled his bosom, as he denounced curses on Zittau's head. It was evident they were plotting his death, but he returned to his chamber.

Lulled into security, of late his confinement had been less severe. He was suffered the range of a corridore to walk in when the weather had been tempestuous, and this indulgence had yet been continued. At the usual nightly visitation of his lamp he affected to be very drowsy; but he thought Gudolvo eyed him with more than common attention. Yet no particular caution was used; and he listened till the sound of footsteps had ceased. He then made for this corridore, leaving behind his lamp, lest it might awaken suspicion. But how was he surprised on perceiving lights through the crevices of apparently a temporary flooring of boards, so old as to allow him to view a large room underneath. He listened if all was still, and at length placed his eye through the interstices of the platform, from whence a knot from the wood had slipped. He beheld his uncle at a table, surrounded by the banditti, who were drinking very freely; and he found himself to be still the principal feature in their conversation. He eagerly devoured every word they uttered. Zittau expressed his fears of the emperor; and he heard them say, "we swear," after which they ejaculated, "he dies." Again they resumed their seats, and the means were debated, how they should accomplish their horrid purpose. Gudolvo mentioned poison, but this was objected to as dilatory. At length, when they had been by Zittau wound up to a frenzy, by intoxication, they agreed to enter his chamber in numbers that very night, and asleep

---

1 *blazonry*: A heraldic device, or collection of heraldic devices (*OED*).

or awake to butcher him upon the spot; that Adelaide also should be murdered, after being shewn the dead body of Albert, without she would consent to be united to Count Zittau, and by her own hand-writing declare that Albert was killed in attempting the life of his uncle. "Execrable villany!" exclaimed the distracted Albert, as he started from the floor. "Oh! Protector of innocence! thou wilt not suffer these wretches to put their threats into execution. For myself I will sell a life I am tired of, dearly and honourably. But must my Adelaide, dearest maid, she who, oh heaven, has obeyed thy dictates without repining; she, who is all goodness, must she be butchered by the blood-thirsty villains? Must her delicate form be disfigured with wounds, ere she will consent to espouse the murderer of him she loves. Will she blast the reputation of him she adores, or must she feel the assassin's vengeance. 'Tis madness, oh God! 'tis too much.

"Wilt thou then forsake me," groaned Albert, with agony, while drops of perspiration chased each other down his face. "Oh! gracious Father of Heaven! wilt thou withhold thy thunder at such a deed." Tears at length burst from his eyes; they allayed the fever of his brain; they flowed fast. Yes, the courageous, the high-minded Albert wept. Had he not, 'tis probable, reason would have vacated her seat in his brain. These tears, however, he soon wiped away. "Foolish boy," he exclaimed, "will these complaints nerve thy arm; summon a stern resolution." A supernatural strength seemed to revive him, he tore a bar from the scarce to be reached casement; he breathed a prayer for Adelaide, and waited in suspense fully resolved to sell his life as dear as possible. Despair seemed to strengthen him. He longed for the combat; but all was silent. The hurricane whirled round the battlements, and the sighs of ghosts appeared to vibrate in the breeze.

(To be continued.)

(Continued from page 281.)

CHAP. VI.

Here have we war for war, and blood for blood;
Controlment for controlment!——SHAKESPEARE.[1]

A DREADFUL silence now pervaded the castle, while Albert, nerving himself with resolution, awaited his coming death. The clock tolled the heavy hour of twelve; "another ten minutes," he exclaimed, "and all will be over;" he staggered to his couch, but the iron bar still remained in his hand. "These eyes," said he, "which have never withheld their tears for another's distress, will be soon sunk in death. This heart which now firmly beats, will throb no more. To be thus plunged into eternity, in darkness; thus to have the cup of youth dashed from my lips, and to go I scarce know where——requires some serious thought. There is a heavy dread lying at my breast, in despite of all my philosophy. Oh, Adelaide!" he exclaimed, and his soul was wrung with agony; he threw up his eyes to Heaven in speechless grief; his head turned round, but he heard noises, and his wonted energy returned. They approached nearer; "they come," he cried, "now, oh God! thou only art my only refuge; strengthen my arm with self-defence; deliver me and my Adelaide." He hears the fastening of a distant door unclosed with care: they doubtless hoped that he slept; but he has placed his back against the wall; he feels strong as the enraged tiger; and behold the door slowly opened, and by the glare of a torch, Gudalvo[2] attended, enters his apartment. They stand aghast at seeing him thus pre-pared, and their fears were not decreased, on hearing him exclaim, "Come on, ye blood-suckers; take the life of your victim, but be assured he will sell it dearly." He then drew his dagger, and with the half of the bar which he had torn from the window, parried their

1 From King John's speech in *King John* (1623), Act I, Scene 1, by William Shake-speare.
2 In this first part of Chapter IV, "Gudolvo" is erroneously spelled "Gudalvo."

thrust, and did some execution. Two soon lay dead, or exhausted at his feet; the rest became furious. At length he is seized by the throat, his courage no longer avails him, and Gudalvo's sword prepares to drink his blood: but his prison is crowded with men; the bugle rings through the castle; the vassals of the Countess Bruhl, rescue him from his fate. Fortune at length seems weary of persecuting him, numbers lay bathed in blood. Albert ranges the castle, fury guides his steps; he hopes to meet Count Zittau, but he, too cowardly to assist at the hellish schemes he had planned, had left the castle that night; and Adelaide, his dear Adelaide, returns him no answer.

It was Albert's first care, as soon as order was restored in the castle, to enquire after Gudalvo, for on him rested all his hopes of the discovery of his partner in tyranny. He had been carried to a chamber, where he lay weltering in his blood. The agony of a wounded conscience, the pain of his wounds, and the fear of punishment, all contrived to give him the appearance of a dying dæmon. It was with difficulty the blood which flowed from his wounds was stopped, but life was dear to him; he opened his eyes. At the promise of conditional pardon, he put a key into the hand of Albert, and saying enough to give some clue where Albert might find his Adelaide, charged Sebastian to watch him carefully, and to arrange matters that no surprise from the escaped banditti, might once more get them into their power.

Alas! Albert was not yet to gain the object of his dearest solicitude; he found her not. Gudalvo had mistaken his request, and came back for further explanation; but the only man that could give it, seemed fast sinking in death, and it was some time ere the few cordials he drank revived him. He was severely wounded, and the impatient Albert was obliged to wait in agonizing suspense in his chamber until the following morning.

Albert arose early, somewhat refreshed; but when he spoke to Gudalvo, the wretch gave a vacant stare, then turned from him without an answer. Sebastian repeated his master's request, but the same silence ensued; when Albert again repeated his promise of pardon, and conjured him to say, where they had confined the young lady. Gudalvo muttered the word pardon, to himself, several times; at length this was followed by his expressing more audibly—"but you will not, you cannot forgive such a wretch as I have been." "Recollect, sir," continued he, with earnestness, and attempting to rise; "it is I who have sought your life; no, you know not half my crimes, or I am sure you never would forgive me. Yet if you could, I would con"——here the poor wretch became exhausted——"yet, I think," added he, "you would not repent your mercy." Albert repeated his former assertions in the most solemn manner. The repentant Gudalvo, however, could give no account of the object of Albert's enquiry; she was confided to the care of some other man, by Count Zittau;—but he gave him the keys of all the caverns, and again Albert commenced his search, but with a heavy and desponding heart. Long did Sebastian and Albert pace along, lighted by the paly-torch:[1] steps ascended and descended; caverns they entered, where the foot of man had not intruded for years; hopes were raised and blasted; till at length they entered a large recess, which they presumed was handsomely furnished. A bed was in the centre, but it was unoccupied: and at the further end of the recess, he perceived a female, whom he imagined was his Adelaide: but his agitation, his fears for her health, in not knowing how to discover himself without alarming her, kept him irresolute in what manner to act, and he continued contemplating her at a distance, though scarce able to refrain from snatching her to his bosom. She appeared to sleep; her eyes were closed; but he perceived by the rays of light that burst through the iron bars of her prison, that her sighs interrupted her repose. On one hand reposed her head; her black hair hung down in disorder, while a long white arm reclined on her knee; no hue of health seemed to visit her cheeks; they were pale—wild disorder and ruin reigned around her. "Unfortunate girl!" exclaimed Albert, "what has thou not suffered while in the hands of these miscreants, and I have been the cause of it all!

"Not content in bringing down the vengeance of Heaven upon my head, I have also made thee a partner in my misery; wilt thou not hate the man who has thus been the occasion of all thy unmerited sufferings?

"How piercing would be the sensations of thy mother did she view thee thus pale, dejected, the inhabitant of a loathsome den; would they not execrate the villany of Zittau?" She moved, she

---

1 Unidentified but may be a torch made of pales (pickets) bound together.

rose from her couch, but her movement betrayed a delicate frame nearly worn out with suffering, and the following ejaculations burst from her lips; "Another day is come and going:" "another day of misery shall I pass"—"am I never to be released, cruel Zittau? and dost thou suppose all thy terrors would make me leave thee for my beloved Albert?" "Ah, my mother, believe not the suggestion of falsehood; Albert, my love, is innocent." "Not a drop of water to moisten my parched mouth: cruel jailors, will ye then leave me another day to starve?—but I shall soon die! I feel my chills shake my frame—I cannot long survive!—but I will leave the world, blessing thee my mother, and my dearest Albert——and my poor father." "Why, oh death, art thou so anxious to close the eyes of those who are happy, and yet wilt not bear the prayer of those whom misery looks forward to for thy release. Perhaps, even now, thou hoverest over the child of affection, of virtue, and of fortune. Unavailing are the mother's tears, the father's groans, or the sighs of relations. Alas! nothing prevents thee claiming thy victim."

★   ★   ★   ★

"Adelaide," softly exclaimed Albert; "ah," she said, unconscious of reality—"still that sound in my ears, still I hear him call; beloved Albert, I come, I vowed to join you, but it will be in the tomb; 'tis for thee I have dared to confront horror in all its shapes. Your uncle's menaces, I only feared on your account." Here she placed her hand on her forehead, her ideas appeared to wander; again she recovered.

"'He,' cried the unfeeling Zittau, 'shall first be murdered, if you refuse to save him.' In vain I knelt and prayed; by this time he is no more. I see his many limbs torn by the"————she fainted. Sebastian had returned with water, it revived her; as the sun breaks through a misty cloud, so recollection dawned in her mind: she was then at length convinced that Albert was once more restored to her. "Do I hold his hand?" she exclaimed, "do I really speak to him? or if I do not, if it is fiction all, oh let me not know it; do not say that he lives not." She gazed wildly on him, she laughed, then became senseless, and it was long before she could be moved, or that her nerves recovered their usual tone. Messengers were dispatched to the countess with the joyful tidings, who sent conveyances, and it was not long before they left the gloomy turrets of Hereitzein castle, accompanied by the repentant Gudolvo, whose strength appeared to be far from re-established. The transports that revelled in the bosom of Adelaide in viewing once more the landscape of nature in its gayest liveries, was almost too much for her strength; nay, it required all Albert's persuasions to quell those sensations which filled Adelaide's bosom. At length the castle of her mother appeared in the distant twilight embosomed with trees, still lightly gilt by the last ray of the nearly-departed sun. Eager they passed the extended lake, unruffled but by the sportive swallow, or the whitened sail that glided along unmindful of the overhanging rock that seemed about to crush it with its premeditated fall. Nature was sinking to rest; one hue of colouring only prevailed; and the tired husbandman was seen

> "Plodding home his weary way."[1]

The silence was only interrupted by the twinkling of the sheep-bell, and the cooing of the stock dove. A scene so placid, so holy, inspired Adelaide with the most tender ideas, and filled her eyes with tears of sensibility. It was not lost on Albert, who in breaking to Adelaide the death of her father, robbed her of some share of those regrets which she felt, and which another relater would have made more piercing. Adelaide, conscious that she had no father now to welcome her return, felt even, if possible, more eagerness and more sensible of the worth of that parent which Providence had left her; and nowithstanding the shock she felt on sinking into the maternal arms of the countess, joy checked the rising tread, and night closed upon them before they could even tell the extent of the pleasure they experienced. Although the countess had been inconsolable and constant in her regret for the murdered baron, she was fully sensible that she owed some portion of thankfulness to that Providence who had restored to her a daughter. Thus happiness was not altogether forbid the castle; her faithful followers she thought deserved some exertions from her. The goblet was filled,

---

1 An allusion to Thomas Gray's "Elegy Written in a Country Church-yard" (1751).

her vassals were rewarded, and the hall had once more echoed the sound of rejoicing; and however the absence of him, who once gave zest to the feast, would sometimes give a pang to their festivity, yet the jocund bowl was passed till morn broke forth in the East.

Gudolvo was the only one absent from the banquet. As the supposed murderer of Count Bruhl, Albert was silent as to the character of his guest; and he wished to be alone. There buried in a chamber, where the noise of revelry could not reach him; he was found constantly by the attendants at the castle, either writing, or with folded arms apparently soliciting mercy from Heaven, attentively perusing a missal, or throwing up his eyes to the martyr'd saints, who in gay attire dignified his chequered window.[1] Content now lodged at Gibheline Castle. Adelaide visited every spot as soon as her renovated health permitted, which was endeared to her from infancy; and while she stooped to arrange some flowers, which the storms of the elements had bent to the ground, she compared them with herself, as having been, by the machinations of her enemies, nearly bowed down to the earth. She sat not long, in a hermitage formed by nature, before Albert made his appearance, to inform her of his plans with regard to his uncle. He was still his relation; ought he then to shed his blood? No! he would throw himself at the feet of his emperor; he would demand his right: should Zittau deny him this, he resolved to cast down the gauntlet of defiance, and to let the battle decide his fate. In those days of blood, the terrors of death, when unaccompanied with infamy, were not so much dreaded as they now are, even by the fair. Yet Adelaide, shocked as she had been by the horrors she had just suffered, trembled for the fate of her hero. She however saw no means of diverting him from his purpose but the hope that the merciful Gustavus[2] might deem his the language of truth, and disgrace Zittau as a false knight, without this terrible proof of his faith.

On their return the unoccupied chair of the baron brought tears into their eyes. 'Tis true Albert now occupied it, but something seemed to say, alas! why does he not come? "I see him, yet he is not

---

1 A stained glass window featuring images of saints and alternating coloured squares.

2 The emperor.

present; he beckons his hand like the white son of Colmar;[1] but he vanishes like a cloud through the misty heath of Mona."[2] Adelaide had as yet kept her friends in total ignorance as to the cause of her detention, and they had feared to speak to her respecting it, lest the revival of scenes, where her sufferings had been so acute, might unnerve her. She now informed them of her sudden disappearance; the countess trembled, Albert was all anxiety, but her memory was defective. She was obliged to collect her ideas, and first arrange the circumstances of her detention, which indeed bore all the illusion of a dream; they would have begged her to defer the recital, but being determined to relieve their mind, after a little pause she commenced in the following manner.

(To be continued.)

(Continued from our last Volume, page 323.)

CHAP. VII.

> "One daughter only have I, no kin else
> On whom I may confer what I have got.
> The maid is fair,
> And I have bred her to my dearest cost,
> In qualities of the best. This villain
> Attempts her love; I pray thee, good young man,
> Join with me to forbid him." SHAKESPEARE.[3]

"THE convent bell," said Adelaide, "had just rung for vespers, when I entered the grove of poplars which leads to its holy walls, and tranquillizing my mind, as my eyes were fixed on the gleams of departing day, with a hymn to the Virgin, I was interrupted by

1 "white son of Colmar": possibly Jean Roesselmann, a 12th-century hero and native son of Colmar.
2 The isle of Mona, also called Anglesey, off the northwest coast of Wales.
3 From the Old Athenian's speech in *Timon of Athens* (1623), Act I, Scene 1, by William Shakespeare. The third line is abridged from "The maid is fair, o' the youngest for a bride" and "This villain" is often printed "This man of thine."

footsteps, some of which appeared near me, while, at a distance, I saw horses fully apparelled, standing in a glen beneath my path. Unconscious of danger, I proceeded onward, when I was seized by some rude hands, who dragged me off in silence,—for fear had completely enchained my voice. I presume that I fainted through their violent conduct, for it was night ere I was awakened to a full sense of my situation. Consternation made me brave, and despair urged me at first to make the utmost resistance I was capable of. This soon proved useless: the hollow forest only resounded my agony, my resistance was futile, my demands unanswered. I found myself fast bound to the horse, that rapidly conveyed me across the country; and, on the next morning's dawn, fearing that I might by my cries obtain succour, the villains tied a sash across my mouth, and continued to bear me over plains which seemed to have no end, till an immense forest checked the rapidity of our motion.

"I see, by your countenances, my dear friends, how much you participate in my sufferings; indeed they were too severe to describe. On the following morning my enemies seemed to think themselves secure, for they ventured to alight; they placed me on the ground, nay, they even partially unbound me, and offered me refreshments. Alas! you may easily conceive, after such conduct, that hunger had little share in my sensations: they soon ceased to proffer me what I sullenly refused. At length they were alarmed by the rustling of leaves; their pistols were cocked; men appeared between the copse. I was hurried on my horse, but not before I had seen the plume of your helmet, Albert, waving in the air. Good Heavens! what then were my emotions! The villains allowed me to shriek but once; the bandage was replaced, and hope vanished from my sickened sight. When the wretch left his fellows to sustain the shock of your valour, he seemed to think me too precious a treasure to risk the loss of. Alas! I was soon aware of his cruel purpose. He did not halt with me till he arrived at my prison; there he left me to ruminate on my misfortunes. My courage was now quite exhausted; I threw myself on the ground in the greatest mental agony, and burst into tears. Fatigue, and the dreadful ideas which I imagined that my dear friends would experience by my absence, at length threw me into a severe illness. 'Tis true, assistance was procured me, yet some time passed in a delirium; and my first return to convalescency was greeted by the appearance of Zittau, whose proposals, too shocking for me to relate or you to hear, caused the dawning of a dreadful truth to be awakened in my soul. He had the temerity to make me an infamous proposal. On my refusing him with firmness, he left me, menacing vengeance; and, when he told me that he had you in his power, that you should also suffer for what he termed my obstinacy, agony was too poor a name for my sufferings. Not to trifle too much with your feelings, my story shall be brief. I was now a stranger to all indulgence; bread and water was all the sustenance allowed me, and, for the last week of my existence, although I wished to die, yet something seemed to call me back to life. Ah! how well do I now recollect my falling into that sort of non-entity, that state of mere vegetation, in which you found me; and how long I fancied I was dying, when that healing power was very far from me. The last evening I remember was that when my light was expiring for want of oil. I had before this endeavoured to beguile away my time, by my musical talent, and attempted to sing aloud, but to no purpose. Once, indeed, I fancied I heard some one in return, but reflection readily told me it was unreal; and becoming at length too weak for such exertion, never after did I attempt it. I made an effort for the last time to trim my lamp; then threw myself on a couch, waiting for death. 'Poor emblem of myself,' I exclaimed, 'am I not, like thee, nearly exhausted? Life, 'tis true, flutters about my heart, but without comfort soon will it beat no more.' The light was nearly extinct; it burst forth in a blaze, sunk, emitted a smoke, and all was darkness. 'Thou art but gone before me,' I said, and closing my eyes as if that would expedite my death, the murdered forms of my father and you, my Albert, flitted before me. I followed you with my eyes, I stretched out my arms towards you, but you vanished; yet again you appeared, you appeared bleeding, and seemed to reproach me. What happened after I know not. Until I was delivered by you, to whom I owe my existence, all was involved in obscurity." She then offered her hand to Albert, who appeared deserving of her affection, while her cheeks were suffused with the liveliest tints of nature. Some little explanation now took place with regard to the singing, and other circumstances, while the countess, smiling as she did through her tears, pressed her daughter to her bosom, and felt all the luxury of a mother's love.

The following day registered those orisons in heaven which, consecrated by the holy father Ambrose, were vented in the chapel. In the maternal supplication to the father of mercies, forgiveness of enemies was not omitted. The organ's peal once more harmonized the thanksgiving of Adelaide, while the tear of gratitude stood in Albert's eye. If the dark soul of Zittau had been open to conviction, he would have confessed the power of religion, and resolved to sin no more. In the disposition which they were now, all enmity was at an end: they were considered not as enemies, but as objects of compassion; and Albert, at the suggestion of Adelaide, prepared to visit the chamber of the repentant Gudolvo. But astonishment was again raised, by finding that that part of the castle, which he was wont to occupy, was left vacant; and the attendants could obtain no account of the fugitive. Albert began to apprehend all was not right, that, his repentance being the offspring of fear, he might still suffer from his diabolical machinations; Adelaide trembled for the consequences; while the countess, sunk upon the floor, and in accents of terror, besought St. Francis to interfere for her welfare.

The appearance, however, of Father Ambrose, quieted, in some measure, their alarms: he desired them not to be apprehensive for the consequences; he had heard the confession of Gudolvo in the morning, and could not conceive after receiving absolution, that he would return to profligacy. What that confession was, he could not utter; the laws of the holy church forbade it. "What he may choose to inform you of himself," said Father Ambrose; "this scroll will disclose: this he put into my hands: take it, my children; 'tis yours; and may your fears be at rest: here I leave you: forgive the tardiness of age; I ought earlier to have relieved your anxieties; but, ah! the blood creeps in that current which eighty winters have frozen. Adieu!" No time therefore was lost in the perusal of the manuscript, which unfolded to them the following words.

(To be continued.)

(Continued from page 23.)

CHAP. VIII.

"A deed without a name!"

SHAKESPEARE.[1]

"Is it possible that a wretch like me, whose sins are numberless as the stars of heaven, can be permitted to live and to flatter himself that he might yet be happy but for thee, oh conscience! who art a hell within me: oh, my merciful protectors, how well you spurn the serpent from you, whose life you have preserved when you finish my narrative; and you, my kind hostess, how will you abhor me, when you learn that I was the murderer of your husband; but I fly from you for ever; never more can my guilty face, after this confession, be opposed to yours: 'twas I who murdered him, my coward-hand struck the fatal blow: ah, my brain burns; recollections yet would madden me: I tremble; the pen falls from my hand.

*   *   *   *   *   *

"Once more I endeavour to continue my detail; oh, merciful heaven! if such a wretch as I am, may ask for mercy, here humbled to the dust, let me invoke thee, and suffer me, in peace, to expiate my crimes by a candid confession.

"Austria gave me birth; my father's name was Rudolpho; but I neither remember him nor my mother; they died during my infancy, and were spared from witnessing the profligacy of their son. I am related, as you are, to the wretch Zittau; to him I owe all my misery, but he will in the end be punished. Being left without a friend, my only dependance was on your uncle. When I attained a proper age, and was tolerably schooled in iniquity, I entered the

---

1 Spoken by Hecate and the witches in *Macbeth* (1623), Act IV, Scene 1, by William Shakespeare.

German service, where, as in most camps, I found vice in all its gradations, and profligacy reign triumphant.

"Night followed night in one continued round of licentiousness, and I joined in every enormity without one idea being entertained, how soon I might meet the blow of an avenging God, from the mouth of the enemy's cannon on the following morning. I was soon taught to believe that there was no avenging Power; this I had no wish to discredit, and Zittau had even more reason than myself to hope the opinion was true.

"The war being concluded, having already murdered one man in the prosecution of my pleasures; as my money became entirely dissipated, the mansion of Zittau was my only resource; he was also my superior officer, and his will my law. Never was a wretch so abused in return for the services I had rendered him; he instilled into my mind every base sentiment, and sapped the foundation of every religious principle. Before this last return to Zittau, all my faults arose from imprudence, now they became the designs of the sophisticated murderer; there was not any crime I would hesitate to execute; no virtue but what excited my ridicule.

"Pedatra was the daughter of Count Zittau's steward, whom he desired; I will not say he loved her, for that would be profane. Her parents were poor, and unable to resist his inclinations: Pedatra was surrendered to his arms. Weary in a little time of the object of his passion, Zittau resolved upon her destruction; and no one appeared so proper as myself to accomplish his guilty purpose. He proposed a bribe, which I accepted, and conveying her in secret to a place suitable for so horrid a deed, a poignard ended her life, and that of an innocent babe, the fruit of his lawless and transient amour.

"Inhuman wretch! methinks I hear you exclaim: ah, you know not indeed the blackness of this heart; but you must yet wade further with me in blood, and read the last outrage to humanity, of which I was guilty. Time and reflection had brought me to a sense of my deeds, when Zittau entered my apartment: 'Say, Gudolvo,' uttered he, 'can thy heart murder a man? thy arm has shed infants' blood? couldst thou meet thy fellow in open combat?' This suspicion of my courage I could not bear; I dared him to expose me to any being. Stimulated, alas! by this bravado, and by hopes of further reward, your friend, the Baron Holstein, became my next victim; and your death it was resolved should follow. But you may wonder what could possess me to riot in the blood of those who never offended me; I must recall some circumstances to your mind to solve this apparent mystery. 'Gudolvo,' said Zittau, 'I have something of consequence to unfold: I have had many proofs of your fidelity, and have given you many testimonies of my friendship: but I must put your regard to another trial: thou knowest the youthful Albert is thine enemy; he is now nearly of age, and about to enjoy his patrimony: thou knowest also, how inconvenient it is for me to restore those effects, that I have converted to our mutual use. This boy, friend, is enamoured of Adelaide, the daughter of Count Holstein, at whose castle he is become a frequent inmate; and so pleased is the maid with his love-sick nonsense, that they have agreed to be united in marriage. Holstein's demands I cannot meet: for his daughter's interest, I shall be called upon for an ecclaircissement[1] of Albert's claims, and as I cannot restore the money I have secured, except at your destruction and mine, let Holstein be dispatched, and Albert's inheritance shall be yours: yes,' added he, emphatically; 'half the fortune of your implacable enemy.'

"I remained for a time immersed in thought; when Zittau fearful that I might relent, recounted with vehemence the insults I had experienced, and the injury I had received: painted in glowing colours the charms of Redora, whom Albert had wrested from my arms; and described the strength of our castle in the forest, to which, after the murder of Holstein, I might retreat; and inflaming my passions to the highest pitch of vengeance, left me capable of doing any deed of horror. A little time after, aided by the steward, whom we corrupted to poison the ear of the countess, the baron by our hands met his fate."

The countess here swooned at the horrid recital, and was conveyed to her apartment. At her departure, a horrible curiosity impelled them to continue the memorial, which further disclosed, that the steward died by poison given by Zittau; and the awful death of this man, for the first time, awakened contrition in the soul of Gudolvo; but let his own words relate the dark feelings of his soul.

---

1 *ecclaircissement* (éclaircissement): A clearing up or revelation of what is obscure or unknown; an explanation (*OED*).

"The baron fell from the first wound I inflicted, and my too ready companions in blood finished the deed. And now, my lord, adieu for ever: you know the rest; and let your joint maledictions fall on my head. The life of penitence I have sworn to live, will be horror indeed: and, oh! I dare not die: yes, I go far from you, deserving young man; it is not fitting that the same country should retain us: I water the path with my tears; I seek some distant monastery to shelter me; I beg the mountains to hide me from myself: oh! pray for me, pity me; for you can never know the poignant regret of the repentant Gudolvo."

An awful silence pervaded the apartment; horror and grief sat on each brow: they took a sad farewell, that Adelaide might visit the countess, whose endearing attentions soon expelled the gloomy sensations Gudolvo's tale had inspired. They recovered her so much as to make her resolve to finish it by herself on the morrow; and when Adelaide was about to return to Albert, she begged that masses might be offered up for the soul of the repentant sinner. The detention of Albert's estate, was a serious evil; but while his mind fluctuated between leaving his wife in the first months of connubial felicity, in order to regain them, and the dread of experiencing his uncle's resentment, a stranger demanded an interview with Lord Albert, and was ushered in the armory. He was the bearer of a packet, which required immediate perusal; and retiring to Adelaide, Albert broke the seal, and read the following words:—

"Once more, my lord, the repentant Gudolvo addresses you; he informs you, that you are fully revenged, for your enemies are no more; your uncle, the once detested Zittau, has met with that death his atrocious life demanded. Batoni, the bearer of this, witnessed his fate; accompanied solely by him, a few days after the dispersion of our gang, Zittau was thrown from his horse, down an immense precipice; his companions heard him fall, and the next morning beheld his mangled limbs scattered below. Once more, my lord; adieu! adieu for ever."

No time was now lost in arranging the affairs of Albert: he was again put in the full possession of his estates; and the fascination of his wife had so far recovered the spirits of her mother, that one evening she did not hesitate to entertain them with anecdotes of her early life; and amongst others, she related the circumstance of the Mysterious Dagger, of which, Albert now begged a solution.

"Wear it my child," said the countess, "for ever; and although in the contemplation of it, I may regret the memory of my lost lord; yet in its becoming the property of the restorer of our family honours, I can view it without any alarming emotions. It was the property of your grandfather, Adelaide: engaged one night in a feudal quarrel, three persons sought his life; his courage would have availed him nothing, had not a gallant stranger interfered, who crying out, 'forbear,' mingled in the fight: they soon became masters of the field; but the stranger knight, after receiving our hospitalities, died in Palestine. On this dagger, a present from Sir Hugh, we had the word 'Forbear,' as a motto, engraved. It was this weapon that assisted in saving the life of Count Holstein, who presented it to his son. Behold it, Albert," said the countess; "it is of a singular construction: used in the ordinary way, the embellishments of a German eagle only appear; but clutch it violently, you touch a spring which throws out a double point; press it thus slightly, you see it as quickly recedes."

Struck with the invention, and the service it had performed, Albert regarded the dagger as an interposition of Providence, and held it in veneration.

The dilapidated castle of Albert, restored to its former grandeur, now resounded with music and joy. His dependants now shared in his happiness; and in the school of Adversity having learnt the true value of life; in the endearments of his wife and children Albert experienced unsullied felicity. When the rude tempest rocked the battlements, seated in dignified repose he related to his offspring the tale of adverse times, and in what manner he overcame "the Banditti of the Forest."

C.

THE CHILD OF SUSPICION,

A ROMANTIC TALE.[1]

CHAP. I.

MORTIMER HALL, the ancient residence of the noble family from whom it received its name, stood on the confines of an extensive forest, in the county of Essex; and although it was no longer the favourite retreat of the family, it had not been suffered to fall into entire decay. Some parts had been occasionally modernized, according to the varying fashion of the times; yet still many apartments retained their original heavy and gloomy appearance; and the mansion being much larger than the family had of late years any occasion for, these Gothic chambers had gradually been deserted, and were even regarded by the ignorant domestics with superstitious apprehensions.

During the absence of its owner, the care of this noble edifice was left to an old man, who had formerly been steward and factotum in the family; but Humphrey had filled that post at a time when stewards were content to take care of their master's property without enriching themselves, or lending a helping hand to their patron's ruin. It was owing to this unambitious disposition, or perhaps to the deficiency of his education, that Humphrey had grown hoary-headed in service, and still thought himself well off, to be allowed a comfortable maintenance at the hall, where he had nothing to do but eat, drink, and sleep; or, when his aged limbs were attacked with rheumatic pains, have them wrapped in warm flannels, by the assiduous Mrs. Winifred Morgan,[2] *ci-devant*[3] house-

---

1 Vol. 11, n.s. (1811): July, 31-38; Aug., 87-93; Sept., 124-130; Nov., 266-272; Vol. 12, n.s. (1812): Jan., 2-14.

2 Referred to variously as "Winifred," "Morgan," and "Mrs. Morgan."

3 *ci-devant*: formerly (*OED*).

keeper, and now, like himself, on the superannuated[1] list. This good old couple would, perhaps, have found it difficult to have supplied their own necessities at times, had they not been assisted by an active little girl, the grand-daughter of Humphrey, then about nine years of age, whose lively prattle was their chief amusement.

One evening, about the latter end of March, as this little party were sitting round the fire, gossipping over tales of times past, and anticipating pleasures to come, when their master would bring home his young and beautiful bride to restore comfort and hilarity to the long neglected mansion, their discourse was suddenly interrupted by a mournful and unusual noise. "Merciful goodness!" exclaimed Winifred, "what can that be?"—"I heard nothing," replied the old man; "but you are always full of these fears and fancies."—"I tell you, Humphrey," replied the piqued dame, "that I heard it plain enough; and if you are deaf, I am not; it was like a groan."—"I heard it too, grandfather," said Jane; "but I dont know what it was like; I think it was the wind."—"Most likely, child, most likely," muttered the old man; "see how the candle flares; aye, aye, it was only the wind, sure enough."

Mrs. Winifred was not very willing to acknowledge herself in the wrong; but as the wind did, indeed, just then rise and increase to such violence, as to make every casement rattle, and almost shake the building to the foundation, she thought it best to let the subject drop. "Well," said she, "I am sure we shall have cause to rejoice when Sir Herbert comes home again; for we have had a dismal moping life of it, these last five years; though, to be certain, he has never suffered us to want any comforts; but still one wishes to see a little of life, and the face of one's fellow-creatures, which one hardly does here, I am sure."—"Ah, Winifred," said Humphrey, shaking his head, "when one considers every thing, one cannot wonder that Sir Herbert dislikes this place; to be sure, it would not become us to say any thing against our betters: Sir Herbert has been a good master to us, and that is all we have to trouble our heads about."—"Why, grandfather," interrupted Jane, putting her hand upon the old man's knee, and looking earnestly in his face, "is not Sir Herbert good to every body?"—"Yes, certainly,

---

1 *superannuated*: Disqualified or incapacitated by age; old and infirm (*OED*).

child," exclaimed Winifred, hastily; "I told you so always, you know I did."—"Aye," replied Jane, "I know you did, Mrs. Morgan; but I thought my grandfather meant, just now, that he was only good to you; and I remember too, that the other day, when you were in that fine long gallery, shewing me the pictures, you stood before one of a beautiful lady in a veil, and you said to grandfather, 'Sir Herbert acted a cruel part by her;' but you did not tell me the lady's name."—"Hush! hush! child," cried Winifred; "for God Almighty's sake never repeat a syllable of that again; I quite forgot what I was saying then; I had no meaning in it; no meaning at all."—"Come here, child," said Humphrey, pulling her rather roughly towards him; "you know I never did beat you in my life, but if ever you say a word about what you then heard, I will punish you so severely, that you shall remember it; aye, and shut you up in the haunted rooms into the bargain." Jane, terrified, fell upon her knees, and humbly promised that she never would hint at it again; and she received a kiss of reconciliation from her grandfather, which effectually restored harmony.

At that moment, however, a groan, louder and nearer than the former one, was distinctly heard by the whole group; terror chained the tongue of every one, and they gazed upon each other in the greatest consternation. It was repeated, and succeeded by a stifled scream, which sounded as if it proceeded from a female. "Heaven defend us?" ejaculated Winifred, "what can all this mean; now I hope you are convinced I was right; but you are always so obstinate, Humphrey."—"I will go out and see, however," said the old man, catching up a lanthorn; "the sound came from the back part of the premises." Winifred started from her seat, and dashed the lanthorn out of his hand: "Why, Humphrey; surely, Humphrey, you would not be so fool-hardy as to go out now; you must be certain it is nothing human, at this time of night," muttered the old lady, retaining the flap of his coat in her terrified grasp. "And I am sure," replied Humphrey, "I should be nothing human, if I did not; I have never done harm to any one, and why should I be afraid? So prithee, dame, let go my coat."—"Nor I neither, for matter of that," repeated Winifred; "but I have no notion of running my head into mischief out of idle curiosity; so, if you will go, I will stay here and say my prayers. Come, Jane, kneel down."—"I would rather go with grandfather," returned the girl, creeping up close to him. "Then I am sure I will not be left alone here," rejoined Winfred, mustering up her small stock of courage, and hobbling after her fellow-servant.

Humphrey proceeded cautiously along, inspecting every corner, without success; and was just turning back to the house, when the mournful noise was again repeated, though less distinctly than before. "Hark!" said the old man, "I am certain that sound came from the shed behind the dairy: nay, now Mrs. Morgan, why do you tremble so; if you are afraid, go back." Winifred, who was as much terrified at the thought of returning alone as of proceeding forward, thought it best to assume the appearance of courage, and therefore continued to follow, still holding by him, and with her apron thrown over her head, that she might not encounter any terrific sight. Nor was the precaution wholly unnecessary; for when Humphrey entered the hovel, and held down his lanthorn, to take a survey of it, a sight most dreadful and alarming presented itself. On the straw scattered floor lay extended, apparently in the agonies of death, a female, of no mean appearance, but in a most miserable plight; by the side of her was a bundle, and in her arms a new-born infant, which she vainly attempted to clasp to her bosom.

Humphrey uttered an exclamation of horror, which almost petrified the terrified Winifred, who, notwithstanding the precaution she had taken, could not help looking round: no sooner did the good woman behold the wretched object before her, than every sensation of fear gave way to the impulse of humanity, and snatching the almost lifeless infant from its expiring mother's feeble arms, she wrapped it carefully up in her apron, and hurried back to the house; where, seating herself before the fire, she chafed its little limbs, poured a tea-spoonful of cordial down its throat, and then busied herself in hushing it to sleep. Humphrey, meanwhile, was not less assiduous to the mother; and, giving the lanthorn to Jane, he raised the poor creature in his arms, and bringing her in as gently as possible, laid her upon his own bed. Winifred then resigned her tender charge to Jane, with strict injunction to keep it warm, and not handle it roughly; and directed all her cares to the fair sufferer; who, after proper restoratives had been administered, recovered sufficiently to express her gratitude; and although her dress was of the most homely kind, her language was that of a person who had been accustomed to better days. Unfortunately, however, all their benevolent attentions were unavailing, for, towards morning, the exhausted sufferer fell into successive shivering fits, and expired, without being able to make her real name or circumstances known. Winifred, who had no idea of her immediate danger, had not tormented her with impertinent questions; and the unfortunate object of her compassion was too weak and agitated to enter upon any explanation.

Humphrey and Winifred were unspeakably shocked, by an event which placed them in a most awkward predicament. The nearest village was three miles distant; yet, as soon as day dawned, Humphrey saddled his old mare, and prepared to set off, in order to consult with some of his acquaintance as to the manner in which he ought to act, and also to try if he could learn any particulars concerning the deceased. Just as he put his foot in the stirrup, he recollected the bundle he had seen in the shed, and which had till then slipped his memory, and he judged it best to examine the contents, before he proceeded any further. He accordingly returned to the shed, and having secured the important bundle, brought it to Winifred, that together they might examine the contents. This, unfortunately, afforded them but little satisfaction; it contained a few changes of baby-linen, neat and plain; a green silk purse, with a few pieces of silver coin in it; a miniature, set in gold; and a pearl necklace, wrapped in the cover of a letter, directed to Mrs. Ebrington, but without any address. The portrait represented a young and handsome man, in a naval uniform, whom Winifred naturally conjectured to be the father of the child; but whether its parents had been married or not, was a matter of doubt.

Humphrey accordingly commenced his journey, and, as soon as he reached the village, made diligent enquiries of all he knew concerning the unfortunate traveller; but could only learn that a female, answwering the description he gave, had passed that way at seven o'clock on the preceding evening, and the person who saw her asserted that she had a bundle hanging upon her arm, the weight of which seemed almost to overpower her. "I pitied the poor soul," added the man, "for she was not in a situation to be tramping about; I asked her to take share of a pint of ale, but she did not seem to like the proposal; so I let her trudge on her way."

This communicative friend was a carpenter and undertaker in the village, and no sooner learned the embarrassing dilemma in which old Humphrey was placed, than, having an eye to his own profit, he very sagaciously advised him to make no more noise about the affair, observing, "that there were many evil-minded persons who might take it into their heads to occasion him much trouble; besides," he added, "it is a great way to B——, where you would be obliged to go, to lay the affair before a magistrate; and perhaps Sir Herbert, when he comes to hear of it, may not be best pleased at your making yourself so busy. Now, my advice is this: the burial of the woman shall not come to much; let it be done decently and quietly; give out that she was a relation of yours, and nobody will trouble their heads about it. Who knows, but she may be come of some good family?"—"Who knows, indeed!" returned Humphrey, musing; "and if that is the case, it would be a thousand pities to throw her poor remains upon the parish: but then the child!"—"Oh! it is ten to one if that lives many days," replied the undertaker; "and then, you know, there will be an end of the business."—"Well, well," said the old man; "you may as well go back with me, and we will consult Dame Morgan about it."

This being accordingly agreed upon, the cronies jogged onward to the mansion-house, with all the expedition they were capable of. They found Winifred still occupied with her innocent charge; who, now properly dressed and fed, nestled close to her bosom, and was in a sweet sleep. "See, grandfather," cried Jane, as Humphrey entered, "what a pretty little boy it is; its eyes are as black as beads."—"It is, in good truth, a beautiful babe; but, lack-a-daisy, what shall I do with it?"—"Nurse it, my good Mistress Morgan," said the loquacious carpenter: "Egad! any body would take you for a young woman, to see how cleverly you handle it: I am sure you are too tender-hearted to send such a precious cherub to the parish."—"Sweet lamb!" exclaimed the tender-hearted Winifred, "I should be sorry to do that, sure enough; but you must know, Mr. Chipwood, that Sir Herbert is going to be married, and intends to bring his lady down here, and then, if that should be the case, what a pretty hobble I should be in."—"Why," returned the carpenter,

a little disconcerted, "that would be awkwardish, to be sure; however, if you are disposed to be compassionate to the sweet baby, and
the worst comes to the worst, I dare say my wife would have no
objection to take charge of it, for the matter of a trifle a week."—
"At all events, then," said Winifred, "I will try what I can do; the
poor innocent shall not be turned upon the parish if I can help it;
for I can shrewdly guess it ought to be better off in the world."

This being arranged to their mutual satisfaction, Master Chipwood returned to his home, not a little pleased with the thought of
having secured a job; and that if any good should result hereafter,
he had a hand in it, and should be entitled to a share of the reward.

(*To be continued.*)

(Continued from page 38.)

CHAP. II.

ALL was soon in a state of bustle and confusion at Mortimer
Hall, a courier arrived, with intelligence that Sir Herbert and his
lady were upon the road, and would reach the hall by sun-set; and
the necessity for immediate preparation was so pressing that the
sleeping infant was scarcely thought of. The notice was so short,
that the beds were unaired, the poultry not killed, the milk not
skimmed, and poor Winifred had her hands so full of business that
she scarcely knew which way to turn. At length, however, owing
to the most assiduous and unremitting exertions, every thing was
in proper order, and the bell at the great gate rung just as Humphrey finished brushing his best snuff-coloured coat, in which
he designed to receive the noble owners of the mansion. The
remains of the unfortunate woman had, on the preceding day, been
decently interred in the village church-yard, therefore all anxiety
on that score was over; but, just as Winifred was running to her
drawers to look out her last new cap, the loud crying of the boy, just
awaking, filled her with terror indescribable. "What, in the name
of mercy, shall I do now," she muttered to herself; "my lady will

certainly hear the little squalling urchin, and I shall be turned out of doors, perhaps, for my humanity: well, well, this is a pretty piece of business."

At this moment she heard the voice of Sir Herbert, enquiring for her, as he ascended the stairs; luckily, the infant ceased crying, and, consigning it to the ready Jane, the trembling old woman made her appearance. "How are you, Mrs. Morgan?" asked the baronet, taking her hand with much cordiality, "you see I have kept my word, and brought you home a mistress: there, pay your respects to Lady Mortimer, and let her see what accommodations you have got for her." Winifred turned to make a profound reverence to her new lady, but started with unconcealed surprise and disappointment, when she perceived a little square mean looking figure, obviously deformed, and whose squinting grey eyes glanced malignantly upon the agitated old woman. Sir Herbert turned aside to conceal a smile; and, placing his hand on the shoulder of Humphrey, he strove to conceal his untimely risibility, by pointing out a grotesque figure wrought on the tapestry. "Well, Mrs. Morgan," said Lady Mortimer, "when you will have recovered the use of your faculties I hope you will take the trouble to show me to my chamber; I really am not accustomed to be stared at in such an unaccountable way; and but that my servants would, I fear, lose themselves in the intricacies of this barbarous old-fashioned place, I should not submit to be conducted by such an ill-mannered old woman."

Winifred, rather nettled by this ungracious speech, replied, somewhat sharply, "Marry, come up; but, perhaps, I may understand manners as well as my betters, saving your ladyship's presence; and barbarous as this place may seem to your ladyship, there have been generation after generation of my honoured master's family who lived and died in it; aye, and I wish some of them were alive now."—"Nay, my good Winifred," said Sir Herbert, mildly, and thinking it was time to check her volubility, "Lady Mortimer did not mean to cast any reflections upon you in our ancient venerable habitation; and although you did stare at her rather unpolitely, she has too much good sense to be offended at your want of knowledge of the rules of polite society; besides, she is fatigued and hungry, and all that, you know, does not improve the temper."— Nor the looks neither, thought Winifred, if one may judge by this specimen. "I beg your ladyship's pardon," said she, aloud, "if I have given offence, I did not intend it."—"It is no matter," returned Lady Mortimer, waving her hand with an air of consequence, "show me to my chamber, good woman, that is all I require; and let the butler send me up some chicken patties."—"I am very sorry, my lady, but really I do not know how to make any such thing; you shall have a nice boiled chick in a short time."—"Well, well; go along; I suppose I shall be starved to death in this place."

Winifred was too much vexed to reply, but, shutting the door with precipitation, found her chagrin increased by having demolished one end of her best apron, in the warmth of her resentment. At the bottom of the staircase she met Humphrey. "Well," said he, in a whisper, "are the little lady and you better friends yet?"—"Friends, indeed," returned Winifred, with tears in her eyes, "I wish she had never come to this place; here were we hugging ourselves with the idea of Sir Herbert bringing home a young and beautiful bride; that there would be dancing on the lawn, and such revelry: instead of which, lo and behold, here comes an ugly crooked creature, as ill-tempered as old scratch. Well, for my part, I think our master was bewitched to marry her."—"Ah!" replied Humphrey, shaking his head, "money does every thing now a days."—"Money! what could Sir Herbert want of money; has he not got this beautiful estate, and plenty more?"—"You know nothing about it, but I suspect it is as I say; why, do you think Sir Herbert would have had all them beautiful timber trees cut down, if he had not wanted money?"

Humphrey had indeed guessed the truth. Sir Herbert had succeeded to his father's title and estates at too early an age to know what was due to the former, or how to preserve the latter; the consequence was, as usual, mortgage upon mortgage, until all resources failing, a wealthy wife seemed the last and only means of avoiding an inglorious emigration. Miss Lupino, the daughter of a wealthy stock-jobber,[1] had frequently been in parties where he visited, and had distinguished him by the most flattering regard; the pill was not palatable, but it was thickly gilt, and Sir Herbert

---

1 *stock-jobber:* A member of the Stock Exchange who deals in stocks on his own account (*OED*).

determined to swallow it. No sooner, however, was the honey-
moon passed, than the baronet, not choosing to become the butt
of his friends, by exhibiting his fair companion on the box of his
barouche,[1] or run the risk of being annoyed by the visits of her
city connections, he, under the plea of urgent business with his
steward, and a wish to give her pleasure, hurried the lady down to
Mortimer Hall, where, in solitude and deep surrounding shades,
he determined she should remain unseen. Of this determination
he, nevertheless, deemed it most prudent not to give her too early
information, but to leave the disclosure of his intentions to time
and chance; and it was with some vexation he witnessed the inaus-
picious aspect of her first introduction. He accordingly took the
first opportunity of summoning Humphrey and Morgan into his
presence, and, after very condescendingly conversing with them
upon various uninteresting topics, he assumed a more serious air,
and addressed them to the following effect:—"I am unspeakably
sorry, my good friends, to perceive that you have given way to an
unjust prejudice against Lady Mortimer; a prejudice which her
want of personal attraction has most probably given birth to; now
I wish you, as sensible well-disposed persons, to get the better of
such weakness; first, because it is frequently founded upon error;
and, secondly, because it is probable that Lady Mortimer will make
the hall her constant residence; and I should be sorry to compel
such aged domestics, who have served me faithfully, to seek
another asylum, which must inevitably be the case should either
of you seriously disoblige her ladyship, upon whose side I will
promise there shall be no offence given." Humphrey and Winifred
gazed at each other in mute consternation; it was an arrangement
equally unexpected and unwished for, yet neither dared to express
disapprobation. "We will do our best to make things agreeable to
her ladyship," said Humphrey. "*I never affront nobody that doesn't
put upon me,*" murmured Winifred; and Sir Herbert, unwilling to
push the subject farther, expressed his satisfaction. Winifred now
deemed this a proper opportunity to reveal a secret which could
not long be concealed; she therefore bluntly told the whole story

---

1 *barouche*: A four-wheeled carriage with a half-head behind which can be raised
or let down at pleasure, having a seat in front for the driver, and seats inside for two
couples to sit facing each other (*OED*).

of the hapless wanderer and the little orphan, adding, "and now, sir, I hope you will not be displeased at the part I took in it; and I have told you the whole truth, that you might not suspect any thing worse." Sir Herbert smiled. "You are perfectly right, Winifred, to be careful of your reputation; if you can find time to attend to the little bantling I have not the smallest objection, that is, provided it meets with Lady Mortimer's approbation, to its remaining under your care." Of this Winifred almost despaired, but departed highly pleased with the affability and good-humour of the baronet.

At night, when the household had retired to rest, Winifred, whose little charge happened to be more than usually wakeful, heard the voices of Sir Herbert and his lady in high contention; nor did the loud dispute cease for several hours. In the morning Lady Mortimer appeared with swoln eyes, her accent was no longer haughty, her manner no longer domineering; while Sir Herbert was as unconcerned and carelessly polite as before. "Mrs. Morgan," said Lady Mortimer, when Winifred appeared to know what she would choose for dinner, "I understand you have got a young child in the house; I should like to see it." Morgan, highly pleased at this intimation, eagerly hurried after Jane, who soon brought the child into her ladyship's presence. "It is a very pretty child," observed Lady Mortimer, slightly surveying it; "there is a portrait too, I have heard." Winifred immediately took it from her pocket. Lady Mortimer surveyed it attentively: "Has Sir Herbert seen this?"—"No, my lady; he did not think to ask for it, though I mentioned it to him."—"You may leave it with me," said Lady Mortimer, carelessly tossing it into her trinket box, "and I have no objection to the child being kept at the hall, provided you do not let me be disturbed by his noise; for as my health is not very good, Sir Herbert thinks it will be of service to me to remain here some time longer. I do not much admire the place, I own; but perhaps I shall get reconciled to it in time." Morgan had too good a heart to bear resentment beyond the moment, and conceiving that her master was not, in reality, so complaisant a husband as he wished to appear, began to suffer pity to take the place of indignation. "Why, to be sure, my lady, this is rather a dullish place, in the winter most especially; but then, to gentlefolks like your ladyship, who can read, and all that, time cannot hang so heavy upon hand."—"Have we no neighbours at all?" enquired Lady Mortimer. "Who lives in that Gothic building which I see from my window?"—"That, my lady, is Kenersly Abbey,[1] it is a curious old building, and belongs to the Lutterel family.[2] Lord Lutterel died a short time ago, and as there is no rightful heir to be found, affairs seem in jeopard like."—"Who occupies the abbey at present?" enquired Lady Mortimer, with apparent earnestness. "His lordship's brother is just come down," replied Winifred; "he has assumed the title, and taken possession of the estate; but nobody likes him, and so every one wishes that the real heir, the late lord's son, could be found."—"Lord Lutterel then had a son, who is missing?" observed Lady Mortimer. "Aye, that he had," rejoined Winifred, sighing, "and a noble youth he was; I can remember, some twenty years ago, how every body doated upon him."—"By *every body*, I suppose you mean yourself and the servants at the abbey?" observed Lady Mortimer, with a sneer. "Why no, my lady, that was not exactly what I meant; but the servants did indeed doat upon Mr. Osborne, for he was the very moral of perfection; he never gave himself airs, or treated his dependents as if they were not made of the same flesh and blood. But it was not only the servants who loved him, there was one—but that is no matter, I shall say nothing about that."—"I should like very much to hear some more on this subject," said Lady Mortimer; "you will oblige me, Mrs. Morgan, by telling me what you know; I love to hear family anecdotes."—"Indeed, my lady," said Winifred, after a pause, "I am but a poor hand at remembering such things; I know there was some talk of a love affair, but the friends on both sides objected, and so it was broke off, and then the young man went abroad, and I fancy has not since been heard of, but he is supposed to be dead; he may not be though, for all that." Morgan being either unable or unwilling to give any further information, Lady Mortimer soon dismissed her.

On the following day Sir Herbert quitted the hall, and poor Winifred found, to her great mortification, that the old walls were not then to be enlivened with feasting or revelry. For some time

---

1 Possibly refers to Kinnersley Abbey in Shropshire. Variously spelled here "Kenersly," "Kennersly."
2 Possibly refers to the Anglo-Irish Luttrell family. Variously spelled here "Lutterel," "Luterell."

after the departure of Sir Herbert, Lady Mortimer shut herself up in sullen humour, and only let the inhabitants of the hall know that she was their lady by finding fault with every thing sent to, or done for her. At last the morose fit wore off, and she condescended to be particularly pleased with Jane, to whom she made several handsome presents, and often engaged her to stroll about the pleasure grounds with her. Children are easily attracted by the least appearance of good-nature, and the nursing of little Walter was soon considered by her less agreeable than rambling about with a fine lady, who gave her so many pretty frocks and sashes. Walter, it is true, fared the worse; but he was a chearful healthy child, and would roll about on a blanket for hours together, without being clamorous; and his well-formed robust limbs gave promise of increasing vigour and activity.

(To be continued.)

(Continued from page 93.)

CHAP. III.

Such was the position of affairs at the time of the orphan Walter's first appearance at the hall. We must now consider him a youth of fifteen, enjoying the favour and patronage of Sir Herbert, who, having no children of his own, declared it his intention to leave the principal part of his fortune to the young Walter, provided he continued worthy of his countenance. The good old Winifred had been long since numbered with the dead, and Humphrey, though still living, was reduced by old age to a state of second childhood.

Walter, though elevated into consequence by the notice of Sir Herbert, was not ungrateful to, nor unmindful of his former benefactor, but frequently passed whole hours by the side of old Humphrey, amusing him with lively converse, or administering to his wants with the assiduity of a tender nurse. Lady Mortimer alone beheld the young man with an evil eye; for, although she had in one instance suffered vanity to overpower her avarice in bestowing her hand upon a man who was only attracted by her wealth, she looked forward with hope to the period of her emancipation from these hastily imposed trammels, and was unwilling that an obscure orphan should derive advantage from her folly, or the caprice of her husband.

Jane was her constant companion and confidant: the latter, it is true, did not hate Walter, but she was a sufficient adept in the art of dissembling not to let her lady know that Walter's indifference to all her blandishments drew forth many a secret sigh. Sir Herbert, although he did not choose to carry his lady to the metropolis, denied her not the pleasures attainable at the hall; and an intimacy had for some time been established between his family and that of Lord Lutterell, at Kennersley Abbey. Here Walter spent many happy hours, for Lady Monimia, Lord Lutterell's daughter, was the companion of his walks, his rides, and his sports; Monimia had smiles for his joys, and tears for his mortifications; for Lady Mortimer's malice frequently found opportunities of venting itself, even upon the defenceless head of childhood. Walter had too noble a disposition to harbour resentment against any one, but the keen agony of a wounded spirit occasioned him many hours of unknown sufferings, and, as he grew older, he felt, that although he could forgive the persecutions of Lady Mortimer he could never look up to her with esteem or respect.

One day the baronet received an invitation to accompany Lord Lutterell and his daughter in chase of a wild boar, a sport in which Lord Lutterell took great delight. Walter with pleasure found himself included, and at the appointed hour the party sallied forth. Lord Lutterell, eager and impetuous, led the way, regardless of danger, and Monimia knew of his violence of temper too well to betray the least sign of timidity, although he sometimes chose such rugged and precipitous paths as occasioned her momentary alarm. Fatigue at length obliged her to slacken her pace, and Walter would willingly have remained by her side, had not Lord Lutterell and Sir Herbert shouted to him to come forward, as the object of their pursuit was entangled in the thickets, where they meant to surround him. Walter rode forward reluctantly; the attendants eager to witness the sport, rushed unthinkingly forward, leaving the lady Monimia wholly unprotected. She rode slowly on, unthinking of danger, when the loud shouts of triumph, proceeding from her father and his followers, startled her horse, and made him dart forward with alarming velocity for a considerable time. She kept her seat, but at length growing giddy through the rapidity of the animal's pace, she must inevitably have fallen, had not a stranger rushed across the path and snatched the bridle with one hand, while with the other he rendered her such assistance as checked the violence of her descent to the ground. A slight sprain was all the hurt she received, but it was sufficiently severe to prevent her walking; and her horse, having broke the bridle, was already out of sight.

Agitated and distressed, Monimia knew not how to proceed. She explained the cause of the accident to the stranger, and entreated him to find her friends. "With pleasure, madam, would I do so," he replied, "but I cannot leave you here; permit me to escort you to my residence, which is very near, and I will immediately return to seek your party." As delay would be attended with still further inconvenience and danger, Monimia thought it best to comply; but her ancle was so painful that every effort to touch the ground occasioned her extreme anguish, and she again entreated the stranger to let her remain while he sought her friends. "It is impossible," said he, "you know not the perils to which you would be exposed; night is drawing on, and the marauders who infest these forests may be already upon the prowl. Hard by is a hermitage, permit me to bear you thither, there you may be safe for the short time that I will leave you." He then gently raised her and bore her in his arms to a rude recess, hewn in the side of a craggy cliff. An aged man stood at the entrance, he saluted the stranger respectfully and invited him to enter. "Father, I entreat your care of this lady," said the stranger; "I will return quickly."—"What protection these feeble arms can afford," replied the hermit, benignly pressing her hand, "she may command." The stranger then quitted the hermitage, leaving Monimia reclined upon the moss covered couch of the hermit. "Know you that stranger?" asked Monimia. "He is no stranger to me," replied the hermit, "he is called the Count Moresco, a foreigner, but a person of rank and fortune, with a brave heart and generous spirit, lady; aye, and he is reckoned handsome too."—"I have scarcely looked at him," returned Monimia, smiling, "but I think he is not very young." At that moment they heard the trampling of horses and the sound of voices not far distant. "They are found! they are found!" exclaimed Monimia, triumphantly, and the next instant she found herself in her father's arms. Walter alone looked less rejoiced at the meeting than the rest, his eyes glanced on Count Moresco with a look of suspicion and dislike; for, in a moment, the fire of jealousy was kindled, and he feared that the service which the count had rendered Monimia, a service which in the warmth of her gratitude she incessantly dwelt upon, would render him too attractive in her sight. "I did not know I had such a neighbour," observed Lord Lutterell, bowing to the count, "or I trust we should have been better acquainted by this time; pray how far distant is your residence from the Abbey?" "I think it may be twelve miles," replied the count; "the chace has drawn you further than you imagined; I hope, however, it will not be your last visit: I mix little with the gay world, but should be happy to class Lord Lutterell and Sir Herbert Mortimer among my small circle of friends. Your son, I presume, sir?" he continued, offering his hand to Walter, who rather hesitatingly presented his own. "By adoption," returned the baronet. "Enough; I shall be proud of his acquaintance; and now if you will not accompany me to the castle, permit me at least to set you in the right road, lest you should bewilder yourself in the intricacies of this extensive forest."

This was a courtesy not to be rejected; the count accompanied them several miles, and they then separated. It being rather late Sir Herbert and Walter immediately returned to the hall, where the baronet repeated the events of the day to his lady, extolling the graceful manners of the Count Moresco, and chiding Walter for the coolness with which he received his overtures of friendship. "I thought them rather premature, sir," said Walter, colouring, "those who are so hasty in their professions of friendship, where nothing has occurred to authorize it, have commonly some sinister design."—"You are not very philanthropic in your notions, I think, Walter," observed Sir Herbert. "And, pray, young man," asked Lady Mortimer, sarcastically, "what designs could a man like the Count Moresco have upon a poor dependant boy?"—"I did not suspect him of designs upon me, madam,"—"Upon whom, then?" Walter dared not reveal his thoughts, he was confused and agitated. "Upon whom, pray?" repeated Lady Mortimer, fixing her sharp

eyes upon him, spitefully. "Upon Sir Herbert perhaps, or Lord Lutterell."—"Indeed, and so you very politely tell your benefactor to
his face that he has not so much judgment nor penetration as a boy
of fifteen."—"Good heaven! madam, I meant no such thing."—"It
would be hard to tell your meaning, I believe," said Lady Mortimer,
shaking her head, "but I think I am not mistaken in pronouncing
you a hypocrite." The bosom of Walter swelled with indignation,
he looked scornfully at Lady Mortimer, then raising his fine eyes,
suffused with tears, to Sir Herbert, he asked him if he thought he
had ever merited such treatment. "I do not, indeed, Walter," said
Sir Herbert, "but I wish you to be less arrogant in forming opinions; a modest deference to the judgment of others would best suit
your years; I am sorry to find that Lady Mortimer and you cannot
keep upon good terms, but I shall not interfere in your disputes,
although, I think, I could set this matter in its right light. I warrant
now you would be ready enough to do justice to the merits of the
Count Moresco, were you not fearful that the fair Monimia might
be already inclined to rate them too highly."—"Why surely, Sir Herbert," observed Lady Mortimer, "Walter cannot hope to have any
interest in that quarter, Lady Monimia is too nobly born, too highly
sensible of her duty to stoop to an orphan boy, the child of indigence, of suspicion."—"Hush, madam," said Sir Herbert, angrily,
"if humanity has no place in your bosom, respect my authority at
least, and recollect my repeated commands, that such language
may be refrained from. Walter owes nothing to your favour, and
shall lose nothing by your hate." He then abruptly caught Walter's
arm, and casting an angry glance at his wife, quitted the room.
When they departed, Lady Mortimer sought her confidant Jane
and while every angry passion predominated, imprudently made
disclosures which prudence would have bade her conceal. "Would
you believe it, Jane?" said she, "the boy is actually in love with Lady
Monimia."—"I guessed as much, madam," returned Jane, with a
stifled sigh, "he is never so happy as when Sir Herbert takes him to
the Abbey; to be sure it is nothing but pride makes him look so far
above himself, for Lady Monimia is not so very beautiful, I think;
what is your opinion, my lady?"—"The girl is well enough, but that
is nothing to the purpose."—"True, my lady, and Walter may find
girls as handsome without going so far. Her skin is so white and

insipid-like, and her blue eyes (I never thought blue eyes pretty) and then she is as slender as a rush, and a mere child after all, only just sixteen." While Jane was thus describing Monimia, she was taking an accurate survey of her own person, which was certainly far from ordinary, and the very reverse of Monimia's. Lady Mortimer was too much absorbed by her own thoughts to notice very particularly either what Jane did or said, and when she had concluded her long harangue, muttered, "I should not wonder if it was the same man." "Who do you mean, my lady."—"The Count Moresco," replied Lady Mortimer, "I knew a gentleman abroad, who exactly answers the description; I hope I am not mistaken."—"But do you think, my lady, that Lord Lutterell would ever consent to their marriage?"—"I have no fear of that, if Moresco perseveres."—"Moresco," repeated Jane, "I was speaking of Walter."—"I will take good care of that," returned Lady Mortimer, "the secret is in careful hands."—"What secret, my lady?"—"Oh nothing, nothing, child, do not be curious, you know I often tell you things when you ask no questions. So now go about your business, child, and be sure to let me know what-ever passes between Sir Herbert and Walter in your hearing." Jane promised to watch them closely, for it was an office to which her own feelings prompted her; and it was not long before she brought word that a grand entertainment was preparing at the Abbey, where the Count Moresco was expected, and Sir Herbert's family were also invited. Lady Mortimer, anxious to be one of the party, knew that the only method to obtain the desired favour, was to conciliate him by appearing more kind to Walter, she accordingly affected the utmost good humour, frequently pretended to lament the uncontroulable petulence of her temper; and Walter, who was ever the first to pardon a personal injury, returned her advances to a reconciliation so amicably, that harmony was completely restored, and Sir Herbert, in token of his approbation intimated his inten-tion of taking her with him to the Abbey. This point gained, Lady Mortimer triumphed in secret, her face was dressed in smiles of complaisance; but malice and revenge lurked in her heart.

(To be continued.)

(Continued from page 130.)

CHAP. IV.

Observe her mien
Majestic, gentle, and her smile serene;
Her airy step, as lightning from the sky,
The rays cerulean of her humid eye,
In sunny clusters round her forehead bare,
Devolves the light luxuriance of her hair.

Barrett's Woman.[1]

THE most splendid preparations were made at the abbey for Lord Luterell, who had perceived that Moresco was struck with the charms of his daughter; and upon that account he was desirous of making an appearance which, by impressing his guests with an idea of his affluence and liberality, might induce the count to make early proposals. His lordship, it is true, had a suspicion that Monimia had suffered her heart to be ensnared by the youthful Walter. But although he saw nothing to disapprove in the young man, it was not his intention to let Monimia bestow her hand upon a dependent, and portionless orphan; one too, whose birth was suspicious, and who might be the child of dishonour. On the morning of the important day, Lord Lutterell took his daughter into his own apartment, and opening a casket which she had never before seen, presented her with a superb set of jewels. "Take these, Monimia," said he, "and wear them to-day; it is now time for you to relinquish the childish simplicity of dress in which you have hitherto appeared, and let me see with how much taste you can adorn yourself; I wish upon this occasion to behold your natural attractions; heightened by the aid of dress." Monimia smiled. "As your present, my dear father," said she, "these costly ornaments are certainly acceptable, but I am sure your poor daughter will have no cause for exultation in wearing them."—"Why so, Monimia?"—"Because," she replied, hesitating, "I am sure those who will see me to-day prefer my usual

1 From *Woman: A Poem* (1810) by Eaton Stannard Barrett.

mode of dress; and such an appearance of magnificence and osten-
tation will inspire more awe than admiration."—"You are right in
that conjecture, perhaps," returned Lord Lutterell, "and it is as I
would have it. Those whose rank in life does not place them upon
an equality with my daughter, should have their familiar advances
checked by an appearance which must remind them of her superiority. In fact, Monimia, I will speak plainly to you; the partiality
of Sir Herbert for his adopted son, has made me suffer an intimacy
to subsist, from which I augur no good; I therefore wish you to be
more reserved in your conduct towards him, and without giving
offence to Sir Herbert, let them see you are not inclined to encourage any presumptuous hopes." At these words Monimia bent
her conscious eyes to the ground; they were filled with tears, but
her father affected not to observe, or at least not to penetrate the
cause of her emotion. He took her hand tenderly, saying, "I am not
attempting to cast any blame on you, my child, your conduct is irre-
proachable. Go then, attire yourself to my wish, and be assured a
most splendid conquest awaits you." Monimia pressed her father's
hand, but dared not trust her lips to make any reply. In her chamber
she pondered on his words, and found them such as she could not
reconcile in any way to the scheme of happiness which her sanguine imagination had formed. It was evident that he wished her
to renounce Walter, but he little knew how great an effort it would
require to obey him. Still obedience was what Monimia had ever
practised towards her only remaining parent; and no consideration
of earthly happiness could induce her to act contrary to his commands, which she considered as little less sacred than those of her
heavenly father.

Monimia was unversed in the modern theory of self-will and
perverseness. Her education had been superintended by a pious
ecclesiastic, who had carefully instilled maxims suitable to the
habits of the times; and under the influence of these, Monimia
would have considered any wilful act of disobedience as the surest
means of drawing down the divine wrath upon her head. Still,
however, she reckoned much upon the indulgence she had ever
experienced from Lord Lutterell, and was too little versed in the
ways of the world to suppose that an affectionate parent would
be so far deaf to the voice of nature as to sacrifice the felicity of a

dutiful child to interest and ambition. Consoled by this hope, the
artless girl prepared to give the first proof of her desire to please
her father, by arraying herself in a manner which she conceived
instead of heightening her charms would totally eclipse her few
personal attractions; and as she stood before her mirror arranging the jewels which her father had presented her, she frequently
sighed, and exclaimed, "How gaudy! how unbecoming! I am sure
Walter would admire me ten times more in my new camblet,[1]
trimmed with point,[2] and my hair in its natural form; but my father,
ah! he will be delighted with these magnificent trappings, and if he
is gratified I shall be happy."

Thus soliloquizing, she finished the business of the toilet, and
when ready to receive her guests, descended with a palpitating
heart. Her appearance was indeed such as delighted her father, who
gazed on her with unconcealed rapture. Her dress was white satin,
closely fitting her finely turned shape, and falling in graceful folds,
with a train of considerable length, richly embroidered with green
and gold laurel leaves; large emerald studs secured the sleeves and
bosom, and a pointed girdle of gold net-work upon crimson velvet,
with rich tassels, confined her slender waist. From her left shoulder depended a crimson velvet mantle, fastened with a cluster of
diamonds, and looped up under the right arm with a similar ornament, descending again to her feet, and richly fringed with gold;
her luxuriant tresses were confined by strings of diamonds, and
secured on the top of her head with a bodkin[3] of various coloured
gems. Nothing could be more magnificent than her appearance;
yet Walter, while he looked the admiration which he felt, thought
she moved with less grace than usual, and seemed more oppressed
than improved by such stately trappings. Moresco was lavish of
compliments, and every one seemed emulous[4] of paying homage

---

1 *camblet*: A name originally applied to some beautiful and costly eastern fabric,
afterwards to imitations and substitutes the nature of which has changed many
times over (*OED*).

2 *point*: Denoting lace named after the (actual, supposed, or original) place of
manufacture (*OED*).

3 *bodkin*: A long pin or pin-shaped ornament used by women to fasten up the hair
(*OED*).

4 *emulous*: Desirous of rivalling, imitating, obtaining (*OED*).

to her beauty. Lady Mortimer, whose insignificant deformed figure served merely as a foil, could not suppress her mortification. Walter observed it; but instead of triumphing over an humbled enemy, he strove by the most polite attention to soothe her ruffled temper. Of him, however, she thought but little. Moresco was the object who engaged all her notice; and he was so entirely engrossed by the lovely hostess that he had not even recognized in Lady Mortimer his quondam[1] acquintance on the continent; perhaps it was not his wish to recollect that which could bring with it no pleasureable sensations. Such at least was the inference which she drew from his behavior; but she was determined that his forgetfulness, whether real or pretended, should not be of long duration; and accordingly when, after dinner, she found an opportunity of speaking to him, as the party strolled through the pleasure-grounds, reminded him of her claim upon his recollection. Moresco coloured, and affected the greatest surprise; but, with a significant glance, she replied, "Nay, count, you have no occasion to use duplicity towards me, particular circumstances render it necessary for me to say, that I am disposed to be more your friend than you have any right to expect. I can penetrate your views and wishes, and it is in my power to serve you; for once be assured you have nothing to dread from a woman's tongue." Moresco, encouraged by this address, instantly threw off the reserve in which he had before wrapped himself, and in the course of the evening contrived to speak a few words privately, in which he solicited an interview, which Lady Mortimer readily granted. Having thus in part affected her purpose, Lady Mortimer assumed an air of perfect good humour, and the evening passed in social harmony. An invitation was given by Sir Herbert to the whole party, and they parted, highly pleased with each other. Monimia alone retired to her chamber, with a heavy heart. The adulation of the count, instead of affording any gratification to her vanity, filled her with dismay; she began to suspect that her father's expectations were well grounded, and had once in the evening detected them in earnest and animated conversation, of which, by their looks and gestures, she had reason to conjecture she was herself the subject. Filled with this conviction she passed a sleepless night; nor were

1 Former.

her apprehensions without foundation. Moresco had endeavoured to obtain the consent of Lord Lutterell to address his daughter, and had received sufficient encouragement to feel highly elated with his brilliant prospects.

The fact was, that Moresco, however splendid his appearance, possessed no substantial wealth, but owed his subsistence to means which if revealed would have effectually checked his presumptuous hopes of obtaining the hand of the Lady Monimia. The consciousness that Lady Mortimer was acquainted with these resources filled him with alarm; and he no sooner found that she was inclined to befriend him and observe silence on the subject than he determined to court her favour, and leave no means untried to secure her in his interest. By the aid of the obsequious Jane, he was readily admitted to a private conference with her lady. What passed at that interview cannot be at present revealed; suffice it, she found an opportunity of putting her malicious schemes in practice, and Moresco took, as he thought, an effectual method of securing the uninterrupted possession of the desired object, by coinciding with his artful confederate. While affairs were in this state, the day fixed for Sir Herbert's promised fete arrived. Lady Mortimer, anxious to rival Monimia in magnificence, though she could not hope to equal her in elegance, spared no expence in the decoration of her person or apartments. Every luxury that could be procured, was purchased for the occasion; and the arrival of an aged minstrel at the gate, afforded her a triumph, as it would enable her to contribute to the entertainment of her guests by the exercise of his skill and taste in a science of which she was wholly unversed, and which, upon trial, she found infinitely superior to the highly-extolled talents of Monimia. It was with this view rather, than any benevolence of heart, that the aged musician was admitted into Mortimer Hall, and regaled to his heart's content, for several days previous to that of the festival. The poor old man, though blind and infirm, oft time tuned his harp to a merry strain, and drew forth such tones as charmed the enthusiastic Walter, who would sit by his side for hours together, listening to his poetical descriptions of battles, or the more touching effusions of recollected love. From the loquacious Jane, the minstrel had obtained many family anecdotes, which his prompt genius knew how to turn to account, and he seldom failed to adapt his lay to the feelings and circumstances of those whose attention he wished to excite. An unlooked-for event too soon disturbed the harmony which had lately prevailed at Mortimer Hall. Walter, who frequently indulged himself in solitary strolls, one evening failed to return at his accustomed hour. Sir Herbert, at first imagining that he had been detained at the abbey, suffered several hours to elapse without testifying any uneasiness; but when the time of retiring to rest drew nigh, without bringing Walter home, he dispatched a servant in search of him. The man however returned with intelligence that he had not been seen by any of Lord Lutterell's family; and the baronet, heedless of his lady's remonstrances determined on setting out himself, in hopes of being more successful. Sir Herbert returned from his fruitless expedition fatigued and dispirited. No tidings of Walter were to be obtained, and he found it impossible to think of festivity while he remained in such a state of suspence and inquietude; an apology was accordingly sent to the invited guests; and Lady Mortimer endeavouring to conceal her chagrin at the disappointment, by affecting concern and sympathy, shut herself up in her apartment. Left thus to himself, the baronet found no solace but in the soothing strains of the minstrel, who had found the means of interesting his feelings, and calming the perturbations of his troubled mind, not only by the melody of his notes, but by conversation; which had ever for its subject the praises of a youth so deservedly beloved. "You appear to have known better days old man," said the baronet, addressing his venerable companion; "your language is not that of a needy itinerant, your story would amuse me if I could prevail upon you to relate it." The minstrel sighed. "I have indeed known better days, Sir Herbert, but my present sufferings are but a just retribution for the miseries I have occasioned others; and when I acknowledge this, I think you will not be desirous of hearing a story, which can afford you little room for praise or pity."—"You are mistaken," replied Sir Herbert, thoughtfully, "the errors of our youthful days, are sometimes condemned with too much severity; at a more advanced period few, perhaps, can look back on their past lives, and exultingly say, I have never transgressed. Tell me then, bard, your story, without reserve; and if the sorrows which you now labour under are not irremediable, perhaps I may be possessed of power and inclination to mitigate them." The minstrel, gratified by this condescension, bowed his head respectfully; then laying down his harp, and folding his arms across his bosom, began his recital thus.

(To be concluded in our next.)

Concluded from our last Volume, page 272.

"I was," said the minstrel, "the son of a noble house, more famed for hereditary honours than extensive possessions, and at an early age chose the profession of arms. I quitted the bosom of my family, contrary to the wishes of a fond mother; but my father, whose pride was perhaps as strong as his affection, applauded my choice, and encouraged me, with holding out delusive prospects of future glory. I should perhaps have remained satisfied with my destination, had not a passion more powerful than ambition obtained admission into my breast. In the neighbourhood resided a female, young, lovely, and amiable: we knew only to love each other, but she was an orphan, and dependant upon a brother, who was as mercenary as despotic. My parents, whose mistaken partiality induced them to consider me in every way her superior, positively forbade my pursuit of the gentle Adelaide; while her brother, finding it was not likely that any essential advantage was to be derived from the union, seconded their views by the most rigorous measures. Perhaps this injudicious severity served to incease our ardour; we contrived to meet clandestinely, and, after a thousand scruples on the part of Adelaide, I persuaded her to agree to a private marriage. This imprudent step once taken, we flattered ourselves with the hope that our friends would not remain inflexible; but in that hope we were cruelly deceived. The brother of Adelaide, highly incensed at being thus counteracted in his views, turned his offending sister from his house, and her only alternative was to follow my precarious fortunes. For a time the smiles of love seemed to afford us ample compensation for all other disadvantages and privations; but the strength and spirits of my Adelaide suffered under the hardships she was necessitated to share, and the regiment to which I belonged being ordered abroad, I persuaded her to remain in England. It was with extreme reluctance she complied; a sad presentiment seemed to weigh on her spirits, and her last farewell expressed a conviction that we should meet no more. Need I observe to you, Sir Herbert, that the temptations to pleasure and dissipation in a military life are great, and, without a certain degree of experience and resolution, almost unavoidable. Though I had sufficient affection for my wife to avoid licentious pursuits, I was not so wholly proof against the seduction of example as to avoid falling into extravagancies which rendered my remittances to Adelaide both scanty and precarious. Still she remonstrated not, and I pursued my thoughtless career, without reflecting that she was perhaps suffering all the horrors of indigence; till, ashamed to acknowledge my folly and remissness, I suffered several of her letters to remain unanswered. At length I received one which roused me to a sense of my injustice and inhumanity: it was from a person who, interested in the fate of my Adelaide, had afforded her support and assistance during my absence. This letter overwhelmed me with shame and anguish: it informed me that my wife, agonized by my neglect, and on the point of becoming a mother, had come to the desperate resolution of throwing herself upon her brother's mercy. 'It was in vain,' said her friend, 'I attempted to dissuade her from a measure which I considered hopeless, and represented to her the numerous chances which might have occurred to interrupt your correspondence, and assured her of a welcome asylum with me. To these representations she would reply, 'I am already under oppressive obligations, the weight of which lie heavy on my heart. Deserted by the object of my tenderest regard, I have no wish for, no hope of happiness. I feel I shall not want much for myself, but my helpless babe, for it I deem it my duty to seek a protector. My brother, however incensed against me, had a generous and feeling heart; he will not shut his door against a sister he once so tenderly loved; he will not condemn a helpless innocent for the transgressions of its parents: at least, I will make this last appeal to his feelings, if I perish in the attempt.' Firm in this determination, Adelaide set out on her intended journey, too scantily supplied, I fear, for the occasion, for, from the hour of her departure, I have obtained no tidings of her fate. I have written to her, but received no answer, and a dreadful apprehension has seized me that she never put her purposed plan into execution, for I am satisfied that had she been received into her brother's house, I should have heard from her.'

"How can I describe the sensations of self-reproach which I experienced on the perusal of this dreadful information! It was out of my power to return to England, but I immediately wrote to the brother of my Adelaide, who, in reply, assured me that he had never seen nor heard of his disobedient sister since she first quitted his protection." "Good God!" exclaimed Sir Herbert, starting up, "this coincidence of circumstances is astonishing: you must be the husband of my sister?" "I am indeed that unfortunate, guilty wretch," replied the minstrel, "nor will your surprise be diminished when my recital is concluded. From some particulars which I have gathered since my residence at the Hall, I think it not improbable that our regretted Walter is the child of Adelaide." "Of Adelaide!" repeated Sir Herbert, in amazement; "that would indeed be a blissful discovery; but what can induce you to form such an extravagant surmise?"—"Some casual observations which I have made respecting the age, and circumstances which introduced the youth to your protection; but if you, Sir Herbert, will interrogate your aged domestic Humphrey, he can give you satisfactory information, and will perhaps be less reserved upon the subject than he is to others." "It shall be done!" exclaimed the baronet, exultingly; "but I am now curious to learn your motives for this disguise, and why you have not presented yourself at the Abbey, where your presence would undoubtedly occasion great revolutions." "Alas!" returned Osborne, sighing, "why should I seek aggrandizement now, which it is not in my power to enjoy. The sad fate of my Adelaide has clouded all my prospects. I am unworthy of prosperity; and if my hope of finding my son in the amiable Walter is frustrated, it is my resolution to pass the remnant of my days in obscurity."—"That must not be," interrupted Sir Herbert; "Lord Lutterell has no heir; why then should the ample possessions of your ancestors be suffered to decay, or fall into the hands of strangers: know you not that an alliance is in contemplation between your cousin and a foreigner named Moresco?"—"If her heart is not interested in the event," returned Osborne, "my interference shall check his villanous career: I know Moresco."—"As to the heart of Monimia," observed Sir Herbert, "I believe it is secretly and fervently devoted to the lost Walter."—"Then," cried Osborne, exultingly, "all may be as we wish; but I will now proceed to inform you of all the particulars you desire to know.

"I no sooner received the afflicting intelligence concerning my Adelaide with which I have already acquainted you, than I became careless of my existence, and rashly plunged into the greatest scenes of danger. The fate I sought was denied me: I received a deep and dangerous wound, which effectually disabled me from further service, and was sent back to England, with several of my equally unfortunate companions. On our passage we fell into the hands of the enemy, and, instead of being permitted to revisit our native land, were consigned to a tedious imprisonment. My own misfortunes affected me less than those of my fellow sufferers, whose hopes were so cruelly destroyed; yet I was not entirely free from a desire of obtaining my liberty. My patience and uncomplaining docility obtained for me the good-will of my gaoler, who at length permitted me to escape. Furnished by him with this disguise, I succeeded in gaining the nearest port, and secured a passage home. We reached England in safety, but, as I had been so many years absent, I was desirous of learning the exact state of family affairs, before I ventured to appear in my real character; and accordingly commenced my journey on foot, unknown and unbefriended. On enquiry, I found that my parents had been some time numbered with the dead, and that my uncle had assumed the title of Lord Lutterell, in the supposition that I was no more. Not doubting his justice of generosity, should I make good my claim, I yet felt anxious first to ascertain whether or not you had deceived me respecting my beloved Adelaide, and for this purpose obtained admission into your mansion as a minstrel. The first moment I beheld Walter I conceived for him a degree of attachment which I could scarcely account for, and, in consequence, my curiosity was strongly excited to learn every particular concerning him. Every circumstance related by the good Humphrey confirmed me in the opinion that the unfortunate creature who perished under your roof was no other than Adelaide."—"It is indeed probable," said the baronet, thoughtfully; "but, if I recollect right, there were some articles left, which might serve to confirm or to destroy our hopes."

Sir Herbert then gave orders for Humphrey to attend him, and, upon questioning the old man concerning those trifling memorials, he learnt that they had long been in the possession of Lady Mortimer. Surprised at this circumstance, and at her having never mentioned it to him, he made no secret of his astonishment, and was preparing to summon her into his presence, when Osborne again addressed him: "I am fearful, Sir Herbert, that the most unpleasant part of this affair remains yet to be investigated. One of the articles to which Humphrey alludes was a miniature resemblance of myself; the features were no doubt well known to your lady, and this will sufficiently account for her keeping it from your sight." "I am at a loss to comprehend this affair," observed Sir Herbert thoughtfully; "how could your features be known to my wife?" "I must, I see, explain myself more fully than it was my wish or intention to have done," returned Osborne; "know then, Sir Herbert, that when I was on the continent, chance introduced me to Miss Lupino, who not knowing that my heart and hand were devoted to another, honoured me with a distinguished preference, which she did not attempt to conceal: I most explicitly informed her of my real situation, and acknowledged my marriage with your sister. This information, however, did not appear to effect any change in the lady's sentiments, and my disgust at her licentious principles was expressed so unguardedly, as to excite her most violent indignation. To obtain revenge, she encouraged the addresses of Moresco, an artful Italian, whose character was of the most doubtful kind, and I narrowly escaped from a snare laid between them for my destruction.—You are struck with horror, Sir Herbert, and it is with concern I make a disclosure, which must prove so agonizing to your feelings; but that I assert nothing more than fact, you may immediately ascertain, if you choose me to appear before Lady Mortimer, divested of this disguise." "What iniquitous transactions!" exclaimed Sir Herbert; "who knows, but to her malignant influence, may be ascribed the mysterious disappearance of Walter: but tortures shall wring the confession from her." With this hasty resolution, he dispatched a messenger to inform Lady Mortimer, that he wished to see her instantly. Upon entering the saloon, where Osborne, divested of his long beard and minstrel's garb, stood waiting her approach, she gave a start of surprise, and fixing her eyes on him, with manifest tokens of dismay, remained several moments as if struck motionless. "The appearance of this gentleman seems to disconcert you strangely, madam!" observed the baronet sarcastically; "you are, perhaps, better acquainted than I imagined." Lady Mortimer appeared at a loss for a reply: at length summoning up all her assurance, she answered; "The features of the person now before me, do indeed remind me of one long since dead; such resemblances frequently occur, and if I testified momentary surprise, I know not why it should, sir, excite your resentment." "You are not quite so ignorant as you pretend," returned Sir Herbert; "in fact, madam, this is the person whom you, as well as others, imagined could never appear in judgment against you; in him you behold the heir of Lutterell." Lady Mortimer turned pale, a convulsive motion agitated her lips, and sinking into a chair, she faintly articulated, "I am undone." Sir Herbert grasped her arm—"You are right in supposing that I have learnt particulars, which must eventually disgrace you; I have, therefore, only to hint, that nothing but the most sincere contrition, and unequivocal acknowledgment of your misconduct, can preserve you from the effects of my just indignation and abhorrence. On one condition only, will I consent to screen your infamy." "Name it, Sir Herbert," the lady faultered out. "Reveal to me, what has been the fate of Walter: by your connivance, I am persuaded, he has been removed, and if, as I suspect, his life has been attempted, you, and the vile Moresco, shall be delivered up to justice." At this threat, the terrified Lady Mortimer fell on her knees; "I have deserved your suspicion, Sir Herbert," she exclaimed, "but guilty as I have been, Walter's blood has not been shed to my knowledge." "Where then is he concealed?" asked the baronet sternly. "Moresco has secured the person of his rival, but he pledged his word, that no violence should be attempted." "Enough," cried Sir Herbert; "if you have deceived me, dread my vengeance: until the fact is ascertained, a close imprisonment must be your fate." He then conducted her to her apartment, and after taking every precaution to effect her secure confinement, he returned to Osborne, to consult with him concerning the best means of recovering Walter. "Open force alone can effect our purpose," said Osborne; "Moresco commands a strong body of desperate fellows, whose depredations have long been the terror of the country; they lurk in the subterraneous passages beneath the castle, and the entrance is by means of a recess, which to elude suspicion, has the appearance of a hermitage." "I remember the place," replied Sir Herbert; "I will summon all my vassals, arm them well, and attack the castle by surprise; do you hasten to town, and bring a party of the police to reinforce my little army." This being agreed on, Osborne departed with all possible expedition.

Meanwhile the pretended count, impatient to secure the prize, which he feared by some untoward discovery might be wrested from him, urged his suit with ardour, and made such tempting proposals, as induced Lord Lutterell to give his word that Monimia should become his bride on a certain day, named by Moresco. Monimia endeavoured to avert the sacrifice by tears and entreaties, but on that head, Lord Lutterell was inexorable, and Monimia gave herself up to hopeless anguish. The day approached but too rapidly, and every preparation was made for the splendid celebration of those nuptials which were to devote the hapless victim to endless misery. On the morning appointed, Lord Lutterell impatiently summoned his daughter to attend him: she tremblingly obeyed; but determined not to be moved by an appearance of reluctance, which he deemed childish, and unjustifiable, he assumed a sternness of demeanour foreign to his heart. "It is the first act of obedience I have required from you, Monimia, and it gives me pain to perceive that you so reluctantly obey a father who has ever been indulgent and affectionate to you." "I know it, my father, I acknowledge that your tenderness to me has been unlimited, and except in this instance. . . ." "Nonsense," cried Lord Lutterell, interrupting his weeping daughter; "this is the common cant of perverse children; you, Monimia, should be above such caprices; I am anxious to secure you the possession of wealth, rank, and independence, by an union with a man formed by nature to captivate your sex, and one who could not fail to obtain your preference, had not a romantic attachment blinded your judgment, and incited you to disobedience: but learn, foolish girl, that my possession of hereditary wealth and title, is but precarious: intelligence has reached me, that my brother's son yet lives; if this report be correct, our certain ruin must ensue; and by your marriage with the count alone, can I hope to see you placed beyond the reach of that unlooked-for change of fortune. To see you in a state of affluence and security, will mitigate the pangs of disappointment; for your sake alone, are wealth and rank of consequence to me: but no more of this, were it otherwise, my word is given to the count, who now impatiently awaits us in the chapel." Monimia was too much overpowered by contending emotions, to make the reply her heart dictated; she passively suffered her father to lead her forward. At the foot of the great staircase, they were met by Moresco, magnificently habited, who, with exultation in his looks, caught the fair hand of the almost senseless Monimia, and pressing it fervently to his lips, hurried her towards the chapel. The chaplain was punctual in attendance, he opened his book, and the awful ceremony commenced. Monimia for some time effectually struggled against the faint sickness which oppressed her, till at length her exhausted spirits were inadequate to the effort; and as soon as the fatal ring was placed on her finger, she uttered a piercing shriek, and sunk senseless into the arms of her terrified father. Moresco looked more displeased than concerned; but his attention was soon diverted from his fainting bride, by the arrival of a courier, breathless with haste, who eagerly demanded to see the Count Moresco. "Hasten, my lord," he cried eagerly, as soon as the count appeared, "or you will be too late to defend your possessions; an armed force, headed by officers of justice, have attacked the castle; they have already liberated the young man lately brought thither, and traitor-like, he is now betraying all our haunts: our people, disconcerted by your absence, are upon the point of surrendering: nothing but your immediate appearance, can inspirit them to make a vigorous defence. I have with difficulty escaped to give you this information." Fearful of betraying the villanous confederacy in which he was engaged, Moresco would not request the assistance of Lord Lutterell: but enjoining his follower to secrecy, he made a pretence of urgent business, mounted his horse, and rode away at full speed, leaving the inmates of the abbey in extreme surprise at the wildness of his gestures, and his abrupt departure.

Moresco no sooner arrived within view of the castle, than he halted panic struck; for advancing towards him, in triumph, he beheld Sir Herbert, Walter, and a stranger of martial appearance: the former immediately rode forward: "Surrender instantly, Moresco," he cried, "as you hope for mercy." "Not to you," returned Moresco, indignantly; "while I wear a sword, I know how to defend my life and property, as well as to chastise presumption." Encouraged by this boldness, his attendants made a show of resistance. "Must I then stain my sword with the blood of such a vile miscreant?" exclaimed Walter, advancing to attack him. "That is as fate may decree," retorted Moresco: "should you succeed, proud boy, think not to reap the hoped-for fruit of your achievement; the fair Monimia, lost to you for ever, will scarcely deign to bless the murderer of her husband." "Her husband!" exclaimed Walter, retreating with horror and astonishment. "I tell you truth," retorted Moresco, with a malignant laugh; "but I do not wish to daunt your courage, boy." Saying this, he spurred his horse forward, and before Walter was prepared to defend himself, would have plunged his sword into his breast, had not Osborne, perceiving the danger of the youth, opposed his skilful arm, and with one stroke shivered Moresco's weapon, and brought him to the ground. A scene of uproar and confusion ensued; the attendants seeing their leader fall, sought their own safety in flight, but were pursued and taken; while Moresco, finding himself deserted, and overpowered, begged for mercy: he was soon secured by the officers of the police; when Sir Herbert, and his party, consigning the miscreants to the punishment which awaited them, and undesirous of further revenge, rode onward to the abbey. Lord Lutterell, anxiously waiting the return of Moresco, was looking out, and perceived the party who approached, with equal alarm and astonishment. He cordially welcomed Sir Herbert and Walter; but his heart sunk within him when Osborne, alighting from his horse, saluted him as his uncle, and offered to embrace him. "It is then true!" ejaculated Lord Lutterell; "but where is Moresco? Osborne, I recognize your features; think not I would defraud you of your right; but pardon my strange reception; this is a day of most eventful occurrences." The party being readily admitted into the abbey, Sir Herbert briefly recapitulated the preceding events, and unfolded to the astonished Lord Lutterell, the full extent of

Moresco's villany. "Alas!" exclaimed Lord Lutterell; "duped wretch that I was, this is the punishment of ambition; my sweet Monimia has been sacrificed to a vile marauder, who this morning made her his bride." "Do not despond," said Osborne, to the drooping Walter; "since the marriage is so recent, it may soon be hushed up. Moresco must pay the forfeit of his crimes upon the scaffold; and the house of Lutterell shall flourish again. Behold, sir, I present to you a son worthy the love, which even in humble obscurity, he obtained. Walter, Sir Herbert's adopted child, is Lutterell's rightful heir; in him, and your fair daughter, let us unite each jarring interest, and in their happiness cement our own." "You surprise and delight me," exclaimed the gratified father of Monimia; "but let my child be summoned, this will be to her a day of joy indeed." Pale, and dejected, Monimia obeyed the mandate, and descended to the saloon, where the unexpected party were assembled; her eyes instantly selected Walter from the group, and the sudden sensation of joy it occasioned, instantly banished every painful recollection. Heedless of every observer, she rushed into his extended arms. "Walter!" "My Monimia!" was reciprocally uttered; but instantaneously memory brought back the events of the morning; and shrinking from the embrace of her delighted lover, she cried fearfully, "Oh, Walter! we meet too late; I am wedded to another." "I know it all, dearest Monimia;" exclaimed he, gazing tenderly on her pale face, now bathed in tears; "but that detested marriage will soon be annulled, and my Monimia be at liberty to bless him, who has too long been deemed the unworthy object of her choice." "It is true indeed," said her father; "in Walter, you no longer behold the friendless orphan, the child of suspicion; but the rightful heir of these domains, and the acknowledged son of Lord Lutterell." He then led her to his nephew, who affectionately embraced her; and joining her hand with that of Walter, said, "May heaven smile propitious on your union, my children! in depriving your father of these privileges which he has recently enjoyed, I act not under the influence of ambition, avarice, or revenge: to promote your felicity, and that of my son, so happily discovered, and restored to my arms, is my only wish." Mutual explanations then ensued, and Walter took an early opportunity of pleading for his unfeeling enemy, Lady Mortimer. "At your request," said Sir Herbert; "I will not treat her with the severity she has deserved. I will settle on her an annuity adequate to her wants; but never more shall she appear to the world as my wife: but for her art, and malice, I should long ere this have known and acknowledged you, my dear Walter, as the son of my unhappy, much wronged sister."

It were needless to dwell on the succeeding events, which may be already anticipated. Moresco was sacrificed to justice; and as soon as propriety would admit, Walter received the hand of his much-loved Monimia. Ardently attached to the asylum of his infancy, Walter accepted with pleasure, Sir Herbert's invitation to reside at Mortimer Hall. The neglected remains of the unfortunate Adelaide, were removed from the parish church-yard, to the family burial vaults, and again interred with the respect due to a member of that noble house. The old age of Humphrey was cheered by these agreeable arrangements, and by the amiable attentions of Walter, and his fair bride; nor was the village carpenter forgotten, by whose advice, and interference, Winifred had been induced to protect the orphan babe. Lady Mortimer, disgraced, and humbled, quitted the scene of her mortification, attended by the flippant Jane; who, instead of feeling satisfaction at the recent discoveries which had been made, and perceiving the total overthrow of all her ambitious hopes, gave vent to her malice by feeding the malignity which still rankled in Lady Mortimer's bosom. Impotent as venomous, the evil recoiled upon themselves; for, neglected and despised by all, their days were lingered out in cheerless obscurity; while Walter and his amiable bride became the delight of their parents, and the most perfect pictures of conjugal felicity.

[SONNETS.][1]

How have I lov'd amid the dark'ning grove,
When evening's sombrous shadows crept around;
Musing in pensive thought awhile to rove,
List'ning the deep and melancholy sound
That ever murmur'd as the fitful blast
Sobb'd thro' my woodland haunt!—the rustling trees,
Still as the cloudy night-storm gather'd fast,
Tossing their foliage to the hollow breeze,
Such music made as with unearthly spell
Charm'd my rapt soul in sweet, yet solemn mood;
Now softly moaning like funereal knell,
Or convent's piteous dirge; now thund'ring rude,
Like angry billows, that, with deaf'ning roar,
Foam up the craggy rocks along some distant shore.

OSCAR.[2]

SONNET,
WRITTEN DURING A LATE EVENING WALK.[3]

See, now the West, ting'd with the parting ray,
Throws o'er the landscape round its golden gleam;
Soft sheds the evening-star its silvery beam,
And seems to bid my lingering footsteps stay,
Awhile through these delightful shades to stray;
While Fancy, wak'ning from her airy cell,
Binds fast my willing soul with magic spell,

---

1 Vol. 14 (May 1813): 298.
2 See Introduction, Authors and Contributors, xiii..
3 Vol. 15 (Aug. 1813): 118.

And breathes a brighter radiance than the day.
Come, then, sweet sylph! with thee I'll wander far,
Nor heed the darkling glooms that round me lie;
Blest in the brilliance of thine ardent eye,
I'll e'en forget the world's corroding care;
Forget that once I knew no anxious fear,
Forget that ever I have shed a tear.

                                        A.

SIR EDMUND;

A FRAGMENT.[1]

"A tale of the times of old, the deeds of days of other years."
OSSIAN.[2]

TWICE had Sir Edmund's horse fallen; twice had he broken the reverie of his master, who, careless of the driving sleet, and the pitchy darkness of the night, still continued to proceed; his limbs were stiff with intense cold, and at length the fierce spirit of the knight was nearly overcome; he found himself utterly unable to proceed; and he alighted from his charger, in order to warm his sinking frame by the exercise of walking. The depth of the snow prevented his intention; he stood still for a few moments; and gave himself up to reflection. "What!" said he to himself, "shall the mighty Sir Edmund, before whose arm whole hosts of Saracens[3] have so often retreated,—shall a knight of the Cross, who has endured all the rage and peril of the battle, sink before the northern blast? Shall I who have escaped destruction in the very jaws of death,—who have now returned to receive the reward of my toils, become the prey of warring elements? Forbid it, oh power of mercy! Thy shield was before me in the day of carnage and slaughter; Oh! let me yet live to rescue my Eltrida from the arms of the villain Wolfrid." Again he exerted his remaining strength, and mounted his steed; who, as if conscious that the fate of his master depended upon his exertions, dashed forward through the snow with amazing power and swiftness.

---

1 Vol. 16 (Jan. 1814): 12-16.
2 The first line of "Carthon" in *The Poems of Ossian* (1762), "translated" by James MacPherson.
3 *Saracens*: Among the later Greeks and Romans, a name for the nomadic peoples of the Syro-Arabian desert which harassed the Syrian confines of the Empire; hence, an Arab; by extension, a Muslim, *esp.* with reference to the Crusades (*OED*).

Sir Edmund once more held in his panting charger; he had heard a hollow sound strike upon his ear, as if a bell had been tolled at a little distance from him; he listened with anxiety;—again he heard the welcome sound, which seemed almost at hand; it was evidently the bell of some convent, which was now tolling for the vesper prayers. His horse obeyed his motion, and pleased as himself to hear the well known sound of relief, once more bounded forward.

The sound of the bell directed Sir Edmund, and, in a short time, he arrived at the gate of a large building, which was what he had supposed it to be, a convent. With difficulty, he alighted; his blood-less limbs threatened to refuse their office; but at length he suc-ceeded in ringing the gate bell. The sound of merriment proceeded from within, and the first peal was disregarded by the inhabitants of the house. Again he pulled with violence, and after numerous interrogations, and much scrutiny, was admitted within the gate. "Monk," said Sir Edmund, "I have here a faithful beast, who has suffered with me the inclement batterings of the storm: and if you will see him comfortably housed, and plentifully fed, this purse shall be yours." "Your horse, Sir Knight," said the monk, taking the purse, "shall receive every attention; I will myself be his feeder." The knight was now conducted to an apartment, where the Abbot and his monks were seated round the board, which was loaded with luxuries; ill seeming the banquet of religious disciplinants.[1] At his entrance, all rose from their seats; and the attention of Sir Edmund was attracted by a youth, who, clad in armour, started from the table; and, as if seized with some sudden disorder, covered his face with his cloak, and rushed from the apartment.

"Let not my presence disturb any of this assembly," said the knight, "I only ask the rights of hospitality for a few hours, until I and my horse can recruit our exhausted strength and spirits." "Knight of the cross," answered the Abbot, "for your armour bespeaks your order, you are welcome; be seated near the fire. The young man you have seen is also a stranger; and is doubtless taken suddenly ill; excuse my absence for a little time, till I enquire into

---

1 *disciplinant*: A person who scourges himself or herself as a form of religious discipline or penance (*OED*).

the nature of his disorder." Sir Edmund obeyed; and soon the genial warmth restored life and vigour to his almost inanimate frame.

The Abbot soon returned, and brought an account that the stranger who had that night arrived at the convent, and, like Sir Edmund, claimed protection from the storm, was afflicted with a sudden and violent disorder; and one of the monks was dispatched to his assistance. Sir Edmund, after a little time, wished to retire to rest; and the attentive Abbot, taking a lamp, offered to conduct him to his chamber. The storm still continued with unabated fury; and as the knight followed his guide through the long and winding passages, the rapid current of air almost extinguished the quivering lamp. One circumstance strangely awakened the suspicions of Sir Edmund; looking by chance behind him, as he followed the Abbot, he caught a glance of the figure in armour, and which was evidently the same that arose from the board at his entrance; it now crossed the gallery on which they were passing. This employed his thoughts after the Abbot had left him. "If this stranger," thought he, "was so very ill, it is strange he should be at this hour wandering about this cheerless mansion." He laid himself on the bed, without pulling off his armour: and placed his sword by his side. Unused to the attacks of fear and suspicion, sleep soon closed his eyelids; his dreams were disturbed; he beheld in fancy his Elfrida standing by his side; he prepared to rush into her arms, when suddenly his enemy, Wolfrid, rushed between them, and drawing his sword, plunged it into the breast of the fainting female; and then turned his rage upon the knight; who, to his unspeakable horror, found his own sword far beyond his reach. He was roused from his slumber by the violence of his emotions; and beheld the armed stranger quickly retreating towards the door of the apartment. Sir Edmund started from the bed, seized his sword, and taking the lamp from the table, rushed after him. Again he caught a glimpse of the mysterious stranger descending the stair-case with quick steps, holding a drawn sword in his hand. "By heaven, I will unfathom this mystery," exclaimed Sir Edmund, and followed the sound of the footsteps.—He drew nearer and nearer; and at length, at the turning of an angle, caught hold of his cloak; it yielded to his grasp, and he held it in his hand;— he stopped, and holding the light nearer, discovered it to be the well known mantle of his rival Wolfrid. "Accursed villain!" exclaimed

Sir Edmund, "thy intent was murder." All the preceding circumstances rushed upon his memory; and he now easily accounted for
the indisposition of the supposed stranger at supper. He placed the
lamp upon a pedestal, for it impeded his progress; and grasping
his sword, rushed onward by the light of the moon, which faintly
glimmered through the arched windows;—fainter and fainter he
heard the retreating tread; and soon he had lost all chance of overtaking the flying miscreant.—He paused, unknowing how to act;
and listened to catch any sound which might direct him:—A soft
murmur rose on his ear; he advanced a few paces; it was the sound
of music; he followed it; oft the sound seemed lost; again it burst
upon his ear, and at length he arrived at the door on the other side
of which the delightful harmonist seemed to be placed. He gently
opened it; clothed in mourning garments sat a female, whose
fingers, gently drawn over the strings of a half decayed harp, produced the heaven-breathing notes he had heard. At his entrance,
the female raised her head. Good heaven! what was the emotion
of Sir Edmund at beholding, not a stranger, as he had expected,
but, his lost Elfrida! Nor was the surprise of Elfrida less moderate;
she obeyed the first impulse of her heart, and rushed into the out-
stretched arms of the knight. While Sir Edmund held his beloved to
his bosom, he thought not of danger; but a loud and frantic scream,
breaking from Elfrida, aroused him; and, with a convulsive start,
she dashed her lover to the other side of the apartment. The knight
was alarmed, and astonished; but his surprise ceased, when he
beheld the villain retiring once more in confusion.

Sir Edmund rushed forward. "Turn, turn, infernal traitor," he
shouted, "and meet thy reward!" Wolfrid found it was impossible
to escape, and he faced his antagonist; they fought, but the arm
of justice prevailed; Wolfrid soon lay prostrate at the feet of the
enraged Sir Edmund.

R. PORTER.[1]

---

1 Possibly also the author of "Sir Egbert: A Gothic Fragment."

ON THE EFFECTS OF CHIVALRY IN THE DARK AGES.[1]

To the poet or enthusiast, conversant with legendary lore, with the pomp of tournaments, and the wild but expressive minstrelsy of the early bards, an inexpressible charm seems suspended over the memory of the feudal ages; which, in proportion as the rugged features that distinguished them, and the gothic darkness with which they were surrounded, are dissipated or relaxed by the mellowing hand of time, acquires such irresistible force, that the powers of reason are gradually overshadowed, and the heart hurried away in a torrent of romantic enthusiasm.

As our thoughts wander from the present, and lose themselves in the dim lapse of slumbering ages, we find in the contemplation of the crumbling piles of feudal magnificence, images of mingled grandeur and sublimity, and reflections, which now chill the soul with sensations of terror and of awe, now tinge and soften it with the soothing languors of melancholy.

The lofty turret, fast mouldering to decay; the huge port-cullis, tottering to its fall; the massive draw-bridge, long buried in the moat it overhung; even yet remind us of the warrior-forms whose umbered arms once gleamed upon the walls they defended, and whose ponderous footsteps awakened at intervals their remote and slumbering echoes; while the lone screams of the night-bird, the dark flappings of its dusky wings, and the sad moanings of the blast through the broken crevices of the dilapidated edifice, are, indeed, but mournful remembrances of the joyous revelry that rung through its once hospitable halls, when the bard swept his harp to the song, or the knights, "in gay and gallant trim," led their fair mistresses through the swift mazes of the dance.

Time seems in this, as in many other instances, to have smoothed down the asperities of reality, and to have shed a mild

---

[1] Vol. 2 , i.s. (Sept. 1815): 163-169.

and hallowed ray over scenes replete with bigotry, with barbarism, and with horror. Difficult, therefore, must be the task, to bid truth rise victorious over such darling prejudices of the heart, to dash the delicious poison of romance from the lips of the enthusiast, and tear the mystic veil from the sombre and distorted features of that sybil, whose spell has darkened the understandings and hacknied the sensibilities of so many generations.

In a careful survey of the annals of chivalry, the eye is, without doubt, occasionally arrested, and the bosom fired by some act of heroism almost super-human, and some feat of valour that startles the imagination; by instances of austerity and self-denial, worthy the apostolic ages; and a spirit of munificent hospitality, that would not dishonour the most refined æra of civilization. These shed a pure and vivid ray over the solitary pages they adorn, like the blazing coruscations of the heavens, more transcendently luminous, in proportion to the deepening horrors of the surrounding obscurity.

But often, very often, do we find their boasted valour maddening into brutal ferocity; their abstinence and forbearance, the offspring of monkish craft or stoic insensibility; and their renowned hospitality, swelling with the insolence of ostentatious superiority.

With regard to its effects on the religious feelings of its professors, what can be more obvious, than that Chivalry was ever the companion and best-beloved of superstition; that vows and pilgrimages, dispensations and penances, originated in the most trivial occurrences, or were surreptitiously obtained by the intrigues of priestly rapacity; and that the belief in goblins and sprites, those abortive monsters of a crude and timorous fancy, agitated the minds and paralized the faculties of the deluded and credulous world.

Nor did learning deign to smile on regions apparently besotted in ignorance, and warped by credulity; but seemed forced to seek a narrow and darkling habitation in the solitary cell of the recluse, whence its weak and sickly irradiations were rarely ever known to emerge, but as an engine to stultify reason, confound judgment, or rivet the chains of papal subjection. A few, however, (alas! how few!) daring ebullitions of its flame, played round the casque of the warrior, and lighted up the eye of the bard, amidst the wild but sublime ravings of his soul!

With minds thus narrowed by prejudice, and enslaved by bigotry, civil liberty must likewise, in conjunction with other guardian
virtues, have been a stranger to the world. Consisting, as did society
at that period, but of two distinct classes, the lord and the vassal, in
vain do we look around for those social enjoyments, those manifold reciprocations of kindness, and those many endearing chari-
ties of life, which brighten the varying evils of existence, and bind,
in silken bands of benevolence, the universal family of mankind.

Sunk in acknowledged and hereditary vassalage, the miserable
peasant saw himself forced to surrender up his substance, or to
pour forth his blood at the will of his despotic lord; for whom, also,
the shuttle and the spinning-wheel of the matron performed their
perpetual rotations. Nor was this all: the sacred penetralia[1] of their
home, the blooming objects of their parental affections, were all
unsheltered from the bold intrusion and lawless violence of the
obdurate tyrant, whenever anger might tempt him to oppression,
or beauty, innocence, or caprice, urge him to the gratification of his
sensual and depraved appetites. Even royalty itself has been known
to tremble on the throne, and to shrink into the inmost recesses of
the palace, awed by the impatience of controul, and restless turbu-
lence of the haughty and imperious barons.

The land, for the most part partitioned out among these powerful chieftains, was continually, from the injustice of some and
the ambition of others, immersed in the miseries of predatory
warfare, power being the rule by which right was administered; in
fine, when no disturbance from without smothered for a season
the flame of civil animosity, and thereby directed those tumultu-
ous energies, so often exhausted on each other, against a common
enemy, Europe seemed, at times, inhabited by lawless banditti,
intent only on rapine, violence, and murder.

This dreary picture will hardly appear exaggerated, when
we carefully survey, in many of the gloomy edifices of baronial
splendour, not yet wholly annihilated by the fury of war, or the
more gradual devastations of time, that massive strength of walls,
that frowning and stupendous architecture; those humid cells,

---

1 *penetralia*: The innermost parts or recesses of a building; *spec.* the sanctuary or
inner sanctum of a temple (*OED*).

impervious to the cheerful day; those ponderous chains, and other implements of torture, which they are known to have concealed; and, above all, the ferocious and unrelenting characters so often recognised in their founders.

Having thus briefly scanned the Effects of Chivalry on the age, principally with regard to the manners, the habits, and the religious feelings of men; let us now take a cursory view of its influence over the minds and conduct of the gentler half of the species, from whom society, in every age and clime, receives a complexion and a tone at once powerful and decided.

And here superstition tyrannized, with at least equal dominion. Many portions of the day were set apart for the due performance of its manifold ceremonies, and time crept heavily on; amidst the endless recitations of Latin orisons, the edifying occupation of counting rosaries, and the solemn and curious mummery of auricular confessions. The short remainder of their hours elapsed in the more pleasing, and perhaps equally profitable pastime of greedily devouring the narratives of antiquated nurses, or the frivolous tittle-tattle of gossiping chambermaids.

Even in their daily and most ordinary occupations, the love of the marvellous would frequently obtrude itself. Often would they start, like timid fawns, as they paced the long corridors of their gothic habitations, at every blast that wailed around the turret; or anticipate, with trembling anxiety, some fearful or gallant adventure, whenever tempted to exchange the seclusion and monotony of the castle, for the verdure of fields or the fragrance of flowers.

Yet not always thus harmless and insignificant were the occupations of these romantic fair. Placed in conspicuous elevation, as spectatresses of the tournament, the brilliancy of their eyes gave new poignancy to the javelin, and new keenness to the sword; from them also emanated the rewards due to superior valour and address, though the triumph was not unfrequently accompanied by the groan of anguish, the tear of mortification, or the effusion of blood.

Their gentle bosoms, thus early accustomed to scenes of magnificent barbarity, can it be uncharitable to suppose, that those tender sensibilities which hallow and soften the hearts of women, with secret but powerful agency, must lose somewhat of that exquisite tact, that virgin susceptibility, whose witching charm draws round them, as with a spell, the love, the desire, the adoration of mankind?

Nor did this infraction of feminine softness always evince itself amidst the, perhaps, irresistible blandishments of a splendid spectacle; but instances of vanity might frequently be found, accompanied with cruelty the more exceptionable, as nurtured in the hour of reflection and retirement, and in the unillusive[1] soberness of frigid calculation. Of this unamiable feeling, let the following instance, among a crowd of others, be alone produced, as thus curiously and quaintly related by the venerable Leland.[2]

"About this tyme there was a greate feste made yn Lyncolnshir, to which came many gentilmen and ladies; and amonge them one lady brought a heaulme for a man of were, with a very rich creste of gold, to William Marmion, knight, with a letter of commendement of her lady, that he should go into the *daungerest* place in England, and ther to let the heaulme be seene and known as famous. So he went to Norham, whither, within four days of his cumming, cam Philip Moubray, guardian of Berwicke, having yn his bande 40 men of armes, the very flour of men of the Scottish marches.

"Thomas Gray, capitayne of Norham, seynge this, brought his garrison afore the barriers of the castel, behind whom cam William, richly arrayed, as al glittering in gold, and wearing the heaulme, his lady's present.

" 'Then,' said Thomas Gray to Marmion, 'Sir Knight, ye be cum hither to fame your helmet: mount up on yowr horse, and ryd lyke a valiant man to yowr foes even here at hand, and I forsake God if I rescue not thy body deade or alyve, or I myself wyl dye for it.'

"Whereupon he toke his cursere, and rode amonge the thronge of ennemyes; the which layed sore strypes on him, and pulled hym at the last out of his sadel to the grounde.

"Then Thomas Gray, with al the hole garrison, lette prick yn among the Scottes, and so wondid them and their horses, that they

1 Undeceiving.
2 Written in a supposed medieval style, spelling in the following tale has not been updated or corrected. The tale can be found in this version in Walter Scott's "Notes to Canto First" of his *Marmion: A Tale of Flodden Field* (1810, first published 1808), Vol. I, 192-193.

were overthrowan." Leaving the poor knight, no doubt, greatly
rejoiced that death had not put an end at once to his folly and his
life!

And here, we perceive, on the one hand, the noble thirst of
glory giving way to a sentiment of false honour; and the arm of a
warrior, which dignified justice and patriotism should alone have
nerved to slaughter, actuated by puerile and insignificant motives;
and, on the other hand, a torrent of human blood, and the life of
a gallant but inconsiderate soldier, held trifling and unimportant,
when conducive to the gratification of a whimsical caprice, and
measureless and contemptible vanity.

Some allowance may, perhaps, here be claimed, in consideration of the backwardness of this æra of the world; but it may be
answered, that, in the breasts of women, gentleness, tenderness,
and humanity, should ever be felt and acknowledged as their peculiar virtues and inherent attributes, unchanged by the controul of
circumstance or the hues of time.

Having thus endeavoured to delineate the general features char-
acteristic of the feudal ages, which, from the universal prevalence
of chivalrous institutions, and the uniform diffusion of religious
bigotry throughout Europe, must have borne a striking resemblance in every state and empire of that quarter of the globe, and
have therefore been equally applicable to them all. I have now only
to express my apprehensions, that the picture here traced with rigid
fidelity, will be found to startle the imaginations of some, and do
violence to the prejudices of others. To such, therefore, who may
behold, with anger or regret, this rugged outline of a venerable era,
and who have warmed their fancies and regulated their judgments
by the glowing imagery of ancient ballads or modern romances;
to such, I say, be it made known in conciliation, that _he_ who has
thus, with an unsparing hand, laid bare the foundations of a pleasing and fanciful superstructure, and stripped it of its grotesque and
imposing decorations, confesses himself not wholly free from the
enchanting delusion; confesses, that _his_ soul still lingers with delight
over the wild minstrelsy of the bard, and still kindles at the flush
of romantic enthusiasm; resembling therein that false prophet of
old, whose tongue paid miraculously homage to truth, though his
heart bowed in secret to the shrine of deceit. Finally, he affirms,

that he has not hazarded one assertion, nor advanced one solitary argument, unsupported or unenforced by careful investigation and dispassionate reflection, by the opinions of the well-informed, and by the authority of history.

July, 1815. ALPHONSO.[1]

---

1 A frequent contributor of medieval and Gothic content to *LMM*, including essays and poetry.

SIR EGBERT;

A GOTHIC FRAGMENT.[1]

> It is the voice of the years that are gone; they roll before me with all their deeds.　　　　　　　　　　　　　OSSIAN.[2]

THE loud pealing of the thunder shook the wide vault of heaven, the rain fell in torrents, all was darkness, save when the vivid flashing of the lightning disclosed to the wanderers the horror of their situation. Sir Egbert paused irresolute, for he was aware that danger surrounded him which required more than human prudence to avoid. "Bertram," said Sir Egbert, addressing his 'squire, who followed at his heels, "we have thus far traced the monster who robbed me of all I held dear; but here all hope of overtaking him must fail." Bertram replied not to the words of his master; indeed he scarcely possessed the faculty of speech; for the unparalleled danger and distress of his situation had nearly deprived him of his senses. By the incessant flashing of the lightning, Sir Egbert discovered that he was surrounded by high and craggy mountains, which a prior knowledge convinced him formed the most dreary part of the Grampion Hills.[3] He dismounted his horse, fearful lest his next step should plunge him headlong down a precipice, or hurl him to the fathomless abyss of some yawning chasm, and cautiously leading him by the bridle, Sir Egbert continued slowly to proceed; whilst the faithful Bertram followed his steps, invoking his patron saints to rescue him from his present difficulty. Nearly an hour passed away in this manner; when, after a dreadful flash of forked lightning, Sir Egbert fancied he beheld the lofty turrets of a large building. He communicated his hopes to his servant; and making a

---

1 Vol. 4, i.s. (Aug. 1816): 85-88.
2 Opening passage of "Oina-Morul" in *The Poems of Ossian* (1773), "translated" by James MacPherson.
3 Located in the south of Scotland.

full pause, anxiously awaited a renewal of the electrical flash, that he might be certain. He had not long to endure suspense; for, with emotions of extreme pleasure, he beheld a large, though ruinous building, which seemed the remains of an ancient castle, at a short distance from the spot where he stood. Commanding Bertram to follow him, he proceeded towards the ruins. His surmises were just; it was indeed an old castle, which time had rendered untenantable, except by rooks and owls, whose doleful hooting, at the dead hour of night, would have appalled the stoutest heart. Entering a porch, Sir Egbert seated himself on the stone bench, congratulating himself that he had found a place to wait in safety, until the return of day, sheltered from the storm. Bertram was also pleased, though he could not refrain from shuddering, when he reflected on the wildness of the ruins, which, to his terrified fancy, seemed the retreat of robbers, or of beings of supernatural qualities. Sir Egbert was lost in thought: with his arms folded, and his eyes fixed on the ground, he meditated the preceding events; the death of his Ethelinda, and the retreat of her murderer, Oswald:—his heart panted for revenge; and he determined to sacrifice the base assassin to his fury, whenever he should meet with him. He was roused from these reflections by his servant, who, in a voice of extreme terror, desired him to observe! "What?" enquired Sir Egbert. "What dost thou see, Bertram, that can inspire this dread?" "Surely my eyes deceived me," replied the other, "or I beheld the faces of men surveying us from behind that massy pillar." "What pillar canst thou distinguish," said Sir Egbert, "when it is so dark that I cannot even see my own charger that stands by my side? Thy fears have made thee superstitious, friend." "It was when the lightning flashed," replied the 'squire; "and if you watch, we may perhaps again perceive them." More to satisfy his faithful servant, than from any other motive, Sir Egbert obeyed; and bent his eyes towards the spot that Bertram indicated. Twice the porch glowed with the vivid lightning; and nothing was distinguished by the massy walls of the building. The knight was preparing to address Bertram on his unnecessary fears, when, by another stream of light, he plainly beheld a man, with a sword in his hand, cautiously approaching the spot where he stood. "There is treachery," he cried, immediately changing his situation; and drawing at the same time his own weapon. The footsteps of the suspicious intruder were now distinctly heard retreating from the spot, as the arches of the interior of this ruinous building reverberated the sound. "Follow me, Bertram," exclaimed Sir Egbert; "follow me; for, by heaven, I will search the mysteries of this dreary pile, till I have unravelled them." He had no sooner uttered these words, than, brandishing his truncheon, he rushed into the innermost part of the castle, followed by his 'squire, who reluctantly left the comparative place of safety which the porch afforded him. His imagination represented to him broken stair-cases, or ruined floors, where they might fall, and be precipitated headlong, he knew not whither. Indeed, Sir Egbert was quickly checked in his impetuous career by a flight of steps, at the foot of which he had fallen. Rising with renewed determination, he more cautiously ascended, still followed by Bertram. The wild wind whistled mournfully through the wide crevices of the walls, like the sighs of the departed; the owls, the tenants of the moss-covered towers, in horrid tones, hooted forth their mournings; whilst the horror of their situation was increased by the stifled voices of men, which they heard at intervals. No mortal power could appal the soul of Sir Egbert; yet he felt a sensation of horror at these mysterious sounds. Involved in doubt and disorder, the knight paused to consider whether he should go on, or leave the place. It was evident some one had intended to attempt his life; and, surrounded as he was by darkness, he might fall an easy victim to the treacherous wiles of banditti. Whilst engaged in this reverie, he felt some one hurry past him quickly, though he distinguished nothing substantial, except the flapping of a pliable substance on his face, like that of a cloak: the next moment, he heard a well-known voice whisper rather loudly—"Where can he have strayed? He shall not escape me! my revenge shall yet be satisfied." Heavens! what was the astonishment of Sir Egbert, when he heard the voice of his rival, the detested Oswald? He doubted not that chance had conducted them to the same spot, and that the monster, not satisfied with the blood of the innocent Ethelinda, had determined to sacrifice him to his revenge and hatred. The storm had now in some degree abated; and the morning had begun to appear, when Sir Egbert thought he distinguished the person of his enemy a few paces before him. Disdaining to assassinate him when in his power, he addressed him by his name, and bade him defend himself. Oswald started at the sound; but instantly obeyed the summons. The clang of arms now resounded along the lofty arches of the ruined building; and Bertram stood in anxious expectation await-ing the decision of the combat. Scarcely able to distinguish each other in the thick shades of twilight, and the tempest now scarcely dispersed, they fought at random. Thrice had Sir Egbert's sword penetrated the body of his antagonist, who was ready to faint from loss of blood, when the honest Bertram beheld a third person steal-ing close by the wall, with the evident intention of attacking his unsuspecting master. Carefully observing every motion of the assassin, as he dimly distinguished his figure from the dark wall, he grasped his truncheon, and, when he beheld him rising from his couchant posture, rushed forward, and with one stroke cleft his head asunder. Oswald no sooner heard the groan of his dying serv-ant, than a certainty of his own fate rushed upon his mind; and he paused involuntarily. The darkness prevented Sir Egbert from dis-tinguishing that his enemy was thrown off his guard, and exposed to his uplifted sword; or his noble soul had scorned to strike; the force of his arm could not be restrained, and with a horrid groan, Oswald fell on the damp floor: the blood rushed from his wound; but remorse had penetrated his heart; he took the hand of Sir Egbert, as he raised him from the ground, and confessed the inju-ries he had done him; then, in broken accents, proceeded in the fol-lowing words— * * * * * * * * * *

R. P—R.[1]

---

1 Possibly R. Porter, author of "Sir Edmund: A Fragment."

THE VAMPYRE;

A FRAGMENT.[1]

Taken from a Tale of that Title, by LORD BYRON, *just published.*[2]

"SOON after, Aubrey determined to proceed upon one of his excursions, which was to detain him for a few hours; when they heard the name of the place, they all at once begged of him not to return at night, as he must necessarily pass through a wood, where no Greek would ever remain, after the day had closed, upon any consideration. They described it as the resort of the vampyres in their nocturnal orgies, and denounced the most heavy evils as impending upon him who dared to cross their path. Aubrey made light of their representations, and tried to laugh them out of the idea; but when he saw them shudder at his daring thus to mock a superior, infernal power, the very name of which apparently made their blood freeze, he was silent.

"Next morning, Aubrey set off upon his excursion unattended; he was surprised to observe the melancholy face of his host, and was concerned to find that his words, mocking the belief of those horrible fiends, had inspired them with such terror. When he was about to depart, Ianthe came to the side of his horse, and earnestly begged of him to return, ere night allowed the power of these beings to be put in action;—he promised. He was, however, so occupied in his research, that he did not perceive that day-light would soon end, and that in the horizon there was one of those specks, which, in the warmer climates, so rapidly gather

---

1 Vol. 9, i.s. (May 1819): 282-284.
2 Extract from *The Vampyre: A Tale* (1819) 44-48, published anonymously. Also published in the *New Monthly Magazine* (April 1819), where it was attributed to Lord Byron, despite having been written by his friend and physician John William Polidori, who subsequently acknowledged himself the author.

into a tremendous mass, and pour all their rage upon the devoted[1] country.—He at last, however, mounted his horse, determined to make up by speed for his delay; but it was too late. Twilight, in these southern climates, is almost unknown; immediately the sun sets, night begins: and ere he had advanced far, the power of the storm was above—its echoing thunders had scarcely an interval of rest—its thick heavy rain forced its way through the canopying foliage, whilst the blue forked lightning seemed to fall and radiate at his very feet. Suddenly his horse took fright, and he was carried with dreadful rapidity through the entangled forest. The animal at last, through fatigue, stopped, and he found by the glare of light- ning, that he was in the neighborhood of a hovel that hardly lifted itself up from the masses of dead leaves and brushwood which surrounded it. Dismounting, he approached, hoping to find some one to guide him to the town, or at least trusting to obtain shelter from the pelting of the storm. As he approached, the thunders, for a moment silent, allowed him to hear the dreadful shrieks of a woman mingling with the stifled, exulting mockery of a laugh, continued in one almost unbroken sound;—he was startled: but, roused by the thunder which again rolled over his head, he, with a sudden effort, forced open the door of the hut. He found himself in utter darkness: the sound, however, guided him. He was apparently unperceived; for, though he called, still the sounds continued, and no notice was taken of him. He found himself in contact with some one, whom he immediately seized; when a voice cried, "Again baf- fled!" to which a loud laugh succeeded; and he felt himself grappled by one whose strength seemed superhuman: determined to sell his life as dearly as he could, he struggled; but it was in vain: he was lifted from his feet, and hurled with enormous force against the ground:—his enemy threw himself upon him, and kneeling upon his breast, had placed his hands upon his throat—when the glare of many torches penetrating through the hole that gave light in the day, disturbed him;—he instantly rose, and, leaving his prey, rushed through the door, and in a moment the crashing of the branches, as he broke through the wood, was no longer heard. The storm was now still; and Aubrey, incapable of moving, was soon heard by

---

1 *devoted*: Formally or surely consigned to evil or destruction; doomed (*OED*).

those without. They entered; the light of their torches fell upon the mud walls, and the thatch loaded on every individual straw with heavy flakes of soot. At the desire of Aubrey, they searched for her who had attracted him by her cries; he was again left in darkness; but what was his horror, when the light of the torches once more burst upon him, to perceive the airy form of his fair conductress brought in a lifeless corse. He shut his eyes, hoping that it was but a vision arising from his disturbed imagination; but he again saw the same form, when he unclosed them, stretched by his side. There was no colour upon her cheek, not even upon her lip; yet there was a stillness about her face that seemed almost as attaching as the life that once dwelt there:—upon her neck and breast was blood, and upon her throat were the marks of teeth having opened the vein:— to this the men pointed, crying, simultaneously struck with horror, "A Vampyre! a Vampyre!" A litter was quickly formed, and Aubrey was laid by the side of her who had lately been to him the object of so many bright and fairy visions, now fallen with the flower of life that had died within her.

THE LOST FALCON.[1]

TRANSLATED FROM THE GERMAN.[2]

IN one of those beautifully romantic spots, so often met with in the Hartz Mountains,[3] at the sight of which, the ancient days of chivalry and romance, with all of their dark terrors and knightly achievements, rush so powerfully on the mind, stood the lordly castle of Count Rudolph von Swartzburg. It hung frowning over the brink of an inaccessible precipice, surrounded by misshaped piles of dark granite, which seemed to rear their craggy heads, tufted with matted clusters of gloomy pine, beech, and oak, as if in defiance of the huge mass of towers which weak man had dared to raise as rivals in their own awful solitudes. The Count had for some time entertained, with all that generosity and hospitality so well according with the chivalric notions of those days, a cousin of his, Count Albrecht von Sinnern. This gay and high-minded youth was passionately fond of the chase, and scarcely a day elapsed, without himself and his cousin passing the greater portion of it in hawking in the vicinity of the castle; the country, by its deep, woody recesses and hilly situation, being particularly adapted for this noble pastime. Albrecht had a favorite falcon, which engrossed so great a part of his affection that he seldom or ever lost sight of him, and after a day's sport, with many endearments, he reluctantly resigned him to the care of the falconer. It actually appeared as if the little creature understood the gestures of his fond master, and endeavored to repay, as well as to deserve, his kindness by his superior dexterity in pursuit of game. Unluckily, this bird, through the carelessness of the falconer, disappeared one morning. Distracted by the loss,

---

1 Vol. 15, i.s. (1822): May, 267-271; June, 315-319; July, 13-16; Aug., 79-81

2 An original has not been identified, although this claim to translation may be fictitious.

3 The Hartz Mountains (more commonly spelled "Harz") are said to be the setting for many German fairy tales.

Albrecht searched, though ineffectually, every spot in the neighborhood, and would gladly have sacrificed all his remaining hawks and
hounds to have once more obtained possession of his lost favorite.
One day, after having spent many hours in fruitless search of this
remarkably beautiful creature, Rudolph and himself, enticed by
the fallacious hope of succeeding in their pursuit, became more
and more entangled in the lone haunts of the mountains. Rudolph
reminded him how very unsafe it was to await the approach of
night in so wild and dangerous a spot; but so intent was he on the
object of his wanderings, that he entreated Rudolph to return to
a hut hard by, and there await his arrival. At such a time, and situated as they then were, it would have been madness to have left his
friend alone, so they continued to proceed together. "Do you not
hear," cried Albrecht, as the sun's last rays were fading slowly from
the summits of the distant hills, "there he is?" The sound really
appeared to proceed from the bells of a falcon; and Albrecht thinking himself already in possession of his favorite, began to entice
him by the kindest expressions: but in vain; the sound seemed to
recede as they approached, and to mock all their endeavors to reach
the spot from whence it arose. Like a chamois,[1] Albrecht climbed
the most pathless hills, and it was with great difficulty that Rudolph
could follow him. They soon attained the summit of such a one
that it was found utterly impossible to advance, and, unluckily,
equally so to recede. "Good God!" exclaimed Albrecht, looking
over the sides of a steep and perpendicular cliff, "is it possible that
this can be the way we ascended?" Rudolph was amazed; but it
could not have been otherwise, as not the least vestige of any other
path was visible. To return was out of their power, as the first step
towards a retreat, would have been the last on this side of the grave.
As evening began to spread her shadowy veil over the surrounding scenery, their situation became more lone, and to add to the
horror of the scene, they distinctly heard the wolves prowling in
the vicinity for their prey. It may easily be imagined, that they lost
no time in searching for an outlet; but this proved ineffectual. The
broad cliff on which they stood, appeared to them totally separated

---

1 chamois: A capriform antelope (*A. rupicapra* or *Rupicapra tragus*), the only representative of the antelopes found wild in Europe; it inhabits the loftiest parts of the
Alps, Pyrenees, Taurus, and other mountain ranges of Europe and Asia (*OED*).

from the neighboring hills; and they began to suspect, that they had arrived there through the agency of some mischievous demon, the peasantry in the environs strongly affirming the reality of such supernatural occurrences. It must be owned, that the thoughts of remaining the whole night in such a dangerous spot, and seeing no hope of the morning bringing any alleviation to their sufferings, was not very consoling. Strange as it was, even in this terrible situation, Albrecht did not forget his falcon; but often expressed his ardent desire of having him once more in his power. The night grew darker and darker, when suddenly they thought they perceived a light at a short distance; they were not mistaken in their conjectures, and their astonishment passed all bounds on its approaching still nearer, as if by a regular pathway, at last they heard footsteps close at hand. The most beautiful figure had perhaps never afforded more real pleasure to the two young friends than the hideous features of the deformed lantern-carrier did at the present moment, while she, on her part, appeared much surprised to find them there. "Well, my good old dame," exclaimed they, "how did you manage to ascend this rugged rock?" "I might with more propriety ask you that question," replied she, "I am at home in these wilds, but you do not seem much accustomed to such rough lodgings." "And where live you?" they further enquired. "In a hut not far from hence." "In a hut, and to whence a path from this leads?" "Certainly," answered the old woman; "so if you fear to pass the night here, follow me." Such an offer, and at such a time, could not be refused. "I will light on before," said she; "now turn neither to the right nor left, but tread in my footsteps." They followed the lantern according to her directions. Though not quite even, the way was tolerably passable, and they were rather surprised that they had not before discovered it. It was true, the branches of the trees tended much to conceal it from casual observance, and they often found some inconvenience in wading through the wide-spreading boughs that crossed their path. All this could not efface the thoughts of his main object from Albrecht's mind. "Have you perchance seen a stray falcon hereabouts, my good dame?" said he. "Yes," replied our conductress; "was he not very large, with ash-grey wings and dark spots?" "Right!" exclaimed Albrecht, overjoyed; "Oh! if that creature could be mine again!" "Who knows what may happen?" said she; "the whole of yesterday we heard the sound of his bells in our neighborhood; once or twice he flew close by the hut; my daughter, who was struck with his beauty, attempted to lure him in, but he refused the proferred bait, and soaring majestically aloft, was soon lost to our feeble sight; but, perhaps, she may have been more lucky today." "Woman!" cried Albrecht, "you might ask much for that bird." "My wishes," she replied attempting a smile, "know no very great extent; you must make your terms with my daughter."

The way proceeded now without any material change, over craggy steeps, into the most precipitate dells, and again up the sides of the most stupendous heights. At length overcome with fatigue, they stopped to gather a little breath, "Pray, what do you call far, if this is not so?" exclaimed Rudolph. "What! tired already, good gentleman?—well, only a few steps further, and you may rest yourselves; close under that hill lies my cottage." The hill exhausted their remaining strength; but upon seeing a flame ascend from a grotto by the side of the hut, they renewed their efforts, and arrived at last sinking from excessive exertion.

"That is my daughter," said their conductress, pointing to a young female who proceeded from the mouth of the grotto. "How long you have stayed this time," exclaimed the girl; "I have expected you this hour." "As an excuse for my absence, I have brought two guests, who were too unaccustomed with the path to follow me at my ordinary pace." Albrecht and Rudolph were struck with astonishment at the brilliant beauty of the daughter; they had thought such serenity of countenance, regularity of features, and symmetry of figure, could alone have proceeded from the chissel of the Grecian sculptor, and could scarcely believe their eyes when they beheld a human being, arrayed in dazzling white, standing before them, in the midst of such a wild solitude, in all the beauty of a goddess. She appeared to them adorned for the altar, and awaiting the arrival of her bridegroom to lead her thither. The fashion of her dress also differed widely from the neighboring customs. While Rudolph was trying in vain to find a single point or feature about this wonderful being, that could at all authorise the idea of so close a relationship as existed between her heavenly figure and the deformed, dirty, old hag that gave herself out as her mother, Albrecht stood transfixed before her; for the first time since his departure, he seemed to have quite forgotten his falcon. The blissful beam of her dark eye had totally bewildered his senses; unwittingly he spread his open arms towards her; she advanced a step, and her bashful downcast eye soon completed what its tender glance had begun.

"Christallina," said the old woman, who had observed all that had just passed with seeming pleasure, "the falcon we saw yesterday belongs to this gentleman; perhaps you have succeeded in making him a prisoner to-day." "Yes," returned she, "but not to give him up so soon again. You would not," addressing Albrecht, "give me all I require for him." "All," exclaimed Albrecht, "but most willingly myself, and all I possess." "Your riches, sweet stranger, have no charms for me; it is yourself I ask, yourself alone, and for ever!" Rudolph was terrified by the earnestness of her words, particularly when he saw the deep impression they made upon Albrecht. "Thine I will be, and for ever!" exclaimed he, as he clasped Christallina in his arms, and held her to his bosom, as if willing she should remain there to eternity. His friend was much struck by the singularity of the whole proceeding; to give himself up to an unknown and highly mysterious being, was a madness that only those who were present and beheld her superhuman beauty, could at all excuse, and nothing, indeed, but that beauty could have justified in the least the precipitate step he had taken. It would have been useless to remonstrate at such a moment, and his friend hoped to be better able to enforce his advice in the morning, when the first wild burst of passion should have subsided. For this reason he did not touch on the subject when they retired to the room allotted for their night's rest.

(To be continued.)

———————

(Continued from page 271.)

RUDOLPH was too fatigued to remain long awake; but the rising sun found Albrecht still pacing the chamber with agitated step and disordered air; he confessed that he had wandered about the house during the whole night, and that only the earnest entreaties of Christallina, and her repeated threats of never seeing him again, prevented his approaching her chamber. "God be praised!" cried Rudolph; and after a friendly expostulation, he succeeded in showing him his yesterday's mad conduct, in a proper light, and was at last delighted to see his remonstrances take a salutary effect on the disturbed mind of Albrecht. He threw himself on his bosom, and so far perceived and repented his thoughtless levity, that he was even willing to give up his dear falcon, rather than fulfil his engagement of yesterday. The appearance of the loathsome old woman who brought in their breakfast, served to strengthen his resolution. "Good God!" cried he, "that such a wretch was within an ace of becoming my mother-in-law." They were, however, disquieted by the thought that Christallina might keep him to his promise, and were considering the best method of evading it: but their fears on that head were misplaced; for the old woman soon re-appeared, to their surprise, arrayed after her fashion, in sumptuous apparel. She told them she came from her daughter, who awaited them, either to fulfil her engagement with Albrecht, or to give him back his promise; for she thought it wise to avoid precipitancy in such an affair. Overjoyed at these assurances, and from such a quarter, they followed her to the grotto, from whence her daughter came forth to meet them. Her appearance the evening before was but a faint reflection of the lustre her beauty and celestial figure shed around at present. And as her ruby lips opened, and her dark swimming eye, the true pledge of love and ardent passion, flashed on Albrecht, his cousin saw at once all his new-formed resolves consumed in that glance. "Handsome stranger!" said she, whilst a smile of ineffable brightness, that lit up the whole of her lovely countenance, played on her lips, "I owe, perhaps, your promise of yesterday to the earnest desire you expressed of obtaining your favorite. My love for you knows no bounds, and it therefore requires a love as ardent and sincere in return. I require all, or nothing! Go, sweet stranger, leave me, and let me see you no more, or be wholly mine for ever!" "Your's in life, your's until death!" cried Albrecht, prostrating himself before the beauteous girl. She raised and pressed him passionately in her arms; then slowly lifting her lovely eyes, depressed from a sense of her open confession, they suffused a beam of joy and happiness, over Albrecht's manly countenance, that seemed almost divine. The old woman then said to Rudolph, in a tone that bore a strong resemblance to Christallina's, "Man, be thou witness of the blessing I deal to this pair;" so saying, she placed her hands upon both their heads, exclaiming, "Woe be to them and their's that turn my blessing to a curse!" Rudolph stood petrified, for she spoke the last words in so dreadful a tone, that even Albrecht started from Christallina's arms to gaze upon her, and the glance that met his, gave rise to such an inward sensation of horror, that his trembling frame could scarcely support him. But the soft and enchanting sound of Christallina's voice soon re-assured him. "Now," said she, "youth of my soul! you shall have your redeemed falcon,—go and bring him, mother." She went, and returned with the bird on her hand. Albrecht burst forth into an extravagant cry of joy at the sight of his long-lost darling, and when he had secured him on his wrist, fondled him with expressions that proved how delighted he was at having at last attained the object of his tedious search.

It now became every moment a matter of greater wonder how these two beings, in this uninhabited wild, should possess all the articles of comfort to be met with in civilized society. "Who are you?" asked Albrecht, "and how do you live in this lone place?" "Those, my love," replied Christallina, "are short questions that require long answers. My birth-place is now no more of this world; the waves of the northern ocean, on which it was for some time borne, have received it in its depths again. As to any further intelligence, you must have patience until a fitter opportunity." Albrecht then began to think of returning to the castle; and upon offering to take Christallina with him, "No," said she, "go to your home, and think of me. Come as often as you please to me; but I cannot live with you in your habitations; it would only serve to remind me of a still greater splendor I am doomed to miss." A look from Albrecht seemed to ask an explanation; but she shook her head and left them.

The old woman now led the way; at times winding through thick underwoods, at others cut through by mountain torrents that came tumbling down from their sources, dashing their foam from rock to rock, at once impeding their progress, and rendering it unsafe. Albrecht, quite out of patience, asked their conductress, if she knew no better road. "Not by day," said she; "but I will be at the castle-gate with my lantern, every night at nine o'clock." "At the castle?" cried Albrecht; "why, woman, you know not its distance from hence." "Fear not," replied she, a ghastly smile overspreading her haggard features, "those who are well acquainted with the path as I am, will easily find the way." So saying, she left them to pursue their route alone. They gazed long in wonder after the mysterious hag, and neither seemed willing to interrupt the silence that reigned around.

When they arrived at the hut where they had intended to sleep, all its inhabitants participated in their joy at the recovery of the beloved falcon, although much astonished at their nightly ramble in those unfrequented parts. "You ought to bless your stars," observed an old peasant, "that you have escaped without danger; with many it is otherwise: and those who are lucky there may easily lose their road to salvation." "Do you know with any certainty what is likely to befal one there?" enquired Albrecht, a deadly paleness overshadowing his fine countenance. "I know nothing, nor wish I to know any thing," replied the peasant. They now took up their guns, and left the cottage. The conversation that had passed there, did not seem calculated to restore the young men's gaiety; and Albrecht had at most but a few words for his falcon. At length, seizing Rudolph by the arm, he exclaimed, deeply agitated, "Friend of my soul! could it have happened otherwise?" What could Rudolph answer, when he remembered well his own feelings at the time Albrecht's resolution vanished before Christallina's superhuman beauty.

They now arrived at the castle to the great joy of their friends, who began to entertain some fears as to their safety. Albrecht became from this time quite a different man; and it required an explanation, such as Rudolph alone could give, to account for the sudden change in his behaviour, and to comprehend how his former youthful gaiety could, in the eyes of his friends and the world, be superseded by that gloominess of spirit that now sat so heavily upon him. He soon began to suspect that the falcon from the hills was not his own, although the falconer, glad to escape the well-merited blame for its loss, persisted in its identity. Albrecht was himself at first of the same opinion; but he became every day more doubtful. He insisted that the falcon had at times something so terrific about him, that he was obliged to turn from him and his maddening gaze to escape contagion. He was nearly always absent from the castle alone. The neighbors had of late remarked the old lantern-carrier, and being all more or less given to superstition, they argued no good from such an appearance. After some time had elapsed Albrecht seemed partly to have regained his wonted cheerfulness, although his time was still divided between his hawks and hounds; but his present joy had a something about it that nearly bordered on madness, while his usual confidence was entirely withdrawn from Rudolph.

One day, on his return from the chase, he threw his arms round his cousin's neck, crying, "Friend, and more than brother, I have proved myself unworthy of your friendship by the most abominable connections; but my unhappy lot still entitles me to count upon the pity of a relation. I have now for some time past resolved to break those dreadful ties, that most unholy spell. Christallina still persists in concealing her birth and parentage from me, and remains by her first account of the sunken island, telling me, her father was a prince who sought refuge there from misfortunes. Whether this be true or not, I cannot take upon myself to determine; but I must ever look upon her and the old hag who stands in her service, as two awfully mysterious beings. Her beauty is every day new, and that it is which serves to distract me; for although her features visibly change, they still retain that fascination, which first allured me from my duty; but since yesterday, I hold her in such utter abhorrence, that I am resolved never to see her again." "Then," said Rudolph, "I fear you must have discovered something that gives you reason to hold the peasant's tales concerning her not altogether unfounded?" "It is but too true," replied Albrecht; "but there is a dark and fearful veil drawn over all that relates to her, and, woe to me! I am but too deeply entangled in the mazes of her hellish mysteries; but," added he, springing up, "I dare not repeat them." After these words, Albrecht went to the falconry. In a short time, Rudolph's attention was attracted by a loud triumphant laugh. He went to the window, and found it proceeded from Albrecht. He was staring at the falcon he held in his hand with and infuriated eye, while the animal at his last gasp, and bleeding from a wound he had inflicted, appeared to return his gaze with equal fierceness; he dashed his murdered favorite to the ground, and rushing into the room, exultingly exclaimed, "Thank God, I have now one demon less to deal with!" To such a burst of seeming frenzy, Rudolph had nothing to reply. At they stood together by the window, the falcon still stirred beneath the grass, when Albrecht put an end to his sufferings, by ordering him to be covered with a large stone. What occasioned the greatest astonishment, was, that the old lantern-carrier did not appear that night at the castle; they began to suspect she must be acquainted with the death of the falcon, and on that account remained absent. Evening succeeded evening, and the old hag came not. The violence exercised upon the bird, seemed to have broken all the former ties that existed between Albrecht and the inhabitants of the lonely hut. He considered himself now entirely free from their power, and that his present abode might not awaken any unpleasant sensations with respect to his former unhappy connexion, as also with the hope, that change of scene might tend to obliterate those recent circumstances from his mind, he determined upon leaving Rudolph's castle for his own domains immediately. From thence he often corresponded with the Count, and in one of his letters, acquainted him with his intention of espousing a cousin of his, for whom he had long cherished an affection.

(*To be continued.*)

(*Continued from page* 319, *Vol. XV.*)

ONE evening as Count von Swartzburg was present at an entertainment given by a nobleman in the vicinity, he was struck by the appearance of a beautiful woman, in splendid attire, resembling Christallina in all respects. Her extreme beauty attracted universal notice; and upon making enquiries relative to the mysterious stranger, he was told, she went by the name of Marchesa di Terrenci. After the crowd was in some measure diminished, she approached him, addressing him as follows—"You, Count von Swartzburg, have not, I presume, lately heard from your friend,

Count Albrecht?" "No," answered he, "not for some time past."
"Then," said she, "I can tell you, that he has returned to his castle, on
the banks of the Rhine, and as far as outward appearance goes, he
seems happy; but they who think so know not his heart. He is about
to enter into a matrimonial engagement with a relation of his; but
woe be to him and his intended bride! If he dares to accept her
hand, be assured, my vengeance, which those who once feel forget
not easily, shall sooner or later overtake him. The cruel death of the
falcon," added she, "although it tore him from my heart, could not
protect him from my revenge." So saying, she disappeared among
the crowd, and was seen no more that evening. Upon further enquiry, the Count found that nobody was acquainted with her, neither knew they from whence she came, or whither she went, after
her sudden departure from the entertainment. Rudolph, awed
by the solemn manner of her address, and fearful lest disastrous
consequences should follow such a warning, lost no time in com-
municating what had happened to Albrecht, entreating him as he
valued his own safety and the happiness of his intended bride, to
delay the solemnization of the nuptials for a short period. Unhappily the letter came too late for Albrecht to benefit by its contents.
He had already led his cousin Clara, in all the bloom and beauty
of youth to the altar. She had been brought up at a neighboring
convent, and since her mother's death, had been received into her
aunt's family where she was looked upon in the light of a daughter. Albrecht had seen her frequently there, and a mutual affection
having sprung up between them, they were united by the consent
of her guardians. Count Albrecht, young and handsome, possessed
something so noble and commanding in his countenance, so affa-
ble and fascinating in his address, that it was not to be wondered
that Clara became deeply enamoured of him; and she hoped in his
love and protection to ground all her future prospects of happiness.
Alas! poor girl, how much she was deceived! Though possessed of
many noble qualities, Albrecht had imbibed a wildness and ferocity
from his occupations and former roaming life, that ill accorded
with the mild disposition of his gentle mate. These circumstances,
therefore, naturally embittered her anticipated dream of bliss.
Count Rudolph's ill-timed communication, visibly affected his
conduct towards her. He now more than ever wandered about in

the hidden recesses of the forests with his hawks, seeking in vain to dissipate the fearful forebodings that pressed heavily on his mind. On his return late in the evenings, his cold and repulsive manner, added to the dark terror of his contracted brow, caused his wife to shudder at his presence, and in some measure to fear him. This fear had increased since one day, in reply to her remonstrances, as to his not frequenting the chapel at the usual times of service, he answered roughly, "What should I do there?" Towards the evening, poor Clara's apprehensions were renewed, as her husband always returned at that time, and she was used to see his tall shadow glide along the wall of the summer-house in which she retired to read, expanded to a giant shape, as reflected by the rays of the setting sun. His return in itself always conveyed an indescribable feeling, but the dreadful shadow had something so terrible in it, that she ran to the window to convince herself that her husband had not in reality assumed so hideous a form as the shadow represented. One evening in particular, she was more than usually appalled by the re-flected appearance. It came not as it was wont to do with slow and pensive step, but glided across the wall with a quickness she had never before witnessed. Upon rising to ascertain the cause of this extraordinary occurrence, she saw her husband turn the corner; contrary to custom, he did not proceed to the falconry, but came with a quick and agitated step, the bird still on his wrist, directly towards the spot she had retired to.

"Clara, my dear wife," cried he, an ashy paleness overspreading his convulsed features, "prepare, prepare yourself for the worst!" He had scarcely uttered these terrible words, when a woman, wrapped in a black veil, entered the apartment, and, going up to Clara, unveiled herself. "Your husband," so began the unknown, reddening, "your husband has been guilty of a crime against me, as well as yourself; I am, and still continue to be, his first and lawful wife. Consider then," added she, with a sarcastic sneer, "in what light I must look upon you!" "Count Albrecht," said the justly-irritated Clara, "it is for you, not me, to answer this woman, to tell her who we are, and how we stand connected." "Spare your pride until a fitter opportunity," retorted Christallina, "you see by his trembling how little he is in his proper place." "Vile woman!" exclaimed Albrecht, "do you accuse me of want of courage, you, who by hellish arts have ensnared my soul. Avaunt! malicious demon! I defy your machinations. This woman is mine by the approbation of the holy Church, and mine she shall ever remain." "Clara," vociferated the enraged Christallina, "beware, and dread my vengeance; for both your sakes, break off all further connection with him." "Never!" replied she, "that I will not, dare not do. It belongs rather to you to relinquish that which never was, and never can be your's." "You have pronounced your own sentence," cried the infuriated Christallina, her eyes beaming with such an unnatural fire, that Clara shuddered to meet their gaze: "mine he shall remain, even in death, whilst you must content yourself with his shadow." With a bitter smile, she seized the Count and dragged him from the room. Clara vainly attempted to cling to him, but her strength failed her, and she sank senseless to the ground. Her aunt was much shocked to discover her in this situation, and it was for some time before Clara could communicate to her the dreadful scene that had just taken place. Poor Clara was totally insensible to any consolation her aunt attempted to afford her, who after remaining with her for some time accompanied her to her chamber. There she fell into a deep reverie, which, from her excessive agitation, soon gave way to a quiet slumber. She was, however, suddenly awakened by a rustling noise against the wall, she thought she heard her husband, according to custom, hanging his night watch up there. "God be praised!" she exclaimed, "you are safe returned at last, dear Albrecht." She received no answer. Again she distinctly heard the clothes of his bed lifted up, and some person lay down in it. Trembling with affright, she called on him again; but still no answer. She then sprang up, took the shade from the night-lamp, and with a wild and terrified glance, searched the chamber through; but she still saw nothing. She now took up the lamp, and tottered to Albrecht's bed. Oh! what words can describe the icy chill of horror that crept over her agitated frame, when she discovered the bed empty and untouched, and the watch she had so lately heard against the wall not in its place! The cold dews of fear sat on her pallid brow, and pervaded her trembling limbs, as she stared wildly on the lonely bed, and the dreadful presentiment of evil darted across her mind. She had scarcely extinguished the lamp, and returned to her bed, when she again heard a noise in that

of her husband; she listened attentively, and distinguished the loud
breathings of a person sleeping; it became every moment stronger.
She sprang to Albrecht's bed with the full conviction of finding
him there, when, to her inexpressible terror, all was lone and still
as before. Although nobody appeared to be in the bed, she lifted up
the clothes with a palpitating heart; it was empty, and in complete
order, and it was this dreadful order, combined with the foregoing
mysterious circumstances, that almost occasioned the loss of her
senses. The horrid thought now occurred, that her husband must
be dead, and that this was the shadow with which Christallina had
threatened her, come to deceive her with the fond hope that it was
Albrecht himself. To her bed she dared not return, and shuddering
even at the thought of remaining alone in the fearful chamber, she
left it; but although she closed the door after her, the loud noise of
a sleeper still rang in her ears, and followed her as far as the three
rooms through which she passed. At length in an agony of superstitious horror, she threw herself at the foot of a crucifix, erected
in a small recess, in a distant apartment, and there poured forth her
soul in fervent prayer until the morning light burst through the
windows of the room.

(To be concluded in our next.)

———————

(Concluded from page 16.)

HER aunt, terrified at not finding her in her chamber, had followed
her thither, and not knowing the cause of Clara's dismay, was
shocked at the deadly paleness of her face, and the hollow wildness of her eyes. She descended with her, and tried to soothe her
by every consolation and kindness in her power. But Clara soon
found, that even the day was to have its peculiar horrors. After
breakfast, of which she partook to avoid the appearance of singularity, she sprang up suddenly, exclaiming, "Ah! there he is at last."
"Who?" demanded her aunt. "My dear, lost husband," frantically
replied she; "do you not hear him?" upon this she rushed into the
garden, calling upon her dear Albrecht, and searching for him in

every recess of its winding alleys; but receiving no answer, she
returned wringing her hands, and sunk into her chair in a perfect
state of insensibility. She had experienced the same deceit as in the
night before, and heard Albrecht's voice, busied in the falconry,
only she thought the cries of the animals were more piercing than
usual. Her friends, persuaded as to the madness of her assertions,
vainly attempted to overcome her fears by every argument in their
power. She was too certain of the terrible reality to be convinced
she was in error; and taking a book, was left once more to meditate
on the late extraordinary occurrences. The cries of the falcons and
hounds, with the occasional chiding voice of her husband, continued distinctly throughout the day; but as often as she hastened
down in the fond expectation of meeting him, so often was she
cruelly deceived, for not even a trace of what she heard was to be
found. Until this time she had avoided the summer-house, from the
scene that had there taken place, with all its direful consequences,
being still fresh in her memory; but as it could not be more terrible to her than her own chamber, she retired thither towards the
evening. The shadow, that she had before so much dreaded, she
now prayed for as a blessing, as she knew it must be the forerunner
of Albrecht's happy return. "Alas!" said she, sighing, when the sun
had just reached the point at which it usually appeared, "alas! today
I fear the dark resemblance will not come to warn me of his much-
wished approach." The words had scarce died on her lips, when
the gigantic shadow stalked in a bent and melancholy attitude
across the accustomed wall. She then with heartfelt joy sprang to
the window, stretching out her arms more to welcome the sight
than to protect her from its approach. She hastened to the wall, that
she might not be again deceived; the shadow had not yet passed,
and with her hands before her eyes, dreading to search for that
she most wished to find, she precipitately left the room. Clara was
met by Count Rudolph, to all appearance just arrived from a long
journey. "O God!" exclaimed the agitated Clara, "have you seen my
husband?" Rudolph took her hand, and gazing on her mournfully,
broke by degrees the dreadful news that Albrecht had expired in his
arms at eleven the night before, at a strange inn, where he had by
chance found him; and that he just came in time to soothe the last
moments of his dying friend. A dreadful shudder thrilled through

Clara's veins, as she called to mind that eleven was the hour when she first heard the rustling noise in her chamber. With a faltering voice, she asked, how Albrecht had spent the last minutes of his life. "At his earnest request," replied Rudolph, "a priest attended him, at the sight of whom, the mysterious stranger, who tore him from your arms, departed enraged, showering imprecations on the head of her repentant victim. Through me, he entreats your forgiveness for the past, in the hopes of which he departed in peace." "Forgive him," cried Clara, bursting into an agony of grief, "yes, that I do, from my heart; it would ill befit a sinner like me to withhold forgiveness from one, who after a life of misery and woe has been mercifully received into the bosom of his Creator, through a timely repentance, and the reconciliation with the holy church. You, my dear friend, have, and ever must, retain my warmest thanks for your kindness." "And now," said Rudolph, "let me give you some few last lines from him you hold so dear. I should not have interrupted your unfeigned sorrow, by presenting them now, had it not been the dying request of poor Albrecht." "Why not?" replied Clara, stifling her grief, "all that comes from him must be dear to me: give me the letter." She opened it with a trembling hand, and having bedewed it with a stream of tears, read the following words:—

"Dear Clara,

"I die in hope of your forgiveness, and therefore die happy. How well could the bearer repay you for all the pain and anxiety I have caused; believe me, my love, I should leave this world with less regret did I know you safe in the love and protection of my friend. Farewell, my beloved wife, as I trust we shall meet hereafter.

"ALBRECHT VON SINNERN."

"Rudolph," said the weeping Clara, "although my husband's wishes must be dear to me, I have still more sacred duties to perform. At present, I can give no decisive answer. My heart, torn by such a succession of fearful incidents, knows not at present how to decide; but you shall hear from me soon."

The effects of the exasperated Christallina's threat did not, however, cease to pursue their intended victim, and worn down by terror and grief, she at length sought refuge in the convent she had been brought up at, and after a time, recovered a portion of that serenity of mind and calmness of spirit, which a pious observance of holy exercises never fails to pour as a balm on the wounded soul; but she never was wholly herself again. She, of course, refused Count Rudolph's hand, although she held him in the highest esteem. Poor Clara lived many years at this convent in seeming peace, beloved by the Abbess, who being a particular friend of her deceased mother, cherished her as a daughter, and admired by all those who knew her, as well for her kind and benevolent conduct, as for her mild and unassuming manners.

AZIM.

THE HAUNTED MINE.

A Forest Tale.[1]

"What joys are the life of a hunter surrounding,
    For whom foams so richly the cup of delight?
With rifle and horn through the broad forest bounding,
    Or stretched in the shade by the streamlet so bright.
How glorious to see the fleet stag vainly flying,
    The hound in the wild wood, the hawk in the air,
The pastime of princes, all others outvying,
    What sport upon earth with the chase can compare?
Yo! ho! tra, la! le!"[2]

THE bright sun, glancing through the waving branches of the trees, chequered the forest path with golden light, threw a strong illumination upon wild fantastic rocks, which reared their bare peaks amid the umbrageous[3] foliage, and played upon the sparkling waters of a clear stream, as it ran brawling along, sometimes washing the antique roots of gigantic oaks, at others, flinging its white foam in fairy cascades, or spreading into silent pools, ere it stole beneath the overhanging osiers,[4] and hid its limpid current deep in the recesses of the lonely wood. The joyous matin of the birds had ceased, but the forest was animated by the chirp and twitter of the feathered tribe, the glad buz of innumerable insects, and the

---

1 Vol. 24, i.s. (1826): Nov., 259-264; Dec., 325-329; Vol. 25, i.s. (1827): Jan., 25-30.

2 From "No Sport upon Earth with the Chase Can Compare" in *The Universal Songster; or, Mirth: Forming the Most Complete, Extensive, and Valuable Collection of Ancient and Modern Songs in The English Language: with a Copious and Classified Index.* Vol. 1. Translated from Weber by Barham Livius. London: John Fairburn; Simpkin and Marshall; and Sherwood, Gilbert, and Piper, 1825, p. 116.

3 *umbrageous*: Abounding in shade; shaded by trees or the like; overshadowed (*OED*).

4 *osier*: Any of several willows with tough pliant branches used in basketwork (*OED*).

rustling of the four-footed leverets[1] of the glade through bush and brake.

Delighted to escape from his high stool in his father's counting-house at Frankfort,[2] Hermen[3] Sellner thought that he had travelled far enough in search of the rural repose which had been recommended by the renowned Doctor Hotze, as the only means of restoring his declining health. The invalid looked round in the anxious hope of descrying some human habitation; beguiled, by the beauty of the scenery, from his original intention of penetrating as far as the village of Waldensen. A few steps farther onwards, the voices of domestic animals attracted his attention, and he came suddenly upon the *forst haus*, a mean and dilapidated tenement, which peeped from beneath the trees: a bush over the porch indicated that it was open for the reception of strangers; but there was something so painfully revolting in the appearance of an old man who sate on a log of wood at the door, furbishing a rusty rifle, that the horseman paused: indeed, so dark, sinister, and suspicious, was the countenance of this person, that Herman, who was suffering under a nervous disease, would have relinquished his lately-formed design of asking a lodging, but that, at the moment of his resolve to continue his journey, an angel-face glanced from an upper window; the view was only for an instant, but one glimpse of the bright sunny curls, the radiant blue eyes, the brow of snow, and the dimpled mouth of the beautiful vision, sufficed to chain the traveller to the spot; and alighting, he received a surly welcome from the forester; who motioned him to enter an inner room, while a half-clothed urchin, whose patched garments were only fitted for summer wear, led his horse to a shed which served for a stable. Every thing about the place manifested the struggles of some active spirit against the most squalid poverty; the house, though ruinous, was clean; and Herman thought that he could discover the weak endeavours of a delicate female hand to preserve order in the midst of desolation. A few flowers bloomed in pots; a wild vine was carefully trained across the broken lattice; and a pewter platter or two, among the wooden trenchers, shone like silver.

1 *leveret*: A young hare, strictly one in its first year (*OED*).
2 Old spelling of "Frankfurt" (Frankfurt am Main, Germany).
3 After this initial mention, "Hermen" is spelled "Herman."

When the young hostler had groomed the horse to the utmost of his ability, he placed a coarse and frugal meal before his guest. Notwithstanding the hunger produced by his ride, the squeamish appetite of Herman could not relish a mess of stewed cabbage and goat's-milk cheese; enquiring if there was nothing better to be had, the boy, with a sly smile, said, that perhaps the gentleman would prefer a mutton-collop,[1] "though," added he, with a broader grin, "the forest sheep acquire a queer taste, rather too strong for some folks, and the meat may be darker than that you get in town." Vanishing with this speech, he presently re-entered, bearing a savoury dish, which, from its flavour, our traveller shrewdly guessed was composed of more dainty flesh than the animal which had been named could afford; a pitcher of indifferent wine closed the repast; and, during its continuance, Herman entered into conversation with his young attendant, asking sundry questions respecting the cottage, and its inmates. "Ah! sir," said the boy, "this used to be a grand place in the old Lord de Wenebourgh's[2] time; he gave it to my grandfather, who saved his life once in hunting the stag, and both he and my father were chief rangers; father lost that place through the villany of the bailiff, as I have heard tell; and our young lord has been poisoned against him. Poor Gottfried's gone, that used to be the life of the forest; so there is only my mother and me left now." "Is then there no female inhabitant of this house except your mother?" enquired Herman, anxiously. "Oh, yes," replied the communicative attendant, "there is Magdalena."—"Is she your sister?"—"No, but I love her as well, every body loves her, and she is like a sister too, only Gottfried did not think so. But, hush! we must not speak of him. Poor fellow! no one cares to talk of him now; and my father declares, that if ever he attempts to shew his face in the forest, he'll shoot him as he would a kite or a carrion-crow. Those were rare days that I have heard my mother talk of, when Gottfried and my father held places in the Count's service, but that's all over; and all is laid to Gottfried's door; he bears the blame." Herman was about to enquire farther into the delinquent's history, but his attention was suddenly diverted by a voice from without. Drawing near

---

1 Mutton chop.

2 After this initial mention, "Wenebourgh" is spelled "Wernebourgh."

to the lattice he saw his host standing in a cringing attitude, before a young man of a noble and commanding appearance, clad in the green dress of a chasseur.[1]

"What!" exclaimed the stranger, "you old villain! do you deny the fact? why, the very atmosphere around you is impregnated with the steam of venison. By St. Hildebrand, the moon never glimpsed upon a more audacious deer-stealer. Last night, but that my bullet glanced against a tree, I had rewarded thee for all the gallant bucks that have bled beneath thy murderous knife."—"An' it please your excellency," returned the accused, "I am abused in this matter: may the fiend's malison[2] light upon me, if I stirred from my poor hut the livelong night; and as to venison, these lank jaws of mine have not known the taste of meat since your highness vouchsafed us the fragments of the wild-boar feast. Travellers are starved away from my door."—"Knave," rejoined the chasseur, "thou hast gorged thyself, and fattened all thy customers with the ruddiest haunches that ever graced the banquet of a king; but there shall be an end of this; beware how thou dost provoke my vengeance. The very next offence, I'll drive thee, with dog-whips, from the forest, or hunt thee through the district with my hounds."—"Nay, but your excellency," returned the poacher, "it is hard that I should suffer for the deeds of others: inflict the severest penalty of the old forest law, if ever you find Christian Altman pursuing forbidden sport."—"Now the saints grant me patience," exclaimed the chasseur, raising his voice and catching up the rifle which lay upon the log of wood beside him.—"Confess all thy villany, or, by the blessed Lord! I'll send thee unshrived to the realm that gapes for thee." Thus speaking, he aimed a blow, with the butt-end of the fowling-piece, at Altman's head. Herman was in the act of springing through the window to prevent the bloodshed which he feared would ensue, but the stroke was arrested ere it fell; Magdalena bent her fair face from an upper lattice, which, in consequence of the irregularity of the building, was visible from the apartment occupied by the traveller; the moment that the chasseur caught a glimpse of the lovely girl, he dismissed all traces of anger, doffed his cap gallantly,

1 *chasseur*: A huntsman; a hunter (*OED*).
2 *malison*: A curse, a malediction (*OED*).

and placing himself immediately beneath her window, began to converse in a soft low tone: so gently, indeed, that the words were lost to Herman; but his gestures were those of mild entreaty; and it was evident that he employed all his rhetoric to prevail upon Magdalena, to come down and walk with him through the forest. She, however, was inexorable, yet she smiled sweetly upon him, as she shook her bright tresses in denial of his suit.

Christian Altman had never, apparently, felt much alarm at the chasseur's threats, but when he turned to speak with Magdalena, the forester, unaware that Herman's eye was upon him, cast malignant scowls towards the imperious youth, on whom he had so lately fawned with abject servility. Magdalena did not remain long at the lattice; it was evident that those loud menaces, uttered in her hearing, were only intended to draw her from her retreat, and having succeeded in restoring a calm, she cast a conscious look upon the noble suppliant, and retired. The cavalier lingered for a considerable time after she had withdrawn, and flinging a rix dollar[1] at the feet of Altman, he bade him be honest; and then departed. Herman being now sufficiently recruited[2] from the fatigues of his journey, wandered into the forest, which was beautifully diversified, in some places opening into patches of green sward, shaded by maple and linden trees, from whence long vistas, canopied by the spreading boughs of oak and elm, led into deeper recesses; in other parts, thick, gloomy, and almost impenetrable; or forming wild ravines, where a waste of ragged rocks, crowned with the pine, gave an air of savage grandeur to the scene. While thus straying whither fancy led, Herman took care not to proceed to any considerable distance from the cottage, being anxious to obtain a full view of Magdalena, and thinking that she might be induced to come forth, if the chances of encountering the stranger were lessened. He was not deceived in this expectation; bounding like a fawn, the fair girl entered the wild wood, assisting little Frity to gather fuel for household consumption. Nothing but the surpassing beauty of her countenance

---

1 *rix-dollar*: A silver coin and unit of account, current from the late 16th to the mid 19th centuries in various European countries, esp. the Netherlands, the Holy Roman Empire (and subsequently the Austrian Empire), Sweden, Denmark, and Scotland (*OED*).
2 Recovered.

could exceed the grace and elegance of her form; and Herman marvelled to see a creature so superior even to many of the loveliest of her sex, domesticated with mean, not to say, dishonest peasants. She approached the spot where he sate concealed; he arose and accosted her respectfully. Magdalena replied with much courtesy, and a short conversation ensued; but feigning to have employment within, she soon returned to the house, leaving Herman enchanted with the modest sweetness of her manners. He would almost have fancied her a being of no mortal mould, a gentle spirit, etherial as air, haunting the green and silent glade; but Frity, who was at hand, satisfied him that the object of his admiration was a child of earth. Magdalena's history was sufficiently romantic to have created a strong interest in a bosom less susceptible of sympathetic feelings than that of the amiable traveller. Her father, Captain Wolkenhor, a young brother of a noble family, had offended his relatives, by an imprudent marriage with a person of low birth. Oppressed by the relentless persecution of those haughty kinsmen, baffled in every attempt to repair his ruined fortunes, and rendered desperate by repeated disappointments, he joined a faction adverse to the reigning government, and, the conspiracy being discovered, incurred a sentence of banishment; hardly escaping the severer doom which awaited his associates. The path of the exile lay through the forest of Waldensen, and subdued by the anxiety of his mind, and the hardships to which he had been exposed, before he could reach its confines, he was seized by fever and delirium; the hapless companion of his adversity gladly obtained for him the shelter of Altman's cottage. A long and dangerous illness ensued, which terminated in the total loss of the use of his limbs. Thus disabled from making farther exertion, the low state of his finances compelled him to become a resident in the wilderness, whither chance had directed his wandering steps. Unfortunately, the old Count de Wernebourg had quitted this earthly scene previous to the arrival of the exile's family, bequeathing his property to a grandson, then a mere child, under the guardianship of his widowed mother, who resided with her own relations in a distant part of the country.

After the lapse of a few years, the partner of Wolkenhor's afflictions died, and Magdalena became the sole consolation of her bereaved father. An infant at the period of his disgrace, she had never passed the boundaries of the forest; and as she grew into girlhood, the profits of her needle supplied the means of existence; and but for the exemplary industry of the indefatigable girl, and the charity of the Altmans, then fast sinking into poverty, through the misconduct of the old forester, and the dissolute habits of his eldest son, the forlorn exile must have perished in the most abject misery. He died when Magdalena had attained her sixteenth year; and, too grateful for the support which her father had received to abandon those who had given him shelter, she cheerfully offered to assist Gertrude Altman in her domestic affairs; and, though shy of shewing herself to the few customers who demanded hospitality at the obscure spot in which the forester had fixed his abode, was the prop and support of the house.

From the disjointed narrative of Frity, Herman learned that, previous to the arrival of Count Ernest de Wernebourg, who had only lately taken possession of his estates, the Altmans, though dismissed from the appointments which they held in the family, drew their chief subsistence from the forest; but that now, owing to their audacious infractions of the law, it was both difficult and dangerous to pursue the midnight chase. He gathered also, that Gottfried, even more unprincipled than his father, had, when compelled to fly the country, robbed old Altman of his little store of hoarded gold. "Ah!" cried the boy, "Magdalena often tried to persuade my brother to give up his dishonest pursuits, and to work at some farm, until he should be able to take a little land of his own; and, but for my mother and me, I am sure, she would have left the forest long ago, though she had no place to go to, poor thing. It would break my mother's heart to lose her, for she still weeps after Gottfried, and still hopes, though she dare not tell Magdalena so, that he will return and gain her consent at last to be his wife!

E. R.[1]

(*To be continued.*)

---

1 Although no further information identifies the author, "E.R.," in an unusual move, is appended to each of the installments of "The Haunted Mine."

(*Continued from page* 264.)

"He lies deep in earth,
The forest boughs wave o'er him: birds will sing
As blithely, and the fawn shall calmly sleep
Upon an unblest grave, as though he stretched
His limbs on sod unstained with human blood."[1]

HERMAN felt a strong inclination to question Frity concerning the Count, but respect to the fair orphan withheld him; yet he determined to observe the conduct of the parties silently, and to shape his own in accordance to it. His quiet manners and delicate health soon recommended him to Magdalena, and she permitted him to sit for hours by her side; when she would talk to him of her father, and of the traditions of the forest, all of which she herself devoutly believed; more particularly the strange tales related of an ancient mine, which had been long disused, and which was said to be the haunt of the demons of the waste. Magdalena spoke, also, of the motherly care of Gertrude Altman, and of the debt of gratitude which she owed to the family. Herman, however, guessed that Ernest de Wernebourg was the attraction which chained her to the forest; the young man evidently loved her, and lurked about in every spot where she was likely to be seen; but pride checked the proposal dictated by honour, and to no other would the maiden listen. Magdalena, inexperienced, and under the influence of young affection, suffered her sanguine spirit to cherish bright hopes of the future; and the sweet consciousness of being beloved was, in the early progress of their attachment, quite sufficient to create happiness. Herman Sellner looked on, and sighed; he dared not reveal the secret feelings of his heart; for even if Magdalena could have concealed the preference she yielded to another, he was aware

1 Unclear source. A similar speech appears in Giovanni's speech in *The Florentines: A Dramatic Tale* (1830), Scene III, by Emma Roberts. The only differences are the substition of "She" for "He" and "her" for "him," as Giovanni is speaking of his murdered wife. But because of the later publication date, it may be that the author of "The Haunted Mine," E. R., was Emma Roberts, who perhaps drew upon her own work in progress.

that his parents would not sanction his union with one so low in fortune's favour. Notwithstanding all these obstacles, he would not wholly despair; his noble rival would, perchance, relinquish a pursuit which he could only gain by the sacrifice of many prejudices; and if he should shrink from marriage, Magdalena, forlorn and abandoned, might be persuaded to accept his hand, even though he should be compelled to keep his engagement secret from his sordid family. These sweet, yet delusive, expectations kept hope alive; and now grown familiar with the lovely orphan, she, secure in his protection, no longer refused to join the rustic assembly, who frequently met before the gates of de Wernebourgh's castle, to indulge in country sports. The Count displayed his fine figure to great advantage on those occasions: he was a gallant hunter, a graceful dancer, and unrivalled in the athletic exercises of the field. Scorning the invalid, whose pale countenance and nerveless limbs inspired him with contempt, he felt no apprehension when he saw Magdalena lean upon the arm of her debilitated escort; and bestowed a proud civility upon the insignificant stranger, which Herman bore patiently for Magdalena's sake, although his spirit chafed against it. Mounted on a fiery courser, and making rock and dale ring with the echoing hoof and horn, de Wernebourg, at the head of a jovial train of hunters, would sweep through the green wood; and Magdalena's sparkling eye, raised from the book which Sellner was reading to her, as they were seated on some sunny bank, told how strongly admiration was kindled by that noble form, and how little interest was excited by tales and legends of other times, when he, who was dearer than a thousand heroes of romance, appeared, radiant with manly beauty, and foremost in the chase. With what joy, at sun-set, did the delighted girl quit Herman's side to mingle with her noble partner in the dance; and, though careful not to suffer herself to be drawn away from her companions, her smiles and blushes might be seen even in the dim twilight; and, as Sellner was of the party, she frequently permitted the Count to walk with her to the last turn leading to Altman's cottage. Bitter were the mortifications which the slighted lover experienced as he listened to the converse of the enamoured pair, yet, despite of the certainty that a mutual attachment existed between them, he gathered fresh hope from the developement of de Wernebourg's haughty disposition; and though his heart bled at the anticipation of Magdalena's sufferings, when she should discover the cruel selfishness of the Count's intentions, there was a prospect beyond, which he contemplated with the most ecstatic delight.

A few weeks passed away, in which Herman, though frequently saddened by melancholy reflections, enjoyed more exquisite pleasure than had ever blessed any previous portion of his existence; he spent whole hours by the side of Magdalena, fondly trusting that he was gaining rapid advances in her good opinion, and that he might be secure of her friendship, even if he could not succeed in touching her heart. He perceived that his lovely mistress grew hourly more reserved in her demeanour towards the Count: her modesty had taken alarm at some freedoms which he had offered; and she now began to avoid him most sedulously. Sellner was deceived by the calmness of her manner: while relinquishing those interviews which had afforded her so much happiness, he knew not, that, confiding in her lover's attachment, she flattered herself that, their intercourse being restrained, he would openly avow an honourable passion, and make her his wife.

Yet though suffering little uneasiness respecting de Wernebourg's final decision, Magdalena felt much anxiety on Gertrude Altman's account. The forester spent whole days carousing in the neighbouring village of Waldensen, obtaining the means of indulging in continued intoxication by his nightly depredations; and the trembling girl feared that her influence with the Count would be insufficient to save him from merited punishment. Gradually sinking into utter licentiousness, he had grown incorrigible in his habits, and reckless of the consequences, and scarcely took the slightest pains to conceal the dishonest practices by which he supported himself in luxurious idleness.

Herman perceived that this state of affairs could not be of long duration; and very doubtful of de Wernebourg's motives in seeking to gain an interest in Magdalena's heart, looked forward to the rapid approach of that period, when deprived even of the wretched shelter afforded by Altman's roof, she would scarcely have any alternative between accepting the Count's dishonourable proposals, or of becoming the wife of a more disinterested lover. He indulged at the same time in sweet dreams of future bliss, a secret marriage, and precious hours, stolen from the noise and bustle of the city, spent in visits to his secluded bride. These delightful visions were, however, occasionally disturbed by the cruel apprehension that Magdalena's discouragement of de Wernebourg was only shewn in the presence of observing eyes.

One dark night, when the heat of the weather prevented sleep, he arose, and seated himself at the window of his narrow apartment to inhale the dewy air, while sunk in pensive contemplations, a low rustling in the vine awakened his attention; a slight sound, repeated at intervals, kept him vigilant; but such was the extreme caution of the midnight visitant, that, although completely on the alert, it was with difficulty that Herman's eye detected a dark form gliding away into the depths of the forest. The next morning, he would have spoken on the subject to Magdalena, but she had caught a suspicion that the young merchant's attachment was something more than common friendship, and she shunned him, or took care that Frity should make a third in their interviews.

The following evening, Herman's fears were changed to certainty: the figure appeared again; it was too tall for Altman: "and why," he asked, "should he seek clandestine admittance into his own house?" It could, he imagined, be no other than de Wernebourg; and Magdalena's altered looks evinced that the serenity of her mind had fled; tears, which she vainly tried to conceal, chased each other down her cheeks; but she shrunk from the confidence to which Herman, though a prey to the darkest suspicions, invited her. He, therefore, guided by several minor circumstances which passed under his observation, concluded that the Count had disclosed the baseness of his views; and, while keeping aloof in the day, and menacing Altman with the severest vengeance of the outraged laws, stole secretly, at night, to urge a suit which Magdalena, though hearing with anguish, possessed not sufficient fortitude to repel. Alas! it was only too visible that the hopeless maiden's peace was wrecked: and, despite of the weakness of his arm, Sellner determined to front[1] the seducer in his nightly path, and force him to do justice to the innocence, whose injury he meditated, or, die in the attempt.

---

1 Confront.

After all the family had retired to bed, the anxious lover stole softly from his chamber; and wrapping a cloak around him, proceeded cautiously in the direction which led to de Wernebourg's castle. Once or twice he thought that he could discern a moving object in the deep gloom; but he wished to approach the Count as closely as possible ere he accosted him, lest he might only give a warning to one so desirous of concealment, for escape.

A low wind agitated the boughs of the forest trees, and they creaked heavily in the blast; the branches, as they bent to and fro, assumed fantastic shapes. Amid the deep sighing of the woods, and waving of the foliage, Herman fancied that the whole wilderness was peopled with unearthly creatures. A superstitious horror crept over him; he paused, watching anxiously for approaching footsteps, whilst the murmur of the forest increased.

Amid the crashing boughs and rustling leaves, he thought that he could distinguish a blow and a fall, as if some living creature had been smitten to the ground. A fearful groan struck his ear; and as the sound was repeated, the voice of the listener died within him; but though too much agitated to speak, he hurried onwards to the spot whence he thought the cry proceeded. The thunder now rolled too awfully to admit of hearing more; breaking his eager way through the trees, a bright flash of lightning threw a strong illumination upoon the surrounding scene, and Herman distinctly saw a man dragging a prostrate body along the ground. All was instantaneously involved in darkness, whilst peals of thunder rent the sky. Blinded by the rain which fell in torrents, the bewildered youth, after wandering for some time at random, with difficulty retraced his steps to the cottage.

All there was buried in profound repose. His first idea was to call up Altman, that they might search for the track of the murderer with lighted torches; but the old man was not in his bed; Gertrude slept soundly, and he deemed it useless to alarm her by the tale of his night's adventure. Herman waited impatiently for the return of his host, his heart throbbing at the recollection of the black deed which the forest had disclosed.

E. R.

(To be concluded in our next.)

(Concluded from page 329, Vol. XXIV.)

THE shrill clarion of the early cock fell with a startling sound upon Herman's ear, and when day began to dawn, and birds and insects came gladly forth to meet the light, the depression of his spirits increased; all nature seemed to rejoice, and man alone, conscious of the guilt and misery of his fellows, surveyed the lovely scene with disquietude. Every leaf was effulgent with pendant rain-drops, glittering like diamonds in the sun: the heavy clouds wreathed majestically away; the deer roused themselves from their green lairs to browze; and flocks of wood-pigeons, emerging from the depths of the wilderness, urged their flight in search of food.

Regardless of his dripping garments, Herman was on the point of plunging into the forest, in the hope that day-light would enable him to make some discovery, when the appearance of Altman prevented him. To this man he had ever entertained a strong dislike, and when he saw him stealing cautiously from under the trees, a suspicion crossed his mind; and he would have retired to watch his movements, but the forester's keen eye had already discovered that he was recognized. Coming forward with a careless air he said, "This wild night, sir, has drawn you forth; yet 'tis strange to me, that gentles who might sleep softly should be scared from their beds by a summer's storm; an' I had wherewithal to keep the wolf from the door, the owl and the bat might play their gambols alone. But poor folks must live, and as I am sure you are too generous and honourable to betray the unfortunate, I am free to confess that a stately buck lies cold under the brambles by the withered oak." Herman, during this address, obtained time to collect his scattered thoughts, and he became suddenly averse to speak upon the subject of the murder, if indeed his senses had not deceived him; and returning a light answer, he sought his chamber.

The inmates of the cottage were soon stirring; and, resolved to be guided by circumstances, Sellner composed his spirits, and endeavoured to assume the appearance of calmness. A day or two passed, in which Altman, contrary to his usual habits, remained at home, either amusing himself in the house or employed in its outer repair. Signs of uneasiness were visible in the countenances of Gertrude and of Magdalena; both were frequently in tears. The aspect of all things seemed changed. Summer had scarcely passed its meridian, yet its joys were fled, and nothing but gloom and desolation remained.

Herman was ever on the watch; but the nocturnal disturber of his repose appeared no more. He was surprised at the long period which had elapsed since de Wernebourg's last visit to the cottage. "Had he," asked Herman, "devoted[1] his victim so soon?"—The thought was piercing, and he resolved that the heartless libertine should not escape from the punishment due to his crime. Magdalena's anxious eyes were often directed towards the forest, but still the Count came not; and by the report of one of the rangers, who occasionally emptied a pitcher of wine at the door, she learned that his long absence from home occasioned some uneasiness to his household. He was in the habit of repairing to a distant hunting lodge alone; but the servants at the castle had been surprised and dismayed by the intelligence that he had not been seen at the place whither it was supposed he had gone.

A grim smile passed across Altman's face as the ranger related the apprehensions excited on de Wernebourg's account; and its dark expression did not escape the observant Sellner. A sickening sensation came over him; a sudden conviction that no phantom of the imagination had mingled its illusions with the storm in the forest, on that gloomy night. The Count had but too probably fallen a victim to the hatred which he delighted to provoke.

Magdalena listened, pale and agitated, to the ranger's alarming tale; clasping her hands together she fled weeping from the house, and Herman followed; he now caught a sudden glimpse of a woman's garment fluttering through the trees, heard the sobs of feminine distress; he hurried forward at the sound, and, in the afflicted person, encountered Gertrude Altman. Though deeply disappointed, it was not in the young merchant's nature to turn away from human suffering; he sate down beside his hostess, and besought her to confide her grief to him, with the full assurance of his sympathy, if it admitted of no other consolation.

1 Appropriated, i.e., seduced.

"Ah sir," she cried, "I know you are compassionate and will pity the sorrows of a mother; my son, sir, my poor, misguided Gottfried, he is dear to me though all the world should hold him in detestation? it is for him that I shed these tears. I fear some sad accident has befallen him, for he was too venturous in coming back to the forest, when, with all his caution, so many persons would know and recognize him. It is five nights since he has stolen to the cottage to afford me one of those recent interviews which were at once the joy and grief of my heart, for, alas! I dared not let his father know that he had returned."

"It was your son, Gottfried, then," enquired Herman, a weight of anxiety removed from his heart, "whom I have seen at midnight in conversation with some of the family in the porch."

Gertrude replied in the affirmative, and added, "other eyes, I fear, also have observed him: his mysterious disappearance, and that of the Count de Wernebourg, fill me with horrible apprehensions: should they have met, and the event is too probable, one or both may have fallen. Gottfried is rash, and jealous of Magdalena; who, he justly fears, has devoted her best affections to the Count."

Herman felt that he could give no consolation to the afflicted mother; the scene in the forest afforded strong evidence of the commission of a murder, but he no longer suspected Altman to be the perpetrator of the crime, and he rejoiced that he had not denounced the old forester to the civil authorities. The misery Magdalena would suffer when deprived of her only home, deterred him, together with his dislike to subject a fellow creature to the tortures which, he knew, would be applied to extort a confession of guilt, where the proofs were so doubtful.

Absorbed in painful meditations, advancing he knew not whither, Herman involved himself in the intricacies of the forest, and, in endeavouring to gain a more trodden path, approached the precincts of The Haunted Mine.

The spot was wild and desolate, girt around with huge black pines, beneath whose noxious boughs no plant would bloom; the shaft, covered with a coarse vegetation of rank weeds, shewed a dismal gulf which yawned below. Herman had imbibed a superstitious dread of this place, yet he stood as if spell-bound, and bending forwards looked down the dark abyss. Not a leaf moved, not a bird stirred, the inhabitants tenanting this dreary abode were silent, and the very air was motionless.—In the midst of this awful stillness, a wild cry burst upon the stranger's ear, he started and drew back; but, in despite of the appalling horrors which rushed upon his heart, he again stooped over the mouth of the shaft, and now distinctly heard a long and heavy groan.

Ashamed of his fears, and arming himself with the idea that some wild beast had fallen down the chasm, and was perishing for want of assistance, his compassion was aroused, and shaking off those unmanly apprehensions which shaped mysterious dangers in the dreary haunt, he entered the aperture.

The descent was steep, and almost precipitous; but, with care and caution, the adventurer reached the bottom in safety. Again there came a cry, fearful and withering, as if uttered in the last paroxysm of despair. The voice, no longer deadened by a barrier of earth, sounded as if issuing from human lips. Sellner groped his way onwards, and, guided by the renewed groans, turned an angle in this cavern. A faint light now gleamed upon him through a fissure from above, and he perceived a door, across which a heavy wooden bar had been drawn. Removing the fastening, he stepped within; and beheld, upon the floor of a dreary dungeon, the prostrate form of de Wernebourg. The Count grasped the hand of his deliverer; and exerting all his strength, with Herman's assistance, gained the surface of the earth.

Pausing to recruit his failing spirits, the young merchant learned, that the rescued nobleman had been stunned while pursuing his solitary sports in the forest, by a blow, struck by an unseen enemy, on the back of the head; and that, upon recovering, he found himself a prisoner in the mine, under the custody of a stranger; who, by the Count's description, Herman felt convinced could have been no other than Gottfried, and who had probably, leaving his victim to perish by a miserable death, fled upon some alarm; to which he must have been continually subjected, in a place where there were so many chances of detection and discovery.

De Wernebourg now bitterly reproached himself with the ungenerous part which he had acted towards Magdalena; he confessed to Herman, that, repulsed by her steady virtue, he had determined to take advantage of the knavery of Altman, to deprive her of the protection afforded by his cottage, and to oblige her to seek a refuge in his castle from the pressure of poverty. Pity for the abject destitution of the family, and anxiety to gain the fair orphan's good opinion, had induced him to pardon numerous acts of dishonesty which daily fell under his knowledge; but when no longer hoping to succeed by kindness, he descended to menaces, and swore bitterly to Magdalena that he would bring the forester to justice, his own imprisonment in the mine alone prevented the execution of these threats which had been overheard by Altman.

Left to reflection, with the prospect of a lingering death before him, the Count found leisure to repent of his base designs against the fairest flower in the forest; and being rescued from a yawning grave, he assured his deliverer, who generously rejoiced in the prospect of Magdalena's happiness, that henceforward he would abandon every unhallowed thought against her purity, and woo her for his bride.

Three days had elapsed since a scanty allowance of provision, found by the Count in his dungeon, had been completely exhausted; and as the castle was at a considerable distance, he determined to seek refreshment and repose under the roof of Altman's hut.

Evening had closed in before de Wernebourg, weak, and weary from incessant efforts to escape from his subterranean prison, reached the cottage.—Pale, haggard, and exhausted, his eyes dim and glassy, his form wasted away, and his disordered garments stained with blood, he looked more like a spectre than a living man. A ruddy light glanced from a large wood fire: anxious to bask in its revivifying heat, he entered as hastily as his failing limbs would permit, and as the flickering blaze fell upon the ghastly object which staggered forwards from the door, Christian Altman, starting in terror from his chair, exclaimed, "Will the earth yield up its dead? Save, save me from that killing sight!"

"De Wernebourg!" cried Magdalena, and rushed to meet the Count's embrace.

The forester, bewildered, caught the maiden's arm, and held her back; again exclaiming, "It is illusion all! he sleeps within the grave! his blood is still upon these hands! and see, he comes to charge me with the deed!"

"Christian!" shrieked Gertrude, as she placed her hand upon

de Wernebourg's shoulder, "I hold a living man within my grasp, whence then these horrible upbraidings of a guilty conscience? Where is Gottfried?—where is my child? he it was, and not the Count, who haunted our cottage in the dead of night, if—and thy fearful exclamations thrill my soul with terror—if thou hast, in blindness or in madness, encountered a supposed enemy in the forest, know that thou has slain the youth who was once pride of thy doating heart—thy first-born son!"

The old man sank insensible on the floor: partially recovering from the stroke which was rapidly consuming the principles of life, he confessed, that, aware of the Count's determination to punish his repeated aggressions, he, sharing in the belief of Herman that de Wernebourg visited Magdalena at night, resolved to waylay and murder him. The blow designed for another pierced the heart of Gottfried; who, jealous of de Wernebourg, had anticipated his father's intended guilt, and but for this wretched parent's fearful error, the prisoner so providentially rescued from the haunted mine, would, in all probability, have fallen a sacrifice to the vengeance of this daring outlaw.

Christian Altman, after languishing a few days, yielded his troubled spirit to the grasp of death; but before Herman returned to Frankfort, he had seen the frantic agonies of Gertrude soothed by the unceasing attentions of Magdalena, and witnessed the union of de Wernebourg with the fair girl, who seemed born to administer to the happiness of all around her.

E. R.